INK FOR BLOOD

For the three readers who kept me focused
You know who you are

PART ONE

GLOAMING 1898

CHAPTER 1:
THE CLEANSING

For a hundred years, the Great Machine sat upon the coast. Eight insectoid legs in the earth and sea, eight tentacles waving to the heavens. An angel of old, as the church decreed. For the people of Wrotdam and the surrounding countryside, it loomed ever-present on the horizon. Just as it did on a cool December morning while the sun hid behind a thick layer of grey clouds.

Frost glowed on the windows from the lamplight inside. Autocars rumbled along the cobblestone, pushing the old horse and cart off to the edges. The day was predicted to be unseasonably warm. Children formed humanoid shapes out of the vanishing mounds of snow. The markets were bustling from the lower ward to the upper as Wrodamites prepared for the New Year's Eve celebrations that night.

A cascade of bells disrupted the peace. They started in the Mechanical Cathedral high above the merchant's district and moved through the city. The tune rang sonorous and unique. The Alabaster Bell signalling the beginning of the Cleansing.

By the time the chime of the Alabaster Bell reached the Sawbones Barracks, it was already alive in a flurry of motion. An old stone building in Chasmdrop, a district of the lower ward that bordered the gorge splitting Wrotdam in half, it was the first building built when Wrotdam expanded. Originally a hospital, but only for a year, it found better use as a home and training facility for those who killed monsters — and the people who would become them.

Edwin Zhen entered the barracks. He was ready for the hunt, with his branderbuss on his hip and his twin boltblades in an inverted sheath under his signature green jacket. He brushed some dust off the patches and stitches that held the old leather piece together and gave a nod to the young sawbones as they rushed past. He had a sly demeanour to him, holding himself firm with assuredness and intense, dark eyes. Rig met him in the front hall, beard still wet from a bath. He stood bare-chested, an impressive display of human strength.

"I thought you were moving out of the barracks," Edwin said.

"Why?" Rig headed down the hallway to the living quarters.

Edwin followed. "Because you told me you hate this place. Everyone's drunk, fighting, or fucking, your words. Could be good for you, too. There are some nice flats in Copper Street, I'm not saying you have to buy a house."

They passed the central courtyard, filled with straw training dummies torn to shreds and a fighting ring. Training swords had been dropped without care once the bells started ringing.

"No one wants to room with a sawbones," Rig said.

"Not everyone hates us."

"No, they're afraid of us. For good reason." He used a towel to dry off his bald head and tossed it into a hamper. "Who kills the inkbloods before they turn?"

A few sawbones ran past as Edwin and Rig entered a room built for six people. The personal racks were all empty, save one that had a long coat, a branderbuss, and Rig's personal weapons, a large riotsaw. A single-sided chainsaw with two rows of teeth, it was about as subtle as Rig himself was.

"You underestimate people," Edwin said, leaning against the wall. "A lot of them understand we help."

"A necessary evil, as the church would say." Rig tossed on a shirt and checked his branderbuss. The barrel had been charred black and, despite the size, the long firearm was surprisingly light. "Not all of us can be hopeful like you. And not all of us can get married and have kids."

"I know. I'm not going to claim I'm not lucky, but you'll find a gent who accepts you and all your grumpy ways. People don't survive long being an island. Not in our line of work."

"Everyone dies alone, Edwin." Rig swung on his coat and grabbed his riotsaw, hefting the monstrosity onto his shoulder. "If I survive this Cleansing, maybe you can talk to me like your kid. Until then, let's go kill some monsters."

"You could try to be more enthusiastic. Some people think we're heroes during the Cleansing." Edwin jabbed Rig in the ribs. "And it's not every day you get to be a hero."

Rig gave Edwin a dull look. He put on his hat, pulled up his mask, and stormed past, bumping Edwin's shoulder with his own. There was no talking to Rig if he didn't want to. Edwin gritted his teeth and left to join Rig outside the barracks. Every sawbones that wasn't on away missions, about two dozen, gathered in the training yard, waiting for Commander Stringer to give them their orders. She stood on a carriage bench, a battle-hardened woman with a smug demeanour and an old regiment coat.

"We need to get started quickly," she said. "So keep those lips shut while you get your assignments. Surprisingly, the leeches are actually going to pull their weight and rout out the infections in the upper ward. Out focus is going to be on the south side of the lower. Forest Reach, Copper Street, and Ogfen are all within the infected area, but it's spreading fast. Yusuf, Alvar, and Gwendolyn, clear out Forest Reach."

Three sawbones ran off. Stringer read other orders, sending out sawbones across Wrotdam to bring fire to infected areas, ensure the Mire did not spread, and patrol the streets for outbreaks. When the Cleansing was called, nothing was held back.

"Edwin, Rig, and Hitomi," Stringer said. "Franz is already in Copper Street. Get there."

A wild-haired woman leaned back from the crowd, catching Edwin's eye. Hitomi waved to him and pointed at the gate. She swung her wave cannon — a mechanism the size of her torso — onto her back as she left.

Edwin clapped Rig on the shoulder. "You should look for a place while we're over there."

Rig groaned. They left the courtyard and joined Hitomi as she pulled up the autocar. It was a dark grey metal streamlined ride with two bench seats and a trunk Hitomi popped open.

"We're driving?" Edwin asked, leaning on the driver's door. "We can walk to Copper Street."

"It's not for getting there," Hitomi said. "It's for getting away."

"You're crazy," Rig said.

Hitomi pointed at him with a grimace. "You're mean."

"He means paranoid." Edwin walked around the autocar and got into the passenger seat.

"Paranoid isn't better, Edwin," Hitomi said. "Paranoid is crazy. I'm not crazy. Kemper was crazy and a leech burned his body up in Downing Park. I'm focused."

"Kemper was seeing amber, it was different."

"Right." She rolled her eyes. "Maybe we're all crazy. This Cleansing is already feeling like a chaotic state of affairs, I heard people saying the Mire's acting off. A leech claimed he saw an inkblood walk right past a crowd of folks, grabbed a fruit seller right off his cart and tried to drag him into an alley. You tell me, since when does the Mire pick a target? Since when does it abduct people?"

"Since when do you listen to rumours from leeches?" Edwin rested his cheek on his hand. "What leech was this?"

"I don't know. Caleb heard it from Julia who overheard the leech talking to an alchemist." She tapped her hands against the steering wheel in frustration. "All I'm saying is if today goes bad, I'm done. I'm driving back to Osaka."

Rig put his riotsaw in the trunk, next to Hitomi's wave cannon, and used some rope to tie it shut despite the two massive weapons. When he entered the backseat, the autocar sunk several centimetres with him and the trunk's lid bounced against the rope. "What about the ocean?" he asked.

"I'll swim." Hitomi put the autocar in gear and drove toward Copper Street.

The cobblestone streets didn't make for a comfortable ride in the autocar, it was still a new invention to the world. They bumped along abandoned roads, weaving between carriages and autocars left behind by the fleeing citizens. Horses whinnied as Hitomi tore past.

"When was the last Cleansing?" Edwin asked.

"Three years. 1895," Hitomi said.

"That was the last one?" Edwin asked. The buildings whipped by. 1895 was forever ago. The Cleansing came on a rainy March night. Edwin was stuck for twelve hours in the pouring wet, fighting off a horde of sludges in a trainyard. It wasn't a night to forget.

"You've been out of town or something?" Hitomi took a sharp right, heading south down Monti Road.

"Wales," Rig said. "Right?"

"And Scotland," Edwin said. It was that rainy night in 1895 when Edwin returned home to find his front door shattered on the stoop.

"How does the wife feel about that?" Hitomi asked.

A cold night. Front door shattered. Dina Zhen had thrown her body across Thomas and Fei, trying fruitlessly to protect them against the Mire. Their blood soaked through the wood floor of his bedroom. It spread to the carpet around the bed and stained it red. How could that only have been three years earlier?

"She doesn't mind," Edwin said.

They drove past many darkened buildings, lit only by sparse lavender candles. They would dissuade the Mire from entering, though couldn't completely repel them. Their power seemed to be in hope — the person hiding behind them hoped that they worked.

"I heard it's bad out there," Rig said, shutting his eyes. He never liked autocar rides.

Edwin looked back at him. "It's just beginning and people are already saying that? What? Is there a lot of it?"

"Mire's more aggressive this Cleansing. It's going to be a tough day. Or week."

"Well." Edwin shrugged. "If you're going to complain, you could always just lay down and die."

Rig huffed and opened his eyes. "I plan to die on my feet. The world is absolute shit, and you better believe I'm not going to kneel just because it wants me to. Never fall, not even in death."

"You know," Edwin rolled his head back, "there are people who don't know you that would think you're an optimist."

It was dramatic, but it certainly motivated the recruits. No one became a sawbones because they wanted to. It was a life for the downtrodden, those who could put violent tendencies to work, and those who didn't mind drinking raw Ink to keep fighting. But there was power in a defiant attitude like Rig's. Edwin couldn't lie, it motivated him as well.

Hitomi stopped at an intersection, leaving the autocar with one tire on the pavement. The sawbones stepped out. Rig grabbed the riotsaw and wave cannon from the trunk. He tossed the cannon to Hitomi as he gazed down each street.

"Franz!" he shouted. "Where are you?"

There was a bang from a few streets down. Edwin took off. He was faster than his companions and easily vaulted the alley fence as a shortcut. He slid onto a street splattered with black slime. In the middle of the road stood a sawbones wielding a tyrant hammer. A mass of black-grey ooze in a vaguely humanoid shape lunged toward Franz. He met the sludge with a wide swing. Upon contact, the strike plate pushed back and the tyrant hammer unleashed a fiery blast that tore the sludge apart.

Franz turned toward Edwin, covered in muck with smoke twisting out of the hammer's exhaust. He pulled down his mask and squeezed the mess out of his striking blonde hair.

"*Güten tag*, Edwin," Franz said in the thickest Prussian accent Edwin had ever heard. "I hope you have not come alone. The streets are alive today."

Franz ejected the empty Ink canister from his tyrant hammer's head. It was the size of a fist, much bigger than the inkwells that powered a branderbuss. He fumbled in his coat pockets and then pulled out a fresh canister. It took a few hard whacks to get it into place, the tyrant hammer was an old weapon, much like Rig's riotsaw. Franz gave it a spin then rested it on his shoulder.

"Hitomi and Rig aren't far behind," Edwin said. He motioned to the mess. "You've been busy."

"The Mire is fighting back. It's already taken people's hearts. I saw inkbloods go that way before I was distracted."

Edwin winced. Sludges were one thing. An inkblood still looked human. Still bled like a human. "We'll deal with them, Franz."

Rig was first around the corner. He had saw and branderbuss in each hand, ready to fight. Hitomi wasn't far behind, her hair done up in a lopsided bun with the wave cannon strapped to her right arm, holding it by a grip with a trigger. She took one look at the mess then flipped up her hood, pulled up her mask, and snapped on her tight-fitting goggles. No piece of Mire ever touched Hitomi.

"Come," Franz said, turning down the road. "There is one of those nests."

Hitomi fiddled with the wave cannon, turning dials to regulate Ink flow and pressure. With a strike from her palm, the piping filled with liquid fading from amber to blue as it approached the reservoir. Franz led them past an apartment, to an alley that went into a small courtyard between the buildings.

Strung up between the apartments hung a black and grey pulsating mass. Thick strands reinforced with bone and wood hung like spider webs and part of a clothing line went in one side and out the other. A nest that large should've taken hours to form. The Mire was working fast. A bulge grew on the bottom of the main section and dropped a new sludge onto the ground below. In total, three dozen sludges patrolled the courtyard.

"We should push them to the street," Rig said, emotionless as always. "Hitomi can clear them out."

Hitomi raised her wave cannon and gave it an appreciative tap. "I can clear them out right now."

"No." Rig placed his branderbuss over her cannon.

A sludge noticed the onlookers and cocked its facsimile of a head. Other sludges followed, turning toward the sawbones and lumbering forward. Half paid no mind, sitting catatonic beneath the nest.

"Rig's right," Edwin said, pulling up his mask. "You'll hit the buildings. Might hurt the people inside. We'll go through the middle and bait them to follow us. Once they're grouped up, you can get them."

"I'll be waiting." Hitomi ran back the way they came.

The encroaching sludges stretched their arms until bone blades grew out. Some dragged them along the ground, digging distinct gashes in the stone.

"I wasn't thinking about her hitting the buildings," Rig said, aiming his branderbuss at the sludges. "I was thinking about her being gentle and not hitting anything."

"I know." Edwin reached to his lower back, unclipped his boltblades, and let them slide into his hands. Rig was efficient, but cold. Edwin had known him long enough to understand it didn't mean he was heartless, just that he didn't always recognize how much something would affect him until it was right in front of him.

Franz struck first. He batted away the sludge's swing with the hammer grip then slammed the other side into its chest. Sparks danced as the strike plate slid back on its rods. The resulting blast didn't just destroy the sludge, it devastated the three others right behind it. Rig came in next, firing into the crowd with branderbuss shots. A charred sludge grew a bear trap of bones from its chest and snapped at him. Rig swung down with his saw, dismantling the sludge with brutal strength. He fired a few more shots then holstered his branderbuss and grabbed the riotsaw with both hands. Half the hilt slid up behind the blade, striking the Ink reserves and bringing the chains roaring to life.

They pushed forward. Franz and Rig cleared a path with their heavy weapons. Edwin zipped between the sludges, taking out chunks of muck with each pass. The electricity in the blades disrupted whatever kept the sludges together, a finer feat than fire, which burned it out. Still, the Mire could only be killed by destroying the heart, which moved constantly within the body of the creatures. The sludges sitting motionless beneath the nest rose and joined their companions in the fight.

Edwin sliced a sludge half a dozen times and its body simply collapsed into a puddle. The horde pushed back against them. Edwin smiled. The Mire was bestial and fought with pack tactics, it would never run, but it would retreat for a better strike or easier prey. As long as they kept its attention, they could bring it right where they want. They fought the sludges on the move, cutting through the middle until they reached an alley on the other side.

"Keep them interested," Edwin said, deflecting a blow by clapping his blades. "We need all of them on the street."

Rig bull-rushed his way to the centre of the group. He planted himself and, with a roar, spun with his saw outstretched. He sent up waves of black slime. The sludges at the back charged forward, following Rig onto the street. It was more than the three dozen Edwin counted in the courtyard. They stumbled over each other, absorbing the pieces of dead sludge to make themselves stronger. Rig bashed a sludge aside and rejoined Edwin and Franz. They successfully lured them into the open.

That was when Hitomi arrived. "Make some room," she said.

Edwin sliced a sludge's arm off then moved back with Rig and Franz. The horde exited the alley, lining up perfectly for a shot from Hitomi.

"Two times load." Hitomi pointed the wave cannon at the oncoming mass. "Firing!"

The cannon let out a crack and unleashed a chaotic lattice of lightning. Sludges flew back, coming apart through the combination of force and electricity. Hitomi's feet slid across the ground from the force of the blow. The lightning seared the surrounding buildings and turned the street into a slimy mess. Hitomi ejected the Ink canister and reloaded.

"Clear." She slammed the cannon onto the head of a still-twitching sludge. The wave cannon was a powerful weapon. Simple, and restricted in use, but still powerful.

"*Gut gemacht*," Franz said. "I'll burn the nest." He ran off.

Edwin smiled. It was the best a nest clearing could go. But, it wouldn't be the only nest in Wrotdam, probably not even the only one in Copper Street. As if in reply, a sound like a building collapsing came from the south and someone screamed.

"It's not done," Rig said, shutting down his riotsaw and leaning it against his shoulder.

"What's the problem?" Hitomi primed her wave for another shot. "Do you want to go home already?"

"Of course not." Rig glanced at Edwin. "It's not every day you get to be a hero."

Edwin rolled his eyes. "We're moving on, Franz!" he called out, hopping backwards.

Four sawbones ran through a city frozen in time, weapons ready to fight again.

CHAPTER 2:
THE CLERIC

The Cleansing lingered on to the evening and as night began to fall, Adelaide Fisher could do nothing but pray. She sat in a dusty chapel beneath the watchful eye of the Engine Angel, where the setting sunlight reflected off the statuette's eight steel wings to create dappled spotlights. Amid the smell of old wood and smoke, her thoughts drifted to the people in the city below. The Cleansing lingered into its tenth hour, with no end in sight. She let out a soft breath and leaned forward on the worn pew.

"Please." She squeezed her fingers together. "Please keep the people safe on this longest night."

Footsteps echoed through the open chapel door and Archbishop MacMurray appeared at the threshold. His weathered face was a common sight around the Mechanical Cathedral, Adelaide couldn't remember a time before him ambling through the halls with the energy of a much younger man. His hair had been white for as long as Adelaide knew him, and the only thing that changed in his face as the years went on were more wrinkles around his eyes.

"Adelaide," he said, stepping through the door. His robes swept just above the ground, all white and gold with sharp gear-teeth trim. "I thought I might find you here. Why don't you pray in the Cathedral?"

"I like the intimacy of the chapel." Her Scottish accent had yet to fade during her years in the south. She stood, catching a ray of light that made her pale skin glow and smoothed out her amber robes. They matched the colour of raw Ink, as all the Ink Clergy garb did. Her long, half-skirt tail had shifted back during her prayers so she pulled it tighter to the front of her pants to imitate the dresses of the nuns. "God listens to the small voices."

There was also the massive statue of the Machine in the Cathedral. It loomed over the choir, casting a shadow that could swallow Adelaide whole. Not that she would ever tell anyone how it made her feel. The Machine was an angel, and there was nothing to fear from it.

"Walk with me, Adelaide," Archbishop MacMurray said, placing his hands behind his back and turning around. "I have need of St. Zita's Order."

Adelaide fixed the strands of copper hair slipping out of her braid and kept pace with the Archbishop. They walked along the arcade between the chapel building and the main cathedral. The ravine splitting Wrotdam in half could be seen past the academy and gate, separating the structured elegance of the upper ward from the barely bridled chaos of the lower.

Steep-roofed buildings crowded over each other like waves on the ocean, and beyond the Great Machine swayed its eight tentacles through the clouds. Even perched on the distant coastline, the city-sized behemoth was ever-present. It was New Year's Eve, but warm for the season. The snow melted in the evening sun, dripping into puddles at the base of buildings. Adelaide always enjoyed the stillness of winter.

"It's been ten hours," the Archbishop said, tapping his fingers along the arcade's railing. "The sawbones are hard at work, but this is the worst infection I've ever seen. We've evacuated the dockyard and the messengers report at least three of the lower ward districts are completely overrun. The Ward Gate is to be closed."

"Why are we separating the city?" Adelaide asked.

"The upper ward has been cleansed of the Mire, but we must think of the citizens. The lower ward will be quarantined until the sawbones finish their work."

"We aren't…" Adelaide stalled at the thought. "We don't mean to burn the city again?"

"No. We haven't lost the lower ward yet." The word 'yet' hung in the air like a guillotine blade. They stopped near the end of the arcade, where it entered the cathedral, and MacMurray gazed into the distance. "I do hope this mess ends before tomorrow. I enjoy the New Year festivities greatly. It's the last one before the centennial of God sending us His angel, and while I look forward to that, it will be… different than the ones before. I would hate for the event to be ruined."

A hundred years of prosperity. Adelaide hadn't given it near as much thought as she should've. Her job was to understand the Machine and the oil that dripped from its chassis. The celebrations had little to do with that.

MacMurray let out a puff from his lungs and turned on his heel. "But that is then, this is now. Come."

Adelaide followed him into the cathedral. The smell of lavender smoke wafted from the candles melted to the pews. She glanced at the statue of the Machine sitting above the eight-armed cross, swathed in dangling lightbulbs. Waves carved from wood rose from the pedestal to represent the ocean from which the Great Machine first climbed onto the coast. Whoever made that statue must have hated the Machine to make it look so monstrous.

"Tell me, Adelaide," Archbishop MacMurray said, his voice bouncing off the empty cathedral walls. "Have you heard of the True Metal Order?"

"No, your Grace."

"It's a cult that has recently come to my attention. They believe that the Machine is God, rather than being one of his angels. Worse yet, they wish to see the Mire spread." He stepped into the sanctuary and smoothed down the altar cloth. "They revere it."

Adelaide frowned. "That is an interesting take."

"It's heresy. It's idolatry."

"Of the worst kind, your Grace." A belief such as that would be worth investigating, though she must take care not to appear too enthralled. What could cause people to believe such strange things?

"We were given something great." He gazed up at the Machine statue. "God sent us an angel so we could do battle with the Mire, but we must not allow ourselves to slip due to this gift. The Mire is a reminder that we are still being judged."

"Does this True Metal Order worry you?"

"Few things worry me, Adelaide. But you've always been an able observer and interpreter; I would like to send you the reports we have on them. Dissect their beliefs and find their pressure points. The strength of the Mire must be quelled, and only true faith will do that."

Adelaide bowed her head. There were others in the Ink Clergy more suited for information gathering than her, but a request direct from the Archbishop was an honour and solemn duty — even if he did avoid her question. "Of course, your Grace. I will keep one eye on them at all times."

Surely a small cult couldn't threaten the Machine Church, but it wasn't her place to question. A year in the order, and no one had seen fit to give her a purpose. She heard the other clerics whispering. She was no spy. Barely a scientist. They said she only got in through nepotism. That she had no business being there. That she was useless.

"How do you find St. Zita's Order?" MacMurray asked, using the church's official name for the Ink Clergy, though Adelaide had rarely heard anyone call it that.

"It's different. I like the research." She clasped her hands at her waist and gazed up at the mezzanine, the stained-glass faces of saints peeking over the railing beyond. She only joined the order the year before, after spending most of her life in the service. "But I'm overwhelmed with joy at being able to serve the Church in this capacity."

"That's a practiced answer." He chuckled under his breath.

"Only because it's the truth." She beamed, hoping it hid the tremble in her lips. "I've thought it so much it's like scripture to me."

The cathedral door creaked open. A man in a green jacket stomped down the nave, sweat plastering black hair to his forehead and his eyes burning, possessed by rage and fury. Adelaide scowled, confused. Until she saw his weapons.

"Edwin!" Archbishop MacMurray said, taking a step back. "What is the meaning of this?"

"You lied!" He raised a long and weighty firearm, its barrel charred black. A branderbuss, a sawbones's weapon. "They're dead!"

"Uncle!" Adelaide cried. "Stay behind me!" She pulled a collapsible metal rod out of her robes, snapped it out to its full length, and slid in front of the Archbishop. As she struck the rod against the ground, the electric-primed Ink inside it ignited. Fingers of lightning blossomed into a protective wall.

Edwin fired. Spits of flame barked from the branderbuss and disappeared as they contacted the shock shield. Again and again. Energy on energy. The heat pounded against Adelaide's face with each strike and she stepped back into the sanctuary, the shock shield dancing along the floor.

"Guards!" Archbishop MacMurray shouted, moving back with her. "We need guards in the main hall!"

A dozen church guards with ignition launcher rifles poured in from the transepts. They took one look at the crazed man firing at their Archbishop and brought their sights to bear on the assailant. With each pull of the trigger, the hammer slammed down on an inkwell canister in the cylinder.

A dozen congealed flames fired out of a dozen barrels, recoiling the rifles against their shoulders and forcing Edwin to give ground. He sent a glare in their direction as if to say, 'how dare you interrupt me?' In reply, the guards cocked the levers for their next shots and moved in.

Smoke from quick-burning flame shots tickled Adelaide's nose. She kept her pulserod up, in case Edwin made a break for the Archbishop, while her mind raced on what to do. Edwin waited, hunched over like a wild animal. He drew a dagger from the inverted sheathes on his lower back, watching as the guards created a defensive line near the front pews.

"You need to leave, your Grace," Adelaide said. "Out the side door, back to the chapel."

"Adelaide—"

"We can't discuss this! Please go!"

MacMurray set his jaw, but with his niece's urging, he went for the exit, clutching the large cross bouncing against his chest. Edwin's gaze locked on his escaping prey. He rolled his muscles, as if they were trying to pull themselves from his bones, then exploded into motion. The guards unleashed a volley of flames. Too slow, or rather, Edwin was too fast.

The bolts singed across his back as he swooped low, dragging his branderbuss across the carpet and rising to meet the line with a trigger pull. The heat and pressure slammed into a guard's chest, sundering his ribcage and breaking the human barricade. Adelaide cursed and rushed after the Archbishop.

Like water through a cracked dam, Edwin slipped through the line, slicing a second guard across the stomach. Despite MacMurray's head start, Edwin reached the door first.

"MacMurray!" he cried, kicking off the wood with such force the jamb cracked and redirected himself to take the Archbishop head-on.

MacMurray backpedalled, eyes wide in hopeless fear. Adelaide took his place. She pulled up her sleeve and bit onto the metal contraption of straps and tubing around her wrist. Yanking the tab out, the flame gauntlet unfurled. Segmented metal plates shot up her hand, cutting her across the cheek when she didn't pull away fast enough. A nozzle flipped into her palm.

Edwin stumbled to a stop. He must've known what it was. Adelaide ignored the blood oozing down her face and looped the trigger strap around her thumb, clicking the inkwell inset just above her wrist. A viscous amber-red liquid shot through the tubing into the reservoir. With a twitch of her thumb, she unleashed a torrent of flames from the nozzle, driving Edwin back.

A guard swooped in from behind and got his rifle across Edwin's neck, dragging him toward the nave. Taking advantage of the space, MacMurray grabbed the door handle and pulled. It rattled but didn't open.

"It's stuck!" he shouted, taking it in both hands and pulling with everything his old body could give him.

Edwin's kick must've jammed it, Adelaide thought. *Did he plan that?* She pointed across the transept. "Take the other one!"

The guards gave MacMurray as much space as they could. The first still had his rifle across Edwin's neck. Another put his launcher's barrel against his head, searing the skin on Edwin's temple. The guard squeezed the trigger and Edwin turned, dragging the first guard into the line of fire. His head burst into flames and he released the sawbones. The second guard recoiled in horror, stopped swiftly as Edwin thrust his blade up beneath his chin.

There wasn't much the guards could do in close range, and MacMurray couldn't outrun the sawbones to the door. "Cover the Archbishop," Adelaide said, pushing Edwin back with her flame gauntlet. If she could just keep him distracted, make some distance, then her uncle could escape.

The remaining guards complied, circling up around the Archbishop with their rifles at the ready. Edwin was seeing amber. His mind had become twisted from the Ink the sawbones drank. Without a leech around, Adelaide would have to stop him. But Ink Clerics were supposed to fight the Mire, not man. Her knees shook and she wiped the blood from her cut cheek.

She prayed she would only need to drive him off. She prayed she wouldn't need to kill him.

Edwin had other plans. He came in dagger first. Adelaide parried with her gauntlet — and came face-to-barrel with a branderbuss. Fire grew in the dark. She flipped her pulserod up and knocked the gun aside. A shower of high-impact flames scattered into the air, the heat radiating against the side of her face. Edwin put a foot against her thigh and leapt back.

"You are a sawbones!" Adelaide shouted, getting her feet beneath her. "You are supposed to keep the city safe!"

"Lies for the people." Edwin stowed his branderbuss and drew his second dagger, crossing them in a reverse grip. "Truth will crumble the Church." With a flick of his wrists, the boltblades coursed with electricity.

What is he talking about? She couldn't finish that thought as Edwin charged.

She sprayed a line of flames, but Edwin went low. Under the fire and up, he aimed for Adelaide's exposed ribs. Training took over. She caught the blade on a backswing. Sparks filled the air as their two electrically charged weapons met.

Edwin used the momentum to spin back around and strike again. Another parry. Another strike. It went on like this. Spray. Parry. Miss. And Adelaide couldn't shake the feeling she was being toyed with.

Edwin landed a thrust kick into her stomach. The air burst from her diaphragm and she stumbled back. Edwin retreated as well. Fighting a human was entirely different from the Mire — and a sawbones, at that. Edwin bounced and swayed to music only he could hear. Was he enjoying himself? Or was it another symptom of his amberwild madness?

She had to stop him — if only to prove she wasn't useless. To silence the whispers. Digging both feet into the carpet, she charged forth. She twisted the dial on her gauntlet and the nozzle flipped to a second design. Edwin stopped bobbing and went bolt upright. Perfect. Adelaide swung with her pulserod and Edwin ducked — right into her gauntlet. She flicked her thumb to release the explosion.

The gauntlet whirred. Edwin threw himself back as a high-powered burst of force and flames ignited the air before his eyes. The recoil rocked Adelaide, sending her spinning and staggering. She shook her hand, the nerves vibrating all the way up to her shoulder from the impact. She lowered the burst function's discharge and regained her poise. Edwin finished his roll to his feet — his bangs significantly shorter.

"You can still come back," Adelaide said, keeping her gauntlet forward. Her arm still trembled from the last burst.

Edwin huffed, bestial like a bull. An amber light sparkled along the edge of his irises before he charged. Adelaide unleashed a smaller explosion, keeping him back. She tried her best, but once the amberwild took hold, there was no coming back. There was only death now. To protect her uncle, Edwin must be stopped. Permanently. She set her jaw and went on the offensive.

With flicks of her thumb, she set off a chain of explosions. Edwin swayed between the flames, faster than any human had the right to move, a manic smile across his face. She clicked the inkwell to reload and pushed on without missing a beat.

One blast seared his jacket's hem. He was slowing. That, or Adelaide was figuring out his moves. Everything had a pattern; nothing was truly unpredictable. She would catch him. She had to. She swung her pulserod at his leg. Edwin pulled back, putting himself off balance. That was her moment. She brought her gauntlet to his face.

The trigger ticked… and nothing happened. The inkwell was dry.

Edwin adjusted his backward momentum to kick off a pew. He slammed his knee into Adelaide's forehead. Stars erupted through her vision. The Cathedral disappeared amidst the pain and she fell to her knees.

Stupid. Tears welled up in her eyes, and not just from the pain. She was useless. She lost focus. Didn't think about her reserves. Edwin paced around her, flipping his boltblades around. He was a predator, stalking his wounded prey. Adelaide got to one foot, but her head screamed in reply and she fell flat to the carpet. The cathedral breathed, the walls and floor ebbing while Adelaide blinked the pain away.

There was a moment of pause before Edwin's gaze drifted up, toward the wall of church guards and the Archbishop beyond. A tremor rattled his body, curling up his legs to his chest like a coiling serpent until it burst from his mouth. "MacMurray!" he screamed and abandoned Adelaide in a furious charge.

The church guards advanced, firing on Edwin's position. Adelaide covered her head as flame bolts the size of coins whipped by. Ink designed to burn fast and quick. Still, if they weren't careful they would burn the whole Cathedral down.

Edwin slipped between the flaming projectiles. He leapt onto the pew — a bolt slipping past his shoulder close enough to singe the leather — then pushed off. Across the back of the seats, Edwin bounded like a gazelle until he reached the front row and lunged at the guards.

He cut down as he landed. The guard stumbled back, raising his arm for protection. The boltblade barely nicked him, but he seized up and Edwin took advantage to ram his other dagger into the guard's throat.

The room stopped spinning and Adelaide grabbed a pew to pull herself to her feet. She wiped the tears away with the back of her hand. She needed to stop dwelling on her failures; to serve the Church was to keep moving forward.

Edwin slammed his dagger through a guard's chest. He made eye contact with Archbishop MacMurray and walked forward with his blade still in the man's heart. The man grabbed Edwin's arm with his fading movements, feet sliding in shocked instinct. Archbishop MacMurray backed up to the altar, but there was nowhere else to go. Adelaide loaded a new inkwell into her gauntlet and charged in to help, praying she wasn't too slow. Edwin tore the boltblade from the guard's chest and lunged forth. Archbishop MacMurray yelped.

The charged dagger stopped a mere centimetre from plunging into his throat. Three guards surrounded Edwin, holding him back with their shoulders to his midsection.

"Damn it!" Edwin cried, spit flying from his mouth. Black veins crept up his neck. "You bastard! They'll never hear you!"

His feet slipped on the wooden floor as he tried desperately to get that last deadly stretch. The guard's braced themselves, then lifted Edwin off the ground and carried him away from the Archbishop. They tossed him back. Edwin landed on his feet and moved to reengage when Adelaide slid in his way. She twisted the dial on her gauntlet and unleashed a torrent of flames upon Edwin.

"Don't get involved!" Adelaide ordered the guards. She was keeping Edwin occupied, if the guards attacked it brought his attention to the Archbishop.

Adelaide fired the flamethrower in controlled bursts, pushing Edwin back to the aisle. Forward through the last licks of flame, Adelaide rushed and struck Edwin across the face. A thunderclap filled the cathedral. She finally got him.

Sparks leapt at the point of impact and Edwin tumbled back — yet recovered with a roll onto his feet. Adelaide paled. A hit like that should've knocked out any normal person.

Any measure had to be taken to ensure the Mire's corruption didn't spread. Edwin spat out a mouthful of black bile and the amber twinkle in his eyes grew dark. Adelaide primed her gauntlet, then pressed the inkwell two more times to overcharge the launcher. She switched back to burst and widened her stance. This was going to hurt.

"Dog of the Church!" Edwin screamed, hunching over.

"Heretic." Adelaide twisted the nozzle to full discharge and fired.

Flames and light filled her vision. Ten rows of pews turned to splinters and the carpet became ash, charring the stone beneath. Her shoulder cracked as the recoil hit her. Smoke and embers filled the nave, dispersing into the wings and ceiling. Edwin was gone. No corpse.

Had she won? Something hit her back and she went sprawling.

Edwin stood behind her, coolly batting away the embers on the edges of his charred jacket. She tried to raise her flame gauntlet, but her shoulder refused. The last explosion must have knocked it out of its socket. She went to strike her pulserod, but Edwin stomped on her hand.

He loomed over her, each breath scraping out of his lungs. For just a moment, the whites of his eyes faded to a pure, dark amber. *This can't be it*, she thought. God must have a purpose for her more than this. She set her jaw. She wouldn't cry at the end. Edwin screamed with rage and lifted his weapon.

A bolt of electricity struck him in the back, jerking his shoulder forward and sending him tumbling into the carpet with a puff of ash. Adelaide rolled to her knees. A figure dressed in black robes with a crimson scarf stood in the transept, a boltrifle pressed against their shoulder. Electricity coursed through the gaps in the barrel as they took considered steps forward. A grey, beaked mask disguised their features, but the charred edge of their scarf was familiar. Adelaide gasped and smiled, hoping it was her old friend.

"Are you alright, Adelaide?" the leech said.

"Dayla!" she exclaimed. Of course it was Dayla. Dayla would always come for her.

Edwin groaned. Adelaide snapped her gaze at him. He rose to hands and knees and crawled toward the cathedral doors. Black fluid dripped from his lips. Adelaide fell back on her heels, her arm hanging limply from her shoulder and bells sounding through her skull. She couldn't pursue — but Dayla could.

The leech stepped into the aisle and pulled the trigger. The boltrifle snapped, like a mini-lightning strike. The light in the barrel went out and a glowing spark shot from the muzzle. Edwin spun around and clashed his boltblades.

As the blades touched, they let out a burst of energy. It cast Dayla's shot aside, scouring across the cathedral wall. Dayla hummed and pulled back on the slide, filling the barrel with electricity, and launched another bolt. Again, Edwin clashed his blades and the bolt ricocheted past Dayla's ear. It put a char across the edge of her mask, but she didn't flinch. Instead, she planted her feet, brought her cheek to the boltrifle sights and gave one last shot. Edwin ducked under it, letting it sear across the cathedral doors, and was gone.

Dayla stepped next to Adelaide. She kept her eye on where Edwin disappeared. Seconds ticked by like minutes. Then, with a sigh, she turned her boltrifle off.

"Dayla!" Adelaide stumbled to her feet and wrapped her good arm around her old friend. A flood of every conceivable emotion welled up within her. She squeezed Dayla like a life raft. "If you hadn't—"

"It's fine now." Dayla broke the hug and stepped back. She scanned Adelaide up and down from behind her bird-like mask.

"We can't let him get away," Adelaide said, turning toward the door.

"Wait." Dayla caught Adelaide by the arm. She removed her mask, revealing a brown-skinned woman with braided white hair and deep lines on her face from many decades of hard living. She stood tall yet was short by most standards. Despite the rest of her grandmotherly features, her sharp eyes told the story of a predator. "We'll find him," she said. "But you're injured. Someone should look at that shoulder."

"Adelaide!" Archbishop MacMurray hurried over. A few guards stayed close to him while others rushed over to deal with the fire Adelaide left behind. "You're injured! We must have that shoulder looked at."

Dayla chuckled. "What did I say?"

"I'm fine, Uncle — er, your Grace," Adelaide said. She grabbed Dayla's arm and leaned close. "Please, Dayla. You must find that man and make sure he doesn't hurt anyone else. I looked into his eyes and there was nothing but fury and hate. He's seeing amber, it won't be long before he becomes inkblooded."

"Then the sawbones will have further prey." Dayla smiled at her. "This will be dealt with. Have no fear. For now, take care of the Archbishop."

Adelaide nodded. Dayla rested her rifle against her shoulder then headed out the front doors, stepping around the guards stomping on the embers.

"Come," Archbishop MacMurray said, taking Adelaide by her good arm. "Let's bring you to the infirmary."

Adelaide relented. She removed her gauntlet's trigger from her thumb and allowed the Archbishop to lead her away. The pain in her shoulder grew as her adrenaline faded, so she supported it with her other hand. They left the main hall and walked across an arcade, the Church guards keeping an eye on them with ignition throwers at the ready.

"I wish you hadn't done that, Adelaide," Archbishop MacMurray said. "It was very dangerous."

"I'm sorry, your Grace." She bowed her head. *But I saved you,* she thought. Appreciation was too much to ask; she must be content with her own assurance she did the right thing.

"Don't apologize. I'm simply stating a fact. Sawbones are incredibly dangerous. They train for years, some from birth, to fight the Mire. They don't think like normal people and we can't treat them as such."

"But they protect Wrotdam."

He huffed. "If the Governor listened to me St. Zita's Order would still run the Cleansing, not amber-swilling animals."

Adelaide bit her tongue. They entered the infirmary in the north wing. Adelaide wrinkled her nose at the smell of heavy sterilizing chemicals, but there weren't any patients in the beds against the walls. A doctor entered at the sound of her footsteps, lowering her eyes in respect upon finding the Archbishop entering her ward.

"That which can protect can also destroy." MacMurray motioned for the doctor to take Adelaide. "The sawbones are... noble, of course. They sacrifice everything, willfully consuming Ink to fight. But, that's why they need to be controlled by a higher authority. If a sawbones falls from grace as angels did long ago, they become demons just the same." He placed his hand on the doctor's elbow. "She's hurt, ensure she is well taken care of."

"Yes, your Grace," the doctor said. She led Adelaide to a free bed with Archbishop MacMurray keeping pace right behind them. "What seems to be the problem?"

"My shoulder." Adelaide sat on the bed, letting the doctor feel along the joint.

"You must take better care of yourself," MacMurray said, sitting next to her. "Your position in the Church is to observe and learn. I would never be forgiven if anything happened to you."

"By God?" She winced as the doctor's hands brushed her shoulder.

He smiled. "By my sister. She looks down on me from Heaven, I can feel it. Please, for her sake, keep to the reports."

The doctor stepped back. "It does appear to be dislocated. I'll get you some ice. Keep that arm still until I get back." She left the bed. A nurse handed her a notepad as she exited the infirmary.

"Rest well," MacMurray patted her knee and stood to leave.

It wasn't Adelaide's place to question, and yet she couldn't help herself. "May I ask you something?"

He stopped and nodded.

"Why do you think that man attacked you?"

"You can't get into the mind of an amberwild sawbones." He circled the room, lingering at a depiction of human anatomy hanging on the wall. "They're foreign beasts once the Ink takes over. It can be directed, or it can be random, but madness is madness."

Adelaide frowned. "You knew his name."

"Edwin Zhen. He did good work for the Church. It's a shame he's lost his mind."

Adelaide ran her fingers along the bindings on her gauntlet. Edwin Zhen didn't seem insane, not in the gibbering way she imagined. Odd, sure. Passionate and angry, of course. But she expected something more. But maybe that's what made it so insidious. The devil hid in plain sight. In the flesh of the sawbones who succumbed to the amber Ink.

MacMurray let out a sigh. He ran his hands over his face and dropped the practiced demeanour of a clergyman. "It's been three years since the last Cleansing. I dared to hope we would never need to ring that bell again. Since dawn, I've prayed for the insight of Old Archbishop Williams. He formed the Machine Church in a time when the people were terrified and the Mire ran wild. He led the St. Zita's Order to fight back before the College of Sawbones even existed; how am I supposed to match up to that legend?"

"You don't need to match up to his legend," Adelaide said. "God has a purpose for all of us. As long as we serve Him, our legends don't matter."

MacMurray chuckled, nodding his head. "The Order is lucky to have someone as intelligent and faithful as you. I'm sure you'll do great things for them."

"Thank you, your Grace." Calm washed over her. Seeing the Archbishop express his doubts eased her concerns about her own. "I will do my best to serve the Church."

"Adelaide." MacMurray wrung his hands together. He had a few false starts, trying to find the words he needed to say.

"I have not forgotten about your request," she said. "I'll start investigating the True Metal Order as soon as I am able."

Archbishop MacMurray blinked, then smiled. "Yes. We've already taken steps to quell their influence, but we need to know more about them and their dangerous ideas. I know you prefer the more scientific pursuits of the Ink Clergy, but there is no one I would trust more with investigating this cult. We must protect people from these heretics."

He had paused for a moment, an instant that hadn't escaped Adelaide's notice. "That is what you wanted to say, correct?"

"Well." He rubbed his chin. "It doesn't matter. Focus on getting better. I'll check on you later."

He squeezed her good shoulder then hurried out with the guards. The nurse returned without the doctor, bringing a sling and ice. What did her uncle want to say? Usually, he spoke his mind. He seemed especially stressed, even before Edwin's attack — no surprise there considering the Cleansing had been going for most of the day.

The True Metal Order must be more of a threat than he's letting on, she thought. *If Wrotdam's in danger, I must discover how.*

She joined the Ink Clergy long after they stopped being the first and last lines of defence against the Mire. She served Wrotdam by serving God. Now, she could do both. She prayed for God to protect the people, but she could be the answer to her own prayers.

She sat in the infirmary, cooling the pain in her shoulder. No more patients were brought in after her. Soft footsteps and the occasional whispered conversation drifted by like a swaying tide. She twisted the key on her gauntlet, furling it into the safe position. Locked, she slid the tag back into its slot.

Emotions crashed down upon her at once. She nearly died. If Dayla arrived one second later... She couldn't think like that. She was alive. She still had a purpose, even if she didn't know what it was.

No. She knew what her purpose was. That's why she was alive. In the quiet, Adelaide made a promise to herself. God had given her a mission to protect the world He created. She would bring peace to a world in distress, not through prayer, but through action.

The Obsidian Bell rang, signalling the end of a long Cleansing.

CHAPTER 3:
THE LEECH

As the sun reached toward the western horizon, Dayla Singh leaned on the Leechwold's back balcony, overlooking the Wrotdam Woods. The lamps flickered on in anticipation of the coming dark and she waited patiently for Arash, the alchemist, to explain why he interrupted her on the Cleansing.

"Dayla, I've noticed something strange," he said.

He was a thin man who normally held himself with some severity, and always had a red tinge to his skin like he recently finished a run. But the man who stood in front of Dayla shook like a flag in a storm and clutched the long-beaked mask of a leech to his chest.

"I was in the lower ward," he continued, "clearing the sections the sawbones have cleansed. I was ensuring that the obelisks weren't detecting any more Mire. I put down my boltgun for a moment and went to inspect one when it started spinning. I tried to hide, of course, but the obelisk house was terribly damaged. I saw inkbloods, sludges, and even a gnasher. They walked right past me into the sewers."

"Perhaps they didn't notice you," Dayla said, running her fingers along her chin.

"One of the inkblood looked right at me. But I might as well of been a plant to it because it kept moving."

Dayla looked out over the forest, lips pursed in frustrated contemplation. The Mire never showed intelligence. It attacked and consumed, adding to its number thoughtlessly. It wouldn't walk past a target unmolested. Arash was a well-respected alchemist, he wouldn't lie for attention. There was always something about him that reminded Dayla of a face long locked away in the catacombs of her mind. That was probably why she ever gave him the time of day. Few others deserved it.

"Why tell me?" She tapped her fingers along the mask on her knee.

"You weren't the first one I talked to. I told my story to Deacon Brahim. It went all the way up to the Archbishop, but he dismissed it. He told me that God had protected me. But it doesn't feel that way." Arash took a seat at a table. "It feels like the Mire was going somewhere and didn't have time to deal with me. But the Mire is mindless. It should have…"

"Which is why you came to me?"

"Something is going on." Arash leaned on his elbows. His gaze jerked from side to side. "I couldn't tell the sawbones. A sawbones would kill them, but not learn anything. An Ink Cleric, maybe, but none would act against the Archbishop's word. I feel it in my heart that we must find out what this means."

This was a man who volunteered to work in the worst parts of the infection, cleaning the Mire away after a Cleansing or checking the obelisks abandoned in a fight. He wasn't one to get scared easily. Seeing him wracked with confusion put a spike in Dayla's side.

"I'll do it." Dayla slid off the railing and snatched her boltrifle from where it leaned against the balusters. "Where did you see the Mire?"

"Obelisk Twenty-Seven. Northeast, near the dockyard distillery." He wiped the sweat off his forehead. "Good luck, Leech Singh."

She slung her weapon over her shoulder and smiled. "Luck is for the foolish. I have cunning." She clapped Arash on the back and left the balcony.

Candles wafted lavender scents through the Leechwold's stained wood halls, not for light but for the sweet smoke that drove the Mire away. Here, those who watched for signs of infection trained. Dayla walked those halls for nearly forty years, watching over Wrotdam, predicting outbreaks, and a leeches most solemn duty — the cleansing of amberwild sawbones.

It wasn't an easy life, to kill the people who once pledged to protect the city, but Dayla knew there was no return from the amber. In four decades of service, her kills were countless.

She left her autocar in the garage, the streets would be terrible to drive through, and took off on foot. The upper ward had been deemed clean over an hour earlier, but the people didn't risk stepping outside. Even if the inkbloods and sludge were cleared, the Mire could seep in again. Only the occasional bravest souls rushed past Dayla as she stepped over a crumbled barricade.

The Mechanical Cathedral towered above her, a behemoth and architectural marvel of glass and stone. Eight flying buttresses on each side. Eight stained windows on the front. Eight spires on its roof.

Why would Archbishop MacMurray disregard Arash's testimony? she wondered. *If the Mire is acting oddly, the Church should care.*

That question burned enough she cut across the street and entered the connected abbey, where the ministry lived. Someone needed to give her an answer. As soon as she stepped inside, she spotted Deacon Brahim going the other way. He was easy enough to spot. A large-around man with a great white shock of hair circling like a mane into an equally bushy beard — both contrasting against his dark-brown skin.

"Ah! Deacon Brahim," Dayla said, putting on a sweet tone and hunching over to seem unassuming. "I suppose there is a case for luck. Just the man I was looking for."

"Good evening, Leech Singh," the Deacon said, showing off his pearly whites. "How can I help you?"

"I'm looking for someone. Have you seen Leech Arash Jahan? You know, the alchemist?" She waved her hand about. "I heard he was around here."

Deacon Brahim paused. His smile faded for a moment, just long enough for Dayla to notice. "No. I haven't seen him all day."

"Unfortunate." Dayla circled him, bobbing her head side to side as if in deep thought. "What are you doing here? Shouldn't you be in the north? Across the gap in the lower ward?"

"I got called back by Archbishop MacMurray." He rubbed a blemish on one of his rings. "We're closing the Ward Gate."

"Why would we do that?"

"The upper ward is cleansed. We must think of protecting the city. It will be reopened once the Obsidian Bell is rung."

The entire situation stunk. Arash noticed something weird, the Deacon lied about it, and they're closing the Ward Gate. Dayla's skin prickled. "Where is the Archbishop?" she asked.

An explosion was her answer. It came from the cathedral, echoing down the long connecting hallways. Deacon Brahim stumbled back, clutching his cross.

"Stay here!" Dayla shouted. She swung her boltrifle free and charged toward the sound.

A few more of the ministry poked their heads out of their rooms. They disappeared just as quickly when Dayla ran by. As she neared the cathedral, she dug her beaked mask from her robes and donned it. The beak had been shortened to be used with her boltrifle, but still reminiscent of the plague doctors it descended from. She flicked the lock off the boltrifle and pulled back on the priming lever. Electricity coursed through the gaps in the barrel.

She found the door to the cathedral shut, and when she pushed it wouldn't move. Something had jammed it. On the other side came explosions and shouts. She planted her feet then threw her shoulder against the door. It shifted a centimetre in the jamb and rattled her old bones. With a quick breath, she readied herself then charged again. The door flew open and she stumbled through.

Chaos gripped the cathedral. Archbishop MacMurray cowered in the sanctuary surrounded by a dozen guards, most dead. At least twelve rows of pews near the centre aisle laid shattered. In the centre of all the destruction were two figures. Adelaide Fisher, the Archbishop's niece, and Dayla's former ward, was supine. No doubt she, with her flame gauntlet, caused most of the damage. Edwin Zhen, a sawbones, stood over her with a boltblade in his hand.

Dayla's heart seized. Not her. None of the guards made a move to help, too shaken by events.

Useless, she thought.

She aimed at Edwin's back and pulled the trigger. The priming lever sprung forward, and a bolt of electricity shot burned the air. Edwin cried and flew forward. But he wasn't dead. Dayla primed the next shot and moved in.

"Are you alright, Adelaide?" Dayla asked.

"Dayla!" Adelaide cried.

Edwin lifted himself onto his knees. Dayla fired. He jerked around, less injured than she thought, and clashed his boltblades. The shock shield rebounded her bolt. Even injured, he wasn't diminished. Edwin was a sawbones Dayla prayed would never go mad. He was talented and unimaginably fast. If she had the good fortune of a few hundred metres she could've taken him clean, but as it was she could only drive him back.

She fired again and again. The bolts ricocheted about; one coming close to taking off her head. It still scoured her mask — and she had just gotten a new one. She slammed her foot into the ground and readied for a kill shot.

Since when did the amberwild run? The thought tapped against Dayla's brain, waiting for her to open the door. On the same night the Mire acts strange and the Church obscures the truth, Edwin Zhen goes mad? Is there a connection? He glanced over his shoulder and in his eyes was not vacant insanity, but despair.

That pause was all Edwin needed. Dayla fired but, with a final burst of speed, he disappeared out the door. *What a night*, she thought and eased off the priming lever.

"Dayla!" Adelaide lunged at her, taking her in one arm. "If you hadn't—"

"It's fine now." Dayla squeezed her back.

She was still young. Red hair stuck out of her braid in all directions or plastered to her damp skin. Dayla felt an imperceptible tremor through her. How her heart beat with adrenaline. She fought with everything she had and tasted the possibility of death. Dayla nearly wasn't there. She stepped out of the hug.

Adelaide was alive, thankfully, though minorly injured. The Archbishop soon came to take her away for medical attention, leaving Dayla to follow Edwin's trail. Though Adelaide believed the sawbones was amberwild, Dayla couldn't be sure. Edwin might have been seeing amber, but on a Cleansing already so strange, nothing could be taken at face value.

The Church had already proven to be hiding something. The Archibishop stood before Dayla, an audience she could rarely manage on the best of days, but with his injured niece and twitchy guards in the room, an interrogation would be foolish. Not that Dayla believed he would tell the truth. She needed to gather more information.

Bidding farewell to Adelaide and her uncle, Dayla rushed out the front doors, stomping out a spit of ember as she went. Edwin was a concern, he attacked Church officials after all. But Arash's report couldn't be ignored. She was getting too old to be running all over Wrotdam chasing ghosts. Not that she would complain. As long as her heart pumped blood, she kept moving.

Edwin was long gone by the time she stepped out the door. He had a home in the upper ward, but it would be foolish to return to it. Amberwild sawbones didn't look for familiarity, they looked for chaos. Dayla headed to the lower ward. That was where the action was. That was where a madman would go.

She arrived at the great Ward Gate. It towered over the surrounding buildings. An old structure of stone and a wooden door reinforced with iron. It used to be the front gates to the city of Wrotdam, long before they expanded past the ravine. As Dayla arrived, guards flitted about, moving carts and barrels, while others put their shoulders to the doors and pushed.

"Wait!" Dayla shouted.

The guards stopped. They glanced back and took one look at the black robes and red scarf then snapped to attention.

"Lady leech," one said. "What can I do for you?"

"Have you seen a sawbones come through here?" Dayla asked. "Edwin Zhen. Wears a green jacket. He's injured."

"Yes, ma'am. He passed through only a few minutes ago. I tried to ask where he was going but he was muttering something about the docks."

"The docks?" The distillery Arash mentioned was near the docks. They could be connected after all. "Excellent. I'm going through as well."

"But... we were ordered to seal the door. If you go, you can't come back until the Obsidian Bell has rung."

"Do your duty." Dayla stepped through. "I'll do mine."

The gate creaked shut, followed by a thump as the heavy bar sealed it. The bulwark could hold back any assault, all iron and wood. When she was young and had first come from India, most of Wrotdam was within the upper ward. The bridge had been built across the canyon, but the lower was filled with scaffolding and skeletal foundation. It wasn't long before the city spread across the landscape and toward the river in the gorge below.

Dayla's reverie broke with the sound of footsteps. Down the wide and long bridge that connected the wards, a man in heavy leathers ran his fingers along one of the many abandoned autocars. He pushed back his rumpled hat, taking the shade off the mask covering his nose and mouth. A branderbuss dangled off his hip and in his hand, held by a bar bolted to the non-cutting edge, was a monstrous riotsaw.

New sawbones generally preferred smaller weapons, for a beast such as the riotsaw was large and unwieldy. A heft that didn't bother the giant that was Rig.

Dayla turned back to the gate and waited until the footsteps got closer. Rig was a devoted sawbones, but he walked away from the Cleansing. Dayla spent the day in the upper ward, disconnected from the events below. With a Deacon lying to her about Arash, she needed to act smart to discover what was going on in Wrotdam.

"How goes the Cleansing, sawbones?" She smiled back at him. "Quite the day. Isn't it, Rig? Tell me, is your mind beginning to slip?"

"No more than usual." The mask muffled his voice. He took his riotsaw hilt in hand and rested the wicked contraption on his shoulder. Blackened blood stained his long coat. The day had been long for him. "Why are you here?"

She spread her arms to feel the wind. "Don't you feel it? The air this evening? It is a Cleansing like none before. Or at least none you would remember."

Rig let out a growling sigh then made a move toward the gate.

"It's locked," Dayla said

"By who?"

"Who do you think?" She tucked her arms beneath her cloak. "The Church has sealed themselves away."

"Why?" He pulled his mask down. His skin was cool like a midnight sky, with a beard in need of a trim. Still, he was a strong-jawed handsome man with an unfortunate permanent scowl. "The city is under curfew. Why separate us like a quarantine?"

"I told you, sawbones. Tonight is something different. The last time the air had this energy, Ravinetown was sacrificed."

His grip tightened on his weapon. "Are they going to burn the city again?"

"I don't believe anyone but the Church itself knows what they are planning these days. The Mayor may as well be paper." She needed to keep moving. Rig seemed in his right mind. "The upper ward won't reopen until the bell rings. For those who survive the night."

She started down the bridge. The industrial district stood on the other side, full of shops and factories. Rig didn't leave her be, he took long strides and caught up.

"I need in," he said.

"No one's leaving the lower ward. The Church is very good at hiding, my boy." She put on her mask. "What has got you so interested in ascending to the parish? Are there not enough sludges to kill around here?"

"It's not about sludges." He pulled his hat low. "I'm looking for Edwin."

Dayla's gaze snapped to him. Her mask kept Rig from seeing the momentary break in her demeanour. He searched for the amberwild sawbones, just after the attack on the Archbishop and his niece. A sawbones despaired, the Mire acted strange, the Church lied. Coincidences were never simple, Dayla understood that. She should play dumb and let Rig lead the conversation.

"Another sawbones? Is stone-hearted Rig showing some weakness?" Dayla made a show of thinking, running her finger down her mask's beak. "He has family in the upper ward, doesn't he?"

"Yes." He turned up his lip.

"Do you suppose he heard of the gnasher spotted up there?"

He went quiet for a second. "I don't want him to run into trouble."

"You mean someone like me," Dayla said, chuckling. "Edwin is the most stable sawbones I've ever seen. Is he starting to slip?"

"No," Rig snapped.

That was the most emotion Dayla had ever seen from him when he wasn't swinging his saw around. Edwin meant something to him, and though he seemed half-mad in the throes of the hunt, Rig was loyal. One day, Dayla would need to put him down, but until the amber took him he stood with the Sawbones.

Then again, she never imagined Edwin, someone so stable, could fall. The College of Sawbones bore a terrible curse, drinking Ink to fight while knowing it could steal their souls away at any time.

Dayla's curiosity pulled her mind in two directions. Her duty as a leech, or Arash's report on the Mire. They were close, near the distillery at the docks, but time ticked away on both. Fortunately, she had a sawbones, violent and straightforward. If Edwin fell, even if he was his friend, Rig would deal with him. He was that kind of man.

"Very well." Dayla swept her boltrifle off her shoulder. "I still have much work to do. You're in luck, Rig. I saw Edwin not long ago. He was heading away from the upper ward toward the docks. He didn't seem to be in the best of spirits. I hope you can help him." At the end of the bridge, Dayla pointed down a narrow staircase. "I'd take the overlook path. The reports say it's clean."

Rig thumped down the steps. "Appreciated."

"Be careful out there, sawbones," Dayla called. "On a night such as this, it's easy to get lost."

She would have to check on Edwin and Rig after it all resolved. Dayla stretched her legs out then jogged toward Obelisk Twenty-Seven.

The buildings of the lower ward sat closer than in the upper, but the streets were abandoned all the same. As the sun touched the horizon line, the building shadows filled these crowded and twisting corridors until only the streetlamps lit her path.

Still, she knew the way and soon arrived at the little guardhouse that contained the obelisk, a five-foot-tall glass pillar with a layer of Ink at the bottom. Currently, it sat still. Dayla checked around, but all the guards fled, leaving the door open and their meals cold. One of the walls laid in pieces along the street, leaving the room clear to anyone who looked in. No wonder Arash couldn't hide.

The sewer entrance was across the street, where clumps of grey and black muck floated in shallow water. The dying sunlight couldn't reach inside. Dayla grabbed a lantern from the guardhouse and headed into the shadows.

It wasn't far before she found a break in the wall. A slimy trail left the water and went over the stone and mortar into some sort of cavern. It must have been the outskirts of Understone, a natural cave system the homeless lived in. Long ago they were catacombs and judging by the dusty unlit lantern hung inside, no one who needed light had been through in a while.

Dayla moved slow, following the trail down into the earth. She kept her breath steady, though her heart pounded in her chest. She preferred clear sightlines and a long distance. Her rifle rested in the crook of her arm, and she kept her finger hovering next to the trigger. Anything could lurk outside the glow from the lantern, and she needed to be ready for it all.

Within a larger room lined with loculi, now bereft of their corpses, she found an extinguished firepit. She placed the lantern nearby and held her hand over the ashes. Dull, but still warm. Dayla cast her light back and forth. A rat skittered across the floor. Whoever lit the fire fled when the Mire came through, but there were no signs of an attack. Arash was right about the Mire ignoring people. That didn't seem possible. The Mire wasn't intelligent. Was it?

The trail descended and eventually brought her to the cave exit. She stepped into a forest, heavy with the smell of damp dirt, and gazed up the cliff face. Wrotdam sat in two parts at the top of the gorge high above her. Night had fallen upon the city and, from a distance, it looked peaceful.

She doused the lantern and left it by the cave mouth. With her rifle ready, she crept into the forest. Another sludge track came in from her left, and a third from her right. A dozen and more long lines of blood and muck converged on her. She had to be near the end of the trail.

The outskirts held many manor houses. It seemed the richer the Wrotdam elite became, the less they wanted to live in Wrotdam. Among them were villages, places safe from the Mire due to their small population. Normally safe, she reminded herself. Was the Mire attacking them? They would be easy targets without sawbones.

The situation made Dayla's stomach turn. It all felt wrong. The air, the dirt, the trees — everything was wrong. She could see the Machine over the forest, its eight tentacles waving slowly. Would she walk all the way to it? That would take hours. There were sawbones there, living in The Shadow, the town built around the only leg that was ashore. They could deal with any Mire that came through.

But that was not to be. Dayla broke from the treeline into what was once a manor house and acreage, now scant more than a shredded foundation. The remains of inkbloods and sludges littered the lawn. Limbs, grey from the infections, hung off trees like grotesque ornaments. The grass had gone slick black from the Mire being smeared across it at high speeds. She stepped around a part of the roof that blocked the driveway.

Intermixed with the organic debris were pieces of metal. They ranged from the size of a hand to a fully-grown adult. They were too twisted to figure out what machine they could be from. Perhaps a boiler, but it seemed to Dayla that there was too much to be from one house.

She approached the skeleton of the manor. Some explosion had flattened most of the walls, leaving only the strongest supports standing. Could have been two storeys or more, but they had been blown clear. However, there were no burn marks to indicate fire or heat, it was like a strong wind tore everything apart.

In the centre of it all, stood a woman. Blood and muck covered everything from her fine jacket and blouse down to her britches and riding boots. Strands of blonde peeked from beneath the slime, but from a distance, she might as well have been raven-haired. She stared at the ground, hands clenched tightly and shaking.

A piece of wood cracked under Dayla's feet and the woman lashed out. A piece of metal shot from the ground, toward Dayla's face. She knocked it aside with her boltrifle. It flipped through the air in a long arc then turned back toward the stranger.

Eleven other finger-long, crescent moon blades lifted from the ground and surrounded the woman. She held her arms out and they spun around her wrists, while her eyes flicked side to side, as if to take in the scene for the first time.

"I'm not a threat to you," Dayla said, lowering her gun. "Are you okay?"

The woman said nothing. She swallowed hard.

"My name is Dayla Singh." She removed her mask. "See? I'm just a person like you. Not exactly like you though, right? You're a magician. My niece married a magician. He had this trick as well."

The woman's shoulders loosened. Her blades floated into a satchel on her hip. Dayla breathed a sigh of relief. The blades were forged with Ink, and a magician's trick was to control them.

"Can you tell me your name?" Dayla asked, stepping forward. "Can you tell me what happened here?"

The woman looked around. She opened her mouth but didn't make a sound, shaking like a shingle in a thunderstorm. She wouldn't be saying anything while she was in shock. Dayla took off her coat and laid it over the woman's shoulders.

"Come on," Dayla said. "Let's get you out of here."

"Yes," the woman said.

At least you have your voice, Dayla thought.

She led the woman out of the destruction. Questions needed to be answered, but Dayla feared this woman wouldn't be the one to do it. In the distance, a bell rung, followed by more echoing the chime. The Cleansing was over.

CHAPTER 4:
THE THIEF

Understone buzzed like a hive. The degenerates and outcasts from Wrotdam fled the streets as soon as the Cleansing began to beat their bee wings in the catacombs, hoping to get far from the Mire flooding the city above. To be safe in the tunnels. Hush Millions knew too well that idea was a warm blanket, but a harsh lie. The Mire could get anywhere.

Hush bought a stick of lamb from a vendor cooking on an open flame. They were close to sundown, but that didn't matter in the pit of Understone. Off the cliffside, far below, the ruins of Ravinetown taunted with burnt buildings and bad memories. Hush took a bite from the lamb and headed back into the tunnels to meet with Franklin.

"You look sick, Hush," Franklin said. He hopped off a coffin he used for a bench.

"What do you mean?" Hush asked, touching his face.

"When was the last time you looked the sun?" Franklin poked Hush's cheek. "Your bones show."

Hush slapped his hand away. He wasn't a large man, and his days in the underground gave him a ghoulish glow, but he wasn't one to let himself get pushed around. He swept back his long, raven hair and poked Franklin in the chest. "Do you have some meals or not?"

Franklin gave a gap-tooth smile. He gestured with one finger for Hush to follow. Franklin was a slight man who always wore a tattered royal guard's uniform from a bygone age. He stole it off a skeleton from deeper in the catacombs after fighting a gang of inkbloods, or darkveins as the Underslang would go. That was the story he told, at least. One sleeve was pinned up for his missing arm.

He led Hush up the twisting tunnels until they broke the surface in the cemetery. Franklin hopped on top of a chest tomb then scrambled to the roof of a mausoleum. Wrotdam, in all its dark glory, waited for them.

"You're agile for a one-armed man," Hush said, clambering up after him.

"Hush, Hush," Franklin said with a smile. He pointed at buildings in the city. "That jeweller packed up a few big clicks ago, he should be long gone by now. Two empty houses by the ale rig. And if we want to take a walk to Watertown, I looked a few good places we can gobble up."

"What about the richies?"

"Those togs are holed up in their castles with their valuables." He gave a two-finger salute to the shadow of the upper ward. "Besides, heard they're shutting the gate to heaven so it's not worth sneaking through."

Hush somehow paled more. "You remember last time the gates closed."

"It's all bright." Franklin wrapped his arm around Hush. "There's no Ravinetown to burn tonight."

He hopped off the mausoleum and took off at a run.

"There's always something to burn," Hush muttered then followed.

They hit the jeweller first. It was a small place, crammed in the corner of a market between a furniture store and a tailor. It had heavy bars on the scant few windows that existed. They circled through the alley and past the front before Hush decided the best choice was the second-floor balcony in the back. He flipped up his hood, cracked his knuckles, and started climbing.

"See you 'round front," Franklin said, then rushed away.

Every crack in the wood was a handhold or foothold for Hush. Climbing was easy. It was as much intelligence as it was strength. He reached the balcony and swung himself over the railing. Just as he thought, the balcony didn't have a padlock, just latched from the inside. He took the metal slat from his lockpicking set and slid it through the crack in the double doors. With a flick of his wrist, he flipped the latch and entered.

The jeweller was dark, but the late evening sun gave him enough light to move around. He was in a bedroom. The owner took his bedsheets and cleared his drawers, but the locked jewelry box was still full, and a lock wasn't something to stop Hush. He took a handful of necklaces and a few rings and shoved them into his coat pockets. He took a stroll through the building, grabbing a few glittering knick-knacks on his way.

Rather than mess around with the lock, Hush removed the pins from the hinges and moved the entire door aside. Franklin sauntered in with a sack over his shoulder.

"Not too bad," he said. "No wonder I keep you around."

Hush put the door back in place and pinned the hinges. "We'll go through here when we're done."

"Sounds good. Let's clean this place before the angels finish cleaning those muckies."

They went to work, cracking display locks and pillaging drawers. They poured each piece worth anything into Franklin's sack. They took their time, knowing that the Obsidian Bell would warn them when it was time to return to Understone. Franklin dropped the bag on the ground and flopped gracelessly into a chair.

"I've been tinkering about a few things," he said.

"I suppose you're gonna flap about them too," Hush said, dropping a candlestick into the bag.

"I sure am, I sure am. I've been tinkering about our state. About how the togs look down on us scroungers. We work, don't we?"

"We sure do, Frank."

"We're out here with the muckies, doing our natural duty to keep ourselves fed while the castles stay locked. But they treat us like we're some lazy frogs sitting on a log all day. They would never risk their skin for pay. They have us for that. They're the ones we sell this stuff to after all." He leaned his elbows on his knees. "So, why do we work for them? When we can do it for wem?"

"Wem?"

"We. Us. The us that is taking it to the streets to survive."

Hush sighed. "Are you stumbling your way to a point?"

"Not a point. A treatise." Franklin tilted the chair back, balancing on two legs. "Togs don't tinker the way we do. They're piped all differently in the head. They believe they're smarter."

"So, what? You're smarter than them?"

"Not smarter, different. They have their thoughts, I have mine. They have their words, I have mine. The moment you tinker you're smarter than someone, that's the moment you become weak. And you definitely never let someone tinker they're dumber than you. Keep them underguessing you, until you snap the trap."

"Cheers, professor." Hush held up the bag. "I'm done. Let's stomp stone."

He removed the door on the way out but left it resting in the front hall. Next, they headed for the two houses by the distillery.

"Keep your eyes moving," Franklin said. "Some angels might be flitting about."

"This feels grimy." Hush pulled his hood tight over his head. "Usually we sneak past a few muckies on a meal. I haven't even seen a darkvein shambling about."

"Are you missing them?"

"No." His eyes flashed to the alleys as they passed by. "Just saying it's all twisty that we haven't seen one."

"Don't go damping our night. No angels and no muckies is bright with me."

Metal clanged down the street. Franklin drew his revolver. A cat wandered out of the garbage pile. It took a lazy glance at Franklin and his gun, meowed, then carried on its way. Franklin let out a puff of air then holstered his gun.

"Let's get off the stone," he said. "I wanna stash the loot in the ale rig while we hit the houses."

They jogged through alleys and under walkways until they crossed the city to the distillery in the East End. Hush used to know a man who worked there, and he would sneak him some drinks when he could. He ran off with a blacksmith some years back and left Hush without a hook-up for alcohol. He also left Hush with a skeleton key. Using that, they unlocked the back door and walked right in.

"Yeah. No one will be stomping in here," Franklin said, shrugging off his coat and swinging it over his shoulder. He slid the top off a crate and took out a bottle of whiskey. "Let's take a break before work begins again."

Hush put the bag behind a large tank, making sure to push it out of sight. They should be back soon, but if they had to run he didn't want some worker finding their hard-earned spoils. While he hid the loot, he spotted something across the room. Most of the window shutters were closed, littering the distillery with heavy darkness, but a section of the floor looked darker than the rest. Hush crept around the tank.

There was a hole in the floor, revealing a tunnel underneath. Hush knelt next to the pit and peered in. The tunnel dropped quickly into the earth. Scratches and tool marks littered the walls and some had been rocks piled up out of the way. Around the splintered edges of the wood were clumps of black slime. He leaned in, straining his ears for any sound.

Glass shattered. Hush spun toward the noise, clutching his chest. Franklin had broken a whiskey bottle on a crate and currently took it down in deep gulps. He coughed from the burn, spilling drops of it down his chin.

"What's got you all dogeyed?" Franklin asked. He took a step forward, then froze. "Bloody gears. What is that?"

"It's a hole," Hush said. "A hole that muckies came out of."

"Did they do that tonight?"

"They must've broken through tonight, but they had to of been digging for a long time." He turned back to the hole and knelt at the edge. "Unless they can dig fast."

"Are muckies that smart?"

Hush didn't know how to answer that. He'd never known the Mire to be anything more than a mindless monster. But to dig through the earth, to come out in the middle of the North End, that didn't seem like the actions of something mindless.

"Look." Franklin pointed with the bottle at a broken window. "They must've left through here." He walked over and inspected an empty frame. "I said this,

I said don't ever tinker that something is dumb. You underguess it and it gets power. The angels are gonna have one hell of a cleaning tonight."

He took a swig of whiskey. A grey hand grabbed the windowsill.

"Franklin!" Hush screamed.

Franklin coughed up a mouthful of whiskey. An inkblood reached in and grabbed him by the shirt. He slammed the bottle against the inkblood's head, but another appeared and wrapped her arms around his neck. His coat fell off his shoulder to the ground.

"Bloody gears!" Franklin pulled away, but the infected were too strong. A third stomped in and grabbed his arm. "Don't just stand there! Help!"

Hush couldn't move. He could barely think. All he could focus on were the dead eyes of the inkblood. Franklin tore his arm out of the hold and drew his revolver. He fired into one of the inkblood's heads and she stumbled back, but another took her place. They knocked the gun away.

"Hush! You limpback!" His feet came off the ground. "Don't let them take me!"

No, Hush thought. *Don't take him. I need to help. Please move.*

But he didn't. He lay on the floor, staring at his screaming friend until the Mire dragged him out of view.

For a minute, Hush remained frozen. Franklin's shouts grew distant. His coat laid where it fell off his shoulder. Hush wanted to tell himself it happened so fast, but it didn't. He wanted to say there was nothing he could do, but he could have tried. Trying was better than letting his friend — his brother in everything except blood — get taken by monsters.

"Franklin," he whispered, then, louder, "Franklin!"

He leapt to his feet and snatched the coat off the ground. He hit the window running, leaping over the frame. The inkblood Franklin shot turned as he landed on the street. Half her head was blown away, revealing a dark throbbing muck inside. She looked at Hush with one remaining eye.

The other inkbloods had disappeared. Hush felt the paralysis creeping in again, but he refused it. He cried out in rage and charged at the inkblood. With one hand, the inkblood struck him across the face and sent him flying against the distillery wall.

The world went blurry. Hush braced himself on the wall, but he collapsed to his knees. He expected the monster to attack again, but she turned as if he didn't exist and wandered away. Hush tried to stand, only to crumple onto his chest. He spat up a mouthful of blood, leaving behind the taste of metal on his tongue.

He laid there in the street, face wet with tears and blood, wracked with pain, for a long time. He held Franklin's coat to his chest, but the voice of the man who once occupied it had disappeared into Wrotdam. Even if Hush wanted to find him, where would he look? The Mire didn't take people, it killed them. It did everything wrong that night.

Long, draining minutes ticked by as Hush embraced the cold of the stone, hoping it would swallow him up and allow him to die. Soft footsteps padded toward him, so faint it sounded like a cat. Instead, a person stood over him.

Ragged clothing engulfed them, all wrapped up underneath a brown cape swung over their shoulder. They had a wide brim hat that would droop over their eyes if one looked from above. But from Hush's vantage, he could see linen wrappings around their face. Between the shade from their hat and the wraps, their eyes were nothing but dark pits.

"You look like you've had a tough day." She spoke with an American accent. Hush nodded.

"I'm sorry." She barely moved. She may as well have been a statue. "Would you like me to help you?"

Hush nodded again, slower.

The woman turned around. She coughed a few times out of view, followed by a wet squish and when she turned back, translucent slime covered her hand. She bent down and — though Hush tried to turn away — placed it against his cheek.

His jaw clicked back into place and the pain subsided. He spat up the last of the blood in his mouth then rose to his feet. He was a good head taller than the stranger, who kept her brim tilted over her face.

"Cheers." Hush rubbed his jaw. Other than the slick slime remains, nothing felt out of the ordinary. But he couldn't shake the disturbing manner of healing. "I haven't seen you around. I'm Hush Millions." He offered his hand.

The woman stayed silent. She bobbed her head a few times before talking, never looking Hush in the eye. "Mattie Wilkins."

Hush gently pulled his hand back.

"Are you looking for your friend?" she asked.

"Did you see him?" Hush jumped forward.

"Maybe. They've probably carried him far away by now." She pointed east down the street, slime dripping off her finger. "They went that way."

"You're a real shiner, Mattie!" Hush ran in the direction she pointed. "Keep safe out there!"

Mattie tracked his movement, eyes hidden behind her wraps. Hush couldn't help but feel there was something off about those eyes, some spark of light deep in the darkness. Not to mention her healing slime. Where had it come from? He couldn't question it now, though. He spent too long laying in the street, but maybe Franklin wasn't gone.

He kept his gaze moving, not daring to run in case he missed a clue among the Mire's trail. He leapt over a horse's corpse and nearly landed in a thick, dark substance splattered across the cobblestone. The same substance inside the wounded inkblood's head. Further down the road was another spot. A glimmer of hope, and Hush took chase.

A few streets down, something exploded. Blue flames reached over the tops of the buildings in a glorious, but momentary, display. Hush dropped to his knees and hunkered down next to a carriage.

His instincts told him to hide, to scurry back into the underground. It was most likely a sawbones doing battle with the Mire. The docks were close, and they always got hit hard on Cleansing nights. But that was the direction Franklin was taken. Hush squeezed Franklin's coat in his fist. The sawbones could be fighting the Mire who took him. He couldn't allow himself to abandon his friend again. He flipped up his hood and ran toward the explosion.

Building remains littered the intersection. A streetlamp stuck out through the wall of an adjacent home, its socket leaking onto the sidewalk. Hush recognized the location as a church, only the front half had undergone some high-impact renovations. The bodies of inkbloods and long streaks of sludge formed a grotesque welcome mat to the front door.

Hush stepped carefully through the mess. If there was any sign of Franklin, even just a lock of his matted, red hair, he would find it. But there was nothing. For the life of him, he didn't know if he should be relieved. Franklin didn't die in the explosion, but he was still missing. And there was still the church. Franklin could be in there.

Hush entered the remains of the church. His blood went cold. Three large Machine Crosses were propped up around the altar. Old and drawn bodies had been tied to the base of each, not new but miraculously well preserved. His foot moved as if pulled by some macabre force.

One adult and two children. Despite the state of the corpses, the clothing was clean. Someone had dressed them and put them there. Hush couldn't fathom why someone would do such a thing, or whether it was the Mire or a person.

What is going on in this city? he thought.

The hairs on Hush's neck stood up. He spun around as a creature stepped into the blown-out church entrance. A gnasher made of bones and sludge with the skull of a stag. It took one step, cracking a pew beneath a human foot, and Hush fell back. His arm struck something laying on the ground. A branderbuss — a sawbones had been there. Hush grabbed the weapon, pointed it at the approaching gnasher, and pulled the trigger.

A depressing display of sparks dribbled out the barrel.

Hush checked the inkwell. There wasn't one. Staghead grabbed him around the neck with a three-clawed talon of broken arm bones and lifted him into the air. It held Hush close and cocked its head. Hush slammed the branderbuss against its arm, spraying aside the black-grey muck, but it didn't notice or care.

The gnasher jerked upright and looked north. Something ticked inside its skull. Hush put his feet against its rib cage and lifted himself to ease the pressure on his neck.

The ticking stopped and Staghead turned its eyeless gaze upon Hush. In the dark pits of its sockets, a white light appeared. It grew into a searing radiance. A screeching assaulted his ears. The light burned him, brighter than the sun. Was his skin cooking? Was that the smell? The sound drilled into his brain until his thoughts ran away in terror.

Then the cacophony was done. Staghead and Hush had vanished. The Obsidian Bell rang the end of the Cleansing.

CHAPTER 5:
THE MAGICIAN

"This Cleansing is never going to end," Clara said.

Victoria Valjean considered her cousin. Clara could find boredom in a thunderstorm, but she wasn't wrong. The Cleansing had dragged on for hours. It hadn't stopped the party, though. They were celebrating Victoria's engagement after all, as well as the new year. Her fiancé, Henry, suggested doing it on that day, a symbol of how their upcoming marriage would be a new start for them. Unfortunately, her husband-to-be waited outside Wrotdam's locked gates. It wasn't safe to enter during the Cleansing.

"The guards said the upper ward is clean." Victoria ran her hands along her gown. "There's a rumour they're going to close the Ward Gate. Why don't all these people go home?"

"Because they want to celebrate you!" Clara swung an empty champagne flute toward her.

"No one's talked to me for two hours. We should've cancelled the party. It was foolish to think the Cleansing would be done by now."

Men and women filled the elegant ballroom, keeping lively conversation and consuming plates of canapes and charcuterie. None had so much as glanced in their direction, where Clara lounged on a red couch while Victoria sat prim and proper on a chair next to her. She had her hair done up into a swooping braided bun and her make-up applied by the finest artist in Wrotdam to ensure a perfect, natural, look. It took hours to prepare her for the event at Valjean Manor and one bell to put it all to waste.

Victoria sighed and flopped her head back. A crystal chandelier hung glittering above the partiers. Her father's pride, its sixteen lights dazzled off the intricate glasswork.

"Everyone looks at me like I should be pitied," she said. "I'm not sad. Why should I be? This is unfortunate, yes, but it's nothing to get upset about. I got to wear this dress and I love it. And that's just for me."

She patted down the fine yellow silk of her dress. It billowed wonderfully with each spin and movement, all covered in frills and lace. She had seen one like it in a shop on high street but didn't like the colour. It took her a couple of weeks to get it all together but took pride in the results.

"Victoria." Clara stood from the couch. "Everyone just wants to make sure you're having fun. Sure, Henry isn't able to make it, but it's still a party."

"I was having fun. Three hours ago. We should have cancelled as soon as we heard that bell." A wicked idea entered Victoria's mind. She leaned toward her cousin. "What if we sneak out?"

Clara's eyes widened. She sat down and eyed the crowd, afraid that someone might have heard them. "What about the Cleansing? The curfew's only an hour away. Your father will be furious."

"Try one worry at a time. If you attempt them all at once, you're likely to pass out in that corset." She placed her hand over Clara's. "Next year, I'll be married and probably off in London. My parents are just happy I'll be wed before I turn twenty-five, they won't care if I have a little fun before that."

"I... suppose."

"Besides, I'm the greatest magician in Wrotdam." She gave an arrogant smile. "You could be surrounded by sawbones and you wouldn't be as safe as you could with me."

Clara groaned. "Are you still practicing that? What happened to the sewing and the horseriding and the harp-playing?"

"I'll only stop when I perfect something. Then I'll perfect something else." She took the flute from Clara and placed it aside. "Come on, Clara. I'm not talking about raiding the lower ward, but let's go into the forest. We can walk the gorge like we did when we were young."

Clara shifted in her heels. She gazed over the crowd. No one paid them any mind, they wouldn't care if the pair disappeared into the wall.

"Fine," Clara said. "Just to keep you out of trouble."

"Perfect." Victoria stood and took her hand. "Let's get our adventuring clothes on."

She dragged her cousin out of the ballroom, moving slow enough not to draw anyone's attention until they passed through the doors. Once out, they half-jogged toward Victoria's room.

Coming up the stairs, they found a housekeeper polishing a sconce.

"Lady Valjean, Lady Fontaine," she said with a bow. "Is the party over?"

"No, Hera," Victoria said. "Clara and I are simply taking a break. But perhaps you could forget you saw us? It's hard to take a break when everyone knows where you are."

Hera smiled and turned back to polishing the sconce without a word. Victoria and Clara continued past, taking the hall to the east wing. They checked up and down the hallway, then ducked into Victoria's room and shut the door.

"You can borrow some of my clothes," Victoria said, reaching back to unlace her dress. "Hurry up before anyone notices we're gone."

Clara pouted, pulling at her dress. Victoria went behind a paper divider and peeled off her gown, hanging it carefully from the wall. Then came the petticoat, the hoopskirt, piece by piece she disassembled all the servant's hard work. With her limber arms, she loosened her corset until she could unsnap the clips. Tossing it aside, she opened a wardrobe and grabbed a blouse and pants. She tossed them over the divider to Clara.

"Where are we going?" Clara asked. "I hope you have a place in mind."

"I do indeed." Victoria opened the door to her walk-in closet. She ran her fingers down her clothes, deciding which would be the best for the night. "We should go to Hammond's Overlook."

"If we're going to sneak out, why not go see Henry?" Her voice strained. She must've been having trouble undressing without anyone to help her. "He shouldn't be far from town."

"I can see Henry for the rest of my life." She picked up a ruffled blouse. Too extravagant. "Tonight is something special."

She decided on a simpler top and a tapered jacket finished with britches and long riding boots. She stopped by her mirror and admired the fit and line. The perfect outfit for sneaking out, though the casual clothing left her evening make-up ridiculous. She brushed her hands along her flawless, ivory skin. If any of her friends saw her, they'd think she was painted up. If they had more time, she would fix it, but someone was bound to notice their absence before long. They needed to get moving.

She left her closet and stepped around her divider to find Clara wrapped in a black hooded cloak. "Clara!" she exclaimed, placing her hand on her chest. "We aren't sneaking around the back alleys. You don't need to look like the spectre of death."

"Dressing like that makes you comfortable." She pulled the cloak tighter around her torso. "Dressing like this makes me comfortable."

Victoria chuckled. She opened a jewelry box on her dresser. Inside wasn't rings or necklaces, but a satchel with two belts. She unbuckled the satchel and made sure the dozen flying moons were still inside. The blades were sharp, though she rarely had a chance to use them. She wrapped the belts around her hips and thigh, keeping it secure.

"Come on, cousin." Victoria pushed open the nearby window. "Let's go on an adventure."

She swung her legs out the window and dropped onto the roof. Clara followed, albeit more awkwardly. They softly stepped across the shingles, taking care not to alert anyone below, to the trestle on the edge. Victoria climbed down first and helped Clara with the final drop. Valjean Manor backed directly onto the street, so they hurried into the city.

"Isn't this fun?" Victoria said, spinning through the empty boulevard.

"Oh yes," Clara said, rolling her eyes. "This is so much more fun than a ball. All that dancing and laughing."

"I'm starting to think I shouldn't have brought you along. Last chance to go back."

"That would be worse. Pretending I don't know where you are when your father starts yelling."

Clara's dour attitude wouldn't sway Victoria. She spun her blonde hair out of the bun without breaking her quick gait. Her loose braids bobbed as she frolicked. The air was peaceful, with the occasional breeze coolly swimming over her skin. The streets normally filled with people bustling about and autocars honking their horns were now serene. Wrotdam was beautiful in its solitude, and these vacant sidewalks and burning lanterns felt more like home than the crowded ballrooms.

"Someone's coming!" Clara whispered, pulling at Victoria's jacket.

The pair leapt into an alley and crouched behind a stack of crates. An old woman dressed in black hurried by. A red scarf flowed out behind her and a weapon Victoria recognized as a boltrifle hung across her back. Victoria stepped out of the alley, watching the woman take the corner at the rug shop.

"Was that a leech?" Clara asked, hiding behind Victoria. "I thought the upper ward was clean?"

"It looks like she's running somewhere else." A wicked smile crossed her lips and she wrapped her arm around her cousin. "Do you want to follow her?"

"Very funny. Let's go to Hammond's Overlook." She stepped out of Victoria's grasp and dragged her away.

They took the main road to a three-way junction where the city suddenly became a thick forest. It didn't escape Victoria's notice that if her husband-to-be truly wanted to find his way in, he could've just as easily as they walked out. There were no checkpoints or sawbones keeping watch as they were in the lower ward.

Clara kept close to Victoria, jumping at every cracking branch and singing bird. They cut closer to the gorge, where they could look down into the river below and the ruins of Ravinetown. The Machine sat to the northeast, glinting the fading sun off its carapace.

"Have you ever been to The Shadow?" Clara asked.

Victoria kicked a rock over the cliff. "Isn't that the city underneath the Machine? No, why would I go there?"

"Because it's interesting. My mother built a lab there. She doesn't do much of the research herself anymore, but she oversees most of it. She took me one time and I got to meet all the scientists. Some used to be Ink Clerics. And most of them are women."

"Uh-huh."

"Women were the first to make breakthroughs in alchemy, actually. Some of the scientists in The Shadow think we may have an affinity for it and that's why most magicians are female."

"Are you nervous?"

"Why would you ask that?"

"Because you talk when you're nervous."

Clara crossed her arms and stuck out her bottom lip. "I was making conversation."

"All right." She hid an eye roll. "Tell me more about your trip to The Shadow."

Clara talked at length about the city. She droned on about the lab — a private operation of researchers separate from the Church — to seeing the workers harvesting Ink from the Machine until finally bragging about a café where she got free scones from a cute worker. Victoria paid a modicum of attention but mostly took in the lovely view. She saw manors, small villages, and farms dot the way to the Machine's feet.

In a few more minutes they reached Hammond's Overlook. There wasn't much to separate the Overlook from the rest of the landscape, save for a tree growing nearly horizontal out the cliff face before turning toward the sky. The bark had been worn down into a seat from all the people who spent hours there, dangling their feet over the steep dirt hill that led dozens of metres to the ground below. Once Victoria had been one such person.

"We're here." Clara waved her hands at the tree. "Can we go back now?"

"Don't be such a downer," Victoria said, sliding closer to the edge. "How about this?"

She took a deep breath and screamed across the landscape. Clara jumped back in surprise. Victoria's voice carried over the forest and little towns, vanishing into the night sky.

"What was that?" Clara slapped Victoria's arm.

"I don't know! It was something, though." She threw her arms wide, taking in the breeze. "Something more than sitting inside waiting for anything to happen. Sometimes you just have to do *something*."

She winked at Clara — then took a running leap onto the tree. Clara screamed. It shook with Victoria's weight but held.

"Don't do that!" Clara shouted. "I don't want to explain to Henry why his fiancée has two broken legs."

Victoria wasn't paying attention. She spotted something at the bottom of the cliff. Figures stomped out of a cave below. About six, one of them dragged a one-armed man by the foot. It didn't look comfortable. They stepped over a tree root and the one-armed man woke up. He screamed like a banshee.

"Is someone screaming back?" Clara asked, too afraid to look over the edge.

The man kicked against the people dragging him. One of them grabbed him by the shoulders and lifted him to his feet. He cracked the man across the jaw, sending him sprawling in a puff of dirt. The group kicked and stomped on the man until his screams turned to whimpers. That was when Victoria noticed their skin. Grey with black veins.

"It's inkbloods!" Victoria said. "They're dragging some man away."

"What?" Clara covered her mouth to stifle a gasp. "The Mire doesn't kidnap people."

"These ones are."

One of the inkbloods threw the one-armed man over their shoulder and kept walking. The group moved with frightening precision as if they could communicate without talking.

What are they doing? Victoria thought. *I wish I could follow them. Figure out what's going on.*

"Victoria, we need to go," Clara said.

"Hold on." Victoria crouched on the tree. "I want to see what happens."

"Well, I don't, you freak. This trip is over."

Clara held herself firm. She stared Victoria down, unblinking.

"Fine. You baby," Victoria said. Clara, for all her whining, didn't back down once she made up her mind. Victoria would rather not hear about it for the next hour. "We'll go home."

Clara breathed a sigh of relief. Victoria leapt from the tree back onto the ground. She scowled at her cousin, and her stomach flew into her throat. The dirt and rocks gave way beneath her feet. Clara screamed again as Victoria dropped. She clawed for any handhold, but the cliff crumbled at her touch. She slid and tumbled until she rolled across the ground below.

"Are you okay?" Clara shouted.

Victoria shook the sense back into her head. She thanked the clothes she decided to wear, the jacket and pants saved her from getting scratched up in the fall. She looked up the cliff to her cousin's face, wracked with worry, and waved.

"Thank God." Clara dropped to her knees. "Can you get back up?"

"I'll have to walk around," Victoria said, standing and brushing the dust off herself. "I think there's a path down here somewhere."

"Victoria!" Clara pointed behind her. "Look out!"

Victoria spun around. One of the inkbloods wandered back. He had his vacant eyes trained on her, skin slick and dead-like. Black veins pulsed grotesquely along his neck. He clutched a bloody axe at his side and stumbled forward. Victoria unbuckled her satchel. She reached out mentally for the drops of Ink forged in each flying moon, like twelve cold spots in her mind. She swept her hand over the satchel and the curved blades followed her movements. She extended both arms and six moons spun around each of her forearms.

"Stay back!" Victoria warned.

The inkblood didn't slow. If he heard her, he didn't care. Victoria twitched a finger and a moon shot into the inkblood's shoulder.

"It's not going to stop!" Clara cried. "Run!"

More fingers twitched. Three more moons shot forth and stuck into the inkblood's head. Though he stumbled from the force, his feet kept moving. Victoria thought back to the books she read about inkbloods. The Mire moved corpses and could only be destroyed through absolute bodily devastation. Weapons needed to tear, shock, or burn.

I'm the greatest magician in Wrotdam, Victoria thought. *One inkblood is nothing to the greatest magician in Wrotdam.*

She pulled her moons back and swung the lot around her head. The memories of sparring with her tutor came back, turning into footwork and arm positions. Magicians needed to move like the currents of the wind. There were no muscles to push with, and it was easy to pop a blood vessel in your eye if the user wasn't careful. Momentum was a magician's best friend.

The moons collected above her shoulders and began to spin, becoming two whirling buzz-saws. The inkblood raised his axe and Victoria thrust her hand forward, sending one saw into his throat. It tore out blood and gore as the inkblood kept walking. She swung the other saw wide, cutting branches off trees with a humming whine, then yanked it back. They met on both sides and ripped through the inkblood's spine, curling out through the forest and returning to hover above her shoulders. His head sloughed off and landed heavy and bloody in the dirt.

But he didn't stop. A bulbous mound oozed out of the neck stump and formed into some cruel facsimile of a head. The inkblood swung his axe. Victoria stumbled back, nearly tripping over her feet. She separated her buzzsaws into two lines and carved across the inkblood's chest. With each step back, she conducted the symphony of steel. Over and over, until the inkblood crumpled, its body splayed open.

"Yeah!" Clara shouted. "That was amazing, Victoria!"

The moons returned to Victoria's satchel. Her mind ached with exertion. She wanted to go home, crawl into her bed, and sleep for a week.

There was a dull thump and pain shot through her skull. The next thing she knew, she was on the ground. Through a haze of ringing, Clara's scream reached her ears. Blood trickled down Victoria's forehead and to her neck. She felt for the twelve drops of her moons, but a horde of inkbloods descended upon her and pinned her arms. They hefted her onto their shoulders and marched.

"Victoria!" Clara's voice came through the haze.

"Clara!" She fought against her captors, but their grip barely flexed.

Without her arms, she couldn't move her moons. She kicked and wiggled, then stopped. Something moved in the trees, something big. It was black as pitch and dribbled chunks off like sludges but on a whole other scale.

As the tree line broke, she could see the monster clearly. It towered like an oak tree but oozed through the forest as a broad, undulating muck. Chunks of metal stuck out, and as it moved those chunks vanished and reappeared. Smaller sludges and other inkbloods flanked it as if they were escorting it.

And it only got worse. They stepped out from the forest to a well-kept lawn. Ahead, a manor house awaited. Victoria recognized the land as Pembrooke House, seat of Lord Haverstone and his family. She had been to a few balls as their guest, though its current state was like nothing she'd seen before.

Large machines of whirling gears and pulsing pumps had been affixed to the façade and punched through the ceiling. Exhausts poured sulphurous smoke into the air and piping ran from the apparatuses into the ground. The massive sludge stopped outside and expelled pieces of metal into the waiting inkblood's hands. They were building something.

Victoria's mind reeled. How could this be? Such coordination, such planning. Over and over, the experts said the Mire was mindless. How could something mindless create this? And for what reason?

The inkblood carried Victoria into the house. Piping ran through the walls, leaking a grey substance permeating her skin with its rotting scent. They brought her through halls filled with shambling former humans turning valves on the machinery. Her body wouldn't respond as she urged it to fight and her skin went cold with fear.

Soon they arrived just outside the Pembrooke House central ballroom and threw her to the ground. Her head bounced off the wooden floor and her forehead stuck for a second with the drying blood. A pair of bony legs thudded to a stop before her. She couldn't stop her hands from shaking but looked up to see the monstrosity.

The skeletal creature bent down to inspect her. It had the skull of some large dog and its rib cage encased a sludge-like pulsating mass. None of the bones other than the skull were in the right place — one of its legs even ended in a hand. Victoria had heard of them, but she'd never seen a gnasher before.

Now she'd seen two.

Doghead grabbed her by the throat and lifted her like she was paper. She pulled against the grip, aching for a gasp of air. The gnasher tossed her to one with a bull's head. It wrapped its arms around her, keeping her from moving and carrying her into that central room. A metallic whirring filled the air as they entered the ballroom.

In the centre of the dance floor, where all the pipes converged, stood a grinder. Blades stained with blood and flesh spun within a metal mouth. Dark, industrial smoke leaked from the piping and collected at the ceiling. The floor in front was stained red like a welcome carpet. A third gnasher with three human skulls for a head stood by the contraption. It cocked its heads at Victoria and she understood with horrifying clarity they were going to feed her into the machine.

She screamed. Her body finally reacted, kicking with new vigour. Bullhead didn't budge. She reached her mind out for her flying moons, but felt something different. The grinding machine glowed in her psyche. It invited her in. Her teeth were the spinning blades, her skin shell across the bloody gears, her soul the people who fed its hunger. It was thick with oil and death. She wanted it to stop.

So it did. The tearing teeth ground to a halt. Threehead tapped the chassis. It looked at Bullhead, then punched the machine. An invisible force struck Victoria's cheek and she jerked her head to the side. She squared her jaw. Whoever did that was going to pay.

The bolts popped out of a binding and a pipe crashed into Threehead, knocking one of its skulls away. More pipes broke from their setting, pouring blood and black sludge onto the floor. Bullhead dropped Victoria and caught one, lifting it back up into place.

That was her chance. She unbuckled her satchel and drew her flying moons, but another cold spot moved with her. A cold star in the centre of her brain, expanding across her flesh and spirit.

The machine bowed and spun at her call. Her vision turned to dots and colours, but she felt the lines of the machine like a thousand eyes and ears. Her consciousness expanded to the moon and beyond. She saw stars that enveloped planets with cosmic fire. She felt the empty coldness of space like ice in her veins. She heard a million voices screaming at once. Then there was one. One voice to a formless face. It lingered in the machine with her. She pushed back against the voice, but it was the machine that responded.

It exploded. Tore the gnashers apart. Ripped the walls away. The world went white.

She didn't know how long she was out for, but her next memory was her standing on her two feet among absolute destruction. Blood and black slime coated her body like a second skin, its vile taste lingering in her throat. Her stomach turned over and over. She wanted to puke but there was a chance she would never stop until she turned inside out.

There was a sound and Victoria swung toward it, sending a flying moon. The woman knocked it away with the butt of her rifle. A leech. She said something, but it was distant and distorted like talking through water. Victoria tried to respond, but her throat wouldn't work.

"...Dayla Singh." The leech said, removing her mask. It was the same old woman she and Clara saw in the upper ward.

Clara! Victoria thought. *Is she okay? She probably ran back to Wrotdam. I hope she did.*

"See? I'm just a person like you," Dayla continued. "Not exactly like you though, right? You're a magician. My niece married a magician. He had this trick as well."

I don't care about your niece's husband. Just help me. I can't talk. Victoria stowed her moons.

Dayla stepped forward, carefully. "Can you tell me your name? Can you tell me what happened here?"

The manor; ruins around her. The machine; destroyed. The Mire; turned to paste.

No. I can't, Victoria thought. *No one can. Please, help.*

Dayla swept her coat off. She wrapped it around Victoria. The warmth was welcome, but Victoria couldn't help but think of how she stained it.

"Come on," Dayla said. "Let's get you out of here."

Say something, Victoria. She begged her throat to work and her mouth to move. Like pressed her hands into unworked dough, she finally grabbed something. "Yes," she eked out.

It took every bit of energy she had just to make that one syllable. The world came to her in pieces, and the voice she heard in the machine faded into a light memory. Without that voice, Victoria became smaller until she fit her skin. But for a moment, she was the size of the cosmos. And she liked it.

Somewhere, on a distant planet, an Obsidian Bell rang.

CHAPTER 6:
THE CURSED

Mattie Wilkins only came to Wrotdam four months earlier. She took the long journey across the Atlantic, from St. Louis by way of Boston. She spent days crammed into a nook between the wall and a stack of luggage in the cargo hold. She was always a small woman, even into her twenties, built like a birch tree. No one would find her if she didn't want to be found. She couldn't buy a ticket after all. Mattie Wilkins was cursed.

That was the way everyone put it. It started when she noticed the whites of her eyes darkening. After that, her skin faded to a blueish grey. Her brown hair grew into the colour of steel. She cut it almost all off in a fit. By the time they called the doctor, the transformation was complete. Her hair had dulled, her skin was inhumanly colourless, and her eyes were black pits. It was as though everything that made her Mattie drained away, leaving an empty shell behind.

The Mire wasn't unheard of in St. Louis, so people started talking. They said she laid with devils, who cursed her with sludge blood. Priests from the Church of the Machine came by, but they had never seen something like her before. She was still in her right mind, she wasn't becoming inkblooded. They left, promising to return when they learned more. They never did.

But Mattie didn't give up. Rumours reached her of cure-alls existing in Wrotdam, the city the Machine showed itself to. If someone could reverse whatever happened to her, it would be there. She stole some money from her parents, wrapped herself in cloth, and paid her way to Boston, where she stowed away aboard an inkship across the sea.

Wrotdam wasn't kind to her. She asked around for months, alluding to her condition, without any success. Most ignored her like a leper, but those who listened to her had no idea how to help. She never wanted to push too hard, afraid sawbones or Ink Clerics would come for her. She avoided the upper ward as much as possible and slept on the lower ward streets.

When the Alabaster Bell rang and the people started running, she couldn't do anything but follow them into the catacombs below. St. Louis hadn't had a Cleansing in decades, long before Mattie was born; the local sawbones killed any Mire before it could have an outbreak. She found herself a dark corner in the tunnels and prepared to wait the day out.

Her stomach rumbled. She dug into her pocket and pulled out a few coins, the meagre sum she could scrounge through begging. With the money in hand, she headed to the cliffside where she saw people cooking skewers on open flames.

Among the people's hushed mutters, an indistinct voice separated from the pack.

"Bring them," it said.

Mattie spun around. No one talked to her. No one looked at her. But the voice felt close. Right inside her ear.

Must be a weird echo, she thought and went to buy her food.

The cliffside was less busy than the catacomb halls and several small vendors set up along the lip, flirting dangerously with a long drop into the burned village below. Mattie approached one.

"What do you have?" she asked.

"Lamb," the vendor said.

"Bring." The mysterious voice whipped past her like the wind.

Mattie stared at the vendor. The voice was so loud, he had to of heard it. But he didn't react.

"You tinkering about buying?" the vendor said in his Underslang speak.

The coins rattled in Mattie's hands. She nearly dropped them off the cliffside until the vendor snatched them away. He scowled and thrust a lamb skewer at her before shooing her away.

She weaved through the crowd, her eyes darting from side to side but observing nothing. She pulled her wraps away and took an unsteady bite of the skewer. Her condition must be progressing; somehow she hallucinated a voice. If she didn't find the cure soon, there was no telling what she would become.

She took a quick turn into the catacombs and bumped into a hooded figure going the other way.

"Sorry," Mattie said, shrinking away.

They looked back, revealing a dark-skinned woman with hard features. One of her eyes was completely black — just like Mattie's.

Mattie stared in shock as the woman crossed the suspension bridge from the east part of Understone, across the gorge, to the west. She tore off the last chunk of lamb from the skewer and tossed the stick off the cliff before rushing after the woman.

"Excuse me!" Mattie shouted. "Excuse me! Can I talk to you?"

The woman stopped halfway across the bridge and turned around. She was tall, lithe and with a posture like a snake. A bundle of grey robes hung off her in loops and folds fastened with belts. She had skin like fall leaves and in her billowing clothes, she seemed ready to blow away. She cocked the eyebrow above her black eye as Mattie approached. The bridge swung gently above the violent drop into the burned city below.

"I, uh." Mattie clutched onto both ropes, forcing herself not to look down. "I noticed your eye."

"What about it?" The woman crossed her arms.

Mattie took a deep breath, then pulled down part of her wraps, revealing her black eyes and grey skin. The woman nodded and looked past her, making sure no one had followed.

"Come with me," she said, continuing toward the western side.

Mattie replaced her wraps and followed. Understone was quieter under the upper ward. Most people fled the streets and planted themselves as soon as possible, on the east side under the lower ward. The people on the west side made homes from crypts and strung tents between pitons hammered into the wall, settling in for a weary life in the forgotten tunnels.

"What's your name, girl?" the woman asked without looking back.

"Mattie Wilkins."

"American?"

"St. Louis. So, uh, yes, ma'am."

They reached a tent set up between four stone coffins. The woman pulled the curtain aside, revealing a hovel filled with pillows and blankets most likely pilfered from the aristocrats above — something that could be cozy if not for the death surrounding it.

"You can call me Asha." She motioned for Mattie to enter first.

Mattie crouched into the tent and found herself a soft sack to sit on. Asha sat across from her. She flipped down her hood and considered Mattie with her one black eye.

"Show me," she said, lounging back on her pile of pillows.

Mattie had been careful to keep her appearance a secret from everyone. The ones who shied away from her were easy, but others screamed or threatened her. Even the humble Wrotdamites huddling in Understone treated her like she brought on the infection. But if she couldn't trust Asha, she could trust no one.

She removed her hat, revealing her messy, steel hair as it fell across her eyes. Asha made no motion for her to stop. Mattie took a breath and slowly unwrapped her face.

"Oh my." A smile crept across Asha's lips. "I've never seen it so... Is the Mire strong in St. Louis?"

"Not particularly." She pulled off her gloves and clutched them in her lap. "We don't have any sawbones, but we have what you would call leeches. They deal with any infections. What's happening to me?"

"No one knows for sure." She leaned forward, looking Mattie over from toe to crown. "It's a consequence of the Mire, a rare one. Have you had any run-ins with sludge?"

Mattie thought back. The past Spring had been uneventful. She spent a lot of time with her friends, but a monster had never come up. Surely, she would remember that.

"No matter." Asha tapped her fingers along a coffin's lid. "You've been infected. Most become inkbloods, but some have a different reaction. The Mire lives inside us, but it's ever-sleeping. I wouldn't fret, it's harmless. More than harmless, you're immune. It's a blessing — if you can get around the stares everyone gives you."

"It doesn't feel like a blessing. I couldn't leave the house without children throwing rocks at me. Without people whispering as I walked by, calling me a monster or a witch." She scrunched up her face. "They wanted to burn me, and if I stayed, they might have."

"Blessings don't always make sense. You're looking for a cure, aren't you?"

"Yes!" Mattie grabbed Asha's hand. "Do you know of one?"

"Many have asked." She pulled her hand away. "There are rumours, there are always rumours. Rumours that the Church is hiding a way to *fix this* — if there's anything to be fixed at all."

"Why would they hide it?"

"Because if the people ever turn on them, they can throw us to the wolves. Wouldn't be hard to make us scapegoats." She flipped back her curly hair. "Course, I don't believe any of that. I don't think there's anything to cure. If our minds are being spared, it's for a reason, and the Machine will tell us what it is. Have you heard the whispers?"

Mattie's thoughts turned to the voice in the tunnels. "Whispers?"

"A call from the Machine, telling us of the True Metal God. He's not in Heaven, not anymore. The Lord has come to earth in a vessel that will bring Paradise to us. The eight-legged one, not a Him or a Her, but a Machine."

"You think... the Machine is God?"

"I'm not the only one. Doctrine says the Machine is an angel, but angels are messengers. The Machine is not a messenger, it's the message." She went to her knees and leaned forward, her non-black eye lit up like sparks. "The Order sees people like us — people with the eyes, the skin, and the hair — we are the Machine's chosen."

"I don't want to be chosen; I want to be normal." A wriggling grew in Mattie's guts.

"But you are so much more than normal, Mattie Wilkins. You have truly been gifted by the Machine. The whispers must be shouts to you."

A buzzing filled Mattie's skull with each word Asha said. She clutched her stomach and ran out of the tent. Her knees crumpled and she barely caught herself from cracking her head. Something crawled through her intestines, churning its way up into her throat until it burst from her mouth. A clear and viscous liquid poured onto the stone. It clung to her lips in long strands with the taste of rotting fruit.

She caught her breath and blinked tears away, squeezing the rock beneath her hands. Something moved in the liquid. She focused her eyes. It was small, writhing, grey worms.

Mattie screamed and scrambled back, bumping into Asha's legs as she stepped out of the tent. Asha looked upon the strange worms, a smirk lingering across her face. She crouched, gazing down upon the worms Mattie had thrown up.

"Do you wish to see the true power of your gift?" she said, rolling up her sleeve and unwrapping a bandage, revealing a deep cut along her forearm.

Mattie's fingers trembled, horrified as Asha scooped up the slime and put it on her wound. The flesh tensed and the skin knitted together until the cut was gone. Asha held it up to Mattie, but it wasn't a trick of her eyes. It had been healed in seconds.

"Look upon this wonder." Asha swept her hand over the worms as they crawled across the stone, disappearing into cracks and soft dirt. "Few carry these creatures and have this ability, among many more. You're evolving. The True Metal Order can show you how to become what God has chosen you to be."

Mattie's knees shook as she crawled backwards, away from Asha and the worms. It couldn't be real — she was trapped in a nightmare that went on forever. She wanted to go back to St. Louis, with her friends and her family. She wanted to gossip about boys with her friend Amelia. She wanted to sneak out to swim in the river. She didn't want to puke worms on the floor of some cave across the sea. She scrambled to her feet.

"Mattie Wilkins!" Asha shouted. "You forgot something!"

Mattie stopped and turned around. Asha tossed her hat and gloves at her feet. Mattie snatched them up and covered herself once again. She glanced at Asha, smiling with her black eye, then ran. She crossed the bridge, even as it bounced precariously she didn't stop. Eyes looked down on her from all directions. Did they know what lived inside her? She held her wrappings against her face, but she knew they could see her skin. She needed to get away from the eyes. The buzzing stayed in her mind and she couldn't tell if she was going where she needed to go, or where the buzzing drove her to.

"Bring them," the distant voice said. "Bring them."

Up she went. Up through the tunnels where the eyes couldn't see. Understone was a labyrinth at the best of times, easy to get lost in. As she took turn after turn through identical caverns of loculi and crypts, that's exactly what happened.

By the time she slowed, she was far away in the cobweb-filled tunnels no one went to. The sconces were bare. No sun could reach her. It should have been dark — but it wasn't. She rubbed her eyes, but she could still see. The world was shades of grey and amber, but she could make out the rough texture of the walls and the dripping water from stalactites. Asha was right, she was evolving.

Feet slid against the stone and she jerked toward the sound. Four inkbloods lumbered down the tunnel she was heading toward. They were too close for Mattie to run, so she pressed herself against the wall and froze. An inkblood dribbling black liquid from its lips brushed past, its arm touching her hat but it kept moving ahead. The largest one carried a person bleeding from his head on its back, breathing shallowly.

That man isn't dead, she thought, stuck to the spot. *Why are they taking him? What's happening?*

The grim procession carried on. Mattie waited until their footsteps faded and ran out the way they came, finding a broken wall with the sunset shining through. She climbed over the rubble into a construction site near the docks. Crouching next to a stack of bricks, she tightened up her wraps. She couldn't get her hands to stop shaking or her thoughts to stop racing as she pulled the linen over her nose.

"Let me go!" someone screamed and Mattie threw herself against the bricks. "Help!"

A man sprinted past her hiding spot. A moment later, a congealed, black slurry caught him by the ankle. His upper body continued forward and he cracked his head on the ground. The black mass twisted and tensed then began dragging the man's limp form backwards. Mattie peered out from behind her cover.

A sludge led another group of inkbloods through the site, carrying people on their shoulders like sacks of grain. The man who had fallen groaned as he was dragged over loose gravel, the black mass revealed to be the sludge's arm. He looked up, blood coating his face, and focused his eyes on Mattie.

"Help!" He thrashed with a sudden burst of desperate energy. "Help me!"

Mattie squeezed the bricks. An inkblood dripping black fluid from a wound on its neck lumbered forth, following the man's scream. Mattie's legs locked in place, unable to run as the inkblood met her eyes — and looked beyond. It couldn't see her.

"Help!" the man shouted again. Tears poured down his cheeks. His fingers tore against the gravel as he fought the sludge pulling him back.

The inkblood turned away from Mattie and stomped on the man's hand. A second inkblood dropped the captive it carried and drew a hammer. The Mire swarmed around the man.

A part of Mattie wanted to help, but what could she do? She wasn't a sawbones or a leech. Those infected by the Mire were stronger than a regular human, and the usual means couldn't kill them. Mattie would be like a fly attacking a horse. All it would take is a flick of its tail for her to be obliterated. Besides, people didn't care for her, why should she care for them?

The inkblood raised its hammer. The man screamed and cowered. Mattie's heart leapt into her throat, turning to words as it passed her lips.

"Stop!" she screamed.

The inkbloods froze. With mechanical precision, they turned, realizing Mattie existed for the first time. The sludge released its grip on the man's leg, breaking its arm at the middle, leaving a chunk of itself undulating on the ground while the stump reformed into a bone claw. It pushed through the inkbloods and loomed over Mattie, staring at her without eyes. There came a violent turn in Mattie's stomach and she puked again.

The worms poured from her mouth, then writhed across the ground to the sludge. They drilled through its foot and into its body. The sludge trembled. One of its arms shot out and crushed the skull of the inkblood with the hammer. It didn't kill the inkblood but gave the captive man a chance to kick the muck off his leg and jump to his feet.

"Thank you," he said, pausing briefly as he passed before sprinting through a hole in the construction site's fence.

For the first time in nearly a year, Mattie felt good. The true emotion in the man's face, the gratitude, she couldn't help but smile.

The remaining captives, a pair of women, woke up amid the chaos. They saw the sludge convulsing, dripping worms from its body, and screamed. The sludge pulled at its arm, tearing it off and stumbling back against a stack of rebar.

"Run!" Mattie cried, backing away.

One of the women helped the other one to her feet and they bolted. The sludge hammered against the rebar pile, its body ebbing as the worms pushed through its muck. A couple of the inkbloods turned on Mattie, only to get grabbed by the sludge's convulsions and pulled away.

The inkblood who got the worms dumped on him fell to his knees, trembling violently. A sludge head bubbled up from his neck stump, only to come apart in worm-filled clumps, turning pale and watery. He reached for Mattie.

She kicked his hand away and ran. She leapt onto a stack of bricks and dove over the fence, crashing into the trashcans on the other side to somewhat soften her landing. Adrenaline brought her back to her feet and she took off into the streets and alleys. She didn't even know what she was running from anymore. Her thoughts came in flashes of emotion and broken sentences.

The worms that came out of her had saved those people — she had saved those people. But what did that mean? Her affliction had uses, but now she couldn't help but feel the movement in her stomach, the worms that lived inside her. She was further from human than she had ever been before. She had come to Wrotdam to be cured, not to evolve.

Asha said the Church could have a cure. She could go to them and prostrate herself before their mercy, to burn the worms out of her. Or would they kill her? The cursed monster she was.

An inkblood stepped around the corner in front of her. Muck dripped down its face from a missing piece of its head. Like the others before, it ignored Mattie. She was invisible to the Mire until she drew its attention. It wandered past, and Mattie continued.

Around the next corner, the city grew familiar again. She was outside the distillery. A figure slumped by the wall, in full fetal position with his face on the stonework street. His breath came slow and occasionally became whimpers. Fresh blood splattered against the street and wall. Mattie crouched down; her old instincts to hide taking over. He looked so pathetic, crying into the drain. She waited for a while, hoping the man would get up and wander off. He never did. She covered her ears, trying to drown out the whimpers that seemed to only be getting louder. She looked at her hands. She could help him like she helped the people get away from the Mire.

Her mother always said she was too kind for her own good. They lost count of the number of stray cats she snuck into the house. But her parents said kind people were taken advantage of. So, she turned away.

Damn it, Mattie, she thought.

She turned back and walked toward the injured man. He didn't notice her until she stood right over him. He was sickly-looking, with dark hair and a gaunt face. He clutched onto an old royal guard's uniform, red and dirty. His jaw rested in a weird position and blood leaked out of his mouth, mixing with the tears streaming down his cheeks.

"You look like you've had a tough day," Mattie said.

The man nodded. He didn't seem to realize how bad his injury was. She should leave him, as he would leave her. Kindness can come back and bite someone. But she couldn't forget how good it felt to help the others. The man even said thank you.

As she looked into the injured man's eyes, she felt something. It wasn't words, but a feeling washing over her. The man was looking for someone. Someone he lost. There was so much pain in his heart. She couldn't leave him like this, or she would be no better than the people who hated her.

"I'm sorry," Mattie said. "Would you like me to help you?"

The man nodded again.

Mattie turned around. She lifted her hand to her mouth and coughed until the slime oozed onto her glove. She flicked the worms away then turned back to the man. He recoiled, but she placed the slime against his cheek. The man's jaw clicked back into place. He spat up a mouthful of blood and stood. He towered over her, so she kept her hat brim low to hide her face.

"Cheers. I haven't seen you around," the man said. He extended his hand. "I'm Hush Millions."

Oh great, she thought, ignoring his hand. *Now he's talking to me. Why couldn't you just leave?* "Mattie Wilkins." The feelings still came out of him, injecting directly into her brain. Somehow, she knew things she shouldn't know. "Are you looking for your friend?"

"Did you see him?"

"Maybe. They've probably carried him far away by now." She didn't know who his friend was, but she knew where the Mire was taking people. She pointed the way she came. "That was the direction they went."

"You're a real shiner, Mattie!" Hush ran at full sprint down the street. "Keep safe out there!"

He was happy, if only for a moment. Mattie knew it wouldn't last, though she hoped it would see him through at least one night.

"You are a kind person." It was Asha.

Mattie spun toward her. Asha wasn't alone. Three other people who wore the same ill-fitting robes stood at her sides. They each had marks of the infection that Mattie possessed. One had steel-coloured stripes in his hair. Another had grey patches on her face, reaching down her collar. The last had a black eye like Asha, but his other one was bisected by the same black colouring. A gang like that usually had sticks and rocks, not open arms.

"How did you find me?" Mattie asked.

One of Asha's followers held up a jar with some worms in it.

"We know how to talk to the worms," Asha said. "They found their way home. Didn't it feel good to help that person?"

"I don't like you following me."

"You are everything we've dreamed of, Mattie Wilkins. God has brought you here to do its work. The Machine will move, but we need you to direct it. You can help more than one person. You can help all the people. All the people who threw you away."

"Why would I help the people who don't want me?"

"The same reason you helped that man." Asha extended her hand. "You're a kind person. The Machine's will flows through you. We can bring this world into the new century."

Mattie squeezed her cloak. She had been deluding herself, thinking there was a cure to make her normal. This was her life. Black eyes and dulled skin. But maybe Asha was right. She helped Hush, and she helped those people near the tunnel. She couldn't have done that if she was normal.

In the distance was an explosion. Mattie looked toward the sound. Wrotdam was falling apart. It needed help. She could do good. Even just a little bit.

"Can you truly teach me to use this?" Mattie asked.

"No one can," Asha said. "But we can help you discover yourself."

"Then I'll do it."

Asha smiled. "Welcome, Mattie Wilkins, to the True Metal Order."

The Obsidian Bell signalled the end of the Cleansing, but the beginning of Mattie's new life.

CHAPTER 7:
THE SAWBONES

Rig, covered in dirt and viscera chunks, cradled his skull. He ran his fingers over the skin on his bald head. A thumping hid between his thoughts, making it hard to think. The sun sank below the many spires of Wrotdam, quickly spreading shadows over the claustrophobic streets. Corpses laid around the bench he took his break on. They weren't human, not anymore, the signs of becoming monstrous were clear. Dark veins, vacant eyes, and slick skin. Inkbloods. The Mire had taken hold.

He pulled the stopper off a small glass vial and drained it of Ink. The dark-amber liquid had a bizarre, vacant taste — like taking down a gulp of liquid air. It quelled his headache and for a moment there was nothing. No pain. No fear. No thoughts. He felt renewed. With a belly sigh, he stood from the bench and stepped over the bodies.

He crossed the great bridge to the railing that looked over Wrotdam. Steep-roofed, crowded buildings stretched out before him like waves on the ocean. Beyond them, close to the coast, the Machine rose from the horizon. Its eight mechanical tentacles waved slowly.

Rig stepped back from the railing. He needed to focus. All he knew was the Machine. All he had was the Cleansing. He gave his life to the Church to keep Wrotdam safe. Keep his home safe. But all he seemed to get in return was a town full of monsters and the smell of blood and Ink. He replaced his hat and half-mask, meant to keep the corrupted blood out of his mouth during the Cleansing. He was down to the last of his inkwells, not counting the ones designed to power his weapons. But he wouldn't want to drink those — more likely to burn out his insides than give him peace. The day had been long, but the night ahead looked longer. He wasn't hunting monsters anymore; he was searching for a friend.

He grabbed his riotsaw out of an inkblooded Wrotdamite's chest. He flicked a piece of meat off the chains. Blood caked the teeth, but Rig was confident in its ability to work through any potential clogging. Weapon in hand and branderbuss on his hip, Rig continued down the bridge to the upper ward.

An aching stillness held over the city. The Archbishop called a curfew until the latest scourge of the Mire had been dealt with. Citizens hid inside behind lavender candles to ward the monsters away. The city was frozen, and it would remain so until the Obsidian Bell rang. Rig ran his hand along an autocar left on the bridge. During the day, the wealthy rode up and down the streets. They jumped from ball to ball, blind to the struggles of the lower class. On a night like that, they would be feeling safe and warm within their manor walls.

Rig approached the other side of the bridge. A black-robed figure stood at the Ward Gate, staring at the great iron bulwark. A crimson scarf hung off their shoulders, the ends draped over a boltrifle strapped across their back. The garb of a Church leech.

"How goes the Cleansing, sawbones?" the woman said with a chuckle. She peered over her shoulder and shot Rig a cocky smile. Her wrinkles accented the grin with joviality. Dayla the Leech. "Quite the day. Isn't it, Rig? Tell me, is your mind beginning to slip?"

"No more than usual." Rig rested his saw on his shoulder. He'd crossed paths with Dayla many times in his career. The sawbones had a name for her behind her back. The Reaper. Few other leeches led as many retirements for amber madness as she did. "Why are you here?"

"Don't you feel it?" She turned back to the gate and threw her arms wide. "The air this evening? It is a Cleansing like none before. Or at least none that you would remember."

The leech spoke nonsensical, obscure ramblings. He didn't have time for it. He stepped around her and moved toward the gate.

"It's locked," Dayla said.

"By who?"

"Who do you think?" She looked up at the buildings towering over the wall in the ward. "The Church has sealed themselves away."

"Why?" Rig pulled down his half-mask. "The city is under curfew. Why separate us like a quarantine?"

"I told you, sawbones. Tonight is something different. The last time the air had this energy, Ravinetown was sacrificed."

"Are they going to burn the city again?"

"I don't believe anyone but the Church itself knows what they are planning these days. The Mayor may as well be paper." She started across the bridge, back toward the industrial district. "The upper ward won't reopen until the bell rings. For those who survive the night."

Rig kept pace. His mission couldn't be stopped by something as simple as a locked door. "I need in."

"No one's leaving the lower ward," Dayla said. She grabbed a brown, beaked mask from within her robes and put it over her face. "The Church is very good at hiding, my boy. What has got you so interested in ascending to the parish? Are there not enough sludges to kill around here?"

"It's not about sludges. I'm looking for Edwin."

"Another sawbones? Is stone-hearted Rig showing some weakness?" Dayla pondered, slowly running her fingers over the leather mask. "He has family in the upper ward, doesn't he?"

"Yes."

"Do you suppose he heard of the gnasher spotted up there?"

Rig tapped his thumb on his riotsaw's hilt. It wasn't an honest question. Dayla knew. Leeches always knew. "I don't want him to run into trouble."

"You mean someone like me." She cackled. "Edwin is the most stable sawbones I've ever seen. Is he starting to slip?"

"No," Rig snapped. Dayla cocked her head. Maybe he had spoken too fast and made her suspicious. Rig didn't believe Edwin's mind was failing, but the leeches weren't ones to see shades of grey. A suspicion was enough for many of them to cleanse a sawbones.

"Very well." Dayla swept her boltrifle off her shoulder. "I still have much work to do. You're in luck, Rig. I saw Edwin not long ago. He was heading away from the upper ward toward the docks. He didn't seem to be in the best of spirits. I hope you can help him."

They reached the end of the bridge; the same place Rig first came from. If Edwin had left the upper ward, he must have found his family. That, or he was locked out as well and was looking for another way in. Maybe down the river?

Dayla pointed down a steep and twisting staircase. "I'd take the overlook path. The reports say it's clean."

"Appreciated." Rig peeled off toward the steps.

"Be careful out there, sawbones," Dayla called after him. "On a night such as this, it's easy to get lost."

A stiff wind pulled at Rig's long coat. He looked back and Dayla was gone. Obtuse and distant. The signature state for a leech, seeing as there was a near assurance they would have to kill those they worked with. The small hint was huge coming from Dayla. There was no real way he could thank her other than dealing with Edwin. Whatever that meant.

The sun set, replaced by a silver moon that cast a pale light over Wrotdam. It reflected off the calm drift of the river below, and the remains of the burnt town that filled either bank. The overlook path soon strayed from the cliff and Rig was back into the tight walkways. Citizens had abandoned carts and autocars. He wandered past the shredded corpse of a horse still in its harness.

Lamps flickered on, illuminating the streets. Occasionally there would be one that had run out of Ink and stayed dark. A lampsman wouldn't be by to replace it until morning. They left heavy shadows that made the hairs on the back of Rig's neck stand on end. He pulled his mask back over his mouth and readied his branderbuss.

The smell of lavender candles floated through the air. A barrel rolled out of an alley in front of him, thumping from pavement to the street. He aimed his branderbuss at the shadowy passage. A black and grey oozing figure crawled into the lamplight. It coalesced first into a humanoid form then into something more amorphous. Rig kept his breath steady, allowing the sludge to make the first move.

It rolled over the barrel and flopped onto the cobblestone street. With a deep, gurgling noise, it formed into a hunched-over humanoid with exposed ribs. It turned its head and stared at Rig through an eyeless gaze. Rig levelled his branderbuss with the sludge. Neither of them moved.

The candle smell irritated Rig's nose, but he refused to falter. A rotten scent wafted by. It was so slight he almost missed it. He hefted his riotsaw off his shoulder and spun around, driving its teeth into the side of the sludge that had snuck up behind him. The saw tore the sludge in half through weighted force alone, sending its torso splatting against a nearby building.

Whipping back around to the first sludge, Rig lifted his gun. The sludge had its arm raised, stained bones jutting out from its semi-solid skin into a claw. *Whu-pum!* A hundred spits of flame flew from the branderbuss's mouth. The burst removed the sludge's head and upper chest. Rig clicked the finger-sized inkwell next to the trigger, priming it for the next shot. It wasn't as technically efficient as the electricity-based Faraday weaponry, but explosive enough to work all the same.

More sludges gushed out of the sewer grates and off the tops of buildings. They struck the ground with wet thumps then reformed. Inkbloods, veins as black as pitch, stumbled into the street holding swords and axes. Had they set up an ambush? Could they set up an ambush?

Rig fired three more times, blowing three more sludges apart. They were coming too fast for him to prime. He hooked his gun back onto his hip and took his riotsaw in both hands. Pressing the lever down in his right hand, he slid the upper section of the hilt up behind the blade. It struck the igniter and the two chains roared to life. The pair of teeth spun in opposite directions, turning the cutting edge into a gnashing maelstrom of steel.

A sludge lunged forward. Rig caught it on the collarbone and pushed through its body, sending blackened blood flying in all directions. Keeping a wide stance and a two-handed grip, Rig swung messily through a group of three sludges. He stamped one foot down then reversed his momentum. Keeping his right hand on the trigger plate, he sliced one-handed through a sludge's skull. The riotsaw vibrated viciously. He grabbed it by the backbar to keep it from shaking out of his grip.

An inkblood thrust forward with her sword. Rig leapt aside and drove the hilt into her face, then chopped straight down. The two halves of the inkblood dropped, only to be stomped on in the advance of the others. The Mire had truly taken hold.

Readying himself for the next onslaught, Rig spotted Edwin in the distance. He wore his usual green jacket, now charred and bloody, and crossed the street far away from the fight. He took a large cross from the front of Courtrise Church and rested it against his shoulder. His movement was focused, and his shoulders rose and fell with heavy breaths.

"Edwin!" Rig shouted over the sludges.

An inkblood took advantage of Rig's momentary distraction and caught him with an axe on the shoulder. Rig screamed and slammed his elbow into the inkblood's jaw. Edwin didn't notice, or didn't care. He and the cross disappeared into the church.

Rig disengaged from the fight, stopping his riotsaw. He scrambled on top of a nearby carriage and drew his branderbuss, blowing away an inkblood that reached too high. The horde rattled the carriage, threatening to topple it. Rig tossed his riotsaw up onto the balcony of a nearby house. The wood of the carriage groaned like a ship in a wild sea. He leapt to the balcony and pulled himself over the railing just as the carriage's wheels snapped and it flipped onto its side. Rig collapsed to a knee, holding the shoulder wound gushing blood.

The balcony's curtains fluttered behind the closed door. "Go away!" a woman inside the house shouted.

Rig pounded on the door, leaving a bloody handprint. "Open up or I break the lock."

There was silence, then a *chunk* as the latch moved aside. Rig grabbed his riotsaw, threw the doors open, and pushed through the curtains into a dark and drab bedroom. A woman wearing a nightgown slammed the doors shut and locked them. She went about lighting more candles, even though there were already a dozen lining the room.

"I won't be long," Rig said, placing his riotsaw on the floor and taking a knee next to the bed. His shoulder leaked a steady stream of blood, only made worse from his recent climb.

"I don't care," the woman said, lighting her eighteenth candle. "Just get out of my house. I don't want one of you murderers here."

The townsfolk weren't shy about their hatred of the sawbones. They slew the Mire, but they also killed those suspected of harbouring an infection — though they never acted without a leech or Church official's say so — and, of course, there was the amber madness. Best the general populace could say, sawbones were a necessary evil. They weren't part of the Church, easier for the people to blame them without it falling back onto the clergy. Rig didn't care about any of that. He had seen the darkest side of the Mire. There were worse evils. Or, at least, that's what he told himself.

He pulled an inkwell out of his coat, his last one. He gulped it down and the pain in his shoulder dulled into nothing. He could fight again, even if his body began to fall apart. But, without his Ink, his night could soon be coming to an end. He took a bandage from his pocket and shoved it hastily over the wound, hoping to keep at least most of his blood inside, and peeked between the curtains. Sludge and inkbloods wandered the street, but they were too dim to figure out how to follow him.

The chapel lay a dozen metres away. He had found Edwin, but there was something wrong with him. He didn't notice the massive fight going on a few metres away or Rig's cries of pain. He needed to get to that chapel.

"Unlock your front door." Rig grabbed the riotsaw by the backbar.

"Hell no!" She crossed her arms and held her ground. "The sludges will come in an instant. This is your problem, sawbones."

Rig cast her a hard glare. She narrowed her eyes. She had no fear of him, only the monsters outside. Rig looked around the room. The bed was too big for one person. There were two bureaus against the far wall. The woman had a gold band on her ring finger. Yet, she was alone.

"Okay," Rig said. He unlocked the balcony doors and opened them, pushing the curtains aside. The beasts below groaned, but the scent from the candles kept them away. Rig backed up. "You can lock the doors after I'm gone. I'm... keep them locked."

The woman's expression softened. Maybe she knew what he was trying to say. Rig dug his boots into the wooden floor and charged forward. He leapt to the railing, then soared high over the Mire's heads. He landed with a roll just behind the furthest back inkblood and continued with the momentum. The chapel Edwin disappeared into was ahead. Rig ignored the sludge that reached for him and rushed through the heavy doors.

Inside, he dropped the drawbar across the doors and took a moment to catch his breath. He inhaled a strong lavender scent. Someone had been burning candles. Rig turned away from the door and his jaw dropped.

Edwin knelt at the base of three machine crosses. Dim lights barely lit the hall, but enough to reveal the horrible display. Chained to the bottom of the eight-armed icons were three bodies. One larger and two smaller. Edwin had a wife and two children. But these couldn't be them. These weren't recent corpses; they were almost mummified.

Rig leaned his riotsaw against a nearby pew and stepped carefully toward the altar. "Edwin?"

"They said they would come back," Edwin said through deep breaths. He had been crying.

"Who's 'they?'" Rig asked. The chapel door began shaking. There were no lit candles, only the remnants of smoke and smell. It wouldn't keep the Mire out for long.

"The Church!" Edwin spat. He stumbled to his feet. His branderbuss dropped from his lap and clattered to the ground. "They said they would bring them back and set me to work. I thought everything was fine. Dina, Thomas, Fei, they would be back. The things I did for the Church... Rig, does this look like they're back!?" He thrust his hands toward the three figures chained up to the crosses.

"What did the Church do?" Rig regretted leaving his riotsaw at the door. "How can they raise the dead?"

Edwin spun around. His black hair, normally swept back, stuck to his face with blood and sweat. "How do you think, Rig? With Ink. With that Ink that we lap up like obedient dogs. Praising its miraculous properties while ignoring the monsters it unleashes within us."

"Ed—"

"There's something above the Church, Rig." He motioned to the grotesque shrine behind them. "I'm trying to commune, but they aren't listening. We mean nothing to them. We question nothing."

Rig was within lunging distance now. He offered his hand. The banging at the doors intensified. "Edwin. They're going to break down the door."

"They don't matter." He drew his boltblades. Rig jumped back. "Nothing matters. We'll all return to the sea one day. I don't want to be alone when the waves take me. They're sympathetic, Rig. They'll listen to pain."

Rig retreated, careful not to make any sudden movements. "Put those away."

"I need pain." Edwin's brown eyes faded into something even darker. The whites of his eyes dimmed.

Rig drew his branderbuss. Edwin pressed the switches on his swords and lightning danced across the blades. Rig fired, and Edwin clashed his weapons together. A shock shield burst out for a moment, but long enough to defend against the flame spits.

Rig dove toward his riotsaw. He snatched it and ignited the chains as he spun back toward his old friend. Edwin closed the distance in a flash and brought both swords down. Rig caught them with the flat of his saw and pushed them aside. He thrust the saw forward, but Edwin dropped back onto a pew and rolled over his shoulder, back to his feet.

Edwin slid back and pushed one foot onto the arm of the pew. Rig stepped forward. Edwin stomped on the arm and the entire bench flipped sideways. He shouldered the pew and pushed it forward. Rig widened his stance and held his saw out. The pew collided with the teeth. The wood gave way under their tearing motions.

Dodging around the bench, Edwin thrust an electrified blade at Rig's side. Rig had to abandon his saw inside the pew and leap away. Edwin's sword nicked him, sending a charge through his body and turning his dodge into a crash.

He staggered to his feet. Edwin pulled the pew to the ground, sending Rig's riotsaw toward the rattling doors. The cut on Rig's side was small, but that wasn't where the pain of Edwin's weapons came from. He didn't have many more hits in him.

Rig unhooked his branderbuss and fired, primed, then fired again. Edwin blocked both then lunged past the barrel. Rig raised his arms in defence, taking a slice across the arm. His coat stopped the cut, but the electricity coursed through him. He seized, kicking Edwin away and falling prone.

Blood dripped from Rig's mouth as he crawled away. His body began to fail. Edwin was too fast, faster than he had ever seen him before. The Mire changed him. This was a job for a leech, not a sawbones. Rig glanced over his shoulder. Edwin had closed his eyes and swayed side to side. Black ooze seeped out of his pores and flowed over him. Was this the true form of amber madness?

Reaching forward, Rig's hand landed on Edwin's branderbuss. The wood was nicked and the metal was beaten. Edwin had gotten it from his father, Rig remembered. The inkwell glittered in the candlelight. He yanked it out and forced himself to stand and face his fallen friend.

Edwin opened his eyes. They were black with strings of amber thread swimming within. Muck dripped from his knuckles and the oozing substance nearly turned his green jacket black. He spun his swords, sending crackles of electricity into the air.

"I'm sorry," Rig said, squeezing the inkwell.

"We are imperfect," Edwin spoke with a thousand voices from one throat.

Rig tossed the inkwell forward then swung his branderbuss up. Edwin prepared to clash his swords together. Rig shot at the inkwell. It exploded just as Edwin brought up his shock shield. The Ink ignited against the sparks and pushed a chain reaction through Edwin's swords to the inkwells in their hilts. Edwin had a moment of realization, then his barrier exploded.

A wave of electricity and force swept over Edwin. It tore through the front of the chapel just as the sludges shattered the drawbar. Rig covered his head. Debris rained down upon him. When he opened his eyes, the front half of the chapel lay in pieces about the street. A bloody stain and scraps of clothing remained where Edwin once stood.

Rig, battered and beaten, managed his way out of the gaping hole and onto the street. Pieces of wood lay in all directions. There was not a whole sludge or inkblood to be seen, only charred pieces. His riotsaw stuck out of the top of the overturned carriage. Placing one foot against the roof, he yanked it free. Both chains had snapped and the igniting pin was missing. Still fixable. He dragged it behind him as he forced the remains of his body to keep moving. If he stopped, he might die.

He came to the overlook above the gorge. From the upper ward, the Obsidian Bell rang. Another bell echoed its chime elsewhere in the city. Then more. The Cleansing was over. Rig looked toward the Machine on the horizon. Its tentacles continued to wave toward the sky. In the moonlight, they looked like arms praying to God.

The night was just beginning, but thankfully his job was done. The Ink Clergy could clean up. Rig wanted to get home.

Edwin was gone, lost to the whisperings of the Mire. His family died twice. The Church could bring Edwin's family back in some capacity, but somehow that went wrong. The bodies still sat in the chapel far behind him — a grim reminder.

As the wind howled through the Wrotdam streets, Rig could only wonder what truly happened to Edwin Zhen that night.

CHAPTER 8:
THE FALLEN

Before the explosions, the blood, and the death, there was a moment of peace for four sawbones. For hours, Edwin and his team had battled against the Mire. They moved from nest to nest, killing sludge and burning the infection out. More inkbloods appeared as the day went on. No matter how quickly they worked to cleanse Wrotdam, the Mire always reached the citizens.

They had just finished burning a nest formed in a half-built school in Forest Reach and sat down to catch their breath. Franz took out a bag of peanuts, tossing them for Hitomi to catch in her mouth. Rig picked the gore out of his riotsaw's teeth. At that moment, they could almost pretend they were the only ones in the city.

Until an engine roared up. Edwin clicked the inkwells into place on the back of his boltblades and peered through a gap in the schoolhouse wall. An autocar had parked outside. A young woman stepped out and looked around. Edwin tapped on a hanging piece of wood, banging it so the woman could hear. She jumped at the sound, but relaxed when she saw who made it.

"Edwin Zhen?" she asked, shielding her eyes against the sun.

"What's this about?" Edwin leaned against the wall.

"Um, I'm Sister Antonia. I was — erm, Father Smithson wants me to bring you to him."

Edwin raised his head, a slight motion that hid a flurry of thoughts. A priest of the Church asking for him? He had done his work for them. Why would they distract him on a day as important as the Cleansing?

Edwin turned toward his companions. "I'm leaving. Keep the fight alive."

Rig stepped toward Edwin but was stopped with a look. Hitomi laid her hand on his shoulder. She led Rig away and glanced over her shoulder to Edwin. They were as confused as he was. No, they were more confused. Even if the timing was strange, Edwin knew what was going to happen. He stepped through the open wall and entered the passenger seat.

"Where are we going?" Edwin asked as Sister Antonia drove him away from the school.

"Oh, uh, Courtrise Church," she said. She held her breath at every turn.

"Is something wrong?"

"What? Why are you asking?"

Edwin sighed. "Because you're nervous."

"I don't much really like or enjoy being on the streets outside during the Cleansing."

"Then why are you?" *She a rational one, at least,* he thought, adjusting the bandage just under his sleeve.

Antonia squeezed the wheel, tensing her shoulders. "I was asked. I was asked to get you."

"You should learn to say no."

"I'm a servant of God." Her gaze flicked from side to side as she crossed an empty intersection. "It's not my place to question."

"Of course it's not."

They arrived at Courtrise Church, a small building wedged between the split as one road became two. It was close to the docks and the smell of fish brought in up the river wafted by. Some Church guards waited outside with ignition throwers. Three massive eight-armed crosses leaned against the outside, abandoned by the people of Wrotdam.

Antonia waved goodbye to Edwin as he entered the church, already filled with the sweet smell of candles. Father Smithson stood on the pulpit, looking up at a landscape painting of old Wrotdam when the Machine first appeared and there was no upper or lower ward. He was an elder priest, with silver hair cut close to his head. He turned at the sound of the door closing and smiled at Edwin.

"Thank you for coming," he said.

"You asked for me, Father," Edwin said, taking slow steps down the aisle.

"The Church requires your service."

"I'm already serving the Church." He pointed toward the door. "The city's in the grip of the Mire."

Father Smithson stretched his back, standing straight. "There are other considerations than the Cleansing. We know where the True Metal Order is. Or, at least some of them."

"Can this not wait? The Mire—"

"The Mire is a symptom of an infection. It's heretics like the True Metal Order that invite the Mire to rise. We had three years of peace due to your efforts, Edwin. This cult is ruining that work. Why run around burning nests when you stop it at its source?"

"If it's so noble, then take your guards and your Ink Clergy and deal with them yourself." Edwin took a threatening step forward. "Or are you so afraid of the people finding out what the Church of the Machine is truly like?"

Father Smithson leaned on the podium. "People don't understand what's best for them. They need us to tell them. They'll lash out, yes, but that doesn't mean we are wrong. We must keep them safe, even when they don't want us to. And you should not forget the deal."

"I remember the deal. I've been keeping up my side! I go where the Church demands to do whatever it wants. What about your side? When am I going to see my family?"

"Soon. It's a difficult process. But you must have faith and God will reward you. Continue the good work, Edwin."

Edwin made the call a long time ago to grin and bear what he would have to do to please the Church and get his family back. The promise of miraculous resurrection was an alluring prospect. His faith in the order carried him for a year, but in time it faded to horrible practicality. He'd already done his worst, no sense turning back now. It was the only thing that kept him sane in the darkest moments.

"What do you need me to do, Father?" Edwin asked.

Father Smithson gave a self-satisfied smirk. "There's a graveyard in Ravinetown. Do you know it?"

"I've seen it."

"The True Metal Order has taken root in the former caretaker's home. We don't know how long they'll be there for, and they must not be allowed to slip away. You must… show them the error of their ways."

"As it is decreed." Edwin shot Father Smithson a last sneer before spinning around and stomping out. He hated the thought of letting the Church use him as a tool, but he had gotten good at turning off his emotions over the past three years.

Antonia spotted Edwin and started the autocar. He waved her off. He knew the path down the gorge to Ravinetown, and it wasn't fit for an autocar. Part of the cliff had fallen and people had been dumping garbage and building supplies for years. Edwin shoved his hands into his pockets and began his descent.

With each step to Ravinetown, the smell of old ash intensified. The river ran painfully loud against the terrible stillness of the burnt city. Edwin pulled his mask up to not breathe in the air. He crossed the river on a simple stone bridge and walked the narrow spaces between wooden buildings charred a dusty black. By the time he reached the graveyard — nothing more than a small plot set in a shallow cavern — his green jacket had turned grey by the ash that shot up when he stepped on the remains of Ravinetown.

Next to the graveyard was a two-storey home that had weathered the fire without too much damage. As Edwin stepped forward, a window on the second floor banged open.

"Who's there?" a voice shouted. The window was dark, with planks of wood hiding the man inside.

Edwin stopped. "Just a man."

"You're a sawbones." There was a metal click as a rifle bolt drew back. It sounded like a slug-throwing firearm. Bad for killing the Mire, good for killing people. "What are you doing here?"

"Didn't you hear the bell? The Cleansing is on."

"We heard the bell. The Mire doesn't come down here anymore. We don't need sawbones."

"I wanted to make sure." Edwin took casual, almost meandering, steps toward the house. "Why aren't you living with the others in Understone?"

"Stop moving!"

Edwin didn't. "I like your house. The neighbourhood could use work. But if you can get past the atmosphere, it's quaint."

Crack! The ground a few metres from him exploded as a bullet tore up the dirt. Edwin kept walking. He didn't need to reach the door, he just needed to get close.

"You seem scared," Edwin said. "You could hurt someone."

"Go away!" The man fired again, still nowhere close to Edwin. "We don't need the Church here. Their lies cannot sway us."

"I know. But their lies are very important to me."

Edwin bent his knees, then uncoiled in an explosive display of speed. The man in the window fired, but he was untrained and slow. Edwin hit the front door with both feet out, disintegrating the door frame and riding it in. There was a cry of pain as the door crushed someone underneath. Edwin drew a boltblade and drove it down, silencing the person below the door.

A man leapt from the dining table, pulling back his jacket to try to draw a revolver. Edwin drew his other blade and rushed forth. He kicked the table, slamming it into the man's stomach so he dropped chest first. Edwin stabbed the man through the back, piercing his heart. Using the boltblade as a handle, Edwin pulled himself over the table and kept moving.

From the next room, a woman charged in with her revolver out. Another man leapt down the stairs with a rifle in his grip. Edwin slipped his blade through a cup handle and flicked it at the rifleman. The rifleman batted it away and Edwin lunged toward the woman.

He dodged around the revolver barrel and the woman fired. Flipping his boltblade around, Edwin stabbed it into the woman's arm. She pulled back, but the blade was stuck. Edwin spun and aimed the woman's revolver at the rifleman.

With a twist of the blade, the woman's arm seized and pulled the trigger. The bullet punctured the rifleman's chest and he tumbled down the stairs dead.

The woman grabbed Edwin by the neck. He elbowed her in the ribs. The gun went off again, but she released him. Edwin twisted around and sliced the woman's throat. She teetered back, clutching her bloody neck. With the last of her strength, she fired. Edwin jerked his head aside. The bullet grazed his forehead and the woman fell.

Something wet trickled down Edwin's brow. He wiped it away and brought back his fingers with spots of blood. Was he getting slower? He didn't feel like it.

Above him came a series of thumps. Edwin followed the sound with his gaze. He put away one boltblade and grabbed his branderbuss. The footsteps slowed, the person above acutely aware of the silence below. Edwin raised his branderbuss, pointing at the ceiling and waiting for a target.

The floor creaked.

Edwin fired.

The ceiling broke.

A man fell through the flame spits, his leg catching on fire. He landed on a chair, splintering it apart and crumbling. He let out a harsh puff of air — then lurched up like a spring man. Edwin threw his boltblade. It stuck in the man's chest and he fell back down.

No, Edwin thought. *I'm not getting slower. Just getting distracted.*

He stepped toward the dead man. A gun went off behind him — the bullet whizzing past his head. Another woman had picked up the fallen revolver. She fired again. Edwin moved, but not fast enough. His shoulder lit up with pain. He kept his feet beneath him. The woman pulled the trigger again, but there was a striking click as there was no bullet to fire.

The woman went pale. She threw the gun at Edwin and ran to the back of the house, through a heavy curtain. Edwin groaned, taking deep breaths against the pain in his shoulder. He dug in his coat and pulled out a vial of Ink. He drained it and the pain subsided. He shook the haze out of his head, took his boltblade out of the body, and stomped after the woman.

He stuck his blade through the gap in the curtain and yanked it aside. The woman leaned over a trap door in the floor. She turned at the sound of Edwin entering, revealing what she hid in the hole.

Children. Six children, ranging from young child to early teen, were halfway into the trap door. They held each other, staring with tear-filled eyes at Edwin — the monster at their door.

The woman grabbed a nearby knife. A blunt butter knife, but she held it like a sword. She put herself between Edwin and the children.

Edwin's mind went blank. The facts gave way to pain. The emotions he turned off for so long broke through the wall and tore their way into the light. His family's death bled through him like a fresh wound in his mind. He stumbled away from the room with the trap door, letting the curtain fall into place. Then he was outside. Then he was climbing the gorge path. He moved faster until he was sprinting.

The guards at Courtrise Church watched Edwin come running up, his weapons in his hands, and readied themselves. One shouted something that Edwin didn't hear. Edwin cut through the trio of soldiers in a half-lived onslaught. He pinned the last one to the door and stabbed over and over until the wood cracked and softened under the blood. He threw the corpse aside and yanked on the door, entering the church.

Father Smithson stood halfway down the aisle, on his way to investigate the sound outside. What he found was Edwin, covered in blood and soot. The priest turned to run, but Edwin swept forward and kicked his feet out from under him. He landed hard on his back before Edwin drove his knee into his chest and slammed his boltblade into the carpet next to his face.

"Did you know there were families!?" Edwin cried.

Father Smithson stuttered, "What?"

Edwin turned on his blades, letting the electricity reach fingers toward Father Smithson's face. "There were children there. There were families there. Did you know?"

"…No."

Edwin dragged the dagger closer to the priest.

"There's always families, Edwin!" Father Smithson shouted. "Did you think these people were alone? This is the price of piety. It is unfortunate that heretics bring their loved ones into their deviance, but we must stay strong in God's faith."

"No more sermons, Father. I want my family."

"Edwin—"

Edwin drew back his dagger. He grabbed Father Smithson's hand and plunged the blade through it. Smithson screamed until Edwin leaned on his throat to silence him. Edwin's eyes faded to black, then snapped back to their normal colour.

"Bring them." Edwin leaned in. "Now!"

Father Smithson nodded vigorously. Edwin yanked his boltblade out of Smithson's hand and pulled him to his feet. Smithson clutched his hand and refused to look at the wound.

"They're here," he said. "Through the office."

Keeping his hand on the scruff of Smithson's shirt, Edwin pushed him toward the back of the church. They went into the office. Father Smithson pointed a shaking finger at the back wall. Edwin pulled Smithson by the shirt and prodded the spot. He ran his fingers along the panels in the wall. There was a gap between it and the moulding. With a sharp tap, the wall swung open and revealed another room.

"Please stay calm, Edwin," Father Smithson said, speaking in a whisper.

Hanging lamps barely lit the next room, creating dark shadows in the corners. Three medical beds sat side-by-side against the far wall, each with a body wrapped in rags. Their skin was drawn tight against their muscle and bones, holding an unnatural yellow-grey colour. Despite the years of decay that should have occurred, Edwin's family was preserved. His boltblades clattered to the floor. Tubing ran from machines next to each bed, injecting dark yellow liquid into their bodies, while others removed it. Crosses littered the room, hanging from walls and bedposts. Hundreds of them of various sizes.

"This isn't them," Edwin said, almost a sigh.

"I told you it was a difficult process," Father Smithson said, clutching his wounded hand to his chest. "We are still perfecting it."

"What are you doing?"

"Ink, infused with various substances. Chemicals, salt water, blood."

Edwin moved toward the beds.

Father Smithson continued, "We had success with rats and dogs. But humans require something else. Help from above."

"God?"

"God is an old idea, but a useful one to understand what we have seen. We have been reaching out to the stars, seeking communication with the intelligences that created the Machine. To expand our minds into something greater. It's not an easy thing to understand. God is a simple way to comprehend it."

Edwin reached out with trembling fingers. He brushed Dina's arm. She was warmer than he expected. At his touch, her fingers twitched. "What are you talking about?" he asked.

"We are communing with beings greater than us, so that we may become greater ourselves. That is why we need you, Edwin." Smithson took a step forward.

"You need me?" Edwin drew his branderbuss and pointed it at Father Smithson, stopping him in his tracks. "You need me to get rid of the Church's enemies because of these greater beings?"

Father Smithson threw his hands in the air. "We need them to listen to us. We need them to know we will accept their gifts."

How would these greater beings that Smithson mentioned bring Edwin's family back? What even were they? The inside of Edwin's skull itched incessantly. He watched his wife's chest rise, hold position, then fall into a sunken pit.

"I want to talk to the Archbishop." He scooped up his boltblades while keeping Smithson at the end of his gun barrel. "Bring me."

"He can't—"

"Now!" Edwin stowed his blades and pushed Smithson with his gun. "I have questions. And demands."

He led Father Smithson out of the church. They would have to walk to the upper ward. Edwin kept Smithson moving down the road at a steady pace, taking the overlook path along the lip of the gorge. Looking over, Edwin felt awash with guilt, remembering the bodies he left below and the faces of the children who escaped.

"You don't need to do this, Edwin," Father Smithson said.

"Be quiet."

"You're confused. I was confused too when I was first told the truth. Most in the Church don't know, they don't need to know. Perhaps we shouldn't have kept you in the dark. You've done so much for us after all, but it doesn't have to end here. These mistakes can be rectified and we can continue our work."

"I can't—" Edwin paused, composing himself. "I won't kill for you anymore."

"Not even for your family?"

Edwin threw Father Smithson against the overlook path stone wall, bending him over the deadly drop with a branderbuss to his chin. "You haven't brought them back! Three years and nothing!"

"N — not nothing! You should have seen them a year ago!"

"That isn't life," Edwin said. The wind blew past carrying a chilling, wordless whisper only Edwin could hear.

"Edwin." The Father rested his hand on Edwin's arm. "Only the Faceless Gods can help them. They are sympathetic, they feel our pain, they'll listen to your pleas. But our voice must be unified. That's why we can't abide conflicting ideas, they muddy the message. Archbishop MacMurray will say the same thing. He can't help you any more than I can."

"Then I'll kill him."

Edwin grabbed Father Smithson's legs and flipped him over the wall. Smithson screamed, until the impact. Edwin leaned on his elbows and his eyes flashed black again. His vision faded to an amber tinge. His body ached with pain; a full-body pain that felt ancient. He drank another vial of Ink and it disappeared. It was getting hard to think, but emotions were coming easy. He wanted to hurt Archbishop MacMurray. It was MacMurray who approached Edwin and told him that his family could be brought back. It was MacMurray who made Edwin do all those terrible things.

If I kill Archbishop MacMurray, Edwin thought, drawing one boltblade. *Then I will be redeemed. Then God will return my family to me.*

He was moving. He couldn't remember when he started walking, but he was already nearly to the ward bridge. Each step made him surer, but also increased the haze. A voice shouted out to him, but the words were lost. He glanced back and saw Rig. Hitomi and Franz were behind him, but they headed away from the upper ward. Edwin needed to go to the upper ward. Rig stared at him, confused. Hitomi yelled at Rig to keep moving. Edwin made no indication that he cared Rig, or any of the other sawbones, were there. He focused on the ward gate and increased his pace.

Everything became a blur. It was as though he was watching his actions from six feet behind himself. He wandered the upper ward as if he'd never seen it before. He passed landmarks that seemed familiar in form, but foreign in purpose. At one point he may have passed his house, but there was no way to be sure. The pain returned when he found the Mechanical Cathedral, so he drank another Ink vial before entering.

He found Archbishop MacMurray inside, instantly filling with rage. An Ink Cleric with an exploding hand rebuffed him. Edwin nearly beat her, but a sharp bite to his back brought him down. His senses returned for a moment. A leech fired upon him, the Ink Cleric was getting back on her feet, and there were still the church guards around Archbishop MacMurray. Edwin was outnumbered. He decided to run.

He made it outside and took down his last Ink vial. The world sharpened. Going after Archbishop MacMurray was a mistake, of course he would be protected. Edwin was starting to slip. He needed to bring himself back to the real world.

God won't bring my family back to me, Edwin thought, limping through the upper ward. *But... those Faceless Gods can. The Church is sure they can. I need them to listen.*

Edwin's heart beat faster. A guard at the ward gate asked him where he was going and Edwin brushed him off with a mention of the docks. The ocean was the key. The Machine came from the ocean. Everything came from the ocean. Edwin's skin felt like seaweed and his breath tasted like salt. Everything was falling apart and drowning around him. Pain came faster. He needed more Ink.

As he left the ward bridge and stumbled into the lower ward, Hitomi rushed around the corner, nearly knocking them both down.

"Edwin!" Hitomi said. The arm not carrying her wave cannon bled, but it didn't bother her. She had Ink. "Where have you been? We got separated by a gnasher and I've been looking everywhere for Franz or Rig."

Edwin's head pulsed like the waves against the shore. He needed the Ink.

Hitomi looked back the way she came. "Let's find the others and finish this. Most of the obelisks have stopped spinning."

Then her chest bled. Edwin's boltblade pierced through her back. She shook, confused at what just happened. Edwin couldn't remember what actions brought him to that point. Hitomi collapsed, dead. Edwin pilfered her pockets and took all her Ink vials. He yanked the stoppers out then drank them all at once. The ocean became louder. Beneath the crashing waves was the sound of mechanical grinding.

Edwin stood unsteadily, swaying side to side. He took a deep breath and was outside Courtrise Church. The three crosses leaned against the outside and stuck in his brain like needles. Surely the Faceless Gods would listen to those. He took another breath and was inside Courtrise Church. His family knelt before him, fastened to the crosses. Their skin was healthy and pink, but they didn't move. Edwin laid his branderbuss across his lap. The ocean grew louder.

"Please," Edwin whispered. "Please bring them back."

He placed the branderbuss barrel against his chin.

"Before I slip into the sea forever, bring them back."

His eyes flickered black and amber. His hands shook.

The Faceless Gods need more blood, Edwin thought. *That's what it is. If they're sympathetic, then they'll come. If they see pain. They'll come. I need to bring more pain.*

He set the branderbuss back onto his lap. He needed more Ink. He needed more blood. The door creaked open behind him then slammed shut. Edwin wouldn't slip, not until his family was safe. He stood and let out a ragged breath.

He wouldn't hear the Obsidian Bell.

END OF GLOAMING 1898

PART TWO

AURORA 1899

CHAPTER 1

One Year Later

Ophelia Plante had gone to the Church for help. She sat on a bench outside the Mechanical Cathedral with her hands folded, waiting for the Archbishop to see her. Talking her way up the Church hierarchy had been a draining process and she wanted nothing more than to slump over and fall asleep. She flipped up her collar against the wind and shoved her hands into her pockets. It was getting cold.

A horse came plodding up the street, keeping to the side of where the autocars drove. Callen Dust tied his horse up next to Ophelia's and jogged up the stairs.

"Have you talked to them yet?" he asked.

Ophelia stood from the bench. She took off her knit cap, scratched her head, and said, "I talked to a deacon, who talked to a priest, who talked to another priest, who talked to *another* priest. But that last priest, she said I can talk to the Archbishop."

"We're getting an audience with *the Archbishop*?" Dusty wiped the sweat off his brow. "What're we doing, Ophelia?"

"Hoping someone will help us." Ophelia couldn't believe she was the one the village council sent. She was no orator, she could barely convince the birds to stop eating all her grass seed. "How about you, Dusty? Were the Sawbones receptive?"

He shook his head. "They listened, but they said they can't officially send anyone without Church authority."

"So much for sawbones being independent." Ophelia looked up at the Cathedral. "Then I suppose the Machine Church really is Dawnhallow's only hope."

"Not necessarily," Dusty said. "The Commander offered a suggestion. We could hire some help."

"Who? Sawbones?"

"Anyone who can fight the Mire."

Dawnhallow didn't have much money. The citizens were simple people who scraped by with their farms and small businesses. The richest person in the village ran his gang out of his manor just outside the city limits. He didn't care what happened to them. The people of Dawnhallow were on their own.

Archbishop MacMurray exited the Cathedral in flowing robes. Mother Shore, the last priest Ophelia had talked to, came out behind him and pointed at Ophelia.

"Good morning," Archbishop MacMurray said with a friendly smile. "I hope I didn't keep you waiting for too long."

"Of course not, Your Grace." Ophelia knew how to talk to the clergy. She had grown up attending church every Sunday. Of course, the Archbishop of the entire Machine Church was a different beast. She could feel her knees clattering together. "My name is Ophelia Plante, and this is my companion, Callen Dust."

Dusty tipped his hat. Then, with a slight jump, he yanked it off his head.

"Come in," Archbishop MacMurray said. "It's much too cold out here for a conversation."

He led Ophelia inside with Dusty at her heel. Dusty kept whipping his head back and forth — cities made him nervous. Cities simply made Ophelia sad. Every year they got bigger and louder. Mother Shore took her leave as they made their way down the Mechanical Cathedral's nave.

Ophelia mentally prepared herself to give her practiced plea again, when she spotted a dark-clad figure approaching from the transept. A leech. Ophelia had never seen one in person, but the bird mask was unmistakable.

"Archbishop MacMurray," the leech said. "I've been trying to meet with you for some time."

"Ah, hello, Dayla." His entire body tensed up at the sound of her voice.

"Did you read my proposal? Some access to old records is all I require."

"I have not." He gestured toward Ophelia and Dusty. "I have matters with the public, as you can see. Let us save this chat for another time."

"Of course, your grace." An ounce of tension held in her words. She swept the eyeless gaze of her mask over the visitors before marching off, her charred scarf fluttering behind her.

Great, Ophelia thought. *Now I'm making waves. This entire excursion is a pain.* She fixed the braid coming out from under her cap and faced the archbishop head-on. "Did Mother Shore tell you about us?" she asked.

"Some." Archbishop MacMurray eased his old body into the pews. Ophelia and Dusty sat next to him. "I would prefer to hear it straight from the source. Now, you're from Dawnhallow, is that right? I've been there before, a few decades ago, of course. You have a nice church."

"It, unfortunately, burned down a few years ago," Ophelia said. "We've been having services at the inn."

"Ah, that's resilient of you. Though I imagine from the way Mother Shore spoke, your worry is about something more than a burned-down church. Tell me, what is the predicament?"

"We spotted the Mire outside Dawnhallow," Ophelia said. "A bunch of sludges crossed a farmer's field, killing most of his crop."

"Are you sure that's what you saw?" Archbishop MacMurray leaned back. "I'm not sure if you know, but sludges are not the first sign of an infection. It starts with a sickness. As well, the Mire doesn't attack small towns. You needn't be worried."

"It's more complicated than that," Dusty chimed in. "We saw something similar last year. About four sightings over a week, I spotted some myself after my goats got out in the middle of the night. There was a big sludge, like, really big. Big as a barn. And it had all these weird pieces of metal sticking out of it. Later, one of the local kids followed these things to Pembrooke House and said they were attaching metal devices to it. They were building something. We sent word to the church. I don't know if you ever got it."

"When was this?" MacMurray asked.

"Last year, early December. We thought they would come for us immediately, so for days we lit lavender, but they never did." Ophelia grabbed the pew in front of her. All the memories of that terrible day flooded back to her. "But, a couple weeks later, we *were* attacked. It was the same day Wrotdam had their Cleansing. They came in broad daylight and they didn't even try to infect people. They just took them. The rest of us, who could, lit our candles, but the Mire just broke down our doors anyway. The lavender barely slowed them down. They dragged people out, killed anyone who got in their way, they—" She took in a shaking breath, trying to calm herself. This was why she shouldn't have been the one to go, she figured, she was too emotional. "It's going to happen again, your grace."

Archbishop MacMurray sat in silence for a long time. Ophelia squeezed onto the wood of the pew until her fingers ached.

"This is quite a fantastical story. I understand you think you're in danger," Archbishop MacMurray said, diplomatically. "Much of what you said is, quite simply, impossible. The Mire is not intelligent. It does not build things. It does not abduct its prey. Its power is the fear we give to it. This child probably didn't know what he saw, and, though exceedingly rare, it's not unheard of for the Mire to attack a small town. Especially when there is an outbreak in a nearby city. As for the alleged abductions, the Mire is strange and though you did not see it infect your neighbours, does not mean it took them anywhere."

"It took them!" Ophelia insisted. Dusty gave her a meaningful look. She added, "Your Grace. It took… it took my sister. Tore her right out of our house. Do you think we're lying?"

"I think grief and distress can play tricks with the mind." He stood. "Come with me. I'll ease your fears."

He stepped into the aisle. Dusty looked at Ophelia. He smiled at her, strained as it was. He was close to giving up. Ophelia wasn't far off herself. She squeezed her fist until the pain of her nails driving into her palm stopped her from crying. She hadn't spoken of Aisling in a year, and the wound still hurt when poked.

Archbishop MacMurray brought them out of the Cathedral hall and to a small outbuilding down a corridor. It was a laboratory, with beakers of chemicals lining the walls and various tools and apparatus carefully labelled in their designated positions. A woman with her red hair in a messy bun leaned over a desk, scribbling into a book. She didn't notice anyone enter, too engrossed in her duties. She pushed the sleeves of her amber robes up when they slipped down.

"Adelaide," Archbishop MacMurray said. "I hoped we could ask you a question."

Adelaide jumped. She whipped off her glasses and took in the intruders. "Of course, Your Grace."

"This is Ophelia Plante and Callen Dust. They're from Dawnhallow. Adelaide is one of our brightest researchers in St. Zita's Order and she is the best person to ask about anything Mire-related. Tell me, Adelaide, have you ever heard of the Mire taking prisoners?"

"Uh." Adelaide looked down at the papers that covered her desk. "There haven't been any reports of that occurring. At least none that have crossed my desk. Should I have known? Should I start a file?"

"No, that's fine. What about the Mire building anything? Construction some sort of machine?"

"I have never heard such a thing."

"Exactly, thank you." Archbishop MacMurray turned to Ophelia and Dusty, a hint of smug satisfaction on his face. "As you can see, there is nothing to be afraid of. Tell Dawnhallow to keep their candles lit if they are feeling unwell, but they have nothing to worry about when it comes to the Mire taking them away."

"We know the candles are just a deterrent. Couldn't we have a few sawbones or a leech?" Ophelia asked. "Even an Ink Cleric would put people at ease."

Archbishop MacMurray sighed. "Ms. Plante. If the Church responds to every worry by calling out the troops, people will become afraid. The Mire is motivated by our fears."

"I don't mind investigating," Adelaide said, raising her hand. "What is it that's going on, exactly?"

"Absolutely not. There is nothing to investigate. There is nothing to fear. Tell Dawnhallow to rest easy for they are safe."

He stood firm until it was clear he was expecting them to leave first. Ophelia grabbed Dusty's arm and dragged him away. They passed judging eyes from deacons and parishioners on their way out of the Cathedral.

"That didn't go well," Dusty said, pulling his hand away once they were outside. "Did he seem worried to you?"

"He seemed evasive," Ophelia said. They descended the stairs toward their horses.

"There were armed guards watching us."

Ophelia cocked her head. "Where? I didn't see any."

"On the upper floor. At least three with ignition throwers."

"In a church?"

Dusty shrugged. "What do we do now?"

"We tell everyone they're going to die." Ophelia pulled off her cap and placed her forehead against her horse's warm neck.

"Well, aren't you the pessimist."

"I was named after a woman who went crazy and drowned."

"Ophelia."

"That's the one."

"No." Dusty poked her in the shoulder blade. "Someone's coming."

The black-cloaked leech they'd seen inside wandered down the Cathedral stairs, the same charred red scarf indicating who it was. She marched straight for Ophelia and Dusty, now holding a boltrifle slung across her back.

"Hello," Dayla said, bowing her head. "I take it from your expressions your meeting with the Archbishop didn't go well."

"I thought you left us," Dusty said. "Were you listening in? I didn't see you."

The leech turned her lifeless gaze to Dusty, making him shrink away. "I'm very hard to see when I don't want to be."

"Oh." Dusty swallowed hard. "Alright."

"You sounded very passionate."

"For all the good it did," Ophelia said. "The Archbishop didn't believe us."

"It's hard to change the facts in your mind when you're so sure they're the only truth." Dayla clicked her tongue. "The Church is invested in that fact that the Mire is unchanging and mindless."

"Even if it means letting people die?"

Dayla didn't react. Maybe she smiled under the mask. Maybe she frowned. "What will you do now?" she finally asked.

"Go home," Ophelia said, untying her reins from the post. "Should've known better than to expect anyone would care."

"You're giving up?" Dayla cocked her head.

"We don't have to," Dusty said. "We have some money. We'll hire people willing to fight. Sawbones."

"Sawbones won't fight for you. Not if the Church is denouncing you. They won't want to risk their salaries or their Ink access. But where are my manners? We haven't been formally introduced." She removed her mask. She was an old woman with dark brown skin and deep wrinkles. "My name is Dayla Singh. I believe you."

Ophelia narrowed her eyes. "Why?"

"Why not? It seems like a silly thing to lie about. Besides, you just said you're going to pay."

Dusty laughed. He mounted his horse. "And you said no sawbones is going to help us. We need an army."

"You have an army. You have a village."

"We can't fight the Mire," Ophelia said.

"Anyone can fight. You simply need to fight well. That's where I come in, and a few others."

"You have some people in mind?"

Dayla scratched her chin with the beak of her mask. "A couple. Maybe we'll find more on the way. I'll drive."

The leech was peculiar. Ophelia knew she wasn't telling the whole truth. Dawnhallow didn't have many options, though. The Mire would return, but there was no telling when. Last time, it was two weeks. Even if they assumed a similar timeline, it wasn't much time for them to prepare. Dayla had a gun and the capabilities of a leech. It was good enough.

"Go back to Dawnhallow," Ophelia said to Dusty, tossing him the reins of her horse. "Tell them… tell them everything's going to be fine."

Dusty grinned. He nodded and spurred his horse on — Ophelia's keeping pace next to his. Ophelia put her cap back on her head, pulling it down over her cold ears. Dayla had wandered toward a black autocar parked down the street. Ophelia jogged and caught up.

"Where are we going?" she asked.

"Burdenbrough." Dayla put her boltrifle in the backseat. "Nice town."

"And we'll find someone who will help there?"

"If he hasn't wandered into the sea." She knocked on the autocar's roof and bobbed her head back and forth, weighing the options in her mind. "Right. He may take some convincing, but we want him at our side."

Dayla sat behind the wheel. Ophelia rubbed her hands together, getting her energy up. Somehow, with everything stacked against them, she began to see a chance for Dawnhallow to be saved.

CHAPTER 2

Ophelia found herself sitting in a pub that had seen better days. There wasn't a table that hadn't been hastily repaired with crooked nails. The walls were wood planks littered with cracks and notches. The bar had a dark stain that Ophelia was sure was blood. She sat at a table next to a portrait of someone's mother — or possibly father — waiting for Dayla to return with the man she was looking for.

A group of hoodlums came through the door like a pack of wolves.

"Where is he!?" one of them shouted.

"There!" Another pointed to a table with a large man sitting alone, nursing a beer.

The leader of the group, a young man with a flat cap and a waistcoat, walked up and slapped the patron on the back of the head. The victim slammed both his palms into the table and stood. He loomed like a mountain over the room, arms the size of a horse's haunch and chest as broad as a barn. The hoodlum recoiled slightly until one of the six gangsters standing behind him shoved his shoulder.

"What do you want?" the giant asked. "I'm busy."

"You put my cousin in the hospital," the lead hoodlum said.

"Who?"

"Rory Sabini!"

The giant scratched his head. "Rory tried to cheat at poker. Drew a gun on me. What are you, some kind of gang?"

The group laughed. There was a chorus of metal as they drew knives.

"Yeah," the hoodlum said. "We're the Hawkland Mob. Haven't you heard of us?"

The giant took a moment. "No."

Ophelia had. It was the gang headed by Richard Hawk, the owner of Briardown Manor, the acreage just outside of Dawnhallow. They had a wide reach and seemed to have their fingers in everything; highway robbery, burglary, horse theft, and, of course, extorting the people of Dawnhallow. She had no idea their influence stretched all the way down to Burdenbrough.

The patrons rushed out. Ophelia stayed in her seat, partially from shock and partially intrigued by what was happening. The bartender also remained. He leaned over the bar.

"Let's keep this civil, or take it outside," he said.

The Hawker leader ran his finger over his long, curved knife. "That'll be up to Rig, here. Do you feel like being civil?"

Rig shrugged. "You already ruined my night. I'm fine with ruining yours."

He punched the Hawker leader square in the nose, complete with a satisfying crunch as it exploded into gore and the leader dropped. The other Hawkers scrambled awkwardly into action. Rig grabbed the chair he had been sitting on and broke it over one's head. Another thrust forward with their knife. Rig grabbed his arm and jabbed him in the throat. The Hawker dropped his knife and fell to his knees, wheezing for air.

The Hawkers couldn't touch Rig. He came in with overwhelming force, knocking opponents away like rag dolls. He caught a Hawker by the arm and swung her in a full circle, slamming her into another Hawker before tossing her across the room.

She landed close to Ophelia's table. With great effort, the Hawker turned over and drew a revolver. Seeing this, Ophelia took her beer bottle and smashed it over the Hawker's head, knocking her out. Ophelia dropped the remains of her bottle and looked back at Rig as the leader of the group stumbled to his feet, holding his nose and his knife.

"Are we done?" Rig asked.

"We're done, when I say we're done," the leader said.

"George." Rig turned to the bar where the bartender, George, cowered. Rig reached behind the bar and pulled out a sword over five feet long. It had two rows of serrated teeth that, when Rig grabbed the hilt and slid half of it up with a *snick*, roared to life. The Hawker went pale.

"We're done," he said, dropping his knife and running out.

Rig turned off his riotsaw and rested it on his shoulder. He looked at the state of the pub. Bodies were strewn about with tables broken and bottles busted. His gaze fell on Ophelia and he cocked an eyebrow.

"That was impressive," Ophelia said.

Rig stared at her for another second, then turned to leave. Dayla stepped inside.

"Ah, I was told you might be here," Dayla said. She looked at the unconscious gangsters. "You certainly do find trouble wherever you go."

Rig narrowed his eyes at her.

"I have a job for you," Dayla continued.

"I don't work for the Church."

"It's not for the Church. Just listen." She motioned for Ophelia to talk. "Tell him your story, my dear."

Ophelia stood from her seat, smoothing down her shirt to look presentable. She stepped over the Hawker she knocked out. "My village is going to be attacked," she said. "By the Mire. The Church is unwilling to help so I'm hiring soldiers of my own. You seem... capable."

"How do you know this?" Rig asked.

"Because they did it last year. Same night as Wrotdam's Cleansing, December 31st. We're seeing the same things that led up to that attack again. If we don't get help, Dawnhallow will be destroyed." She swallowed her fear and faced up to Rig's massive frame. "So, will you help us?"

Rig grabbed a half-full glass of beer off the bar and drained it in one gulp. "No," he said and walked out.

Ophelia opened her mouth to protest. Dayla stopped her with a reassuring look and followed Rig out of the pub. Ophelia caught up with them as they were walking down the dirt street.

"She's going to pay, Rig," Dayla said. "Maybe you can buy off some of your gambling debts."

"I don't worry about my debts," Rig said. The people of Burdenbrough gave them plenty of space as they walked. "Also, you can't predict where the Mire will attack."

"Then it will be easy cash for you." Dayla swept in front of him. She was much smaller, but Rig stopped like she was a brick wall. "The Mire isn't simply going to attack them. It's taking people."

"The Mire also doesn't do that."

"Are you telling me you didn't notice anything weird during the last Cleansing?" Dayla stretched up. "The Cleansing that occurred while Dawnhallow was in peril? As I said when we met on the bridge, it was a night like none before."

Rig leaned down to Dayla's face. "What do you get out of this?"

"What we all want. Answers."

Ophelia perked up. *Answers?* she thought. *Answers to what?*

Rig narrowed his eyes. He looked over his shoulder at Ophelia. "If you think your village's going to be attacked, leave it."

"It's not as simple as that," Ophelia insisted. She wished it was, but all she could hear was Aisling's voice whenever she packed her bags.

"It is. Don't get attached to things. It's a weakness." He turned to Dayla. "Isn't that right, leech?"

Dayla shifted in her boots. "We aren't talking about me."

"No one's ever talking about you, are they? You can be anything that'll get you what you want. You can be kind, nurturing, or a killer, but you're never *there* to be talked about." Rig stepped around Dayla. "Word of warning, kid. Don't trust her. She's using you for something and you won't even realize it until someone's dead."

Dayla clicked her tongue. "You've gotten more talkative over the past year."

"Hey!" Ophelia sprinted in front of Rig. She had to walk backwards when he wouldn't stop. "Dawnhallow is alone out there. The Church doesn't believe us. A gang runs our streets like their little kingdom. I don't care about your opinions or your demons. I care if you'll fight for some people who really need you! Will you stop!?"

Rig slammed his heel into the ground, coming to an immediate halt. Ophelia took a few extra steps before stopping. Rig glared down at her with dark eyes. His face was as unreadable as Dayla's mask. The slightest indication that something clicked in his head was when his mouth twitched.

"You said you have money?" he asked.

Ophelia breathed a sigh of relief. "You'll get paid. Thank you."

Rig grunted. "Ten minutes."

He stomped off without another word. Dayla crept up with a grin plastered across her face.

"That was very inspiring," she said. "Rig used to be a sawbones. He'll be a great asset to us."

"Are you sure?" Ophelia asked. "He can fight, but it doesn't sound like he wants to."

"Rig used to be the most dedicated killer of monsters in Wrotdam. Or... maybe the second most."

"What happened?"

"He's an emotional man who plays at being heartless. Nothing hurts more than the pain you didn't know you can feel." Dayla walked toward her autocar parked across the street. "Come on, Ophelia. I have another lead."

If Rig was the kind of fighter Dayla could conjure up with no warning, Ophelia was thrilled to see who could be next.

CHAPTER 3

The band played a simple tune, one even the clumsy would find easy to dance to. Of course, Victoria Valjean wasn't dancing. No one wanted to dance with her. Reputations were hard to shake in high society, and Victoria's was shattered. Ever since her engagement broke a year earlier, her social life had all but ended. She found it hard to care, though. Her mind would drift to far-off places. Past the shine of the chandeliers and the glamour of the ballgowns.

"Hi, Victoria," Clara Fontaine said. She sat next to her cousin and looked out into the crowd. It was a risky move for most people, but Clara could be expected to comfort family. "That's a nice dress. Did you make it?"

"Huh?" Victoria looked at her blue gown. It was pretty enough and fit well. "No. My mother bought it from some place. I haven't had time to sew. I've been practicing."

"Practicing what?"

Victoria smiled at her cousin. She rubbed her thigh through her dress until she felt a clasp give way. With a wave of her hand, Victoria pulled a flying moon out from beneath the hem and into her palm. "I didn't even have to look," she said.

"Victoria!" Clara tossed her hankie over the moon before anyone could see. "Are you kidding me?"

"I need to practice."

"It's my engagement party." Clara placed her hand over Victoria's. "Couldn't you try to have fun? Raj's brother is a banker and I bet he would love to dance with you."

"I don't care about dancing, Clara." Victoria pulled her hand away. "I don't care about any of these people. I make dresses with more character than them. It's all shallow. It doesn't mean anything. I have seen stars explode. I have felt the cosmos inside me and I could control it like a sword. These people are nothing before that."

Clara crumpled. "Am I nothing?"

For just a moment, Victoria thought *yes*.

"I hope you start feeling better," Clara said, standing up. "I miss my cousin."

Raj called across the dancefloor for Clara to join them. Next to him was a young man with a bright smile. He was cute, but so were dogs. Victoria concentrated on the flying moon in her hand until it hovered just above her palm, still hidden by the hankie. People would never understand her. They would never understand the greatness she held for just a moment.

A clattering of pots broke her concentration. The moon shot sideways, tearing through the hankie and embedding into the leg of the end table next to her. She grumbled and turned toward the sound. Two kitchen hands scrambled to clean up a couple of pots they had dropped.

Why are they carrying around empty pots? Victoria thought.

One of the workers took all the pots and scampered away. The other one scanned the room and made eye contact with Victoria. He was incredibly pale with messy raven black hair that looked like a blind barber had cut it. He seemed almost sickly. Victoria had never seen him before, though she hadn't been to the Fontaine Estate in the last year, so he could be a new hire.

"Sorry," the worker said. He turned back toward the kitchen, holding his stomach. He wore a chef's coat much too big for him. There was a peculiar shape under his clothing. He was too fit to have a potbelly like that.

Victoria leaned back in her chair and considered the situation. It was probably a gun, she figured. A big gun. Perhaps a shotgun. Maybe even a branderbuss. It seemed they were planning on robbing Clara's engagement party. The guns would be for show. It wouldn't do for a criminal to kill any of the Wrotdam elite unless they wanted the full force of the law to come down on them.

Victoria pulled her moon out of the table leg and swept it back up her dress and into her satchel. She walked slowly around the edge of the dancefloor. No one paid attention to her while she found a set of chairs near the back of the ballroom and took a seat. Victoria had never seen a robbery before.

She observed men and women with unwashed hair and desperate eyes taking places in the room. They each held a cooking pot with a lid in their arms. Though the partygoers noticed them, none cared enough to ask them what they were doing. Victoria steepled her fingers and waited.

A few more minutes passed, then across the ballroom, a shot rang out. Women screamed. The people with the pots lifted the lids and pulled out revolvers.

"No one move!" a voice shouted. "If you're in a chair, stay seated. If not, take a lie down."

Slowly, the crowd lowered until the people were prone across the dance floor. Some were like Victoria and were in chairs, frozen to the spot. Victoria was pleased she picked such a comfortable seat.

There were ten robbers. Each was armed with a revolver except one, the pale one who held a branderbuss with both hands. The one leading the crew was a black woman with dreadlocks and a scar on her brow. She stood on a chair and shouted over the room.

"I don't wanna look any one of you tinkering about moving." Her Underslang was so strong it was nearly indecipherable. "Keep your noses to stone and it'll be all bright."

The robbers moved through the room, shouting at people to throw their valuables into the bags they carried. A woman approached Victoria gun held out.

"Put it all in the bag," she said.

Victoria unclasped her diamond necklace and tossed it into the sack, followed by her rings and bracelet. She noticed another robber ignore a man's watch, recognizing it for the cheap make it was. They had their plan set, though occasionally the leader barked out new instructions.

"Pat them down, Numbers!" she shouted. "Make sure they're not burying anything shiny."

Victoria ground her teeth. A pat-down would reveal the flying moon pouch on her thigh. She couldn't let them take her weapons away or she would be as useless as the rest of the people in the room.

The woman who had taken Victoria's jewelry jerked her gun up and ordered Victoria to stand. She began patting down Victoria, starting at her torso. If she had worn a dress with a wider silhouette the robber wouldn't be able to feel the pouch.

This is what I get for choosing a lazy skirt, she thought, holding her hands to her chest.

There were ten robbers and twelve flying moons. Victoria could take them all out at once — she would have to if she didn't want them to start shooting. It would be good practice at controlling all her moons at once. She reached out with her mind and felt the twelves drops of Ink in her blades as the robber reached her hip.

A siren from outside the manor broke the mood. The robber shoved Victoria back into her seat and spun around with her revolver out. The other robbers did the same, causing the hostages to shake and mutter.

The woman with the dreadlocks cursed. "What happened!? What grimy soul told the devils we're here?"

Of course Fontaine has a hotline to the police, Victoria thought. Her father had bragged to everyone who would listen about the silent line he had to call the police, but Duncan Fontaine was a restrained man. No one would know he had a way to contact the police, especially not some people coming to rob him.

Panicked murmurs passed between the hostages. The woman with dreadlocks stomped on a chair in anger, breaking its seat in half, and motioned for the robbers to group up. The only one who didn't join was the pale man. He waited near the kitchen, head swaying about like he was lost in a dream. He shifted his weight back and forth between his feet. He didn't want to stop moving.

A few of the hostages made moves for the doors. The robbers shouted and spread back out across the room to their original positions. The woman moved back to Victoria's chair again, now visibly shaking. If the police weren't careful, the situation could easily become a shootout. As interesting as that would be to see, Victoria would rather not take a stray bullet for such a boring crime.

"We need to get out of here," the woman with dreadlocks said. "Grab some hostages and let's stomp stone."

Clara's scream reached Victoria's ears clear as a bell. One of the robbers had grabbed her and dragged her away from Raj. Raj lunged for her arm, but the robber gave him a swift kick to the stomach. Victoria squeezed the armrests. Typical. Clara always had to be the centre of attention. She swung her foot back and kicked the leg of her chair, breaking it off and tumbling to the ground with a shout.

The shaking robber jumped at the sound. Victoria began whimpering and curling up.

"Hey," the robber said. "Uh, come on. Get up."

Victoria stood halfway, then with great effort turned her heel and tumbled back down.

"Six, what are you doing?" The woman with the dreadlocks called across the room.

"This woman keeps falling."

"I said grab someone and go!"

Six nodded. She grabbed Victoria and pulled her up. Clara had already been taken to the kitchen door, along with two other party-goers. Praneet Khare, one of Raj's family, and Armand Artegon, a playboy from London Victoria had seen at a few events. Her old acting classes did have a purpose; Victoria had succeeded in becoming a hostage.

A man booted open the kitchen door where two more robbers waited. That brought the total up to twelve. They had bags full of valuables taken from the rest of the manor. The help staff was tied up and gagged in the corner. Blood stained the chef's face from a wound on his scalp.

"What's going on, Zero?" a robber asked the woman with dreadlocks.

They're using numbers as code names, Victoria thought. *How adorable.*

"Someone brought in the devils," Zero said. "We need an exit."

A large man with a messy beard grabbed Praneet. "Let's tell them to let us out or we start killing."

Praneet started to shake. Clara put her hands over her mouth, barely keeping in her tears. Victoria wracked her brain to come up with a plan. Six still had her hands on her shoulder, there was no way she would be able to do the movements necessary to move her moons without someone noticing.

"Wait," the pale man said.

Zero pinched her nose. "Not the time, Eleven."

"It's just..." Eleven ran his finger along his branderbuss's trigger guard. "A castle like this has a secret back door, for sure. It'll walk us past the devils."

The gang glared at Eleven. Zero took an extra moment to consider him. It seemed like the rest of the robbers didn't like Eleven much.

"Are you sure?" Zero asked.

"I think so." Eleven turned to Clara. "This is your castle, tog. Where's the way out?"

Clara's jaw trembled. Eleven rubbed the back of his neck. He had the branderbuss but was unwilling to use it.

"Tell them," Victoria said.

"Traitor," Armand snapped.

"If they start shooting, we're just as likely to get killed as they are." Victoria lowered her voice. "So shut up, Army."

Armand straightened his tie and sulked. Clara made eye contact with Victoria and her shaking stopped. Victoria nodded.

"It's in the second ballroom," Clara said.

"You have a second ballroom?" Eleven rubbed his eyes. "Just... just show me."

Zero spun her finger in the air. "Tie them up."

The bearded robber pulled out some rope and each of the prisoners had their hands bound behind their backs. Victoria was losing control of the situation. She still had her moons, but she couldn't use them. If only someone hadn't called the police everything would have been fine. She grumbled curses under her breath as Clara showed the robbers where to go. They moved carefully through empty halls. The robbers had their loot sacks over their shoulders and their guns at the ready.

The second ballroom was reserved for smaller get-togethers or for when there were too many guests to fit in the primary ballroom. The main feature was a fireplace with a massive mirror above, reflecting the room into something even larger. To either side were golden lighting sconces.

"There." Clara motioned with her head to the right sconce. "Turn that one to the left."

Eleven grabbed the sconce and twisted it. The wall next to it popped open. The pale man looked back at his allies, a smile risking its way across his face.

"Do the devils know about this?" he asked.

Clara shook her head.

"Good." Zero holstered her revolver, hiding it under the staff outfit she wore. "We're going home. Blind them. Keep 'em quiet."

Someone gagged Victoria with a piece of cloth. Clara's eyes were wide, pleading silently with Victoria before a bag was put over her head. Armand and Praneet were nearly catatonic and were summarily blinded. Victoria took a few deep breaths.

Interesting, she thought before the bag was lowered and she was in darkness.

CHAPTER 4

Ophelia sat on the hood of Dayla's autocar, watching the police lead people away from the Fontaine estate. Dayla had told her and Rig to wait while she went to see what was going on. Rig sat in the backseat with his eyes closed and arms crossed. His riotsaw leaned against the seat next to him and his branderbuss rested across his lap. He hadn't said a word the entire drive — no one had.

"You used to be a sawbones, right?" Ophelia asked.

"Yes." Rig spoke without opening his eyes.

"How was that?"

"Dangerous."

Ophelia slid off the hood and wandered toward the back. "Thank you for agreeing to help."

Rig opened his eyes but didn't look at her.

"It's been a hard time," Ophelia continued. "No one wants to believe us. There are even people in Dawnhallow who think we're being foolish. It's like they'd forgotten what happened last year."

"Then why insist?"

"Because I can feel it. I know I'm not good at this whole, talking to folks, thing, but I know what I know. I was hoping the village council would send someone with a bit more charisma to plead our case, but I guess I was the one causing the ruckus. I just don't understand why people won't believe the Mire is capable of this."

"Why would they? The Mire's been the same way for a hundred years."

Ophelia leaned on the door. "Why would we lie?"

"People do plenty of things I don't understand." He looked out the window at an investigator talking to a witness. "I don't think you're lying."

"Thank you."

"I just think you're wrong."

Ophelia sighed.

"I've fought or trained to fight the Mire for as long as I can remember," Rig said. "When it starts, you look for patterns, for reason or meaning. It's not there. The Mire is chaos. Any thought we see in it is our own fancies. I knew a sawbones who thought a specific sludge was targeting her and following her. She didn't last long."

"Are you saying it's impossible the Mire would abduct people?"

"I think the world is a cruel place. I think we look for meaning in cruelty. Let me give you a life lesson; don't die for people. They don't care."

Ophelia stepped back from the autocar. She nearly bumped into an officer who shouted at her to get out of the way. They helped a woman from the estate with mascara lines running down her face. Everywhere, men and women wrapped themselves in blankets and coats to be comforted by friends and family.

"Thank you, anyway," Ophelia said, leaning her back on the autocar door.

Rig looked at her for the first time in the conversation. He seemed about to say something, then thought better of it. He shut his eyes and returned to his statue-like position. Ophelia couldn't get upset that he didn't act in the way she wanted. He was hired help. It was a business transaction, not a personal relationship.

A shock of red hair among the crowd grabbed Ophelia's attention. Adelaide, the Ink Cleric from the Cathedral, broke from the mob. She spotted Ophelia and waved.

"Ophelia!" she called and hurried over. "I'm glad I found you."

"I didn't know you were looking," Ophelia said.

Rig gave them a side-eye.

"After you left, I got the full story from Archbishop MacMurray," Adelaide said. "About what the Mire's doing in Dawnhallow."

"How did you find us?" Ophelia looked around as if expecting to see a tail she missed before.

"Finding things is part of my job. But in this case, I caught your friend Dusty on his way out of town and he told me Dayla had offered to help. I simply had to find her car."

"Does this mean the Archbishop has reconsidered?" Ophelia's face lit up.

Adelaide gave a tight smile. "Unfortunately no. It's not his fault. The Church can't be seen reacting to every rumour that comes through its doors. The people would lose trust. But I believe if the Mire is truly acting in a way we haven't seen before, it's our duty to research it."

"If she's right, then it's going to be a fight," Rig said, leaning out the window. "Not a field study."

"I'm still a Cleric of the Ink." She held up the flame gauntlet on her wrist. "I can fight the Mire if the need comes up."

Rig grunted, satisfied, and reset his position with his arms crossed. Ophelia stepped between him and Adelaide.

"Thank you," Ophelia said. "I'll take all the help I can get." *And I won't have to pay you,* she added mentally.

"It's my pleasure," Adelaide said. "Where is Dayla?"

Ophelia pointed at the Fontaine estate just as Dayla reached the bottom of the stairs. She slowed for half a second, lingering her foot over the bottom of the stairs and staring at Adelaide, before resuming her walk back to the autocar.

"I didn't expect to see you here," she said to Adelaide.

"I would not miss the opportunity to investigate Ophelia's claims," she replied. "And with you involved I have no fear."

"This is possibly incredibly dangerous, my dear. You have never truly battled the Mire and with your uncle—"

"The Archbishop made his decree, but I am not only beholden to the Archbishop." She placed her hand over her chest. "We are taught to follow our hearts. To march forth along the path we have chosen as those saints of the Machine's arrival did. Old Archbishop Williams, Father Ezekiel, Vera the Clean. They saw the divinity in the Machine and its Ink and I feel the same pull they once did."

Ophelia had stopped listening early into her speech, trying to wrap her head around something Adelaide said. "The Archbishop is your uncle?"

"Yes, but..." Adelaide straightened her spine. "I am my own woman. I must go with you. The Mire potentially showing intelligence? This is what the Ink Clergy was made for."

"And spying on people," Rig called from inside the car.

"I don't believe we've been formally introduced," Adelaide said with forced politeness. "I am Adelaide Fisher. And you are?"

"Rig."

"Many people use two names, Mr...?"

"Rig."

"Your name is Rig Rig?"

Rig gave her a dull look. Ophelia cleared her throat and turned the attention back to Dayla.

"Did you find who you're looking for?" Ophelia asked.

Dayla shook her head. "She was kidnapped. Some criminals from Understone crashed the engagement party and made off with the bride-to-be and some guests. Including Victoria Valjean."

"How do they know they were from Understone?"

"They spoke in the slang." She pointed away from the estate. "They apparently took an underground passage to another house down that way and disappeared. Probably back in Understone by now."

"Is this woman important?" Adelaide asked.

"Very." Dayla pondered. "She's a talented magician. We would want her at our side."

"If she's rich, then money isn't going to sway her," Ophelia noted.

Dayla grinned. "She'll come for another reason. Trust me."

"Why don't you just tell us?" Rig asked.

Dayla ignored him. "We'll need to get her away from these people. They used numbers as codenames. Maybe they've done this before."

"I can find them," Adelaide said. The group cast her a confused look. "I told you. Finding things is part of my job."

"Adelaide…" Dayla started.

"Our conversation is done." She lifted her chin.

Dayla inhaled sharply before a smile crept to her lips. "Fine. As you wish."

"Then let's not waste any more time." Ophelia got into the front passenger seat. "It's not something we have a lot of."

Dayla jogged around the autocar while Adelaide approached the back door. She looked at Rig, the riotsaw next to him, then back to Rig. With exaggerated effort, Rig moved the riotsaw to between his legs and slid over so Adelaide could get in. Ophelia felt light as a feather. She had gathered three allies and was on her way to a fourth. Dawnhallow's future looked bright.

CHAPTER 5

Hush had pulled the short straw. That meant it was his job to watch over the prisoners. He had changed out of the kitchen worker's clothes and into something more comfortable. Franklin's old regal coat. The last reminder of a lost friend.

He sat on a creaking wooden chair and kept his eyes on the prisoners. Three of them were unobtrusive, though not content. They had been pushed into a makeshift cell at the back of the Numbers Gang hideout in Understone and had the sacks taken off their heads. The fourth, a woman with a sour look, hadn't stopped staring at him. Hush adjusted the branderbuss he had across his lap and tried to ignore her. He kept his hand over the spot where the inkwell was supposed to be.

"When are we getting out of here?" the sour-faced woman asked sharply. She was the one who convinced the others to reveal the secret passage. "You aren't going to kill us. So what? Ransom?"

"I don't know," Hush said. The woman was smart. Too smart. Likely enough to frustrate the other gangsters. "Zero's tinkering it out."

Hush hadn't signed up for kidnapping. He just needed some money to feed himself and heard the Numbers Gang was known for quick in and out jobs. It figured that the one he went on would go badly. Nothing had gone right for him since he returned. He counted it as five months, but time was difficult to process. He needed to get back to his normal life, rather than hang on to something no one would believe. In time he would forget how he spent the first half of the year. In time he had to.

"Could you at least untie us?" The woman jerked her head to her hands tied behind her back.

"I was just told to watch you. That's all I want to do."

"You're watching us just fine. What's your name?"

Hush leapt to his feet, knocking his chair back. "Stop asking me questions!"

The prisoners jumped. The other woman, Clara, curled up. The dandy, Armand, stared at Hush, wide-eyed. Hush took deep breaths.

It's a simple question, Hush, he thought. *It doesn't mean anything. This is real.*

He ran his fingers along the branderbuss's inkwell slot. Empty. Same as when he found it. He rubbed the slot a few times and calmed himself down.

"Don't antagonize him, Victoria," Praneet said.

Strangely, Victoria was the only one who didn't look frightened by Hush's outburst. She was shocked, but it quickly turned to curiosity. Hush would have to keep his eye on her the most. He picked his chair up from where it toppled over and righted it before sitting down.

"No more questions," Hush said quietly. Then he added with venom, "Victoria."

Victoria smiled. It made Hush's skin crawl. "So," she said without losing the grin. "Why don't the others like you?"

"They like me just fine."

Victoria let out a noncommittal noise.

Hush wasn't an idiot. He knew the Numbers Gang wasn't a fan of him, not many criminals in Understone were anymore. He had heard the whispers; he was weird and unstable. He had outbursts. He would lose focus. But he was still a talented thief. He still had a purpose. Plus, he had the branderbuss. Sure, it wasn't loaded, but people didn't know that.

"Eleven!" Zero shouted from another room. "Come here!"

"What about the hostages?" Hush kept the branderbuss pointed at them.

"Leave them."

Hush walked backwards out of the room. Victoria kept her hollow gaze on him until he was outside and shut the door. He hurried toward the front room where Zero called from. Everyone was there with their guns out. Three and Four were pressed next to the window with the blinds drawn. They were nearly identical twins except one of them had a burn scar across half her face. Zero paced the middle of the room, tapping her revolver against her head.

"What's grimy?" Hush asked.

"Someone's been asking questions about us," Zero said.

"Devils?"

"Eight, tell him."

The large bruiser with an unkempt beard stepped forward, shotgun resting against his shoulder. "I looked a sawbones, leech, and cleric all asking around town. Asking about four kidnapped togs."

"And I'm trying to figure out what an angel wants with us!" Zero slapped a bottle off a table, smashing it against the wall and sending whiskey to the floor. "They're supposed to be wiping muckies, not crawling for criminals. This is all pig twisty, Eleven."

Hush kept his mouth shut. Zero didn't want advice, she wanted an audience. The same feeling Hush had in the estate crept up again — the worry that someone was going to get killed. If the Numbers Gang started shooting hostages, Hush didn't want any part of it. But he wouldn't be able to stop them either. As long as he kept things from spiralling out of control, everyone could get out of there alive. Including the folks in the cell.

"I think someone ratted us out," Zero said. "Someone made a call."

"But why to an angel?" Three asked.

"I don't know!" She kicked a chair across the room. "I'm trying to hold this together! Knocking over a castle was going to be our big score but one of you went dark and I wanna know who!" She pointed her gun at Three. "What about you, Three? You kept going out. Maybe you talked to someone."

Three threw her hands into the air. "I was getting food!"

"Zero," Six said softly, stepping carefully toward her.

"Damn it! Burn it all down!" Zero swung her revolver around, each person flinching as it passed over them. And people said Hush was unstable.

A knock came from outside. The gang trained their weapons on the door. Zero motioned for Three to answer it. Three swallowed then crept forward. She wrapped her hand around the knob and pointed her revolver at the wood. She looked back at Zero and mouthed counting down from three. At zero, she opened the door wide.

A woman with her hair stuck into a knit cap stood on the other side. She recoiled as all the guns were shoved in her face and threw her hands into the air. She certainly wasn't a sawbones, leech, or cleric.

"What are you doing here?" Zero shouted.

"I'm looking for someone," the woman said.

"Who?"

The woman shrugged. "Uh, well."

With a sudden crash, the ceiling fell in. A massive man landed between Three and Seven and laid them out with two mighty punches. Eight turned with his shotgun, only for the newcomer to tear it from his grasp and crack him with the stock, knocking him out.

Four raised her gun, but a bolt of electricity shot through the open door and struck her in the chest. She went rigid then dropped into a heap, twitching on the floor. Hush dove aside as a second bolt went over his head and struck Two. One and Five landed in front of him, tossed aside by the giant sawbones in the centre of the room.

Zero shouted and fired wildly, missing everything. Electricity flew past her and burned the wall next to her head. She froze, smoke billowed out of her barrel. The sawbones trained his stolen shotgun on the two gangsters still standing, Ten and Nine. Eight crumpled into a heap in the corner, covering his head and shaking.

The woman at the door stepped in, flanked by a leech in her dark robes and a woman in some strange variation of church garb. She had to be the cleric, Hush surmised. An Ink Cleric, to be precise.

"Maybe we can talk now," the leech said, her boltrifle trained on Zero. Lightning coursed down the primed barrel. "We're looking for some people."

"I don't know what you're talking about," Zero said.

"Let me, Dayla." The cleric laid her hand on the leech's shoulder and approached. "My name is Adelaide Fisher. Are you the one they call Zero?"

Zero nodded, eyeballing the strange woman.

"Could you put that gun down, Zero?"

Zero looked at her gun. She considered it for a long time, then knelt and placed it next to Three's unconscious body.

"Thank you." Adelaide had a sweet smile that could warm the coldest heart. "We know you were at the Fontaine estate today and you took some people with you when you left. I don't think you were planning on doing that. No one wants anyone to get hurt. We just want the people you took."

Zero chewed on her lip. Hush let out a puff of air, finally breathing. Dayla snapped her boltrifle at him without looking and Hush's breath stopped again.

"We can ensure the police are lenient with you," Adelaide said.

"Or we can ensure they never have to know," Dayla added.

Adelaide cast her a shocked look. "They broke the law. Even without the kidnapping, they stole from these people."

"This is about something more important, wouldn't you agree?"

"I don't. They broke the *law*."

Zero cleared her throat. "I would like to accord with the angel-killer."

"Look at that," Dayla said with a smile. "It seems we have a deal."

Adelaide looked at her disgusted. She stomped next to the woman waiting at the door.

"Eleven." Zero pointed at Hush. "Bring our guests."

Dayla lowered her rifle, taking its sights off Hush. Hush scrambled to his feet and rushed to the cells. The sawbones, the largest of the group, had his eyes fixed on Hush's branderbuss. Was he angry? Did he think Hush stole it? Hush kept his head low.

Victoria sat right where she was a few minutes earlier. The rest crowded against the wooden bars, hoping to see what was going on. When Hush entered, they wriggled back. "I'm letting you out," he said, grabbing the key from the wall.

Victoria cocked her head while the others exclaimed with glee. Hush unlocked the door then cut their bonds loose. They practically sprinted out of the cell when Hush was done.

"Good to see you're all safe," Dayla said as they returned to the front room.

"I want your true word," Zero said, stepping toward Dayla.

"Of course!" Dayla turned to the hostages and spread her arms wide. "We have decided it would be best if we all pretended this didn't happen."

"What?" Praneet exclaimed. "What do you mean?"

"Quite simple. You were released, but you have no idea who it was who kidnapped you or where you were taken."

"That's absurd!" Armand smoothed his hair down. "These people are criminals and should be punished."

"These people have made a deal with me for your safe release. Or, you can go back in the cage and we can try to work out a new deal."

He went pale.

"Just keep your mouth shut," Victoria said. She had her arm around Clara, holding her close. "This is fine."

"Victoria," Dayla said. "Just the magician I wanted to talk to."

Victoria nodded, almost imperceptibly. "Hello, Dayla."

Dayla turned to Adelaide. "My dear, could you lead these poor people back to the surface? Except for Victoria. I need to talk with her."

Adelaide nodded tersely and stepped outside to lead the way. Clara clung to Victoria as she walked until she had to let go. Still, she kept her eyes on her, only turning when Adelaide laid her arm across her shoulders.

Hush's gaze flicked between each person in the room. *What is going on?*

"How have you been, Victoria?" Dayla asked, as though they were friends meeting on the street.

"I'm well. Considering the circumstances," Victoria said.

Dayla smiled and nodded. She gestured toward the woman who had knocked on the door. "This is Ophelia. She has hired us to protect her village from the Mire."

"This concerns me, why?"

"It seems like perfect practice for an up-and-coming magician."

"I'm not an up-and-coming magician," Victoria said, stepping forward proudly. "I'm the greatest magician in Wrotdam. I'm also not for hire."

"Forgive me, Victoria. I just thought we would be lucky to have your help on something like this. You see…" Dayla gave a deliberate pause. Her eyes twinkled mischievously. "She lives in Dawnhallow. It's a small village to the north. They were attacked last year too, around this time. The Mire took their people and carried them far away. Far away as Pembrooke House."

Hush listened intently now. The Mire wasn't supposed to abduct people, but he knew for a fact that wasn't true. Franklin was abducted a year ago. Was it going to happen again? And if so, how did these people know about it?

Victoria had a dark look. "I'll come. Just to see what's happening. I'm curious is all. If it's as bad as you think, Dayla, you definitely will need my help." She brushed past her. "I need to change. I'll meet you in Dawnhallow tomorrow."

Victoria didn't appear to be afraid of walking through Understone, despite the ballgown she still wore.

Dayla waved to her companions to leave. "Come now, Rig. This was a very good show."

Rig opened the shotgun's breech and tossed the two shells across the room. While Ophelia and Dayla were leaving, Rig stomped toward Hush. Hush stumbled back, pointing the branderbuss at the oncoming sawbones. Rig threw the shotgun away and grabbed the branderbuss.

"Let go!" Hush shouted as Rig twisted the gun out of his grip.

Rig inspected the branderbuss, running his fingers over the notches in the wood and metal. His gaze lingered on the spot where an inkwell should be. His expression went soft, but only for a moment before he spun on his heel and followed Dayla and Ophelia.

"Hey!" Hush shouted, jumping after him. "That's mine! Give it back!"

"It's not yours," Rig said.

Hush kept after him as they exited the hideout and entered the Understone streets. A crowd had gathered to see what had happened, and the screaming madman gave them a new show. Hush's shouts grew more panicked. His heart turned into the clomping of horse hoofs. Soon everyone was looking at him. Too many eyes. There were always too many eyes.

"Give it back!" Hush jumped for the gun, only to have Rig hold it over his head. "You're fake! You're not real! That blaster is real! Give it back!"

Rig put his hand on Hush's chest. The lights strung about the cavern walls grew dark. Breath refused to enter his lungs. Understone spun around him. Faces blurred together until they became formless. Still, he clawed at Rig for his property.

"Rig," Ophelia said. "Give that poor man his stuff."

"It's not his," Rig said, pushing Hush away.

Dayla stepped between Rig and Hush, exuding an aura of calm. "Let's take a moment here," she said to Hush. "What's your name?"

Hush seized up again. He kept his gaze on the branderbuss in Rig's hands. *Easy breaths,* he thought. "H…Hush. My name is Hush. Is what you said true? Is the Mire coming to take folks?"

She jerked her head at Ophelia. "She believes so."

"Why would it do that?"

"We don't know." She looked Hush from toe to crown. "Does that bother you?"

"I want my gun back." His feet wouldn't move. They sank into the floor as they did when Franklin got grabbed. Like when he was too cowardly to help. More people were going to be taken. Like he was taken. "I want my gun back and I want to come with you."

Ophelia turned to him in surprise. "Why?"

"Just give me my gun." His hands started to shake. "Let me look at it. Let me know it's real."

"Can you fight, Hush?" Dayla asked.

"What are you doing?" Ophelia took Dayla by the arm, leaning in like he wouldn't be able to hear what she said next. "Look at him. There's something wrong with him."

Dayla eased Ophelia's hand aside. "You want fighters. I'm recruiting." She turned to Hush. "You want to come with us. Maybe you want to help some people who need it. Maybe if you do that, Rig will give you back your gun."

"No," Rig said.

"He'll think about it."

Rig rolled his eyes.

Hush rubbed his hands together. It seemed real enough. When Franklin was taken, Hush failed him. He couldn't fight the Mire at that point. This could be his redemption. Or it could be a trick. Whatever the outcome, he needed to get his gun back.

"I'll do it," Hush said. "But I want my blaster first."

"Rig," Dayla said with a sweet, but forceful, tone.

Rig narrowed his eyes. Slowly, he lowered the branderbuss. Hush wrapped his fingers around the stock. His heartbeat slowed. He felt the nicks and the gap where the inkwell should be. It was all as he remembered it. Rig grabbed him by the wrist and pulled him close.

"That's not yours," he growled. "Just remember that." And he shoved him back.

Hush clutched the gun to his chest. He felt grounded again. But what had he gotten himself into?

Victoria told Clara to explain everything to her parents once they were street level again.

"Aren't you coming back with us?" Clara asked.

"I need to go to my house," Victoria explained. "I have some important things to do with those people who rescued us, so I need to grab some clothes and my autocar. It would be a hassle to explain. I'm just hoping they're still at your place so I won't have to sneak around them. I'll spend the night at our summer home outside of town, I suppose."

Clara wasn't happy about it, but there wasn't anything she could say to stop her. Victoria hiked her gown up and began the long trek back to Valjean manor. She was fortunate to catch a ride with a family that saw her walking down the street and rode in their autocar the rest of the way. The entire time Victoria kept looking over her shoulder. It felt like something was watching her.

As they pulled up to Valjean manor, her heart sank. Her parent's autocar was in the driveway. She would have to sneak in. With a curt appreciation for the people who drove her, Victoria circled the outside of the manor. After the events of the past year, her parents removed the trellis that she normally used to climb down from the roof. She put her hands on her hips and looked up at the roof lip about four metres above her.

With a flick of her wrist, she pulled four flying moons from underneath her dress. She kicked her heels off then tossed them onto the roof. She floated the moons in pairs and stepped back. Rushing forward, she jumped off the moons like steps and grabbed onto the roof. A jolt of pain shot through her hand, but she held on. She pulled herself up onto the shingles and rolled onto her back.

A loose nail had pierced her hand, dripping blood onto her already dirty gown. She cursed silently and pulled the flying moons into her satchel. She grabbed her heels and crept toward her window.

Inside her room, she grabbed a sock and wrapped it around her palm tightly. There were no sounds in her house, but she was sure her parents were somewhere downstairs, so she kept her movements deliberate and slow. She slid out of her gown and got into some clothes better suited for going out of town. Breeches and tall boots, with a waistcoat over her blouse for an accent. It would do, but she would need to pack more. No telling how long she would be gone.

She was putting on her leather jacket when a soft voice came from her window.

"Excuse me," it said.

Victoria spun around. A figure squatted in her open window wrapped in ragged clothing. She wore a white mask with black lines coming from her eyes like tear streaks. A wide-brimmed hat cast a shadow down to red lips. Victoria drew all her moons, floating them around her, ready to attack.

The stranger threw her gloved hands forward. "Wait. I'm sorry I scared you."

"Keep your voice down," Victoria said. "I'm trying to keep a low profile."

"Oh, sure," the stranger said, quieter. "I didn't mean to frighten you. It can be tough, as I think you can see." She indicated her mask. "But I saw what happened in Understone."

"What of it?" Victoria lowered her moons but didn't put them away. They floated just above the carpet.

"I know what Ophelia and her companions are doing. I want to help. I want to come along."

"Then why not ask them, rather than stalking me back to my home?"

The stranger lowered her head. "I would not want to approach a group like that. Between the sawbones, the leech, and the cleric, I don't know who to fear the most. But if I come with you, they'll have to accept me."

"What are you talking about?"

"It might be better to show you." She reached for her hat. "But please don't be afraid."

Victoria's skin tingled. Her moons fell flat to the carpet and she stepped forward. The stranger removed her hat, showing a head of short, platinum hair. She grabbed her mask and pulled it aside. Victoria's eyes flared. The stranger had dull grey skin and her eyes were black as voids.

"Wow." Victoria reached out. The stranger flinched, so Victoria moved slower. She touched the stranger's cheek. For some reason she expected her to be cold, but she wasn't. "What is this?"

"It's an infection from the Mire," the stranger said, sliding out of Victoria's reach. "But don't worry, it's not contagious. You can't get it from me. People have tried. You can see why I didn't want to approach someone from the Church."

Victoria nodded. She had never seen the Mire affect someone in such a way. There was something morbidly fascinating about it. "I'll take you with me," Victoria said. "What should I call you?"

"Mattie Wilkins." She moved to put her mask back on, but Victoria caught her hand.

"My name is Victoria Valjean."

Mattie looked at the blood seeping through Victoria's makeshift bandage. "You're hurt."

"Yeah." She held it up to the light. "Found a loose nail."

The sound of vomit came from Mattie as she leaned out the window. At first, Victoria assumed she must've had a weak stomach for blood, but when she turned back her hand was covered in a translucent slime.

"Can I see your wound?" Mattie asked, slightly out of breath.

Victoria unwrapped her hand carefully. Mattie pressed the slime into it. There was a tingle and Victoria's breath caught in her throat. The wound knitted together before her very eyes. Victoria poked the skin, but other than the blood, there was no indication she was ever hurt at all.

"Well, Mattie," Victoria said, leaning in. "I think we're going to be very good friends."

Mattie smiled weakly.

CHAPTER 6

It was a tight fit in Dayla's autocar with the five of them. Dayla drove while Ophelia sat in the passenger seat, resting her head back after the longest day in recent memory. The familiar old-growth forest loomed at their sides, snow piling up in the shade, telling Ophelia they were almost to her home. The shadows of thin branches swept across the backseat where Adelaide, Rig, and Hush crammed in shoulder to shoulder. As they took a sharp turn, Rig's riotsaw felt against Hush's head.

"We're not exactly an army," Hush said, pushing the saw back to Rig. "If the Mire's coming to take people, is this all we have?"

"We have an army," Dayla said. "We have Dawnhallow."

"The people there aren't sawbones," Ophelia said. "We can't fight the Mire."

"I told you before, anyone can fight the Mire. Besides, you have us to train you."

Adelaide leaned forward. "People can do amazing things to protect their home. You found us, after all."

Ophelia beamed. It had been a long day, and though she couldn't get the backing of the Church, she had gathered quite a group together. With Dayla's help of course. Ophelia never believed she would be capable of such a thing. Perhaps, she thought, watching deer bound through the woodland, Dawnhallow would surprise her as well.

"What about that gang?" Hush asked. "Would they wipe some muckies for us?"

"I don't think they care." Ophelia sank into her seat. "If push came to shove, they would probably just hide in that manor of theirs. That place is built like a fortress."

"Sounds like we should get our hands on it," Rig said.

"Do you think they would listen to us?" Adelaide asked.

"They don't have to."

"Not everything has to come to violence, Rig."

He grunted. "Funny how it usually does."

Adelaide furrowed her brow. She squeezed even deeper into the small spot she had. Ophelia glanced back. Hush still clutched his branderbuss to his chest. She kept thinking back to his outburst when Rig tried to take it from him. He was the only one for whom Ophelia still had concerns. Dayla wanted to bolster their ranks, but how useful would a thief be?

"So, Hush," she said. "Where'd you get that gun?"

"Found it." He held it tighter.

"In an exploded church at the docks?" Rig asked.

Hush jerked a wide-eyed stare in his direction. "How did you know?"

Rig crossed his arms and shut his eyes. Hush turned his body, trying to get the branderbuss away from Rig. Ophelia sat back in her seat and watched the trees whip by the window.

"It's a fun drive," Dayla said.

They arrived in Dawnhallow just before sundown. It was a quaint village of a couple dozen buildings spread out over a few streets. They parked outside the Carefree Inn. Lights were on inside and the occasional shadow would block the window.

"Come on," Ophelia said, stepping outside. "I'm sure they have some rooms for you."

Adelaide, Rig, and Hush came tumbling out of the back. Dayla chuckled at the antics. She opened the trunk and swung her boltrifle over her back. Ophelia spotted her and Dusty's horses tied up outside. He must be there.

They entered the inn to a restrained celebration. It was the happiest Ophelia had seen Dawnhallow in some time, though to most people it would seem like nothing spectacular. The room went quiet as the group stepped inside.

"Ophelia!" Dusty shouted from the back. He pushed his way through the crowd. "Are these the people who are going to help us?"

"Yes, they are," Ophelia said proudly.

Dusty leaned in and spoke quietly, "There's not a lot of them."

"We have another one coming. A magician. Also, they're going to teach us to fight the Mire."

"It's better than nothing I suppose." He looked at the group with worry. Then, a smile spread across his face. "I have a surprise for you too. Apparently, after we left, someone came into the village offering to help. He used to be a sawbones actually! We have to pay him, but he seems capable." Dusty shouted over the crowd. "Sir! They're here!"

The crowd parted. A rough-looking man in a long coat with dark circular glasses stepped up. He reached up with gloved hands and removed his glasses, displaying eyes that were an unearthly electric blue.

"This," Dusty said, gesturing. "Is Edwin Zhen."

Rig, Adelaide, and Dayla raised their weapons. The crowd leapt back. Hush jerked his head side to side, then raised his gun as well.

"What are you doing!?" Ophelia shouted, looking between Edwin and her hires.

"You're dead," Rig growled.

Edwin looked down. He lifted his coat apart and inspected his body. "It doesn't seem that way."

"Why are you here?" Dayla primed her rifle. "How are you here?"

"I'm here to fight the Mire." He gently laid his glasses down on a nearby table. "How… is a little more complicated."

"You were consumed by fire." Rig stepped forward. "I saw you."

"But did you see a body? It's those little details that always get you. You were never good at taking in the entire battlefield, Rig. I was blown up, and I should have been dead. But there was a bright light and—" He paused. "I hesitate to say *saved*. I was fixed."

He grabbed the lapels of his coat and let it fall to the ground. A collective murmur ran through the room. Edwin's arms were metal. Transparent domes along his biceps and forearms contained a flurry of electricity. He pulled off his gloves and let the energy course between his fingertips. He grinned.

"I'm here to fight, Rig," he said. "If it must be with you, so be it. But I cannot let the Mire take this village."

"Everyone stop!" Ophelia slammed her foot down. The room went quiet. Even she was shocked at her sudden display. It had been a long day. She was exhausted. Rather than let this moment of courage fade, she drove it on. "We are on the same side. If either of you wants to get paid, then act like adults!"

Edwin laughed. He swept his coat off the ground and put his dark glasses back on. "I'm going to bed. Leave if you want to throw a tantrum because I'm staying and I don't need you."

Edwin spun on his heel and went upstairs, the crowd giving him plenty of room. Rig took some deep breaths and followed.

"Where do you think you're going?" Ophelia asked forcefully.

"I'm just going to talk," Rig said.

"Leave your weapons."

Rig stopped.

"Now!"

Rig slammed his saw and branderbuss onto a table, nearly breaking it. He dug his hands into his coat pockets and stomped up the stairs after Edwin. Ophelia exhaled and nearly fell back, finally letting fear take her. She actually stood Rig down.

"That was exciting," Dusty said.

Slowly, the room returned to normal, albeit quieter. Adelaide and Dayla lowered their weapons, but their muscles stayed tense. Hush shrugged. He had as little idea what had just happened as Ophelia.

"What was that?" Ophelia asked.

"We have a history with Edwin Zhen," Dayla said, depowering her rifle.

"I thought he was dead," Adelaide said.

"Rig certainly thought he was."

"What were those things on his arms?" Ophelia asked.

Adelaide rubbed her bicep. "I think those *were* his arms. I've never seen a prosthetic like that. It's beyond anything we're capable of."

"It doesn't matter." Dayla was deathly serious. "Edwin Zhen had fallen to the Mire the last time I saw him. He was amberwild."

Ophelia noticed a few of the townspeople were listening in. She pushed the group toward the bar. "He didn't look crazy. He looked weird, yes, and aggressive, but so do you."

"You don't come back once you see amber," Dayla insisted. She stared at the bar, talking to herself rather than Ophelia. "We have to keep an eye on him. He's incredibly dangerous."

"I agree," Adelaide said.

Dayla walked away with Adelaide in tow. As long as they weren't killing each other, Ophelia couldn't be too upset. She looked at Hush, who scratched his head awkwardly.

"I'm, uh..." He sighed. "I'm regretting coming."

"Thanks, Hush," Ophelia said sarcastically. She looked at the stairs to the rooms. Hopefully, Rig and Edwin were talking it out, rather than fighting.

Rig stood outside the door he had just seen close. Emotions flowed in and out of him like the tide. He went from relief to anger to fear, then through countless other feelings before starting the process again. Seeing Edwin again had been a slap to the face. His best friend, or his only friend. He raised his hand to knock, then decided against it and just opened the door.

Edwin lounged on the open windowsill, taking in the cold evening breeze. His strange arms crackled slightly when the door opened and he turned his head to Rig.

"You know," Edwin said. "I think I may win our next boxing match."

"How did this happen?" Rig shut the door.

"I don't know." Edwin looked over his metal hand, flexing it open and closed. "I don't know a lot of things from last year. It feels like I read it in a book that I'm forgetting. I'm sure I did some bad things, things I'll have to atone for. The only thing I remember with absolute, terrifying clarity is you killing me."

"You were amberwild. We agreed that if either of us fell, we would kill the other before the leeches could."

Edwin slammed his foot against the window frame. "I didn't think it would be me!"

"Dina is—"

"They've been dead for years. I was told they could be brought back. I killed for the Church, burned down homes, and stomped out anybody that questioned their authority. I was a one-man inquisition for them, and it didn't matter. They couldn't bring them back."

Rig noticed a frame leaning against the wall. He tipped it back. It was a mirror, turned around to face the wall. "You said there was something above the Church. What did you mean?"

"Father Smithson talked about these things he called the Faceless Gods." Edwin slid off the window and paced. "He said the Church was trying to communicate with them. I don't understand it now, but I did before. At the end I understood everything. I could hear these Faceless Gods like drums in my skull. Then there was you." He cast Rig a vicious look. "Then nothing. A month ago, I woke up in the ocean below the Machine, with these arms. I had escaped, but I don't know what and I don't know how."

"Why come here?" Rig asked. He looked for the punchline to some cosmic joke. He killed his oldest friend, that had to mean something. And yet here he stood.

Edwin tapped his forehead. "I can still hear it. Whatever talked to me while I slept, its tongue still licks the inside of my brain. Not words, but feelings." A mad smile spread across his lips. His electric eyes crackled behind his glasses. "The Mire is coming to Dawnhallow. It will take everyone here and throw their bodies into the Machine. Eat them like slaughtered pigs. Blood, bones, and gristle. I'm going to stop it. Starve it. And I don't need *you* to do that."

"You are still mad." Though that wasn't entirely accurate. When Edwin saw amber, he was wild. The man who now stood before Rig had an intensity, like a spring ready to fire, but all wrapped up in a haunting serenity. He wasn't amberwild, he was something else.

"We steal oil that drips from between the plates of a thing we call an angel. We twist it, change it, turn it to fuel. You and I have drunk of it and tasted the emptiness it gives us. Madness doesn't come into it anymore. Humanity has replaced its soul, its blood, with Ink." He fell back against the windowsill. "I have my purpose, madness or no. Just get out, before one of us gets hurt."

Rig started, like he had any kind of rebuttal to what Edwin had just said. But there was nothing. And he was tired. He turned to the door, but stopped. "I do... I do wish I could have saved you."

"You didn't." Edwin looked out the window.

Rig squeezed his fists until his knuckles popped. There was no use talking to him. Rig was right, Edwin did die. This was someone different. He left the room, slamming the door hard enough to rattle the wall.

CHAPTER 7

With the dawn, Ophelia lay in bed, wondering if everything had been a dream. She looked at the sun streaming in past her frost-covered windows, able to imagine for a second she had nowhere to be. But once she headed out onto Dawnhallow's streets, she was immediately hit with a reminder of reality as Adelaide came stomping out of the Carefree Inn with Dayla on her tail.

"I am here now," Adelaide said, planting herself at the foot of the inn's porch and facing Dayla. "You cannot change that. This is my choice."

"If I could simply bend your ear—" Dayla said.

"You already kept me up much of the night with your doting." She spun on her heel and spotted Ophelia approaching. "Ophelia! The pipes in my room are currently frozen. With the boys occupying their own rooms, the innkeeper told me of a washhouse in town."

"Oh, it's not really a washhouse, but the post office has a tap and soap in the back." She pointed just off the main street to a red-roofed building. "We all use it if we can't get our own water. There's a lock on the door, but it's not much."

"It's quite alright, I'm not fussy." She nodded politely at Ophelia and cast Dayla a withering glare before heading down the road.

"Dayla," Ophelia said, clasping her hands behind her back. "You were the one who said we needed all the help we can get."

"Adelaide is…" She tapped her fingers along the mask on her hip. "…a unique child."

"She's a full-grown woman."

"That she may be. But when she was young she was my ward. I had no children of my own so I had plenty of time watching over her, perhaps I have simply grown comfortable in that position."

"Sounds like you see her as a daughter." Ophelia breathed out a lungful of vapour into the cold air. "My mother rarely let me out of her sight before the sickness took her."

"I'm not sure I would go that far." She chuckled, though Ophelia detected a hint of surprise in the laugh. Dayla always acted indifferent when anyone read into her. "But I do see her as a responsibility of mine. Responsibilities are not something to take lightly." She tilted her head to the side and looked past Ophelia's shoulder. "Speaking of which, I believe one of yours is about to come knocking."

Ophelia looked back and spotted Stephen Dixon marching down the street, eyes fixed on her. When she looked back, the last flip of Dayla's scarf vanished through the Carefree Inn's entrance.

She certainly knows how to avoid a conversation, Ophelia thought, facing Stephen down.

"Ophelia," he said with a polite nod. He was the owner of the mill and de facto leader of the village council — the one Ophelia was least excited to have to explain what happened in Wrotdam to.

"Stephen." She nodded back.

"Cold today." He squinted into the bright cloud cover.

"Yeah."

"Is this, uh…" He waved his hand limply toward the inn. "Is this what the Church sent to help us?"

"Not exactly. The Church refused to help."

"They refused?" He huffed and ground his teeth. "What did you tell them?"

"Exactly what we discussed. All the evidence. The facts. They wouldn't listen."

"You must've done something wrong. They wouldn't simply ignore us." He shook his head and circled around, never deigning to look her in the eye. "Instead you return with this gaggle of brutes."

"I never wanted to do this." Heat flushed into her cheeks. "You're the ones who sent me to get help."

"The village council sent you to request the Church's aid, not bring in some mercenaries from who knows where." He turned on her, staring down his rosy nose. "And you're the one who got the village whipped up into a frenzy over nothing. Perhaps it's fortunate the Church refused us, all the more proof this entire fantasy of yours is just that."

"You were there last year!" Ophelia stamped her foot, cracking the layer of frost over the mud. "You saw them take people as much as I did."

"I took care of my family, as all noble men do. And the Mire did what the Mire does, attack like a rabid dog. Perhaps if someone with some authority entreated the Church they might set up an outpost in the area. If Dawnhallow is large enough to attract the Mire, surely we must be well on our way to being a fine city. That is good for business, not doomsaying."

Ophelia clenched her jaw until her teeth hurt. The blood rushed to her ears and all she could hear was Dusty's gentle voice in her head telling her not to knock Stephen Dixon's teeth out.

"I talked to the council," he continued, unaware or uncaring of the fury building inside Ophelia. "We're holding an emergency meeting at town hall. You'll be speaking. Bring your mercenaries and we'll decide what to do next."

He brushed snow off his shoulder and marched on. Ophelia had been certain her job was done after getting the mercenaries to Dawnhallow. Just the thought of having to stand up and talk to the village made the cold wind grow colder. At least she had backup in the form of well-armed mercenaries. She turned to the inn and found Hush standing on the porch, his eyes wide.

"So, uh…" He pointed in the direction Stephen walked. "That guy's a croakin' pig."

"I assume that means asshole?" Ophelia asked.

He nodded.

"Sorry about him." Ophelia rubbed at the headache growing in her temples.

"It's all bright." He rested his hand on the bottom of the branderbuss tied across his back. He was never out of contact with it, she noticed. "I'm used to togs not wanting me around. You must really love this place to stand up to him."

"You know, it's funny, I don't think I do." She sat on the porch next to Hush's feet. She'd only been up for barely half an hour and the day felt done. "This time last year, I was thinking I'd be across the Atlantic in somewhere like Halifax."

"Why?" Hush asked, sitting down beside her, spinning his branderbuss around across his lap.

"Because I could. It's almost the 20th Century, you can cross the ocean in under a week. We aren't stuck here like our parents were." She gazed up at the clouds. "We can go anywhere. It was my sister who loved Dawnhallow."

"So, she'd want you to stay?"

"Absolutely not. She'd want me to go. She said if I travelled the world I might find something to care about — which sounds mean, I know. But that's how Aisling was. She wanted people to be happy, whatever that happiness meant."

"What happened to her?"

The wind blew a flurry of snowflakes down the road. A brave bird called out, echoing its winter song into the dawn as Ophelia's thoughts drifted back to that unseasonably warm December the year before.

"She was taken." Ophelia wrapped her arms around her knees. "We didn't expect the Mire to come, even after they'd been spotted outside the village. Aisling had heard that maybe there was a Cleansing going on in Wrotdam, but it didn't mean anything to us. We had chores to finish. Out here you don't deal with the Mire. Maybe a leech or a sawbones comes by talking about a nest out in the wood. Maybe if it gets real bad you set up some lavender and wait the night out."

She let out an uneven breath. How long had it been since she talked about that day? Had she ever done it before?

"We heard the screams before we knew what was happening. We lit all the candles we had and huddled beneath our beds. I didn't realize we left a window open, and one of the candles got blown out. I told Aisling to leave it but... she didn't. She struck the match and I saw a mass of something inhuman take her by the arm and drag her out. She screamed, but I couldn't move. I didn't move until the next morning when someone found me."

"I'm sorry." Hush tapped his thumb on the empty inkwell loader on his branderbuss. "I also lost a friend that day. The darkveins took him right in front of me, and I couldn't help. He was right there. Right in front of me." His gaze grew distant. "Sometimes I would be in his place. Sometimes I would grab him. But even when I saved him, I didn't."

"What do you mean?" Ophelia asked.

"I mean, it feels like I played that moment over and over, but it never worked out." He hopped to his feet. "I understand how you feel. It's grimy. Before that, I thought I was brick, but we failed the people we care about. I don't wanna fail no one else."

Ophelia bobbed her head. She hadn't expected any of her hires to understand her, much less Hush, who she never wanted to bring along. "I don't want to sound ungrateful, I'm thankful for each of you for coming, but it's fairly obvious most of you have some kind of... ulterior motive." She caught sight of Dayla just as she crept down the inn's side alley. She gave Ophelia a wave before carrying on. "But you're all here, so I don't know how much more I can ask. I do wonder why *you* were so insistent to come. Why are you here?"

"I don't want anyone else to be taken, and..." He looked down at his red coat, strands of his black hair covering his face. "I want to find more reasons not to fear the sky."

Something about the way he said those words made Ophelia understand, even if they sounded like nonsense. She'd been afraid since her sister had been taken. Aisling had been the strong one. She'd been the one to plant herself, while Ophelia floated about looking for purpose. But purpose had come to her.

"Hush." Ophelia rose from the porch. "Let's gather up our team, we have a meeting to go to."

There was not a vacant seat in the town hall. Everyone from the farmers to the shopkeepers packed into the little room off the side of the schoolhouse. They waited with soft murmurs that hushed as Ophelia took the stand. Her courage waned with the crowd before her. Dusty, who had done his best to ease her mind a moment before she stepped on stage, gave her an energetic smile.

She looked out over the waiting faces. Dayla and Adelaide were close by, sitting in the front row. Rig hid in the furthest corner, with Edwin in the opposite one. Hush leaned against the wall with an amused look on his face and the branderbuss held against his chest like a stuffed doll.

Ophelia took a deep breath and said, "By now I'm sure you all know the situation."

"Why isn't the Church helping us?" someone shouted, followed by supportive chatter.

"They said they don't believe this is a real threat," Ophelia said, her gaze flicking to Adelaide for a moment.

"Wouldn't they know?" another voice said.

"Exactly," Stephen Dixon said, standing up. "If the Church doesn't think it's a threat, then why should we waste our money on hiring some mercenaries?"

Ophelia set her jaw, anger taking the place of courage. "I think in this case; the Church is wrong."

The room erupted into pure sound. Some agreed with Ophelia, while others backed Stephen. It was hard to tell where the majority lay. Rig shook his head and picked at his nails. No help there.

"Hey!" Ophelia slammed her fist against the podium. "We know what happened last year. And now we saw the Mire in the woods again."

"Tom Sully's kid saw the Mire," Stephen said, stroking the edge of his mustache. "If he's to be believed."

"It's the exact same thing Dusty saw last year. My sister saw it as well, and it came for her. The Mire came for her." Ophelia met eyes with Hush, bolstering her resolve. "We all lost someone because they were taken. The Church says it's impossible, but we saw it with our own eyes! Who do we believe? Them, or ourselves?"

A soft whisper ran through the room. Stephen scowled.

"It's happening." Ophelia leaned on the podium. "It's happening again, and we need these people."

"Them?" Stephen sighed. "Even if so, even if the Mire somehow conspiring around our village, there's only five of them."

The council hall's doors swung open with a bang. Victoria Valjean sauntered in like a marching queen. Another person wearing a wide-brimmed hat and a strange mask crept in behind her.

"Sorry if I'm late," Victoria said with a smile. "But I brought some more help." She motioned to the stranger.

"There you go Stephen," Ophelia said. "More than five."

"Yes, seven." Stephen gave an exaggerated sigh and returned to his seat. "Much more impressive, I'm sure."

Victoria went to join Dayla and Adelaide, only for her smile to fade when she saw Hush in the corner. "What is he doing here?"

"We hired him to help us fight," Dayla explained, shifting aside to give her a seat.

"He kidnapped me." Victoria crossed her arm.

"Actually, Zero kidnapped you," Hush said, stepping away from the wall.

"You helped!"

"Helped keep you alive."

Victoria pushed up her sleeve and thrust her finger at him. "Is that how you see it now?"

"Look, you can tinker you're brick all you'd like. But those people were real grimy so the only way any of you were gonna be bright was if someone untwisted them."

Victoria blinked. "Could someone tell me what the hell he just said?"

"Victoria." Ophelia held her hand out to calm her. The last thing they needed was Stephen and the village to see them bicker. "We'll talk about this later."

Victoria crossed her arms and took a seat next to Dayla. Her companion kept to the edges of the room until she could take her place beside her. She kept her hat low, but Ophelia was certain she saw a mask. Her team was getting stranger and stranger.

"It's not just these seven," Ophelia said, turning back to the room. "They will teach us how to fight the Mire. Make us ready."

"You expect us to fight?" Stephen laughed like a barking dog.

"Yes. We can't hide our heads in the sand. If Dawnhallow wants to survive, we need to defend it. And they will show us how."

He pushed his hair back and groaned. "And what about the Hawkland Mob?"

Ophelia sighed and leaned on her elbows. "What about the Hawkland Mob, Stephen?"

"If we start building a militia, and it certainly looks like a militia, won't the Mob get worried? They might do something."

"I don't care about the Hawkers!" Ophelia exclaimed. "I want to believe this village is worth saving. My parents and grandparents are buried in the cemetery, and my sister believed this was the greatest place on Earth. You know me. I can't lie to you; I don't want to be here, but I am here. I'm here because it matters. I'm here because no one believes us. I didn't believe my sister when she told me what she saw last year." Ophelia's voice wavered, but only for a second. "And I've been to Wrotdam. They ignore us and say what we saw was impossible, but we saw it. We lost children, mothers, fathers, brothers, and sisters. If those who are supposed to protect us won't, we'll protect ourselves."

A murmur ran through the crowd. It was impossible to tell if it was in agreement. Stephen considered Ophelia for a time, shaking his head.

"Alright." Ophelia leaned forward. "Are we going to do this?"

In half an hour, the council hall was empty except for Ophelia, Dusty, and the seven mercenaries. Ophelia sat on the stairs to the raised podium with Dusty at her side. The meeting left a bucketful of adrenaline in her veins and she needed some time to settle down.

"Well," Dusty said, tossing his jacket over his knees. "At least they said yes."

"Barely." Ophelia looked over her hires. "I never thought that would be the hard part."

"You did splendidly," Dayla said, sitting next to her. "We would have stayed no matter what the village said, though."

Rig grunted. "Speak for yourself."

"Thank you for the kind words, Dayla," Ophelia said. Her gaze landed on the small mask-wearing woman who tried her best to fade into Victoria's shadow. "I'm sorry, in all that mess, we didn't get introduced. I'm Ophelia."

The woman recoiled as everyone turned to look at her. She pulled her hat lower and spoke in a soft voice, "I didn't realize there'd be so many people."

"This is Mattie Wilkins," Victoria proclaimed, brusquely pulling her forward. "She approached me and said she wanted to come along. She's quite the young lady."

Hush leaned forward from his place in the corner. His fingers played along the wood inlays on the branderbuss in his arms.

"Why are you wearing a mask?" Rig asked.

Mattie started to speak when Victoria jumped in. "That's what I was referring to. Show them, Mattie."

Mattie's gaze, partially hidden behind the strange mask she wore, swept over the crowd. It lingered on Adelaide. Mattie took a deep breath and then removed her hat and mask. The dusty sunbeam through the window reflected off her subdued complexion.

"My God," Adelaide breathed.

"What, uh…" Ophelia tried to find the words. She had never seen anyone like Mattie, skin and hair ashen and eyes like dark voids. "What is… that?"

"She's infected." Adelaide looked like she was trying to avoid being drawn in like a moth to the flame. "But I've never seen it so bad."

"Infected?" Dusty said. "That's not what inkbloods look like. Besides, she can talk."

Mattie shrunk into her clothes, clutching hard onto her hat and mask.

"She's right here," Hush said, stepping into the middle of the group. "Don't flap like she's not around."

"Of course." Ophelia shook her head. Hush's words brought her out of a stupor. "I'm terribly sorry."

"It's alright," Mattie said. "I'm used to it."

Dayla approached Mattie with a subdued caution. "This may seem presumptuous, but I don't imagine you came here for the money."

Mattie shook her head. "I'm here because Ophelia is right. The Mire is coming."

Dayla clicked her tongue. "How do you know?"

"Because I'm connected to it. I can feel its will. Most of the time it's unfocused, but recently it changed. It's focusing on this village." She held everyone in rapt attention. "It's building to a peak, getting ready. I don't know when, two weeks maybe, then it will descend upon Dawnhallow."

"At least we'll have Christmas," Victoria muttered.

"Why?" Ophelia asked, pushing past Dayla. "Why this village?"

"Because you're isolated. And you're close."

"Close to what?"

"The Celestial Contraption."

"Is that the machine they were building last year?" Dusty wondered. "The one at Pembrooke House?"

"I don't know," Mattie admitted. She put her hat back on. "But it was last year when I last felt this power. During the Cleansing when the Mire was taking people, this Contraption was what they were being brought to. But something happened, and they failed. They took a year, but they're going to try again. I know it."

Ophelia caught Dayla casting Victoria a glance, but she gave no reaction, only sat on a bench cleaning her nails.

"How do we know you're telling the truth?" Adelaide said, finding her voice amid the flood of information. "You're infected by it. You could be mistaken or lying."

"I... I don't know. I just feel it." She straightened her spine, more sure of herself. "And I'm not lying."

Adelaide flexed her hand, her flame gauntlet creaking with the movement. "The Mire could be controlling you."

"Can it do that?" Ophelia asked.

"I don't know." She brought her hand to her lips in contemplation. "All I know is the Mire has been acting strangely, it's doing things we've never seen before. Anything is on the table now."

"I trust her," Hush said.

"I do too." Edwin spoke from his place leaning against the wall. It was three simple words that took everyone by surprise. They gave him a lot more weight than they gave Hush.

Rig scratched under his hat. "That's kind, but this isn't a democracy. It's an army. Only one person's opinion matters."

All eyes turned to Ophelia. She nearly fell back by the sudden onslaught of attention. "I'm not the one in charge."

"It's certainly not any of us," Dayla said with a grin. "We'd never get anything done."

Ophelia flapped her jaw. Somehow she had become the leader of quite the motley crew. She weighed the options between Adelaide's concern and the benefit of another fighter, especially one who had backed up her suspicions.

"We need everyone we can get," she finally said. "Mattie knows when the Mire will be coming, that's priceless information."

"If she's telling the truth." Adelaide's words were daggers aimed at Mattie.

Mattie turned away from her and put her mask back on. Ophelia looked to Dusty for help, but he backed away from the circle. A hint of a smile lingered on his face. Ophelia had wanted this after all. Sure, it wasn't exactly what she had imagined, but she had seven fighters she didn't have the day before.

"Alright." Ophelia returned to the podium. Surely this wasn't what Aisling had intended when she spoke of Ophelia finding purpose, but it was too late to question fate. "We have two weeks to whip this village into shape. It's not a lot of time considering what we're up against. What do we need to do?"

"Weapons," Rig said, crossing his big arms. "Do you have any weapons?"

"Rifles, for hunting," Dusty chimed in. "Some of the villagers have revolvers too. Other than that? Hammers, knives, sickles. Most of us are farmers, not sawbones."

Edwin snorted and rolled his eyes. He pushed off the wall and left the council hall with a bang from the door.

"I take it that's not good," Ophelia said, her eyes fixed on where Edwin had disappeared.

"You can't kill the Mire with things like that," Rig explained. "You need specialized weapons made by the Sawbones or the Ink Clergy."

"We can't afford something like that."

"They don't sell them."

"So, we're back to asking." Ophelia couldn't stand the thought of knocking on doors again. Was it even possible to convince anyone to lend out their weaponry?

"There's another option," Hush said with a pained expression. "We could gobble some."

Ophelia cocked her head. No one reacted until Mattie spoke up, "He means steal."

Victoria let out a single laugh, but never took her eyes off her nails. Hush shot a harsh look in her direction. A dull thudding grew in Ophelia's brow.

"And now we're stealing from the Church," Adelaide huffed.

"The Sawbones aren't part of the Church, remember?" Rig never smiled, but Ophelia swore there was one hidden in his words. She wondered if she needed to keep a list of who hated who. "That way you can ignore all the bad things we have to do to keep people safe."

Adelaide lowered her head. She took a few deep breaths, letting the stress flow out of her like air. "I don't mean to be a naysayer. I am here to discover what is going on with the Mire, and the more I learn, the more I feel like I knew nothing to begin with. I spent much of that Cleansing you all are referring to in a hospital bed with a dislocated shoulder." She turned to Ophelia. "I am with you. To protect this village is God's will. I feel it."

Ophelia smiled back. They were small words but bolstered her resolve all the same. Even Victoria had stopped preening herself to listen to Adelaide.

"Maybe we're all a bit stressed. It's the first day," Ophelia said. Everyone shook their heads. "Fine, maybe I'm the one stressed. Give me some time to think and we'll come back to this."

"Time is of the essence," Dayla said, resting her chin on her hand. "Two weeks can fly by."

"I know." She leaned back and let out a breath. "Just let me think."

The mercenaries shared looks and slowly filtered out. Hush lingered for a moment at the back of the room. He gave her a sad smile, before leaving her and Dusty alone in the town hall.

"You did great," Dusty said, patting her knee.

"Thank you for lying." She dropped her head forward.

Dusty kissed her on the crown before he left. The only sound was the occasional creak of the shutters from a draft. Even in the silence, Ophelia found little peace.

Dayla caught Victoria's eye as the group returned to the inn. She jerked her head to the side and Victoria nodded in acknowledgement. There hadn't been a moment for them to talk, and there was much to discuss. Dayla faded away, sure that no one would pay attention to the wanderings of an old leech.

Dawnhallow was of modest size, a couple of streets with the main one where most businesses were located — including the Carefree Inn — cutting through the centre. It was the kind of village that ended abruptly, with the backs of buildings up against the wilderness. There wasn't much hustle and bustle, even at midday. A few folks walked the roads or sat on porches, watching time roll by. Kids played in the remains of the last snowstorm.

Dayla found a fenced-off patch of land overgrown with weeds and vines. A garden, in better times, now something abandoned. She leaned on the fence and waited. It wasn't long before Victoria arrived and jumped up, sitting on top of the fence and knocking away a patch of snow.

"How are you feeling about all this?" Dayla asked.

"It's truly an event," Victoria said with a smirk. "That woman's in over her head. Why aren't you leading this whole endeavour if you care so much?"

"Oh, I rarely find myself in charge of events." She turned her face toward the cool breeze. The children had begun grabbing handfuls of snow, hurling them at each other as they laughed. "Ophelia will do fine, even if she requires a bit of guidance."

Victoria scoffed and brushed the dirt from the fence off her hands.

"It's been a while since we'd had the chance to talk," Dayla continued. She pulled off a splinter from the fence and flicked it into the garden. "How have you been doing?"

"Fine," was all Victoria replied.

"You haven't told anyone about last year?"

"I tried." She hooked her feet on the middle rail of the fence and leaned back. "People don't understand. You almost understand, but not quite. I was enough of an embarrassment to run away from my own engagement party, my family didn't need me talking about voices and machines."

Dayla frowned. "An embarrassment?"

"Their words, not mine. I think it's an embarrassment that they won't hear me. You don't know how infuriating it is to listen to the prattles of dust when you've touched brilliance."

When Dayla found Victoria that day, she was shaking like a child. For the rest of the night, as Dayla told a half-truth to her parents, Victoria sat silent, shell-shocked and afraid. Dayla hesitated to say she had recovered in the year since.

Victoria noticed Dayla ruminating. "Did I upset you?" she asked.

"No. I'm simply considering a few things."

"Interesting." She stood on the middle railing and took in the cool breeze. "Most people would be upset being compared to dust. They take it as an insult, rather than a fact. A statement of truth can be neither an insult nor a compliment. I've been thinking a lot about people in the past year. I've come to the decision that they're boring. Or…" She gazed into the distance, straight at a building that blocked her view of the inn. "Most of them are. Adelaide is interesting. Most of the people in the Machine Church I have met are too rigid. She's very curious."

"Ever since she was a child, in fact. She was always asking questions, driving her parents insane, mind you. I'm not surprised she insisted on coming along, perhaps she wishes to drive me insane as well."

Victoria kept her gaze fixed, like could see through the carpenter's workshop and to the inn. A stiff wind swept through her long hair and she shivered, coming back to reality.

"So, Victoria," Dayla said, pushing away from the fence. "This Celestial Contraption your friend mentioned, could it be the machine you found at the Pembrooke House?"

"I don't know. The timing is right, I suppose." She hopped off the fence. "That's why you got involved in all this? Pembrooke House?"

"The Church covered it up. Officially, Lord Haverstone and his family picked up their roots and moved to America a few days before a boiler accident destroyed their home." She tapped her thumb on her mask. "I count myself lucky they did not know I was researching it at the time, else I may have 'moved to America' as well."

"Sounds to me like you think the Church was involved in making that thing."

"I try not to make assumptions. The Church has always valued the image of peace above the reality of it. It's why the College of Sawbones and the Leechwold are kept independent." She lifted the hem of her coat. "Keeps their robes from looking bloody, you see. Perhaps they simply saw Pembrooke House as a sign of something they weren't ready to face yet. It would be best to confirm whether or not this Celestial Contraption is what you saw, as at least you'll know what it does."

"I don't know what the first one did." Victoria collected a handful of snow and began forming it into a ball. "Other than being terrible and wonderful. And if this Contraption is the same machine..."

"You're scared."

"I'm not scared." She scoffed and ran her fingers along the snow, taking care to ensure there were no malformations in her process. "I'm rather curious about what getting close to it again would do."

"Do you believe you'll see the vision again?" Dayla had never gotten specifics on the event, at least nothing that didn't sound like mad ramblings. The wreckage of Pembrooke House gave her little to go on — especially since she had to keep her investigation secret. Once the Church did get word, it was all gone by the next morning.

"I try not to make assumptions," Victoria said, holding the snowball up to the light. The cold snow didn't seem to bother her.

"You can't run away from this forever," Dayla said. "I don't think you want to. You're just like Adelaide, you won't rest until you find out the truth."

"Oh?" Victoria turned to Dayla and leaned in. "Pretending I'm the only one who cares about all this? You already tipped your hand."

"We aren't talking about me."

Victoria laughed.

Dayla donned her mask and huffed, smelling the pleasant herbs stuffed into the beak. She'd been too cavalier and let Victoria see through her armour. They both wanted to discover the truth; Dayla had been searching for years for some form of it. Since she first had the inklings the Church was hiding something. It was an unfounded feeling until Arash came to her with his concerns. But she couldn't seem too invested; she had to protect herself in case things went wrong.

"But yes, I wouldn't mind seeing it again." Victoria rolled the snowball carefully between her hands. "We'll see what decision Ophelia comes to and play it by ear."

"You may want to keep your connection to the Contraption to yourself for the moment." She put her hands in her pockets to get the warmth back into her fingers. "There are those among us who still have suspect loyalties."

"You mean the man with the metal arms?"

"I mean anyone." Edwin was a threat, Dayla knew that for sure, but even Adelaide was still loyal to the Archbishop. Rig was distant enough to be mostly harmless, Hush would be a welcome distraction with all his oddities, but Mattie came as a complete unknown. Better to keep them all in the dark and let Ophelia focus them on protecting the village while Dayla gathered information.

"Sounds good to me," Victoria said. "It's going to be fun."

She clapped the snowball between her hands and tossed the powder back into the snowdrift.

CHAPTER 8

The innkeeper laid the clattering tray of tea in front of Ophelia and gave her a deathly serious look. "So, about our new arrivals," she said.

"What about them?" Ophelia asked, her head whipping up from eating her sandwich. Panic gripped her. Had they done something? Had they gotten in a fight? She wished she could've spent the last few hours thinking about their next move but whenever she got to it, her thoughts ran screaming in the other direction.

"As you know, I have four rooms." The innkeeper was a middle-aged Welsh woman, a fan of drinking, smoking, and spreading gossip. Florence was her name, though she was insistent that everyone called her Flo. Flo was the kind of person that Ophelia needed to be careful talking around. There was no telling what dirt she was looking to spread. "I put that sweet ginger and the old lady in the big one. Mr. Zhen has been quite insistent that he be left alone and while first I let Rig and the skinny man do the same, with Miss Valjean and... the other one here, I'm not sure how best to arrange them."

"I... I suppose..." She shook her head. "No! They're grown adults. Talk to them, not me."

Flo lowered her voice. "Are they safe to talk to?"

"Yes, they're safe to talk to." She poured herself a cup of tea and reached for the milk. "They're going to train us all to fight the Mire."

"Oh, of course." Flo squinted an eye down the sights of an imaginary rifle. "I used to shoot the hares trying to eat our crops back near Wrexham. Never hit one though..."

"That's why they're going to teach us." She dropped a few spoons of sugar and lifted the cup to her lips. "You have nothing to worry about anymore."

Victoria bounded down the stairs, interrupting her before she could take her first sip. "Ophelia," she said. "Have you figured out what we're supposed to be doing yet?"

Ophelia paused and caught the concern on Flo's face. "Not yet."

"Good God. This entire excursion is turning out to be a bore, there's nothing to do in this village other than wait to die." She leaned on the railing and smiled at Flo. "Do you have any crackers by any chance? I spent the night hiding from my parents and hardly had a moment to eat."

"We have some in the larder," Flo said, wiping her hands off on her apron. "I'll get you a plate."

"Get me the box. If I'm going to be sitting on my behind doing nothing, might as well get fat."

"I need to get some air," Ophelia said, slamming her cup down and sending tea splattering over the table. It wasn't time to make her decision, she needed to think. She rushed out the side door into the alley.

She pressed her back against the door and inhaled deeply. How did she get herself into this? Every choice felt like it would doom the village one way or another. She rested her head back and caught sight of Edwin standing on the stairs coming down from the top floor.

"Are things going well?" he asked.

"I think you know." She stepped away from the wall to see him clearer. His jacket and gloves covered his arms, but she couldn't stop thinking about the bizarre metal things beneath. "We need Mire-killing weapons, but the only way to get them is to beg or steal. We might run out of time if we're running around scrounging for gear, but we're already on thin ice with the village council and I highly doubt they want to hear we're going to steal weapons."

"Sounds like a fair amount of problems." He pushed his glasses closer to his face. "I could have told you those people would bring more troubles than they're worth."

"Oh? You're saying you'd protect this village by yourself? Face down a horde of inkbloods and sludges with just your bare hands?"

"You think I can't?"

"I think everyone's right and you are insane."

He chuckled and leaned on the railing. "It's very easy to be a martyr, you know. Die quickly and let others deal with the clean-up."

Where did that come from? Ophelia wondered, squinting up at him. "Ideally I'd like to avoid that. I simply don't know what to do. I'm not the decision-making type, at least not for decisions that affect other people."

"Every decision affects other people. Whether you mean it or not, we are connected in a web of each other's lives and our actions pull on the strings between us. Just make a decision, kid. In every situation, someone needs to make a choice, even if it's a coin flip. If you trust the people around you, in their skills and their abilities, they'll be able to steer you in the right direction. Besides, I thought the entire reason you got a crew together was so you didn't have to make these choices alone."

Ophelia let his words sink in. He was right, they needed to do something. Anything. Indecision could be a worse killer than the Mire. "Thanks, Edwin. Maybe there's some logic in your madness."

"Wouldn't that be exciting?" He turned his face to the cloud cover.

Ophelia rushed back inside, past Flo before she could open her mouth, and up the stairs to the rooms. The only way forward was getting some weapons that gave them a fighting chance.

And she was done asking for permission.

"Hush," she said, swinging the door open to his room. "Do you really think we could steal some weapons?"

"Huh?" The gaunt fellow sat on one of the two beds, branderbuss spread across his lap beneath his coat. He had a needle in one hand as he stitched up a tear in the coat's collar and surprise on his face from hearing his name. "What was that?"

"We need weapons that can kill the Mire." She eased the door shut, making sure Flo wouldn't hear them. "Do you know how we could steal them?"

Rig sat on the other side of the room. His riotsaw laid disassembled across the table and he rubbed oil firmly along the chains, eying the conversation without making a sound.

"I meant generally," Hush said, finishing the stitch and snapping the thread with his teeth. "Anything can be taken, and angels always look to have plenty of cleaners."

"We always lose more sawbones than we gain," Rig said, laying his oil cloth down. "It's not a bad idea to get weapons from them. They won't give them up, but they've got plenty of storage."

"You really think we can gobble from the big house?" Hush asked.

"Not from Chasmdrop, but there are plenty of outposts in the country with grinders and throwers gathering dust." He tapped his fingers on the table as he considered. "There's one near The Shadow that barely sees any action. Could be a good target."

Hush threw on his coat and snatched up his branderbuss. "If you can give me the layout I could cook up a scheme."

"I think I can remember it."

"Perfect!" Ophelia couldn't believe her fortune, pulling in both a thief and a sawbones. Edwin had been right, she simply needed to make a decision and trust her people to help finish the plan. "Grab the others and meet in the big room. Sounds like we have a heist to plan."

Rig shook his head. "It's not a heist."

"I'd say it's a heist," Hush said. "Just based on the count of things we're gobbling up." He turned to Ophelia as she went for the door. "Where're you going?"

"I have someone I need to thank." She left them to get the meeting started and headed for the second-floor exit, where Edwin had been standing.

She stepped outside and found the landing empty. She looked all around but could see no one in the alley. The skiff of snow at the bottom of the stairs lay untouched. Confused, she turned back to the door — and bumped into Edwin's chest.

"Are you looking for me?" he asked.

"Sorry. Yes." She stepped back. From that close, she could make out the electric blue lights behind his glasses. Her eyes itched at the sight of them. "I wanted to say thank you."

"For what?"

"Helping me with a decision. We're going to steal some weapons from a Sawbones outpost."

"Bold choice." He stepped around her and leaned against the railing. "Can't kill the Mire without them, I suppose. Lest you wanna arm everyone with torches."

"We could really use you there helping us." She sidled in next to him. "I know you think you can do this alone, but we're all here for the same reason. Why not use us, at the very least?"

"Even if your words could convince me, they don't want me around. Half of 'em would kill me given the chance."

Ophelia didn't doubt that, considering the demonstration put on the first night they arrived. "Why? Why do they hate you so much?"

"Because I'm an impossibility. A madman that speaks the truth. A flaw in their doctrine. A million reasons more, but it doesn't matter why. Once I fell to the amber and Church law says you don't come back from that, but here's a secret…" He hunched over and leaned toward her. "I don't think I did. Maybe I am still mad, or maybe I will be again. A voice is telling me to take this town, and I hate that voice, so I know I must save it instead. Maybe that's what madness is, a fight with yourself."

"Then we're all mad." She pushed off the railing. "But we're here, and I'd be happy for you to join us. The others will simply have to make do." She took one step back inside when Edwin spoke again.

"You said your sister was taken last year?"

She caught the door with her elbow, freezing at the melancholic reminder of Aisling. "Yes."

"Beware of decisions influenced by sentimentality. It can cause more problems than solutions."

"You know, you sound a lot like Rig. Must be a sawbones thing."

Edwin scoffed. "Must be."

There was a thump from down the hall and muffled shouting. Ophelia's stomach dropped to her feet.

"Sounds like your saviours are getting along," Edwin said with a chuckle.

Ophelia ignored his attitude and hurried down the hall, throwing open the door into the room she told her hires to meet her in. The first thing she saw was Hush on his feet, the chair he had been sitting in toppled over behind him as he pointed at Victoria.

"Not all of us had glitters simply given to us!" he yelled. He had a hand on the branderbuss laying on the table, but everyone knew it wasn't loaded.

Victoria pointed at her ears. "I don't know what you're saying! But if you're talking about money, why don't you just go and kidnap someone again!?"

Rig sat at the table Hush used to be at, ordering Hush and Victoria to shut up, but only adding to the noise. Adelaide sat on one of the beds, clutching her hands on her lap and muttered something under her breath. Dayla, amid all the chaos, sat silently in a lounge chair reading a book, boltrifle leaning against her thigh.

Ophelia slammed the door shut, but it got lost in the bickering. She put her fingers to her lips and blew a shrill whistle. Hush threw his hands over his ears as everyone stopped and stared at her.

"Hi, Ophelia," Mattie said. Ophelia swore she hadn't seen her when she came in, even as the tiny figure sat cross-legged on the floor in the corner. She still wore her mask, but her hat lay on her lap.

"Hi, Mattie." Ophelia put her hands on her hips and paced the room. "What is wrong with you? These people need to see you as a unit. If you're bickering and fighting all the time, they're going to lose faith in you. I don't care if you don't like each other, you need to get along. You need to fight together."

The room was still. Hush picked up his chair and sat down in a huff. No one seemed happy, but at least no one was shouting.

Finally, Victoria broke the silence. "Ophelia," she said, leaning back against the windowsill. "We were simply going over your plan. Something about a weapons heist."

Ophelia rolled her eyes. She sat at the table where Rig and Hush were. Dayla took the last seat, smiling at her in a grandmotherly way. She had the suspicion that when the fighting started, Dayla simply left the table and started reading. Even though she had helped gather the people, it was now Ophelia's show — and Ophelia's headache.

"So, what do we have?" Ophelia asked.

"This is the outpost," Rig said, pushing forward a piece of paper he had been drawing on.

Hush took the paper and Ophelia leaned over to see it. Somewhere within the mess of scribbles and uneven lines was a map. Hush looked at the paper, Ophelia, Rig, then back at the paper. He tapped his finger on the branderbuss across his lap. Without a word, he took another piece of paper and began redrawing the map into something readable.

"It's Outpost Theta," Rig continued. "It's not very busy, mostly a place for roving sawbones to stay the night or refill their inkwells. Unfortunately, that means there could be anything from one to twenty sawbones inside."

"Didn't you say it was near The Shadow?" Mattie asked, slinking away from the corner. "Does The Shadow not get attacked by the Mire a lot?"

Rig shrugged. "It's not a very big town. Mostly workers and researchers."

"But it's, uh…" She pointed to the sky.

"It is under the Machine." Adelaide handed Mattie a cup of tea. "Or at least around one of its legs. But the Machine is what gifts us with the tools to defend ourselves from the Mire, it makes sense the sickness would not step foot in its shadow."

"Which is why it's the best target." Rig reached over and pointed to a part of his disaster of a map. "The basement is filled with unused throwers from when they thought this outpost would see more action."

Hush labelled that part of his map 'Basement.'

"I have a question," Victoria said, kicking her feet out and rising from the windowsill. "Why doesn't the fellow with the blue eyes have to be here?"

"He's…" Ophelia searched for the proper way to explain her recent conversation with Edwin. "He's doing this own thing.

"It's no concern of ours what that man wants to do," Dayla said. "As long as he doesn't try anything."

Victoria sauntered across the room and slid onto the bed next to Adelaide. "What's your problem with him, anyway? He seems quiet enough. I caught a glimpse of those arms earlier today, that's pretty interesting."

"It's difficult to explain. He's somewhat of an enigma, to be sure." Adelaide clapped her hands. "Would anyone like some tea?"

"He's crazed." Dayla tapped her finger on her boltrifle's barrel. "And we need to keep our eye on him. He's up to something, I'm sure of it."

Throughout all of this, Rig was silent, rubbing his thumb on the edge of the table.

"Here's what I tinker." Hush pushed his redrawn map forward. Everyone at the table leaned in and Mattie peered over Hush's shoulder. "The cleaners are in the basement. There's only one way in or out, and that's this staircase here."

"Last time I was there, the staircase had a locked gate," Rig said. "Heavy-duty. I don't know where the key is."

"I could pick it, but…" He pointed at a square room that appeared on each of the outpost's three floors. Too small to be much more than a closet, but even then was minuscule. "What is this?"

"It's a dumbwaiter. The outpost used to be a house."

"A dumbwaiter?" Hush's eyes lit up. "That's radiant. It goes into the basement too. I could climb up to the top and grab the dumbwaiter here. Won't be my first time riding one of those." He put his finger on the second floor. "Then take it down to the basement. I can send the cleaners up to Rig using the same lift."

"And how am I going to get in?" Rig asked.

"You still look like a sawbones, don't you?" Mattie asked. "Couldn't you just walk in? I can't imagine they remember every one of you in the area."

"Technically I'm still a sawbones. It's not so easy to quit a job like that." Rig leaned back in his chair, dangling an arm over the backrest. "If they start asking questions it can get awkward. I'm not supposed to be that far from Burdenbrough. They like to keep tabs on us, active or not."

"That's why we need a clap," Hush said. No one reacted. "A distraction. To get the angels out of the outpost."

"Well." Dayla finally spoke up after taking in all the information. "I suppose I can keep their attention."

Hush turned to her. "You think so?"

Dayla hunched her shoulders and in a wavering weak voice said, "Everyone wants to help a sweet old lady." She dropped the act with a wink. "I can keep them distracted."

"Then we just need a trailer and someone for Rig to hand the cleaners to out the window." Hush pointed his charcoal at Victoria, Adelaide, and Mattie. "Who wants to take that?"

"I was thinking." Victoria leaned forward on her crossed knees. "This whole Celestial Contraption Mattie mentioned, if it's so important to whatever is going on then we should know where it is. Perhaps some of us should find it and see what sort of state it's in."

"I can do that," Mattie said, raising her hand. "Or, at least I can if we get close. My senses aren't very precise, unfortunately."

"It does sound quite interesting," Adelaide said. "I'd like to go too."

Mattie stared at her. Even with her small size, the strange crying mask gave her a menacing demeanour.

"I just want to know what's going on," Adelaide explained, shooting the words out rapidly. "It has nothing to do with you."

Mattie did not move for a good three seconds, then slowly turned away. Adelaide opened her mouth to speak again, but a glance from Dayla told her it was better to stay silent. Ophelia wondered if she needed to start a list of who on her team hated who.

"That's a great idea," Ophelia said. "You three should do that."

Victoria nudged Adelaide with her elbow. "Sounds like all the makings of a fine ladies' trip."

Adelaide's face turned pink. She cleared her throat and shifted away from Victoria. "About that tea?"

"I still need someone near the trailer and to drive the rumbler," Hush said. "We can't just toss the meal onto the ground, someone would notice."

"Dusty can handle it," Ophelia said, rubbing her eyes. "I need to stay in town and make sure Stephen Dixon doesn't start causing a fuss. People still aren't sold on this endeavour."

Victoria threw her head back with a mock superiority, something very close to her actual superiority. "As we're sitting here planning to rob some sawbones, I can't imagine why."

"Right." Hush rubbed his temples. He tapped his finger on the map. "It looks like there's a blind spot for the windows. We can push the rumbler and the trailer here. I would like to do this at night."

Rig shook his head. "Day is better. Fewer sawbones would be around."

"Radiant." Hush groaned. "It's a brunch."

Everyone turned to Mattie. "Daytime break-in," she explained.

"Ophelia!" Flo shouted from the ground floor. Her footsteps pounded up the stairs and Hush and Ophelia were just able to cover the map with their coats when the door burst open. Flo, out of breath and wide-eyed, held herself up with the doorframe. "Ophelia. It's the Hawkland Mob. They're here."

Ophelia cursed and leapt out of her seat. She brushed past Flo and hurried down the hallway.

Edwin waited at the end of the hall, just at the turn to go down the stairs. "Sounds more trouble."

"Are you here to help?" she asked without stopping.

"Let's see what sort of trouble it is first." He leaned his head against the wall and waited.

Ophelia descended the steps to the inn's bar. When Flo said the Hawkland Mob were here, she didn't mean one or two. The table and chairs had been pushed away and eight Hawkers spread themselves around the room. Most sat at the bar, but some stood around a man waiting at the one table that wasn't moved.

He came into the village occasionally, so Ophelia had seen him around. He was a higher up in the Hawkland Mob, not the leader, but certainly a lieutenant. A man with a chestnut complexion and short-cropped hair, the way he lounged back in his chair with one big boot on the table told you he believed he owned the place. His gaze, hard and intense, tracked Ophelia as she slowed her descent before arriving at the bottom of the stairs.

"Guillotine Harry," Ophelia said.

"You must be the Ophelia I've been hearing so much about." He spoke with a French accent that slurred out like a snake. "There has been talk you're building some sort of army."

"It's not an army." It took every ounce of her self-control to keep her gaze on Harry and not on the gangsters that surrounded her. "It's just some people to help us fight against the Mire." *Since you won't,* she added mentally.

"That's right." He shook a finger at her. "You've been telling everyone that the Mire's gonna come and steal them away. Ridiculous. Sounds like cover for something more…insidious."

"It's true! We need to protect ourselves!"

"If you were looking for some protection for hire, why not us?" He spread his arms wide and his gang laughed mockingly. "We would gladly renegotiate our protection contract."

Renegotiate and disappear, Ophelia thought.

Harry swung his leg off the table and leaned forward. "Here's the deal. You're making some people anxious that you do not want to be anxious. Send your friends home, and we'll consider this a momentary lapse in judgement."

"And if she doesn't?" Edwin asked, descending the steps. The rest of her hires weren't far behind.

The Hawkers shot to their feet. Harry held his hand out to steady his gang, but hesitation laid heavy on his face as he looked the seven mercenaries over. Perhaps he hoped to just deal with Ophelia and avoid a fight.

"If she doesn't…" Harry snapped his coat lapels. "She'll find her life getting very difficult."

Ophelia was feeling much more confident. Rig stood to her right, a stoic giant. Dayla was to her left, and Adelaide was right there to watch her back. Each one was willing to stand by her side, even Edwin, despite his attitude. Though, as the Hawkers spread out to encircle the group, Ophelia wished they had brought their weapons. Hush was the only person armed, but his branderbuss was just for show. Bless him, he held it like it wasn't.

"I should warn you," Rig growled. "This isn't my first bar fight this week."

"I didn't agree to fight people," Adelaide whispered to Dayla.

"Sometimes one path leads through another." Dayla donned her beaked mask. "Let's not kill any of them though. Not yet."

Harry pulled his coat aside, revealing the revolver on his hip. He laid his hand on the wood grip and sneered at Ophelia. "So, what's it going to be?"

The front door of the Carefree Inn burst through its jamb. Rig charged out with two Hawkers on his back. He reached over his shoulders and flipped them both onto the dirt. One of the windows exploded and Hush tumbled through clutching onto another. Adelaide followed, cracking her unlit pulserod across the Hawker's back, forcing him to let go.

Ophelia kept back from the brawl; she wasn't much of a fighter. Flo, as well, had taken cover behind an overturned table. Gone was Guillotine Harry's smug disposition, instead, he batted away flying moons with a broken-off chair leg, retreating into a corner. Victoria laughed like a madwoman, swinging her arms side to side with the motions of her blades.

Even Dayla held her own. She kept her distance from a Hawker swinging a sap like a flyswatter. Between each swipe, she darted in for a jab to his ribs, much quicker than Ophelia expected an old sniper to be. The strikes were weak, but a dozen or more added up until the Hawker's legs softened.

While Edwin backed two Hawkers out the front door Rig had opened, Ophelia looked about for Mattie. She was the only one unaccounted for, along with one of Harry's men. Ophelia crept along the edge of the room until she could throw herself next to Flo.

"Have you seen Mattie?" she asked.

"Who?" Flo barely raised her head to respond.

"The small one with the mask."

"Oh, no." She shook her head until her hair came out of its pins. "But a girl that tiny better be hidden."

Mattie was the only one Ophelia still had misgivings about. She was so small and meek, barely making any sound in their meetings. Ophelia peered above the overturned table, where the brawl had mostly progressed outside. Maybe Flo was right, and she had found somewhere to hide.

Harry knocked away a flying moon and lifted his revolver. Victoria's eyes widened. Her moons looped through the stair's balusters, too wide of a circuit to stop Harry's shot.

"Whoops." She leapt behind a pillar.

Harry cocked and fired over and over, tearing chunks of wood from Victoria's cover with each shot. Victoria covered her head and brought her flying moons back to her, slowly twirling in the space around her. Ophelia jerked forward, but Flo held her by her pants.

"You're going to get yourself shot," she hissed.

A piece of wood next to Victoria's head disintegrated into splinters. Harry stowed one revolver and drew his second, firing slower, but circling the pillar for a better shot. Victoria kept pace, ensuring she was always on the other side in a deadly game of Ring a Ring o' Roses. She took a few deep breaths, then flung her arms out to the side.

The flying moons split in half and looped around both sides of the pillar and headed for Harry. He stumbled back, two of the moons catching him on the shoulder, but he still got his shot off. The bullet punched clean through Victoria's exposed arm, casting blood across the floor. Victoria cried out and her moons tumbled to the ground.

Harry gritted his teeth and clutched at his shoulder. He grabbed the moons stuck in his flesh and yanked them out, letting them clatter to the floor and leaving a deep cut on his hand. Victoria stumbled out from her cover, her own blood pouring from her wound, and fell to her knees. Panting and stained red, Harry lifted his revolver toward her.

"Victoria!" Ophelia shouted. "Hide!"

Victoria lifted her head as Harry pulled the trigger. The hammer clicked against a spent casing. He cursed and slammed the gun against his thigh. He caught sight of Ophelia and snarled, but, noticing he was without his gang, tucked the gun into his waistband and scrambled out the front door.

Ophelia crawled over the table and rushed to Victoria's side. Blood oozed from her upper arm, over her elbow to her wrist. She pulled off her coat and collapsed onto her side, the shock fading and giving way to pain.

"Just stay still," Ophelia said. She didn't have much better advice to give. Dealing with gunshots wasn't her forte. "We'll get you some help."

Victoria pressed her hand against the wound, only for the blood to ooze out the other side. Her breath quickened. Her chest rose and fell in disjointed leaps. Ophelia hated to think it, but it was the first time she saw Victoria show anything outside of snark.

"Just, uh…" Victoria gritted her teeth. A few metres away, her moons vibrated. "Just find Mattie."

"Mattie?"

"Yes! Mattie!" She made a conscious effort not to look at her arm. "Just go, you idiot! I've been shot! Go!"

Ophelia leapt to her feet so fast she nearly slipped and rushed out the door. Someone had to of seen Mattie, if only she could grab their attention. The fighting continued in the street, basked in an orange glow as the sun began to set. Townsfolk roused from their evening routines and poked their heads out from windows and doorways. A kid stepped out onto his porch, rubbing his eyes.

"Go back inside!" Ophelia shouted.

The kid's mother appeared from the door and yanked him back. If the villagers wouldn't help, they could at least stay out of the way. Ophelia spotted Hush and Adelaide standing toe-to-toe with a Hawker wearing a knuckleduster.

Hush took a punch across the jaw. He spun with the force and came back pointing his branderbuss at the Hawker. The Hawker faltered, enough for Adelaide to swoop in with her pulserod and strike him on the back of the knee. He collapsed to all fours and Hush spun his branderbuss around to swing low. He drove the gun's stock into the Hawker's brow, sending him over himself and to the dirt.

A gunshot split the air, followed by a strange *ting*, and Hush froze. Edwin stood at his side, coming out of the darkness, his fist right in front of Hush's face. Down the street, Guillotine Harry had his gunsights on Hush while glaring at Edwin with confusion and anger. He squeezed the trigger twice more, and Edwin jerked his hand around accompanied by more metallic *tings*. Edwin raised his hand so Harry could see, and dropped three crushed bullets. Harry went pale. Ophelia's jaw dropped.

"Let's stop playing around." Edwin removed his coat, revealing his machine arms. He spread them wide and electricity coursed down their length, burning away his gloves as he marched forward.

The Hawkers regrouped, staring at Edwin with expressions unfitting hardened gangsters. Harry's arm shook as he tried to keep his revolver up.

Energy swirled within the glass bulbs on Edwin's shoulders, biceps, and forearms. Lightning crackled through the air, brightening the dusk. "We are not going anywhere. This is bigger than some squabbling punks." He planted his boots and pointed at Harry. "You come back, we kill you."

The mercenaries stood at his side. Rig, Dayla, Adelaide, and Hush. They stared down Harry and his gang, surrounded by the glory of the electrical storm. Harry's strength gave out and he dropped his arm to his side.

"Let's get out of here," he said, without an ounce of his usual swagger.

The Hawkers nearly trampled each other as they ran to their autocars. Edwin pulled back his spectacle, drawing the electricity back into his arm bulbs. The villagers murmured, and Ophelia heard them speak of who to be more afraid of.

"Ah! Worms!" someone shouted.

A final Hawker came stumbling out of a nearby alley, swatting at his torso and pants, trying to knock off some minuscule creatures. They did look like worms, but it was hard for Ophelia to tell in the dimming light. He ran after his gang, leaping into the backseat as they started up their autocars and peeled out, sending gravel and snow splattering against nearby porches.

From the same alley, Mattie wandered out, adjusting her mask. She spotted Ophelia and waved. Confused, Ophelia waved back. She inhaled sharply. Victoria. She was still hurt.

"Mattie!" She rushed to meet her. "Victoria's injured. She told me to find you. Why?"

Mattie gasped. "Where is she?"

She pointed Mattie inside, and the little one took off. The rest of the team watched the Hawker's taillights disappear into the forest before noticing the commotion and following. Ophelia took a moment in the empty street to take in the lights in the surrounding buildings. Wide-eyed faces of the young and old stared back. The mother who yanked her child away now hid him behind the curtains. Near the top of the frame was a small hole in the glass. A bullet hole.

She never wanted Dawnhallow to become a battle site. There was little other option now.

CHAPTER 9

Ophelia rushed into the Carefree Inn, finding everyone already circling Victoria as she leaned against the shattered pillar. Flo crouched at her side and held a red dishtowel wrapped around her wound. Victoria sat with her eyes closed taking in deep breaths, her twelve moons orbiting her crown.

"I should really get the doctor," Flo said.

"No, it's fine," Mattie said, kneeling next to Victoria. She looked pointedly at Flo. "We just should go upstairs."

"Whatever," Victoria said. "Just do it quickly." She floated her moons toward her pouch, but only three made their way inside, the rest got caught on the leather and clattered to the floor. Adelaide scooped up the remainder and they all headed upstairs, Rig supporting Victoria.

When they reached the room, Mattie spun around and pointed at Flo. "You stay outside."

Flo opened her mouth to protest, but Edwin slammed the door in her face. Rig knocked aside the map and laid Victoria on top of the table.

"The table?" Victoria whined. "Why? There's a bed right there."

"Take off her bandage," Mattie said, going into the bathroom. "I'll be right back."

Delicately as possible, Dayla peeled away the dishtowel. Ophelia's stomach knotted around itself. Blood poured from Victoria's arm, quickly coating the table on her right side. The bullet must have nicked something vital.

"Is it really bad?" Her skin was ashen. "Am I going to die? That's so boring…"

Adelaide took Victoria's hand. "You're going to be fine."

"You're such a nice lady."

Mattie came back from the bathroom with her mask gone and her hands covered in slime. Everyone waited in silent attention as Mattie approached

Victoria. Adelaide squeezed her hand as Mattie pressed the slime on either side of Victoria's arm. Ophelia crept forward, peering over Dayla's shoulder. When Mattie removed her hands, the gunshot wound had disappeared.

"My God," Adelaide whispered. She dropped Victoria's hand and stumbled back. "What did you do?"

Dayla stroked her mask's beak. "You're full of surprises."

Victoria flexed her arm and smiled. Some pink had already come back into her skin. Adelaide looked between her and Mattie, her expression lost somewhere between amazement and horror.

"Is this because of your condition?" Edwin asked. "You can heal wounds?"

"It's related, yes." Mattie backed away from Victoria, shrinking into the corner where she was comfortable.

"How is this possible?" Adelaide stormed up to Mattie. "How can you perform a miracle so easily?"

She winced. "It's just a thing I can do."

Ophelia stepped forward to intercept. "Adelaide, calm down."

"Yeah." Victoria slid off the table. "It's pretty bizarre but useful, don't you think?"

"Are none of you considering the ramifications of this?" Adelaide spoke to the air, rather than the people around her. "The Mire is a curse. It is pain and evil manifested. Someone so seeped in it should not be able to perform a miracle such as healing a wound. Not even Ink can do that. It doesn't match up with the Church teachings on what the Mire is!"

The door slammed. Mattie was gone.

"You're all muckheads," Hush said, grabbing Mattie's mask from the bathroom and chasing after her.

Adelaide's jaw hung loose. She stared at the door, her lip quivering slightly. She clutched her hands to her chest and dropped into a chair.

"Adelaide," Dayla said with a sigh. "Consider, in the future, trying to speak with more tact."

"I simply wanted to explain the theological implications of her," Adelaide said.

Edwin donned his glasses. "You know there's a person under all those implications."

"In all my years researching the Mire, I've never seen something like her. If I could bring her to the clergy, run some experiments on her abilities."

"You will not take her anywhere!" Edwin's hands crackled with energy as he stepped toward her. "Hasn't the Church had enough of its experiments?"

Adelaide shrank back. "What do you mean?"

Ophelia placed herself between Edwin and Adelaide. Dayla took a more aggressive route. She kicked her boltrifle from where it rested and caught it out of the air. The power source hummed and electricity crackled down the vents in the barrel, threatening Edwin with each burst.

"Settle down!" Ophelia shouted.

"Dayla," Rig said, stepping in her line of fire.

"You know as well as I do how dangerous he is." Dayla shifted to aim around Rig, but he moved again.

"He's upset."

"I'm out of here." Edwin spun on his heel. "Tell you what, cleric. Why don't you ask your Archbishop about experiments? About Faceless Gods?" He opened the door. "You're a child."

He slammed the door, rattling the photos on the walls. Dayla turned off her rifle and tore her mask off. She scowled at Rig. "He's not your friend anymore. You don't come back once you fall. This is some sort of deviation, but he's still sick. And it's my job to put him down."

"No one is putting anyone down!" Ophelia rubbed her temples. "Just a few minutes ago you were all working together."

"It's easy when you're fighting something." Rig's glare lingered on Dayla before he turned away.

Some commotion came through the cracked window, drawing Ophelia's attention from the problem at hand. The sun had finally set, bathing Dawnhallow in moonlight. But on the street below, villagers lit up the night with lanterns in their hands. *Oh no*, Ophelia thought, *I should have known they wouldn't be happy about this*. She pushed the window open and braced for the worst.

"Ophelia!" Rory, the local blacksmith, called. "We saw what happened."

She squeezed the windowsill. She'd brought war to their sleepy village, but if they sent the mercenaries away, they'd never be able to protect themselves from the Mire. It would be trading one threat for another. She would need to convince them it was worth the danger.

"Your people…" Rory's hand with the lantern shook. He was scared, they were all scared. Ophelia needed to calm them down. She readied herself to plead and beg, except, Rory's hand stopped shaking and he smiled. "They faced down the Hawkers and won! No one's ever stood up for us before!"

Ophelia's eyes widened.

"We've been talking," Gracie, the schoolteacher, said. "We're tired of hiding."

The crowd cheered.

Edward the general store owner stepped forward and joined in. "We're tired of ignoring what's going on."

Another cheer.

Isaac, the Carefree Inn's cook, pumped his fist into the air and shouted, "We want to fight. We want to fight for Dawnhallow with your people."

The crowd whooped and hollered so loud that there wasn't one single person in Dawnhallow still asleep. Ophelia had gotten a willing army. *But*, she gazed back at the mercenaries sending each other dirty looks, *their leaders were as likely to kill each other as they were the Mire.*

Without her mask, Hush figured Mattie wouldn't go too far. A cool breeze blew across his neck and he turned away from the stairs to the main floor. Someone had left the door at the end open. On an external staircase sat a small shadow, lit by the moon. Mattie dangled her feet off the side.

"Hey." Hush ducked through the window. "You forgot your mask."

Mattie took it with a smile. "Thanks."

"You don't have to wear it." Hush knelt next to her.

"It helps me feel invisible." She ran her fingers over the mask's nose.

"I can't help but be invisible. I don't know if you remember me—"

"I do. Hush Millions, right? You're looking a lot better."

Hush laughed. "That's not a hard hole to climb out of."

Mattie laughed in return. She placed her mask to the side and stretched back, looking up to the stars through the gap in the alley. They were between the Carefree Inn and the next building over. It felt like if no one wanted to see them, they wouldn't. Hush tapped his fingers along his branderbuss. He hadn't considered what to say to Mattie when he found her, but there was something nice about the silence. His mind felt calm for the first time in months.

"Don't let those people get you down," he said. "They're muckheads, not worth your seconds."

"I can't even remember why I came." She pulled her hat brim down over her eyes. "I'd been doing fine staying in the shadows."

"But you're here. And you did something radiant back there."

"That's what they used to say. Radiant. Amazing. But I just wanted to be normal."

Hush cocked his head. "They?"

Mattie took off her hat and ran her fingers through her hair. "I came to England to find a cure. It was just rumours, but I was willing to try anything. Instead, I found some people who call themselves the True Metal Order."

"I don't think I've heard of them." Hush was surprised. He figured he knew every gang that ran in Understone.

"They believe a lot of things about the Machine. They believe it's God. They believe the Mire is a gift we don't understand."

"The Mire is not a gift. The Machine is worse." He wrapped his arms around his branderbuss, feeling the empty spot where the inkwell should be.

"Why do you say that?" Mattie asked.

"No one believes me, except for when they do, but then they actually don't. That's how I knew it wasn't real. That's…"

Mattie observed Hush silently. A horse whinnied in the night. Hush had nearly broken. He nearly let Mattie in. He held the branderbuss tighter to his chest.

"Never mind," he said. But he didn't yet want to leave Mattie's side.

"Okay." She bobbed her head. "I'd probably believe you, you know."

"Yeah." He let out a breath that turned to vapour. He hadn't noticed the cold at first.

"I remember why I came now," Mattie said, gently breaking the quiet. "To this town. To Dawnhallow. To help people."

"With the Celestial Contraption?"

She nodded. "I spent a long time with the True Metal Order. It didn't matter if I didn't agree with them, I felt safe. Other people had my condition, not to my level, of course. But we all heard the voice last year telling us to build and bring people. But as suddenly as it started, it stopped. Until a few weeks ago." She let out an uneven breath. "This voice terrifies me, Hush. It's inhuman. The rest of the Order can't feel it, or they don't care. They think the Celestial Contraption will herald a new world, but at the cost of people's blood and bodies. They think I'm important to this device."

Hush was dumbstruck. There was more going on in the world than he knew. "Are you?"

"I don't know. But I heard the word Dawnhallow. That's why I came. I can't let good people be hurt for this thing." She scoffed. "Maybe I am too kind for my own good."

"No, you're not. When everything is wrong, kindness is all we have." He nudged her with his elbow. "Kindness from you is the reason I'm alive."

"Which is the reason why you're here." She waved her hand at the sound of people cheering in the distance. "In this mess."

The cheers echoed into the night, replaced by murmuring winds. From Hush's reckoning, their display in the street had won them favour with the villagers. Though, favour tended to be fragile where he came from.

"So, you know why I'm here," Mattie said. "Why are you?"

Hush craned his neck back until he could see the stars. "I want to save someone."

"Who?"

"Anyone."

The hundred million lights sparkled above their heads. Enough that Hush could pretend the darkness between them wasn't so vast. Mattie flopped onto her back, joining him in the view.

"Did you ever find your friend?" she asked.

His voice came as barely a whisper, and barely a thought. "Many times…"

"What was that?"

"Nothing." He turned away. "Just trying to forget."

CHAPTER 10

Victoria descended the stairs to the inn dining room. She flexed her arm, inspecting the healed-over skin. There wasn't even a scar to indicate not long ago there was a hole in it. She lost her calm a bit when she got hit, but in retrospect, it wasn't as bad as she would have imagined. And now she had a story to tell. The greatest magician in Wrotdam needed stories.

A sheet of wood had been laid over the front window. The innkeeper, Florence, cleaned up the dining room to the extent of pushing the broken furniture to the corners and went to bed. Apparently, the barfight shook her. That was fine, Victoria was famished but she could find some snacks herself and wouldn't have to talk with that grating woman. There was sure to be something hiding in the kitchen behind the bar.

She dug through cabinets and shelves, pushing aside towels and tableware until she came upon a pantry. She grabbed a small bag of pork scratchings and a couple apples. Her arms filled with loot, she kicked the pantry shut. She was about to leave when she spotted a bottle of clear liquid on a high shelf. Belgian gin. Victoria was never allowed to drink much more than wine at the manor. She put one of her apples on the bar and replaced it with the bottle of gin.

Lights appeared in the shadows of the dim dining room, and she nearly jumped out of her skin. Edwin sat at one of the corner tables, reading by the slight glow of a single lamp. His blue eyes and the lights in his arms glowed like fireflies in the dark. Victoria shook off her fright and headed over.

Edwin paid no mind to her as she approached. She waited a couple of seconds to see if he would look up, but he never did. She tapped the table with her bottle. "Mind if I join you?"

"Yes," he replied, never looking up.

"Wasn't really a question." She sat across from him and put down her food and drink. With a troublemaker smile, she leaned in and faux whispered, "I heard a rumour you caught a bullet out of the air."

Edwin gave no indication that he heard her and flipped to the next page.

"What are you reading?" she asked.

"Frankenstein."

"Is it good?"

"I've found it relatable, as of late."

Victoria clenched her jaw. "You know, even with metal arms, a normal human shouldn't be able to move fast enough to grab a bullet in flight."

"I'm magnetic."

"Excuse me?"

Without looking up, Edwin tapped his flat palm against a spoon sitting in the saucer for his teacup. It stuck to his fingers and he lifted it for Victoria to see. With a flick, the spoon dropped free.

"Intriguing," Victoria said. "Though revolver bullets are made of lead and copper, neither of which are magnetic. You're giving an easy answer. To get rid of me quicker, I suppose."

Edwin's head twitched, breaking his disaffected demeanour. Though, it could have been a trick of the flickering lantern lights. "You have a more extensive knowledge than I gave you credit for. I apologize."

Victoria waited to see if he would say anything more. The wind whistled through the cracks in the panel over the broken window, and Edwin turned the page. Victoria pressed her lips into a white line, feeling the heat flush through her skin. Edwin hooked his tea with a loose finger and took a slow sip. As the caffeinated liquid poured down his throat, the glass bulbs on his arms crackled with electricity.

"Do those hurt?" she asked, her voice a monotone growl.

"I don't feel anything."

"How did you get them?"

"Found them." He went to put his cup back in the saucer.

Victoria unbuckled her pouch. She drew one moon in a wide spin and dropped it at the teacup. Edwin flicked his finger aside and the moon slammed a couple centimetres into the table. The room froze into near silence, the only sound being midnight winds and Victoria's heavy breathing. Without so much as a sidelong glance, Edwin moved his hand around the blade and returned the cup to the saucer.

Victoria pulled her moon back into her hand, spinning it between her fingers. "Do you have a problem with me?"

"I have a problem with everyone." He took a deliberate moment to turn the page. "But to answer your question, you do specifically irk me."

"And why's that?"

"Because I see the way you look at people. Like they're not real. Like to you, they're simple meat and bone and muscle. It's not the superiority I'm used to seeing from Wrotdam elites, no. You don't just think you're better than people. You think you're different."

Victoria ran her finger along the flying moon. "I am different."

Edwin finally looked up from his book. His electric blue eyes focused squarely on Victoria's. Her skin tingled.

"Do you love anyone?" he asked.

She scoffed. "I was almost married once."

"What happened?"

"I went crazy." She floated the moon from her palm and let it spin around her finger. A wicked smile cracked across her face. "Or at least that's the story. He broke it off."

"And did you love him?"

"He was nice. Pretty. Engaging."

"Oh yes," Edwin said sarcastically. "Sounds like love to me. Besides, that's not what I mean. I'm asking if you love anyone. If you care about anyone outside of what it means to you. If you can think of one person who you would do anything for."

Victoria wrinkled her nose. She didn't need someone she barely knew making judgments of her, acting as if he knew her. No one had proven they were deserving of her love yet.

Edwin continued, "I suggest you find yourself someone to love, someone to ground you. Or it won't be long before you stop seeing people as anything at all. Then you'll really start hurting them."

"You don't know me."

"No. But for a short time, I was you." He returned to his book. "You're a real fine psychopath, Victoria Valjean."

Victoria slammed the moon into the table. The steps creaked and Adelaide came into the dining room. She froze when she saw Victoria and Edwin.

"I'm sorry," she said. "I didn't mean to interrupt. I'm just looking for some water."

"You're not." Victoria forced a smile. "We were just finishing our conversation."

"Well, you, uh, have a good night." She scampered to the bar.

Victoria turned to Edwin and leaned in. "What about her?"

"What about her?" Edwin barely moved.

"I've been thinking about her a lot. She interests me, which is something few can manage these days. I've never met anyone from the Church who has so much… curiosity. Just priests who leer at me while pretending not to. As well…" She rested her cheek on the back of her hand, looking at Adelaide pass through the swinging doors with a small gap in her lips. "Redheads."

"And so, some collection of meat, bone, and muscle has piqued your curiosity." His eyes flared with electric light. "Splendid."

"I'm trying to say, you half-machine freak, that maybe I love her."

"You still have such a narrow view of that word." He shrugged. "Maybe you do. Maybe you will. Maybe I'm not the one you're trying to convince."

"Who else would I be trying to convince?"

"Exactly." He went back to reading.

Victoria scowled at him. She swept her hand over her moon and brought it into her pouch. Bolstered by pride, Victoria grabbed the bottle of gin and swaggered toward the bar. She placed the bottle on the countertop and waited; first standing, then sitting, then standing again, before deciding on a half-lean. The kitchen door swung open and Adelaide stepped through with a water pitcher. She nearly dropped it when she saw Victoria had moved.

"Oh!" she exclaimed. "Hello, Miss Valjean."

"Please, call me Victoria." She gave her smoothest smile.

"Very well. Goodnight, Victoria." She turned to leave.

"Wait." Victoria slid down the bar.

Adelaide paused. She looked at Victoria with a curious expression, waiting for her to speak.

"Uh." She hadn't planned what to say next. She was used to things being more ceremonial, with introductions and dances. Adelaide waited — she needed to say something. "It was a pretty exciting day today, wasn't it?"

"Yes. It was quite full." She nodded. "I'm glad you're feeling better."

"I was going to have a little drink to unwind." Victoria held up the gin. "Perhaps you'd like to join me?"

"That does sound enticing, but I'm afraid I don't imbibe."

"Well, uh, I don't usually either." She motioned to the bottle repeatedly, like she could turn it into something else. "I just found it and thought—"

"It's not any sort of religious abstention. It's more of a personal one." Adelaide clutched harder onto the pitcher and shuffled her feet. "It's simply with all this new information coming to me I believe I need to update my notes. I have lots I need to think about."

"I could help you."

"You could help me… think?"

Victoria felt herself sinking into a pit. She could be a magician, sew, ride, paint, dance, and a dozen other enviable skills, but it seemed casual conversation still eluded her.

Adelaide snuck around the bar, toward the stairs. "Thank you for offering, but I think I can manage on my own. I'm sharing a room with Dayla so if I need help thinking, I'm sure she can." She smiled and gave an awkward half-curtsy. "Goodnight Miss Valjean — er — Victoria." She disappeared up the stairs.

Victoria puffed out a long-held breath and collapsed onto the stool. She tapped the gin bottle against her knee. Suffice to say, it did not go how she hoped or imagined. She looked to the corner where Edwin was still reading his book.

"I bet you enjoyed that, huh?" she called to him.

"At what point after I said, 'I suggest you find someone to love,' made you think I would enjoy watching you fail?"

Victoria straightened her spine like a pencil and snatched the gin. She wasn't hungry anymore, but she sure needed a drink. She hurried past Edwin without a second glance, but as she reached halfway up the stairs paused with one hand on the railing.

"If you die in all this madness…" She ran her finger through the hair that fell over her shoulder. "Could I take you apart?"

Edwin never gave her an answer. Not that she needed one.

CHAPTER 11

The morning came with a layer of crunchy frost on the ground. Ophelia bundled up in a coat and scarf and went to see her hires off. A day had been spent planning, but they couldn't waste any more time. Hush, Rig, and Dayla were going to go procure some weapons, while Mattie, Adelaide, and Victoria planned to scout out the Celestial Contraption.

As Ophelia crossed the street from her home above the general store to the inn, she spotted Edwin standing on the balcony of his room, watching the preparations not far away.

"Hey, Edwin," Ophelia shouted. "Are you sure you don't want to give us a hand?"

Edwin gazed down at her. He pushed his sunglasses up his nose and turned back into his room.

"I guess that's a yes," Ophelia muttered.

Edwin remained a mystery. He elicited a certain vitriol from some of the mercenaries and seemed completely unwilling to be involved in the work of preparing for the Mire. Yet, he scared off the Hawkers when they demanded he leave. Ophelia may not have understood Edwin, but she trusted that he truly wanted to protect Dawnhallow, even if it was for his own reasons. Also, after intimidating the Hawkers, it was good to have at least one of the mercenaries stay in the village.

Rig and Dusty finished hitching up the trailer to Dayla's autocar. Trailer was a generous term for an old wooden cart with a sheet spread over it, but it would do. There wasn't a hitch on the autocar, so they had to tie the trailer directly to the frame. Dusty crawled out from beneath the autocar and knocked the dirty snow off his shirt and pants.

"Alright, that should hold," he said. "I suppose I should be more optimistic. That will hold."

"Good." Rig tossed his riotsaw under the trailer's sheet. "Let's get moving before the snow starts."

Victoria leaned against her autocar and smirked at them. "Are you disappointed that I won't be joining you?"

Hush popped his head over the trailer. "What will we do without a tog to help us?"

"How is that supposed to be an insult? Doesn't that just mean dressing well? What's wrong with dressing well?"

"It's not an insult," Mattie said, leaning out the back window of Victoria's autocar. "It's just the slang."

"Really?" She narrowed her eyes at Hush. "Do you really not mean it as an insult?"

Hush shrugged. "I don't mean *that* as an insult."

"Hush," Rig said. "If you don't get in the autocar, you're riding in the trailer."

The heist team packed into the autocar. Dusty gave a reassuring wave to Ophelia, and Dayla put the car into motion. They rolled casually to the edge of the village and turned north, onward to the outpost. Ophelia silently wished them luck, then approached the back of Victoria's autocar where Mattie waited.

"How do you plan on finding this thing you're looking for?" Ophelia asked.

Mattie held up a mason jar. Inside were little grey worms wriggling in slime. "I have some friends to help me."

Her face turned green. "Oh…"

"Adelaide!" Victoria called, leaning over the hood. "Come on!"

Adelaide came stumbling out of the inn, clutching onto her notebook and three empty jars.

"Sorry. This is a new scientific finding; I need to make sure I can document it." She put the jars in the back next to Mattie then hopped into the passenger seat. "One of the villagers had a spyglass they let me borrow. This is all very exciting."

"It's going to be a fun trip," Victoria said, entering the driver's seat.

Ophelia chuckled and stepped back. Mattie held up the jar and the worms pressed themselves against one side.

"We're going west," she said.

Victoria turned the engine over and tore off, kicking up dirt and snow as it went. Ophelia had to jump back to avoid getting hit with gravel before they vanished into the forest. She took a moment in the calming and cold morning air, then unbuttoned her coat and entered the inn.

◄ ∞ ►

Dayla stopped the autocar on the edge of the woods. She pulled slightly off to the side, trying to hide them from Outpost Theta, a brick manor house that was wholly unremarkable other than the sign that signified it as such. There were a couple of autocars parked outside, as well as a carriage next to the stables. Hush spread the layout map over the hood of the autocar and took in the sight.

"You see back there?" He pointed at the rear of the outpost, near where a section of the building extended out. "Right next to the storage room? That's where we're going to park the trailer. Dayla will be our clap while Dusty and I push the trailer into position. Rig, you—"

"I'll walk in the front door." Rig hefted his riotsaw onto his shoulder. He was done up in his sawbones' garb, with the long coat and rumpled hat. His mask sat pulled down around his neck.

It had been a year since Rig retired from the life as much as any sawbones could, and the clothes were still just clothes, but they hung on his skin like needles. He'd worn the parts, the coat or the shirt, the heavy boots or the hat to protect his scalp, but never all of them at once. With the mask on his face and the branderbuss on his hip, the old life burned in him again with a sickening flame. One all too familiar.

"Are we good, Dusty?" Hush asked, bending over Dusty's legs sticking out from the back of the autocar.

"Yeah, hold on." Dusty rolled out with the chain from the trailer. They couldn't drive the autocar up to the house, so they had to pull the trailer by hand.

"Then let's begin. We'll start pulling the trailer around. Give us a few minutes, Dayla, then you can go."

Hush and Dusty grabbed the trailer's handles and pulled it around the autocar then along the edge of the woods, beginning the wide curve around the east side of the outpost. Dayla opened the autocar door and took off her leech robes, tossing them into the backseat. Underneath she wore a dishevelled pastel sari. She fixed it at her shoulder and hunched over. She played the helpless elder card well.

"So, Rig," she said, standing beside him to watch the outpost. "Does it feel odd?"

"What do you mean?" He pulled at where the mask straps bunched at his neck.

"Stealing from sawbones."

"We'll bring the weapons back." He crossed his arms. "You should be used to stealing from sawbones."

Dayla cast him a confused look. "We don't steal from sawbones."

"You steal everything from sawbones. You steal their lives, their hopes, their humanity. You leave them with nothing."

"We respect sawbones, Rig. They make a noble sacrifice to battle the Mire. Before them, the Ink Clergy would die in droves trying to fight back against the Mire. But that sacrifice is still a sacrifice."

"And yet everyone hates us or is afraid of us. The Church is ready to disown us at a moment's notice. I retired and I still have to check in with the Leechwold."

"And have you abstained from Ink the entire time?" Dayla asked. "There are few who can stay retired for just that reason."

"They ask the same thing every time I check-in." He stuck his hand in his pocket so she couldn't see his fingers twitch. "You know Ink has nothing to do with our skills. We're better than the Ink Clergy because they are, still, clergy. We're trained to live for battle. Ink or no Ink."

"Yet, many cannot live without it."

Rig grunted. "Because we're told not to."

Dayla scowled but soon softened. "You used to be one of the most devout sawbones I'd ever seen. Violent and half-mad, but devout. What happened to you?"

Rig lowered his gaze. His entire life had been serving the Church as a sawbones. He had been abandoned by immigrants on the doorstep of an orphanage. He had been on the path of a troublemaker, getting in scraps with the other kids almost daily before the Commander approached him. He said Rig was strong, and that strength could be used to protect Wrotdam. But why protect a city that hated him? A city that would turn its back on him? A god that didn't care about him?

"I saw the end," Rig said, heading toward the outpost.

"Edwin." She kept pace with his long strides.

"He'd found a way to live an almost normal life, and that was taken from him."

She tucked her hands behind her back and lowered her head. "We are toys to an unkind god."

Rig cocked an eyebrow at her.

"Just something I heard once."

A patch of snow fell from a tree and startled a group of birds. They took flight, then faded into the overcast sky.

"He's not back," Dayla said. "You know that, right? I don't know what devilry it is that allows him to pretend to be in his right mind, but he is still seeing amber. The Ink will reclaim him soon."

Rig stared where the birds had flown, even long after they were impossible to see against the clouds. "Why are you here, Dayla? You're sneaking around the Church just like I am. Do you not believe in God?"

"I may have once." She inhaled deeply through her nose. "But I don't need to believe in God, I need to believe in the purpose."

"The purpose?"

"To help people."

Rig stopped and hefted his riotsaw up onto his shoulder. "Then how did you become a leech?"

"Because I'm good at hurting them." She pulled her scarf over her head and continued on toward the outpost.

Dayla crunched across the frozen ground. Without the intimidating black and red garb of a leech and the dark dehumanizing mask, Rig could see her for what she was. A tired and scared woman, weary from a life as the necessary evil. Or maybe she was just that good at pretending.

Rig waited until she was nearly at the outpost before continuing up himself, pulling his mask over his face. He took handfuls of dirty snow and dusted his shoulders and hat, making it seem like he had been trudging for longer than he had. He didn't have a horse or autocar, but sawbones arrived at outposts in stranger ways than walking.

Dayla was at the door when he arrived. She managed to collect three sawbones listening to her intently.

"He's a tall boy." She made her voice quiver pathetically. "If I can't find him, I don't know what to do."

"Don't worry, ma'am," one of the sawbones said. "We'll find him. Can you tell us any more about him?"

"He has a coat."

Rig kept his eyes forward and walked right past the sawbones without them giving him even a glance. As he went through the front hall to the stairs, he didn't see any more sawbones inside. They could have lucked out after all. Up the stairs and to the back of the house, Rig started to feel confident about the plan.

The window was open in the common room where the dumbwaiter went. There were a few couches spread randomly around the room — moved around by sawbones — and some sparsely stocked bookcases. Rig glanced outside. Dusty and Hush stood beside the trailer staring up at the window. They jumped when the sawbones poked his head out. Rig pulled down his mask and Dusty patted his chest, telling his heart to slow, while Hush swung Edwin's branderbuss he carried onto his back and expertly clambered up the exterior wall.

"Radiant?" he asked, swinging himself over the sill.

"Yeah, it's good." Rig checked over his shoulder, listening for any further footsteps. "Just be fast."

Hush pulled open the dumbwaiter's door. The lift looked like a tight fit and, though thin, Hush wasn't a short man. Still, he clutched the branderbuss to his chest and squeezed in.

"Send me down," he croaked out.

"One thing." Rig leaned in close, even though there was no one to hear him. "See if there's some Miracle Ink down there too."

"What?"

"Raw Ink. It's amber. In a vial about this big." He held his fingers about four inches apart.

"Sure." He glanced Rig up and down. "Do we need it?"

"Just find some." He pressed the button that sent the dumbwaiter to the basement.

Hush descended and Rig leaned his riotsaw against the wall to wait and keep an eye on the door. The common room wouldn't be used much during the day. Mostly it was for some nighttime get-togethers or if someone wanted to sleep away from the bunks. Still, that didn't mean no one would come in if there were any sawbones still in the outpost.

There was a subdued mechanical whirring and the dumbwaiter rose into view, packed with ignition throwers that barely fit in diagonally. It was fortunate the dumbwaiter was so tall. Rig grabbed the weapons and sent the dumbwaiter back down. He returned to the window and passed the rifles one by one to Dusty, who hid them under the tarp in the trailer. Hopefully, Dayla could keep the sawbones distracted, but the heist was going to take a while.

They sent out dozens of rifles until the dumbwaiter brought up something different. A sword with two serrated blades set next to each other. Rig recognized them as grinders, a weapon usually used by novice sawbones before moving on to something more effective. When activated, the blades would move up and down alternatively, tearing apart any Mire in its path. In many ways, it was the younger cousin to Rig's riotsaw and a perfect backup weapon for the villagers. Rig took the bundle in the dumbwaiter and dropped them down to Dusty.

They worked slowly, but efficiently, and after enough ignition throwers and grinders to reasonably suit an army, Hush sent up boxes of inkwells. Most were power sources for the weapons, but there was one smaller box. Rig clicked the latch and his breath stopped as he looked inside.

Twelve amber vials of raw Ink. Miracle Ink. Rig had to consider when he last saw one. Four months ago? Maybe six. He had missed the quiet they brought. While he passed the inkwells down to Dusty, he tucked the smaller box into his pocket. On the next trip, Hush himself rode the lift.

"That's all they have," he said, sliding into the room. "Or at least all that would fit into the dumbwaiter."

"It'll do." Rig grabbed his riotsaw. "Out the window. Dayla can't distract them for much longer."

Hush moved across the room, silent as a ghost. As he reached the window, footsteps came thumping down the outside hallway. They weren't in a rush or trying to sneak. Whoever it was didn't know Rig and Hush were there.

"Go," Rig said, pulling up his mask and putting his riotsaw back down. "Move the cart."

Hush nodded then leapt out the window. He grabbed the sill and spun into a hang before dropping to the ground. The footsteps reached the door. Rig leaned against the window, blocking the view with his wide frame, and waited. The door opened and a familiar face entered.

"Rig?" Franz said, recoiling in shock. "Is that you?"

"Franz?" Rig pulled down his mask.

Franz stepped forward to greet him. "It's so good to see you, *mein lieber!*"

Rig moved to keep Franz from seeing out the window and got swept up into a big bear hug that lifted him into the air. Rig and Franz were of comparable sizes and Rig wasn't used to getting taken off his feet. Franz gave him a few good shakes then let him go.

"I thought you had retired," he said.

"I got a reason to come back." Rig circled Franz so that his back was to the window. "What about you? Not in Wrotdam anymore?"

"No." A severe expression came over Franz. "After Edwin and Hitomi...I didn't feel like I was doing my best there. I'm now a vagabond sawbones."

"A vagabond? Didn't Edwin do that for a while?"

"*Ja.* I follow rumours of rogue nests and pockets of the Mire that attack small settlements. It's good. I still have to make check-ins to get more Ink, or they send a leech after me, but I enjoy the freedom. I'm doing what a sawbones is meant to do. I'm protecting people."

Rig leaned against the back of a couch. "And they accept you into their towns?"

"Many do. Others have rumours that sawbones consort with the devil and bring the Mire upon ourselves." Franz guffawed, slapping his chest. "There is no shortage of stories about us out there. But I don't listen to them. Because I know they can only devise these rumours because they are safe. And that's all I care about."

"That's..." Rig sighed and stepped away from the couch. He spied the trailer out the window, now being pushed far enough away that people would just assume Dusty and Hush were farmers. "That's kind of you."

Franz wrapped his arm around Rig's shoulder. "You are just as kind, even if you don't realize it. When Hitomi broke her leg, you carried her clear across the lower ward. When I fell into that pit of sludges, you dove in like a madman. You were always at the back just so you could keep an eye on us and be ready to jump to the front. That's who you are, Rig."

Rig lowered his head. Those actions were easy for him, he was protecting his companions. But what did that mean in the grander scheme of things? He fought because it was what he knew how to do.

"I know you and Edwin grew up together," Franz continued. "His passing must have affected you greatly. But whatever it is that brought you back, I'm sure it's the right thing. I'm sure Edwin would be proud."

Which Edwin? Rig thought. *The happy Edwin who had a family and friends? Or the metal-armed loner?*

"Perhaps you'd like to join me for a drink?" Franz asked, clapping Rig on the back and releasing him. "I love catching up with old friends."

"I can't." He grabbed his riotsaw from near the window. Dusty and Hush had disappeared. "There's work to be done. Goodbye, Franz."

"*Wir sprechen uns bald*, Rig." He smiled and waved as Rig left the common room.

Rig pulled his mask up and hurried down the stairs. He hadn't seen Franz since the Cleansing the year before. The days and weeks after that day, after his fight with Edwin, were hard mentally. It didn't hit him until he woke up the next morning that Edwin was gone. Then he heard about Hitomi dying in the Cleansing after they were separated. It was easy to leave after that. Rig feared what telling everyone what he saw would mean, as though he would be seen as the mad one after that. Franz likely didn't know the whole truth.

Not that it mattered in the end. Edwin didn't die.

Rig went right out the front door without anyone stopping them. They cared less about sawbones leaving. Dayla and the sawbones she's been distracting were nowhere to be seen. Rig hurried back to where they parked. Dusty was already around the back fastening the trailer to the autocar as Hush waited near the passenger door. Dayla, however, was not there.

"Where's the leech?" Rig asked.

"She did such a good job pretending to be a helpless old lady that it looks like the sawbones drove her to town," Hush said, rolling his eyes.

"That's unfortunate." Rig leaned on the autocar's roof and glanced down the road. "I suppose we should go get her."

"Closest village is only ten minutes away," Dusty called from below.

"Make it quick." Rig tapped the hood. "The others will be waiting."

CHAPTER 12

Victoria's autocar tore down country roads, rolling over hills dusted with white powder. Mattie sat in the back seat, her mask and hat next to her. She rested the jar on her knee. Inside, the worms crawled over each other, leaving their little slime marks on the glass. They wanted to get to the Celestial Contraption, or perhaps just show her the way. She had gotten used to expelling the worms from her stomach, it barely fazed her now. Yet, that is what upset her the most. She had become so accustomed to her condition that even the bizarre parts were normal.

But she could also help. She healed Victoria after all. And now she was helping them find that terrible machine that the True Metal Order wanted. Adelaide still made her uneasy and being in the autocar with her made Mattie miss the days she could hide in a storm drain and be alone. Victoria was there too, but Mattie didn't feel much more comfortable with her. There was something predatory about the way Victoria looked at her.

"Mattie," Adelaide said, turning around in her seat. "What is this Celestial Contraption?"

"It's hard to say. I only have feelings and stories." She ran her finger along the jar lid. "But it's a device that's important in the teachings of the True Metal Order."

"The True Metal Order?" Adelaide nearly jumped out of her seat. "You know of them?"

"Well, I hear things." She looked out the window, hoping it could hide her fearful expression. "That's all. Lots of talk in Understone."

"What's this about a metal order?" Victoria asked.

"True Metal Order." Adelaide settled back. "They're a cult. I've been trying to find them but all I ever learn is their scripture on the Mire and the Machine…"

A slow realization came over her. "They kept repeating this idea that the Great Machine, which they believe is God, is incomplete. There is a second machine that will allow God to fully form. Could this be the Celestial Contraption?"

"They believe it is," Mattie said.

Victoria tapped her hand against the steering wheel. "Hold on. This machine will create God?"

"No." Adelaide stared hard out the windshield. "The Great Machine is not God, in any form. It is an angel and it is His will, but we do not pray to it."

"Considering how the Church talks about it, you could have fooled me."

Adelaide measured Victoria. "Are you not religious?"

Victoria laughed. "My family's devoutness begins and ends at the church doors on Sunday." Concern flashed across Adelaide's face. "But I've always been willing to learn more. If you're willing to teach."

The worms push against the left side of the jar. "Uh, hey," Mattie said.

"I'm not much of a teacher. As an Ink Cleric — St. Zita's Order, I should say — my duty is to ask questions." Adelaide twisted the spyglass in her hand. "It's supposed to be to ask questions at least."

Victoria cocked an eyebrow. "Do you not?"

"I'm supposed to research the Mire, yet if we learn something that doesn't fit our preconceived notions, the Church just casts it aside. How am I supposed to ask questions if the answer to every question is…" She stopped herself, her eyes wide and horrified that she said too much. The wind outside became a rushing river of sound.

"So, Victoria," Mattie said again.

"None of us are part of the Church," Victoria spoke softly. "You don't need to be ashamed if you have doubts."

"I don't have doubts." Adelaide grabbed the machine cross hung around her neck. First tightly, then her grip softened until she ran her thumb along its length. "I have concerns."

Mattie leaned forward. "Victoria."

"What is it?" Victoria snapped.

"We need to turn left."

A country road whipped past. Victoria cursed and turned the wheel hard. Mattie was thrown back into her seat and the autocar jumped off the road, tearing through underbrush before returning to the correct path. The worms — a little shaken from the driving — pushed against the front of the jar.

"It feels like we're close." Mattie's skin tingled with subdued electricity and in the moments of silence, if she focused hard, she could hear inhuman breathing in her mind.

As the autocar moved along, the trees to either side became more evenly spaced and well-groomed. It was a long driveway to someone's house. If the machine that had been built in Pembrooke House was indeed the Celestial Contraption, then they were on the right track.

"I know this road," Victoria said. "The Bilson's have a place here. They throw the loveliest get-togethers every spring. They have a wine cellar bigger than my room."

"We should pull off before we get too close," Mattie suggested.

Victoria eased the autocar onto the shoulder. Down the road, between the expertly landscaped treeline, they could see the white timber of the manor house. Adelaide practically flew out of the passenger door and snapped open her spyglass.

"I don't see any movement," she said. "But there are pieces of metal."

"Attached to the house?" Victoria asked, stepping out onto the roadway.

"It's just laying around. But they're big. You wouldn't just leave something like that on your front lawn."

Victoria scowled into the distance, then approached Adelaide with her hand outstretched. "Let me see."

Mattie crept away and opened the jar. The worms flooded into the fresh air and dug into the ground. The worms always disappeared, Mattie noticed, but she didn't care where. She looked into the distance where winter storm clouds formed. It wouldn't be long before the snow hit them hard.

"This Celestial Contraption," Victoria said, lowering the spyglass. "Could it be a communication device?"

"Perhaps." Mattie tossed the empty jar into the backseat. "Why do you ask?"

"Because." Victoria craned her head back and gazed into the sky. She gritted her teeth, forcing her body to say the words. "Because last year I was at Pembrooke House. And those machine parts look a lot like the parts that were attached to it."

"You were at Pembrooke House?" Adelaide's eyes went wide. "What happened?"

"I don't know. I could interact with it, I supposed because I'm a magician. Then, for lack of a better term, it exploded." She paced the road, her feet crunching the gravel with each turn. "But before that, I heard something, or I felt something — I experienced *something*." A grin crept along her lips. "Something monumental."

"So, you think it's a communication device." Mattie scratched her head. "Like a wireless telegraph? Communicating with what?"

"Everything."

"Or maybe..." Mattie dug her boot's heel into the gravel. "...the Machine?"

Adelaide shook her head. "You think this has to do with the Machine? This is that True Metal nonsense again. How do you know so much about them?"

Mattie shrunk away, but only for a moment. She was part of this team. Hush was right, who cares about these muckheads? Mattie stepped up to Adelaide.

"What happened to asking questions? The answer won't always be what you like. But if you don't listen, you're no better than them."

Adelaide blinked in shock and backed down.

"I'm going in." Mattie straightened her spine and pulled her gloves tight. She was going to ride this feeling for as far as she could. "They don't see me unless I want them to. Is there anything I can look for that will help us figure out if this is the same thing that was at Pembrooke House?"

"A grinder," Victoria said. "To throw people in."

Mattie clenched her fist. She grabbed her mask and hat from the backseat and turned toward the house.

"Wait." Adelaide opened the autocar door and grabbed a jar. She held it out to Mattie. "While you're there, could you get me a sample?"

"Of what?"

"Anything. We can run tests on the Mire, but if it's changing then we need to know how."

Mattie took the jar gently. Adelaide stepped back, hands clutched before her and face wracked with encroaching desolation. At that moment, Mattie felt bad for her. Adelaide's mind was a whirlwind of emotions, facts, and rhetoric. In some ways, Mattie was a part of that. There were things that Mattie thought were impossible a year ago. When she saw them, she needed to believe them or go mad.

Adelaide needed to do the same thing, or she would go mad herself.

CHAPTER 13

Edwin sat in the inn's dining room, as he had done every day and night since arriving in Dawnhallow. The village was slow, even with the looming cataclysm. It was a slowness that gave Edwin moments of solace that quieted his wild mind.

He had just finished reading *Frankenstein* as the early evening crowd came around. He was disappointed with the ending. A creature that regretted his crimes and drifted into an icy sea. When would the deep ocean come to take Edwin as well? He had felt its embrace since he woke up on the shore, his memories lost in the briny pool. The only word that came to him was Dawnhallow. The only memory that mattered was his final night in Wrotdam. The rest? They faded each day, into an endless sea of blank space.

The door to the inn burst open and a young man nearly tumbled over as he rushed inside. "There's people coming!" he shouted.

"Is it the Hawkland Mob?" Flo asked.

"I don't know. They look different."

Every eye turned to Edwin, lounging in the corner. He took a moment. He wasn't going to leave Dawnhallow, especially not because of some gang that felt tough. He placed his book gently on the table and strode across the room — the villagers' gazes following each one of his steps. The young man stepped aside — almost with a bow — and let Edwin out into the street.

The smallest flurry of a snowstorm sent white particles through the air. Dawnhallow wasn't a big place, so it was easy to see the three carriages that had pulled up a few buildings down. Edwin squeezed his fists, the metal creaking and sending sparks into the air. He was ready for a fight as he approached the newcomers.

As the carriage door opened, it became immediately clear that these weren't Hawkers. They were dressed in grey robes that wrapped around their bodies in random ways, the cloth too large to wear without bundling it up. One stepped out of the carriage and raised their head to take in a stiff breeze. Stitched on their hood with white thread was an eight-pointed star. She turned to Edwin as he drew near.

"Do you speak for this village?" the woman asked. She lifted her hood and revealed one eye black as the starless night sky — just like Mattie's.

"I'll speak for myself," Edwin said. "And you'll speak for yourself quickly."

The woman scowled. "I am Asha, and you are addressing the True Metal Order."

Edwin's eye twitched. A jolt of pain shot through his skull like a lightning bolt. Images of corpses brought down by his blades flashed through his vision. Memories hurt a lot more since he came back.

"We're looking for a woman." Asha strolled forward, backed by her many robed companions. "She's a very special and very dangerous woman. She wears a wide-brimmed hat and a crying mask, it's hard to miss her."

"What do you want with her?"

"To bring her home. She's troubled. If we don't find her then people will get hurt."

"Interesting." Edwin scratched his temple, playing up his contemplation. "Big hat. Weird mask. Dresses in a tattered coat?"

Asha's eyes lit up. "Yes."

"Doesn't sound familiar." He gave her a wink. "Good luck though."

"We have reliable information she was seen in this area."

"People make mistakes all the time," he said with a shrug.

She narrowed her eyes. "It is not wise to stand in our way."

The man next to her pulled a revolver from the many folds of his robe. He drew back the hammer and aimed at Edwin's head.

"I find," Asha said. "That killing one tends to make others loosen their lips."

Edwin cracked his neck. "What a wasteful form of interrogation."

He exploded into motion. The man fired, but Edwin came in low under the bullet and caught the gun by the barrel. He slammed his palm into the man's chest and tore the gun from his grasp. Digging his heels into the ground, Edwin spun and fired. Each crash of his palm on the hammer sent up a shower of sparks. The others barely got their guns out of their robes before he shot them out of their hands. Hot from the flurry, Edwin pressed the revolver against Asha's head.

"One more bullet," he said. "Your choice where it goes."

Asha's eye twitched but she otherwise kept her composure. "You seem familiar to me."

"Should I start counting?"

"Fine." She waved her hand and her allies backed off. "There are other towns we can search. But if you see this woman, it's best for all of us that she is returned. You will be rewarded, as we all will be. She is more important than you can imagine."

"One."

Asha retreated. A circular burn mark remained on her temple. The Order hurried into their carriages and urged the horses into motion. Edwin kept his eye on them as they made a wide turn and broke into a gallop back the way they came.

The True Metal Order, he thought. *What are the chances?*

Ophelia came sprinting down the road. "What was that? What's going on?"

"Just some people who got lost." Edwin fired the revolver into the ground, making Ophelia jump. "Nothing to worry about."

He handed the gun off to Ophelia and sauntered toward the inn. Mattie had been a curious thing since she first arrived, but now she warranted a conversation. The True Metal Order had never been openly aggressive before, but Asha and her people were different than the Order he'd grown used to. Militant, even. Maybe it had something to do with him.

The sun set on Dawnhallow as Victoria, Mattie, and Adelaide returned with bad news.

"Four nests?" Ophelia rubbed her eyes. "Is that something we can deal with?"

Mattie sat cross-legged on the bed of Adelaide and Dayla's room, hiding behind her mask. It had become the unofficial headquarters for the Dawnhallow defence, and even Edwin had joined in for the debrief. Adelaide had been concerned with his presence but chose to separate herself from the conversation, inspecting the jar of black and grey tar Mattie had scooped up from inside the manor.

"A team of three or four well-trained sawbones can destroy a nest if they catch it early enough," Edwin said. He leaned against the wall by the window. "But if these are as dug in as you say, they'll take a more concentrated effort."

"The place is filled with sludges," Mattie said. "Inkbloods are wandering the halls. It's a mess."

She had hoped that after going into the Bilson Estate she would've come out with something more than a new specimen for Adelaide. But the walk through the halls filled her with such dread she worried she would drown in it.

Ophelia fell back into a chair. "I guess we're staying on the defensive."

"We also know it's the same machine from last year," Victoria said, half-sitting on the table, looking at Rig's poorly drawn map.

"Are you sure?"

Mattie glanced at Victoria. When they left, Victoria had asked Mattie and Adelaide to keep her relationship with the machine a secret. "For now," she had said.

Mattie nodded. "I'm sure of it. It feels the same."

The door to the room opened. Hush, Dayla, and Dusty entered with their arms filled with weapons. They dumped them onto the table with a bang.

"There are more in the trailer," Dusty said. "I think we're going to find ourselves very well outfitted."

Dayla picked up an ignition thrower and looked down the sights. "They're old."

Rig came in behind them and slammed down a crate of inkwells. "So are you."

Dayla laughed. She returned the rifle and noticed the looks on everyone's faces. "Why all the solemn looks?"

"There are four nests near the Celestial Contraption," Victoria explained.

"We're not going in there," Rig said, turning to leave.

Ophelia leaned on both her hands, looking over the armaments they had gathered. "We're really going to need to teach these people to fight."

"That's why we brought a sawbones." Dayla grabbed Rig before he could get out of the room. "You can train them."

"You're the shooter," Rig said.

"I'll teach them to shoot. You teach them to kill Mire."

Rig grunted. It seemed like an affirmation as much as anything.

Ophelia glanced at Edwin. "How about you? You used to be a sawbones, didn't you?"

Edwin tapped his foot on the ground and let out a sigh.

"Edwin." Rig stepped in. "With four nests, you won't be able to fight alone. I hate to say it, but we need these people to be ready."

"Fine." He pushed off the wall. "I'll be around."

The hopelessness Mattie felt leaving the Bilson Estate gave way. Edwin had been impressive when they fought off the Hawkers, but she worried when he wouldn't get involved in helping them prepare. He had believed her when she first arrived, and it felt good to have him be a part of the team.

"Alright!" Ophelia pounded her fist on the table. "Then we start tomorrow morning. Get some sleep."

The mood brightened. Everyone went to return to their rooms, except for Adelaide and Dayla who were already there. Before he left, Rig grabbed an inkwell and tossed it to Hush.

"You might as well be loaded," he said.

Hush stared at the inkwell as people filed past. As Mattie came by, he looked at her with the strangest expression, like he was terrified of what was in his hand.

Mattie was about to ask him what was going through his mind when Edwin stopped at the door.

"Mattie, a moment." His eyes glowed behind his glasses.

Hush shoved the inkwell into his pocket and hurried off, pushing past Edwin. *The wrong time*, Mattie thought. She motioned for Edwin to lead the way.

He walked out the side door onto the stairs and down into the alley. The snow was beginning to fall in bigger clumps and the smell of wetness was already in the night air. Edwin made sure the door shut completely after Mattie, then turned to face her.

"We had a visit today," he said. "A visit from the True Metal Order."

Mattie was thankful for her mask; it hid the slackness of her jaw and the concern in her eyes.

Edwin continued, "They were looking for a woman. They said she wore a crying mask and a large hat. They said she was special… and dangerous."

Mattie let out a puff of air. She removed her mask and hat. "I'm not dangerous."

"I figured." Edwin crossed his arms. "You don't seem the type."

"I should have known they would come after me." Her heart beat like horses hooves. Once the others found out about her, there was no telling what they would do. "They think I'm important to the Celestial Contraption. Like somehow I'm the one who—"

Edwin raised his hand, cutting her off. "I don't need to know why. I'm just letting you know they came. They're not likely to give up. You need to be careful; they're desperate and coming with the intent to kill."

"They're violent people, Edwin. They want to see the world burn if it means getting their way. Ever since Asha took over last year, it's been getting worse. I hear people talking about the old days and how the Order used to be." Mattie looked at her feet. "Those people are gone."

Edwin was emotionless. He tapped his fingers on his leg and his blue eyes seemed to pulse for a second behind his glasses in consideration. He swept past Mattie up the stairs and opened the inn door.

"Do you have a relationship with them?" Mattie asked.

Edwin paused, like he was going to answer, but instead kept walking. The door shut with a long creak.

Mattie looked to the dark sky, the stars hidden behind a cloud cover. The snow melted against her face. The True Metal Order could come if they wanted, she wasn't going anywhere.

CHAPTER 14

The morning came with a fresh blanket of snow. It was thick, as the temperature hadn't dropped, and stuck against the sides of buildings. As the sun crested the eastern horizon, however, there were already signs of it melting. Ophelia ran around the village, making sure everyone knew that there was to be training that day. When the time came, Rig found himself standing in front of a few dozen men and women next to Dusty's goat farm. It wasn't much of a fighting force, considering the couple hundred or so citizens, but at least they could arm them all.

"Killing the Mire is not the same as killing a person," Rig said, eyeing down the recruits. Among them were Ophelia and Dusty. "To destroy the Mire, you need to destroy the piece of it that contains the heart. The problem is, it's very small and it moves. You could shoot a bullet and get a lucky hit, but that'll be like closing your eyes and hitting a fly. Instead, we use fire, electricity, and weapons that tear or smash."

Rig walked to the trailer and pulled the tarp aside. He glanced at Edwin, standing off to the side. He had yet to add anything to the training, but at least he made an appearance.

"This is a grinder." Rig grabbed one of the swords and held it up. He paced the line so the recruits could see. "For you, this is the last line of defence. So, while we will be teaching you how to shoot right now, don't underestimate how important this is." He pulled out an Ink canister. "This is a canister of refined Ink. Technically this is referred to as a size four, but most people will just call it an inkwell."

He flipped open the grinder's pommel and inserted the canister. He closed the cover then slammed the pommel against his hip. The grinder came to life, its two blades sliding back and forth in the hilt.

"There is an igniter in the hilt. When you push on the pommel, it starts. To turn it off, you do the same thing." He hit the pommel against his leg and the blades stopped. "I suggest you learn how to do it with one hand. If you use this in a sword fight while it's turned on, you will lose. The grinder will be ripped out of your hand, or simply break. In any other circumstance, you turn it on and you don't stop cutting. The heart is surprisingly fragile, and the vibrations from the blade will damage it even if you don't hit it exactly."

He moved to put it down, then stopped.

"Oh right, it can get jammed. Officially you're supposed to remove the blades to clear the obstruction." He turned a small lever just under the crossguard and the blades slid out of their slots. "In reality, if your grinder gets jammed, drop it and run. Try to fix it in a fight and you'll die."

"And grinders are cheap," Edwin said, walking to the front of the crowd. "Well-trained sawbones are not. Know this: sludges and gnashers are the most dangerous opponents, but don't underestimate the toll killing inkbloods will have on you. They look like people. In fact, depending on where they are in their transformation, you can kill them just like people. But they are not. Their insides have melted and they are nothing but husks for the Mire to use. The only way to make what you have to do easier is to remember that they are already dead."

Hush raised his hand. "Does that work?" Rig didn't remember him joining the line.

"Sometimes." Edwin pushed his glasses up his nose and walked away.

He was always the sensitive one, Rig remembered. It seemed that he hadn't lost that in his strange resurrection. Rig snapped the blade back into the grinder and tossed it into the trailer.

"Dayla will take you through shooting," he said.

Dayla finished putting up some man-shaped targets on stakes and turned to the group. "We're going to use regular rifles for now to practice your aim. Best not to waste the Ink we have. An ignition launcher isn't that far off, it just has less recoil and a slightly shorter range than these twenty-twos."

Dayla continued her instructions as Rig caught up to Edwin joining Mattie and Victoria. They set themselves up on a nearby fence to watch the training, Mattie's feet hooked on the bottom while she sat on the top. She wasn't wearing her mask. Instead, she had wrapped her face in linen bandages, risking some of her grey skin peeking through.

"Where's your mask?" Rig asked.

"It seemed a little silly to wear something like that." She pulled at her bandages. "It's rather conspicuous."

"And wrapping yourself up like a mummy isn't?" Victoria asked.

Mattie pushed her hat brim down in reply.

"That was quite the speech," Victoria said, looking between Rig and Edwin. "I'm certainly feeling ready to fight."

Rig cocked his head. "Why aren't you training with the others?"

"I don't think I need to join the rabble." She gestured toward the recruits as they took their first shots. The targets remained unscathed. "You can just show me some tips later."

"If you want to train, you'll train with everyone else. Hush is there."

"Yes. But Hush is… Hush. Besides, I'm not like them. I'm the greatest magician in Wrotdam." She swung her hand into the air and fell back against Mattie's legs. "I won't be using some gun or grinder."

Rig narrowed his eyes. He knew Victoria would be trouble. He couldn't fathom why Dayla would be so insistent to bring her along. There were better magician sawbones in Wrotdam. One's that were more tolerable at least.

"Besides, Adelaide isn't down here." She twirled a loose bandage on Mattie's hand around her finger. "She's off doing experiments with that muck she got from the Bilson Estate."

"Adelaide is an Ink Cleric. I know she can fight. But you are just a spoiled rich girl who can make her toys float." Rig stepped forward until he loomed over her. "Get over there and start practicing so I know you won't be getting yourself or, more importantly, me, killed when the fighting starts."

Victoria stuck out her bottom lip and scowled. Still, she unbuckled her moon pouch and joined the recruits.

"You know, that may have been the longest I've ever heard you talk," Edwin said. "You'd make a good Commander."

Rig growled and turned to Mattie, who stood bolt upright. "What about you?"

"I can handle the Mire," she said. "I'll be fine."

"How's that?" Edwin asked.

"It…I would rather not say." She shrunk away.

"Why?"

So quietly that Rig could barely hear it, she said, "Because sawbones kill monsters."

"Are you a monster?" Rig asked.

Mattie somehow became even smaller. Rig looked to Edwin for help, but he just shrugged and stepped back to watch. Rig put his hands on his hips and gritted his teeth. Mattie was another person scared of sawbones. But she didn't call Rig a monster, she called herself one. It wasn't Rig she was afraid of. There was another round of gunfire and Mattie seized up. Rig softened. A familiar sadness grew in his chest. He understood what Mattie was going through.

"Mattie," Rig said softly. "You are one of us. You are not a monster." Franz's words rang in his head. "Sawbones don't kill monsters. We protect people. And if you need me to, I will protect you. But I also have to know if you can protect yourself."

A smile crept across Mattie's face, slowly at first, then it grew into a huge grin. "Okay. But I warn you, it's kind of weird."

Rig settled back and crossed his arms. "I can take it."

Mattie put her hand in front of her mouth. She made a few gagging noises, then pulled her hand away. In the middle of her glove lay a small pool of the slime she healed Victoria with and some wriggling worms.

"They live inside me." She wiped away some of the remnants on her lips. "The slime can heal. The worms do a lot of things, but if they get inside a sludge or an inkblood, they can control them."

"You're right." Rig scratched his cheek. "That is weird. But thank you for showing me. I'm sure that will be very useful."

Mattie shook the worms off onto the ground. "Should I tell the others?"

"If you want." He paused, thinking. "I would consider Dayla and Adelaide as 'need to know basis.'"

"Agreed," Edwin said.

Mattie laughed and nodded.

Edwin leaned into Rig's ear. "Good job, Commander Rig."

"Save the promotion for when we survive this."

The recruits fired again. Three puffs of straw broke from the targets.

"Look at that," Edwin said. "Maybe we have a chance."

CHAPTER 15

Days went by and the training continued. The villagers progressed slowly, but surely. They were becoming more accurate under Dayla's tutelage and eventually moved on to using the ignition launchers — after a small accident where one of them nearly burned down a barn. In the evenings they sparred, though Rig was quick to remind them that fighting the Mire was nothing like fighting a person.

"People have survival instincts," he said. "The Mire does not. Defend yourself when you can, but when you have a choice, always attack."

With each day, more of the villagers able to fight chose to. Ophelia smiled when she saw the trailer each morning, empty of weapons. The people were willing, but they had other problems.

"It's a shit place to fight," Rig said.

Ophelia and her seven mercenaries sat around a map of the village in Adelaide and Dayla's room. They had been talking for most of the morning. With the villagers' training going so well, they had moved on to formulating a battle plan. That had not been going as well. Mattie's predictions gave them another week at best, just before the new year.

"There are a few good sightlines," Dayla said, pointing at some buildings. "But no great ones. The best I can think is we hide our shooters here around the main street, lure the Mire in, then fire on them once they're trapped."

"Trying to trap the Mire has never worked," Rig said. "Inkbloods, maybe, but a motivated sludge can squeeze through a hole the size of a shilling. We'd be too spread out. The Mire will come from all directions and these people can't take them in close quarters."

"What about lavender candles?" Victoria asked.

"Once they start firing, the candles mean nothing."

She frowned. "Don't they ward them off?"

"Muckies don't like lavender," Hush said, sitting in the corner. "There's a lot of things I don't like that I deal with." He made pointed eye contact with her.

Ophelia paced the room. Dawnhallow wasn't built to fend off an enemy army, it was built for people to live in. All their training would go to waste if they couldn't figure out a way to apply it. She looked at the jar of dark muck Adelaide had been experimenting with. It sat on a dresser as if to watch them and laugh at their attempts. That little murky fluid was their enemy. It almost seemed like a joke.

Rig slammed his hands on the table. "We need a place where we can see the Mire coming."

"You're not going to find that in the village," Dayla said. "And we won't have any cover outside in the forest. Remember all the people we need to protect?"

Rig scanned the edges of the map, hoping to find something they could use. He slammed his finger down on a rectangle just outside the Dawnhallow limits. "What about this?"

"That's Briardown," Ophelia explained. "It's the manor Richard Hawk owns. The one that the Hawkland Mob uses. I don't think they'd be willing to share with us."

A gunshot tore through the air and the entire room leapt to its feet.

"Ophelia Plante!" someone shouted from outside.

Mattie lifted the curtain and peered out the window. "You know how we were just talking about the Hawkers?"

Ophelia rushed across the room. In the street below waited a couple dozen gangsters. The one who fired his gun in the air was an older man with greying hair. He had a well-kept beard and fawn skin tinged with pink from trying to avoid going out in the sun too much. He straightened his fitted suit jacket and looked up and down the road. Richard Hawk, standing with the Hawkland Mob. Ophelia shouldn't have been surprised he'd show his face eventually.

What did take her breath away was next to him. Guillotine Harry had his arm wrapped around Dusty, with a gun to his head.

"They have Dusty!" Ophelia said, backing away from the window.

"We need to end these pests." Edwin tossed his coat aside and rolled his shoulders with a crackle of sparks.

"I hate to be that person again," Adelaide said. "But I don't want to kill people."

"Huh." Edwin cocked an eyebrow. "You could have fooled me."

Adelaide narrowed her eyes.

"We were hired to protect the village," Dayla said, soothing the situation with her soft voice. "Whatever that means. We can't let these people be hurt, and sometimes that means hurting others. They brought guns, Adelaide, they're ready to kill."

Rig grabbed his hat from the table and donned it. "Dayla, where are the weapons?"

"They're around back." She leaned over the map and let out a long sigh. "Alright, fine, listen up quick, we don't have a lot of time. I have a plan."

The bulge of the revolver in the back of Ophelia's trousers made it awkward to walk. She did her best to ignore it. She was headed toward Richard Hawk and wouldn't want him to notice anything odd. Rig walked at her side. He had a gun stashed on him as well but moved comfortably with the weight. Ophelia spent the last week shooting targets. Hopefully, that meant something.

"Ophelia Plante," Richard said in a joyous tone. "You know, I do actually recognize you. I thought I might. I hear there has been some trouble. I'm hoping to solve that."

Gangsters backed Richard, armed with long guns and sour looks. Ophelia recognized a few of them from the scuffle a few days before. They didn't look happy to be back. Guillotine Harry had his arm wrapped around Dusty's neck with a revolver pushed against his head. Blood trickled down from Dusty's hairline and his hands were bound.

"Sorry, Fifi," he said through a red-toothed smile.

Ophelia took a deep breath and steadied herself. He only called her that when he was in real trouble. "Why are you here?"

"See, I was in London, doing business, and imagine my surprise when I get a telegram saying that the people of Dawnhallow were building an army." He shook his head and laughed as if he had just told the worst joke. "Now it just seems silly to build some sort of army when you already pay me to keep you protected. Might make a businessman nervous that his services might just get refused."

"These people are here to protect us from the Mire. Because you won't."

"Is this about the attack last year?" He groaned. "The world is a cruel and unpredictable place, Ophelia, but even so, don't insult my intelligence with such an obvious lie."

"How else are we supposed to insult your intelligence?" Rig said.

Richard looked at Rig for the first time. "You must be one of the mercenaries. I can beat whatever she's paying you."

Rig cracked his knuckles. The Hawker next to Richard pointed her revolver at him.

"Let's stop wasting time." Richard spread his arms wide. "We can resolve all this with one simple thing. Send the mercenaries away. Oh, and give us your guns. Two things. Or else, my associate Harry here will shoot your friend."

"Don't listen to them!" Dusty shouted, only for Harry to crack him with the butt of his gun.

Ophelia clenched her fist. She resisted the urge to draw her revolver and start firing. That wasn't the plan. Out of the corner of her eye, she saw people sneaking out the backdoors of their homes. Word spread. They stalled the Hawkers for long enough.

"You really should think twice about shooting him," Rig said to Harry.

"Yeah?" Harry spat toward Rig. "Why's that?"

"Because as soon as you do, you've lost your shield."

"My shield?"

Rig pointed at the Hawker aiming at him. "You're first."

A crack like thunder went off and the Hawker's throat popped like a blood blister. Ophelia drew her revolver and fired at Richard. Her bullet cut him across the temple. He pulled a Hawker in front of him to take the next shot and fled. Ophelia and Rig ran in opposite directions for cover, still firing at the gangsters. On the rooftops above, Dayla and Hush kept them covered.

Hawkers fired back at Hush and Dayla, tearing chunks out of the roofs. While Hush held his own, Dayla never missed. Edwin came in from the other side of the street, zipping in and out of sight as he fired into the bedlam.

Ophelia kept her head down and crept around the side of a building. She broke open her revolver and dumped the empty casings. Her hands wouldn't stop shaking. Even knowing what would happen, it was so loud. She peeked around her cover and spotted Guillotine Harry backing up with Dusty. Occasionally he fired in the general direction of someone, but most of his focus was on keeping his shield, just as Rig had warned him to.

"Dusty!" she shouted. She lunged forward but retreated as bullets struck her cover.

Rig took cover across the street against a house. He turned to watch Harry retreat with Dusty before making eye contact with Ophelia. She sent him a pleading look. He was on the right side of the street; he could do it. Rig rolled his eyes, but kicked open the side door to the house.

Go fast, Ophelia thought. She squeezed off a few more shots at the Hawkers. So far, everything was going according to plan.

Rig walked through the house standing tall. He looked out the window into the chaos in the street. Guillotine Harry still dragged Dusty away, but there weren't many places for him to go. Rig crossed into a sitting room, keeping his eye on the hostage.

The house was empty, thankfully. The people in the village got used to hiding when danger came about. It may work for a gang like the Hawkland Mob but wouldn't save them against the Mire. That was a later problem, of course. Rig was still set on getting access to Briardown. Going through the Hawkers seemed like a perfect way to achieve that.

Rig opened a window on the other side of the house and crawled out into a closed alley. The fences on both sides protected a quaint space for the carpenter next door to store his lumber. Rig stepped over the piles of wood and entered the shop. He moved to see where Harry was, only for the front door to swing open and Harry to back in.

"What is wrong with you people!?" he shouted. "There's only eight of them!"

Rig slowed his steps until they were silent against the gunfire from outside. Harry kept backing up, keeping his gun outstretched and Dusty between him and any enemy. He was so focused on the front door, he didn't notice Rig pick up a chair leg until he brought it down like a hammer on his head.

Harry loosened his grip on Dusty, enough for Rig to grab the gangster by the collar and yank him backward. Harry stumbled and crashed back-first onto a half-finished table, falling to the ground. He clutched the back of his head with one hand, his eyes flickering a distant look.

"Look who's lost their shield." Rig tossed the chair leg aside.

Harry's eyes focused. He shouted and brought up his gun, just as Rig brought up his own. They both fired. Rig didn't flinch as the bullet whizzed past his ear. Harry, on the other hand, took the shot to the throat. He drew in ragged breaths, pumping blood down his shirt before his legs gave out. He collapsed into the sawdust, his eyes going blank.

Rig had a thought. He opened his revolver's cylinder. *Last bullet*, he thought. *Lucky me*. He ejected the empty cartridges and turned toward the door.

"Are you okay?" he asked Dusty as he put in the new rounds.

"Yeah." Dusty held his chest, catching his breath. A smile crept across his lips. "I'll be fine."

"Good." Rig's face grew hot seeing the smile. "Keep down." He shook the fog from his head. Focus, he told himself. He swung the door open and started firing.

Adelaide took her place as the fighting started. She hid down an alley off the main street, using a cart filled with hay for cover. The plan was that when Dayla and Hush fired on the Hawkers in the street and Edwin blocked them from the back, they would take cover in the alleys. That was where Adelaide and Victoria — on the other side — would be able to take them out.

She still had her qualms. Fighting humans — even gangsters — wasn't why she was hired. She wasn't a killer. But she had been willing to kill Edwin the year before. She was protecting Archbishop MacMurray, though. Now she protected Dawnhallow. She had a purpose.

A trio of Hawkers came rushing into her alley. They fired back into the main street, at Rig, Ophelia, Hush, and Dayla. They were all relying on her. Adelaide snapped out her pulserod and crept out from behind cover. The ground was cold and easy to walk across. They had no idea she was there.

The closest Hawker was a stick-thin man with a smoker's growl. "We should have burned this whole village to the ground," he said.

Adelaide shifted her weight as she brought her pulserod back. Her foot cracked through the top layer of frost on the dirt. The Hawker jerked around. His eyes widened. His jaw dropped. He breathed in to scream. Adelaide brought her club across his brow and he bounced off the wall. Stealth was gone.

The second Hawker looked over her shoulder, her hands full of revolver rounds she was about to load. "Hey!" she shouted, clenching the bullets in a fist and taking a swing at Adelaide.

Adelaide caught the punch with her forearm and jabbed the Hawker's gut with the tip of her pulserod. What came out was a sound not unlike a duck. As she crumpled, Adelaide brought her knee up. The Hawker took the hit on the nose. In a shower of unfired bullets and blood, the Hawker toppled like a tree. All that time spent in the lab hadn't made Adelaide rusty.

The third Hawker bared his teeth. He snapped his revolver shut and trained it in her direction. Adelaide was faster. She fired spurts of flame from her gauntlet, pushing the Hawker back. He shielded his face from the raging flames. The frozen dirt at their feet melted into mud with each step. He raised his gun again — only to gain a new hole in his crown.

Adelaide jumped back in momentary horror. The Hawker had re-entered the firing range. It was probably Dayla, saving her life again. The street was still a warzone, with bodies, bullets, and blood. It wasn't what Adelaide signed up for. But it was helping people, wasn't it? And sometimes helping people meant hurting others. She leaned her shoulder against the wall. Life sure was easier before she joined the Ink Clergy.

Pop! The wall next to her head turned to sawdust. Another Hawker fled the fight in the street, firing at Adelaide as he went. She scrambled back, sending out spurts of flame to disguise her as a target.

Bullets flew through the fire as she retreated to the cart. The snow at her feet had melted into muddy pools of water and she took care not to light the surrounding buildings on fire. She needed to get out of sight and ambush the Hawker from behind. There was a door around the corner, she could get inside the building and attack from there.

A shot came through the flames and struck Adelaide on the shoulder. She cried out and fell into the mud around the cart. The Hawker swatted at the flames crawling up the arm of his coat. It was a lucky shot.

Her right shoulder screamed in pain, making it hard to maneuver her flame gauntlet. She had little time before the Hawker recovered. She pushed on the inkwell at her forearm, priming more Ink to be fired. Her hand shook and she certainly pressed it more than once. The Hawker tore off his coat and threw it to the ground. Adelaide switched the gauntlet to burst mode.

The Hawker growled, his face turning red with rage. He scowled at Adelaide and took a step toward her. Water splashed and before the sparkling droplets hit the ground, Adelaide extended her gauntlet and fired.

The air burned and popped. The Hawker took the blast full-body. Water and mud flew into the sky, the kinetic force ripping a trench in the alley. The Hawker shot like a cannonball, bouncing off the opposing building's awning. Adelaide cried out in pain. Her arm bled terribly. The recoil from the explosion had torn the wound open even more, and she could barely feel anything more than twitches below the roaring agony at her shoulder.

As she sat there, cold water surrounding her legs, she looked upon the alley. The explosion scorched the walls black and pockmarked them with cooked mud. The ground rippled with the waves of force leading away from her. At least she would be easy to find.

CHAPTER 16

Victoria perked up at the sound of an explosion. Things were certainly getting exciting, but not where she was. She waited around the corner of the alley she was told to protect, crouching against the wall, but no one had come down it. She wanted to get in the fight, but Dayla would be furious if she left her position.

So much of her training had been theoretical; it would be good to put it into practice. She was a skilled fighter against strawmen. There was the inkblood from the year before she killed, of course, but then she got blindsided by a whole gang of them. That was hardly fair. People were more fragile than inkbloods, too.

Victoria snapped her fingers. Her moons went tip-to-tip, furling like a snake. She flicked the bottom one and they all twisted and broke apart. It was fun for a second, but like many things, it eventually gave way to boredom. She leaned her head back against the building.

Wood creaked — but it wasn't from her. She paused, straining her ears to hear something quiet amidst the sounds of battle. Footsteps. She spun to stand. It was the post office. There shouldn't be anyone inside.

Could one of the Hawkers have snuck inside? she thought. *This is technically part of my job.*

She steadied her breath — from excitement or fear, she didn't know — and tried the backdoor handle. It turned with only the slightest groan. She brought her moons close to her and crept inside.

The blinds had all been shut, filling the post office with vertical slices of light and deep shadows. Victoria took soft steps, listening for any sound of someone being in there with her. There was a creak from the next room over, the sorting room. The moons floated next to her arms and she stepped around the counter toward the doorless threshold.

She turned the corner and came face to face with a rifle barrel. She threw herself backwards as the Hawker fired. Victoria tumbled over the counter and landed awkwardly on her knees. A chunk of the counter in front of her face turned to splinters and dust. She scrambled away as the Hawker unloaded, turning the counter into swiss cheese trying to find where she had gone.

I'm not getting shot again, Victoria thought. She circled the counter as the Hawker came around the other side.

At the telltale sound of a rifle reloading, Victoria popped up. She swung her arm and sent two moons flying at the Hawker. The Hawker ducked under the moons. As he came back up, he pulled a revolver from his hip. Victoria cursed and leapt into the sorting room. She dropped to the ground and crawled to the other side of some letter bins. She laid her moons on the ground.

She could barely see underneath the bins. The floor smelled like wet dust that made her queasy. Boots appeared on the other side, carefully creeping into the sorting room. Victoria slid her moons under the bins, keeping them from touching the underside or the floor and making a sound. She only had ten after leaving the two in the other room.

The Hawker moved slowly, each step taken long after the one before it. He fired a round into the wall, trying to scare her. She didn't flinch. The Hawker's next step brought him next to the bins and Victoria flicked her wrist.

A moon slashed across his ankle. The Hawker screamed and fell forward. Victoria jerked her arm upward and the moons followed in that direction. The Hawker's descent stopped at the sound of ten wet impacts. Victoria kept still. The revolver and rifle fell to the ground as blood rained down. Victoria slowly rolled onto her stomach and stood up.

The Hawker laid suspended in mid-fall by Victoria's moons piercing him from his head to his feet. *My supposition was correct,* Victoria thought. *People are fragile.*

She pulled her moons out of the body, letting it collapse. With a flick of her wrist, she cleaned the blood from the blades and left the sorting room. She lifted her last two moons off the floor and brought them all into her pouch. A shadow shot past the crack in the window blinds. Then another one further down. Someone was running down the alley. Victoria cursed and sprinted for the backdoor.

Outside, someone hauled themselves full speed away from the village, heading toward the forest. He looked like the man who seemed to have been leading the Hawkers. Richard Hawk, if she remembered correctly. She pulled out her flying moons and took aim. She bobbed her head from side to side, then put her moons away. Too far.

The main street had gone quiet. Victoria took a last look at Richard running away then turned to leave.

When she got back onto the street, everyone was waiting for her. Hush and Dayla had climbed down from the roofs. Hush still had his branderbuss slung across his back with a rope. Ophelia checked the wound on Dusty's head, while Rig and Edwin checked the bodies littering the road.

"Hey!" Victoria called as she approached. "That Richard Hawk fellow is running away."

"Oh great," Ophelia said. "Where was he going?"

Victoria pointed east.

"He must be going back to Briardown. I'm sure there are more Hawkers there."

Rig pulled back the bolt on a rifle he pilfered. "I think it's time we paid him a home visit."

"Wait." Dayla looked around. "Where's Adelaide?"

Everyone scanned the street. Like Victoria, she had been on alley duty. Her heart leapt into her throat. Could someone have gotten her?

"Adelaide!" Victoria shouted. She dug her boots into the dirt and sprinted for the alley Adelaide was stationed in.

She turned the corner. Her blood went cold at the devastation. The walls were cooked with mud, the ground was carved into a valley, and at the end of it all, Adelaide slumped against a cart. Not moving. From that distance, Victoria couldn't tell if she was even breathing. One by one, the rest of the team arrived, similarly shocked by the sight.

Victoria grabbed Ophelia by her collar. "Where's Mattie?"

"She's back at the inn."

"Get her!" Victoria shoved her away.

Ophelia took off like a bolt. Dayla was already splashing across the puddles of melted snow. Victoria's mind spun. Adelaide couldn't be dead. That would be too unfair. She caught up as Dayla knelt next to Adelaide.

"She's breathing," Dayla said. "Weakly."

"Mattie can fix her." Victoria stayed standing. "I'll stay here. You should go after Richard."

"She's right," Rig said, arriving with Edwin and Hush. "We can't let him have time to prepare."

Dayla squeezed Adelaide's hand and stood. She had a dark and angry look on her face. "Take care of her," she said, leaning her rifle against her shoulder.

Victoria nodded. Dayla, Rig, Edwin, and Hush ran off in the direction of Briardown. Dusty leaned against the cart, still woozy from his injuries.

"She'll be fine," he said.

"I know." Victoria knelt and took Adelaide's hand, muddy and cold.

The world wouldn't be so unfair to Victoria. Adelaide was hers. The truth was crystal clear now, made form by that burst of emotion when Victoria saw her sitting in the mud. Victoria smiled. She wouldn't let anyone take Adelaide away from her.

Rig took the lead of the group, moving at a fast pace through the woods. The more time Richard Hawk had, the more prepared the Hawkers would be for them. But if they brought the fight to Briardown's door, the greater chance they had at succeeding. Even with fewer people.

Dayla had been dark since they left Adelaide. She had put on her mask, making her emotions unreadable. But the way she clutched onto her rifle told Rig that she was ready to kill.

Edwin grabbed Rig's shoulder. "Wait."

They could see the front doors of Briardown. The woods gave it plenty of space to either side and though vines and moss choked the façade, the large gravel driveway left clear sightlines from the front porch. Clearly, Richard Hawk didn't spend much time there, and the Hawkland Mob wasn't much for housekeeping. Part of the wrought iron fence had crumpled under the force of a tree growing through it, yet still held itself proud and strong. Seeing it made it clear — with a bit of reinforcement, would be the perfect place to defend against the Mire.

Hush ducked down next to a log just off the main road. "What do we do now?"

"Yes, Dayla," Rig said. "What's the plan?"

Dayla stared at the manor through the lifeless eyes of her mask. Slowly, methodically, she knelt in the middle of the road, brought her rifle up to her eye, and said, "Open the front door."

Rig looked at Edwin and shrugged. "It's simple."

"We hit them hard and fast before they know what's happening." Edwin drew two revolvers. "Just like old times."

Hush shook his head and left his hiding spot. The trio hurried toward the manor, leaving Dayla in her sniper position. Hush pointed at the second floor.

"I could climb up through that balcony," Hush said. "There isn't a castle in England I can't snap. This way we can bury them from both sides."

"Make it fast." Rig snapped the lever on his rifle. "There isn't going to be a signal."

Hush adjusted the strap on his branderbuss.

"Are you going to use that?" Edwin asked.

"I don't plan on it."

"But you're going to carry it around?"

Hush lowered his head and sprinted toward the manor. Edwin hadn't noticed where the branderbuss had come from, and Rig figured he should tell him at some point. If he was going to, just before assaulting a gang hideout wouldn't be it.

Rig and Edwin set up on either side of the double front door. Hush leapt onto the vines that covered the manor walls. Without dropping his rifle — and the branderbuss bouncing on his back — he ascended the wall as easy as walking. He reached the balcony and rolled over the railing.

Edwin nodded approvingly. "He is very good."

"Dayla's waiting." Rig set his rifle against his shoulder. "Open the front door."

They spun to the door and, in unison, kicked. The lock splintered the wood. It had barely opened when they spotted a Hawker drawing a revolver on them. A bullet whistled through the space between them, hitting the Hawker in the chest. An angel looked over them.

More Hawkers flooded in and opened fire. Rig and Edwin returned with their own shots, clearing rooms as they moved through the manor. They entered a lounge, keeping their eyes out for Richard Hawk. Rig kicked a couch aside and shot down a Hawker as they rounded the corner.

Edwin was more fluid. He slid over the couch Rig kicked like water. A Hawker came up from behind. Edwin stuck his foot under a nearby chair and sent it flying. The Hawker batted it away and Edwin got him with a quick shot, then spun back to shoot another Hawker coming up from the other side.

Edwin moved onto the next room while Rig hung back, keeping him covered. A creak came from behind a lounger in the corner. Rig spun. A Hawker leapt up, shotgun ready to blow him away. The window next to him shattered, and the Hawker took a bullet to the back, folding over the lounger. Rig glanced outside, but couldn't see a sign of Dayla in the trees. Good to know she was keeping up.

Rig and Edwin moved through the manor methodically. Occasionally Dayla sent a shot through a window, never missing and always just where they needed her. Rig winced. That was why she was an effective leech. She didn't have to engage in combat to kill her prey. One shot was all it took.

Edwin hurried into the kitchen. Three Hawkers waited for them. Rig caught one in the chest and took cover, while Edwin bounded off the island like a jackrabbit, bullets sliding past him, and took down the others with two barrels blazing.

Edwin landed on the other side of the kitchen. Another Hawker in the next room stepped into view and fired wildly. He lit off rounds from two revolvers with a third held in his teeth. Edwin rolled and put his back to the far wall while Rig moved forward behind the island.

Bullets filled the kitchen, taking chunks out of every surface and sparking off the dangling pots and pans. Rig peered around the side of the island. Edwin squatted against the wall. He held up his revolvers, shrugged, and dropped them. No ammo. Rig looked around the kitchen, but there weren't any windows for Dayla to fire through.

The Hawker emptied his guns and tossed them aside. He took the one out of his mouth and another from the back of his pants, popping off a few shots before spinning out of view, hiding on the other side of the wall Edwin crouched against.

Rig pointed at where the Hawker disappeared. Edwin nodded and flexed his fingers, sending out crackles of electricity. He braced himself and with a spinning punch drove his fist through the wall. There was a yelp from the other room and Edwin pulled back, dragging the Hawker through and taking most of the wall down with him. He tossed the Hawker backward, sending him sliding along the kitchen floor to Rig's feet. The Hawker raised his gun but only got it halfway before Rig put a hole in his temple.

Blood and bullet holes riddled the kitchen, but nothing moved other than Rig and Edwin. They took a slow turn around the chaos they had caused in such a short time. Another gunshot sent spikes of adrenaline through Rig's chest. They spun to the hole Edwin made as a Hawker's corpse flopped past. Hush stepped in, the last trails of smoke wisping off the end of his rifle. He stared wide-eyed at the missing wall chunk.

"Did you find Richard Hawk?" he asked.

"No," Rig said. "I take it you haven't either?"

"Not yet. But all these castles are laid out the same. I bet I know where his office will be." He turned. "Follow me."

Hush led them to a stairwell and up to the second floor. They walked past scenes of Hush's fight. Hawkers slumped against the walls, with blood splattering sheets protecting the furniture.

"I didn't think you had it in you," Edwin remarked, stepping over a corpse's outstretched legs.

Hush lowered his eyes. His expression didn't seem mortified, or sad, simply haunted. Rig couldn't attempt to understand what went on in Hush's mind. They arrived at the back corner of the manor's second floor. A heavy oak door stood in their way. It should lead to the office, at least according to Hush.

"Watch our backs," Edwin said to him.

Hush nodded. He turned around and scanned the hallway with the barrel of his rifle. Rig and Edwin approached the office door.

"I'm out of ammo," Rig said, holding up his rifle.

Edwin jerked his head toward the door. "He doesn't know that." He grabbed the handle and threw the door open.

Rig swept in first, gun at the ready. Richard Hawk had one leg swung out the window. A bulging duffle bag hung over his shoulder. He froze as Rig pointed his rifle at his chest. Sweat glistened on his brow, despite the cold wind blowing in from outside.

"Step away from the window," Edwin said. "Put down the bag."

Richard hopped awkwardly on one leg and dropped the bag to the floor with a solid thump. He took a moment to smooth out his vest, fix his tie, and flash a smile. With a pull of his sleeves, he was a different person. Calm, collected, though the sweat was still visible collecting in his eyebrows.

"I think we got off on the wrong foot," he said, strolling to his desk. Rig kept his rifle trained. "I'm sure there's some sort of arrangement we can come to. You're mercenaries. Among my personal effects in that bag is around a hundred pounds. Of course, that's not all. Whatever that village is paying, I can easily double it."

"You really don't get it." Edwin approached slowly. "We were never here for you. This is the counteroffer. Leave Dawnhallow. We require this house."

Richard chuckled. He sat at his desk chair and leaned back. "My business is all about faith. The people who work for me must have faith that I will do what needs to be done. There are villages like Dawnhallow all across the countryside that rely on me for protection, not to mention my associates in London who have need of my product. If I start giving up territory, that faith is going to corrode." He smiled. "And what sort of people are we without faith?"

He lunged for the underside of his desk and drew a revolver. In a crackling blur, Edwin grabbed Richard by the head and slammed him into the wall. Electricity coursed from Edwin's hand into the gangster's body. Amid his screaming and seizing, Richard fired his revolver into the floor. A moment later, Richard's brain scattered across the wall.

Edwin stumbled back in confusion, letting Richard's corpse fall. He looked at his hand. The metal between his middle and ring finger burned red hot for a moment from the bullet tearing past. The window Richard had been trying to climb out of sat wide open, with the woods standing silent beyond. What else could the trees say? Dayla made her point loud and clear.

"I think she was upset," Rig said, resting against the desk.

The leaves swayed in agreement.

CHAPTER 17

Adelaide did not see a bright light when she opened her eyes. She also did not see her room at the inn. What she saw was a sparingly used bedroom, judging from the cobwebs and dust, and Victoria sitting by the window. Adelaide sat up and the four-post bed creaked in reply, alerting Victoria that she had awoken.

"Adelaide!" Victoria exclaimed, throwing herself out of the chair and hurrying to her side. "They told me you would wake up when you were ready, but I still have to say I was quite nervous."

"Where am I?" Adelaide asked. She felt oddly refreshed considering the last thing she remembered was bleeding to death in a puddle.

Victoria sat on the bed near Adelaide's feet. "Briardown. We kicked the criminals out, though some decided to stay and help the village. Which is surprising. We also moved all your stuff, including that disgusting jar you've been keeping."

She pointed to the corner of the room. Adelaide didn't bring many supplies, just a bag of personal effects. Fortunately, the Mire sample sat on the floor next to the bag. She was still researching it and wouldn't want to lose her progress now.

"Thank you for that," Adelaide said. "What happened to me?"

"When we found you, you were already injured. You weren't looking good. But, thankfully, Mattie got there in time."

"Mattie?" Adelaide pulled the covers down to see her shoulder, only to reveal her stark-naked body. She let out a yelp and bundled the covers up under her chin, turning red as a tomato.

"Dayla was the one who disrobed you," Victoria said. Adelaide could have been imagining it, but it sounded like a tinge of disappointment in her voice. "I think she's off washing your clothes now."

"I have a change in my bag. Could you…?"

"Oh, of course." Victoria grabbed a long dress from the bag and handed it to Adelaide.

Keeping herself covered with the blanket, Adelaide threw the dress over her head. Her shoulder was not only healed, it felt even better than it did before. It had always felt a little off since she knocked it out of its socket the year before. She pulled the collar of the dress to the side and inspected the skin. Perfect.

Part of her felt sick. She didn't understand Mattie's ability, no one did. From a distance, it appeared to be a miracle. But miracles weren't the place of humans, and certainly not the place of the Mire. Now she owed her life to Mattie — and whatever she was.

"I'm glad you're okay," Victoria said, standing patiently next to the bed. She had her hands clasped before her and looked humbler than Adelaide had ever seen her before. "When I saw you there, I… I was worried I would lose you, uh, we would lose you."

"You don't have to worry about me."

"I do… worry about you."

Adelaide smiled. Her life was always about thinking about others. She had to admit, it was nice to have someone thinking about her.

The door swung open and Dayla entered. "You're awake. Excellent." She held Adelaide's Ink Clergy robes in her arms, now clean and pressed.

"I am awake, Dayla, thank you. I have two wonderful people thinking about me. That's so sweet."

Victoria's eye twitched. "Yes, isn't it so?"

"Is everyone else safe? Did anyone get hurt?"

"Everyone is fine," Dayla said, putting down the robes on the bedside table. "We're just getting settled into the manor, you haven't missed much other than lunch."

"I can bring you some." Victoria turned to leave.

"That's quite alright." Adelaide swung her legs off the bed and stood. "I'm feeling fine. I can get my own food."

Ophelia peeked her head through the open door. "Dayla, do you know where we can put—" Her eyes widened. "Adelaide! You're up."

"Yes, I am. I'm sorry if I concerned you."

Ophelia rushed in and wrapped her arms around her. "I'm just glad to know you're better."

Adelaide froze. Slowly, she softened and hugged Ophelia back. "I would not have taken you for someone who hugs."

"When the situation warrants it." She broke off the embrace.

Hectic foot stomps pounded down the hall before Hush came sliding in carrying a wood crate.

"How can a thief be so loud?" Victoria wondered under her breath.

"I thought I looked you all come up here." Hush put the crate on Adelaide's bed. He blinked twice, then turned to Adelaide herself. "Hi, Adelaide. It's good to look you up and about."

"Thank you, Hush," Adelaide said. "What do you have there?"

"Oh! The underground is full of boxes like this." He pulled off the top. Inside were two dozen short cardboard tubes and some metal disks. "Cannibal poppers."

"Ink-based grenades." Rig stepped into the room. "You use flame-primed Ink in the cap to set off another reservoir in the stick."

"Hence 'Cannibal,'" Victoria said. "That bit of Understone slang I get."

"It's not Understone slang." Rig huffed. "It's Sawbones slang."

Victoria shrugged. "Then that makes even more sense."

"These are only half-made," Hush explained, picking up an empty tube. "But I could get them finished up radiantly. If we put them around the grounds, we can give those muckies a real wrack."

Victoria laughed and leaned toward Hush. "You know how to make explosives?"

"Oh steadily. There were a couple times where—" He froze, still holding onto the cannibal popper. His gaze turned distant and he muttered something under his breath that sounded like, "No, that didn't happen." He put the explosive back in the box and closed the lid. "I can get it done."

"Is he getting weirder?" Victoria whispered to Adelaide.

"He's not getting more normal," she replied.

"Alright, everyone!" Dayla pulled on Ophelia's arm. "We have an entire manor to fill up, we don't all have to crowd into Adelaide's room. That's you too, Victoria."

Victoria looked between Dayla and Adelaide. Then, pouting, she stomped out with the rest of the group. Rig was the last to leave. He paused at the door.

"Adelaide," he said. "It's good you're not dead."

Adelaide gave an amused smile. "Thank you."

Rig tapped on the door frame, gave her a dismissive wave, then left.

CHAPTER 18

"Merry Christmas!" Victoria shouted, standing on top of Briardown's auto pool.

The villagers of Dawnhallow stopped in the middle of their shooting exercise to stare at her, who stood proud with her hands on her hips and a scarf wrapped around her neck.

From the back of the crowd, someone else shouted back, "Merry Christmas!"

The shooting range broke into uproarious laughter. Victoria grinned wildly and leapt off the auto pool roof into a pile of snow. Rig shook his head from his position watching the shooters. They got back into training not long after dealing with the Hawkland Mob. The villagers progressed well, but Mattie made it clear that it could only be a few more days until the Mire attacked. She said something about how she could feel it being anxious.

Edwin took an autocar out to the Bilson Estate the day before and said they had begun constructing pipes on the outside of the house. Not only that, four gnashers stalked the grounds, overlooking the construction like foremen. If he had any consideration of sieging the Celestial Contraption alone, that stopped him dead.

"Come on," Dayla called out, clapping her hands to get their attention. "Back to training. We aren't stopping until each one of you can hit a moving target." She pushed a strawman she had tied to a suspended rope. It flew across the field to where Ophelia waited on the other side to push it back.

Victoria brushed the snow off her coat as she walked. Rig held out his arm to stop her in her tracks. Frowning, Victoria looked at the arm, then at Rig.

"Shouldn't you be practicing?" Rig asked.

"I have been practicing." She unbuckled her pouch. "Look at this."

She dragged her finger over the top of the pouch and a flying moon floated out. She let it rest between Rig and her, then affixed her gaze to it. Nothing seemed to happen.

"What is this?" Rig asked.

"It's vibrating."

Rig put a finger on the cold metal. It shook imperceptibly, but he could feel it.

"You said that vibrations help damage a Mire's heart if you miss." She swept the moon back into her pouch. Her legs buckled for a moment, but she caught herself. With a groan, she put both her hands on her head.

"Headache?" Rig crossed his arms. "I've seen that happen to magician sawbones. Keep practicing. Apparently, it goes away."

Victoria nodded but kept groaning and clutching her head.

"Do you want to get some water?"

She nodded again.

"Dismissed."

Victoria muttered something between an appreciation and a curse and stumbled to the manor. Rig was impressed that she figured out vibrating her weapons on her own. She had been improving immensely. She was a perfectionist, after all.

As the villagers trained, Rig caught Dusty's eye. Mattie gave him some of her healing slime, so he didn't look any worse for wear. As their eyes met, Rig's muscles tensed and he turned away. The moving strawman made another pass. Dusty broke from whatever was going through his mind and raised his rifle, but the strawman was already gone. He looked at the ground, then at Rig, and with a big sigh walked over.

"Hey," he said. "I never really got the chance to say thanks."

Rig gently pushed aside the barrel of the rifle pointing at his leg.

Dusty stammered. "Oh! Uh, I'm just going to put this down." He placed the rifle on the lowered gate of the nearby cart.

"Thank me for what?" Rig turned the rifle so it wasn't pointing straight at him.

"Saving me. You know, Guillotine Harry." He rubbed the back of his neck. "He snuck up right behind me while I was cleaning from training that day. Didn't even see him coming."

Rig looked at the firing line. The strawman swept by. Most made their shot. "It's fine."

"Yeah…" Dusty leaned against the cart, tapping his fingers on the wood. His face turned red. "I was thinking that as a thank you, I could maybe get you a drink. I know we're technically using Richard Hawk's private reserve, but I could pour you a drink?"

"I'm pretty busy. Hush is off digging holes for the explosives and I said I would help him after assisting with the training."

"That makes sense." Dusty turned an even brighter shade of red until it was almost pink. "But there's time. We can find another time." He picked up his rifle. "I should get back to training."

He spun on his heel. Rig casually bent back to avoid being struck by the barrel as he turned. Dusty sulked back to the firing line, shaking his head. Out of the corner of his eyes, Rig spotted Edwin standing back from the training as he usually did. This time, he wasn't staring at the recruits or zoned out and looking at the clouds, he looked at Rig, disappointment apparent in his face.

"What is it?" Rig called.

Edwin shook his head and turned away, appearing to drop it. A second later, he let out a puff of air and stomped toward Rig. "What is wrong with you?"

Rig grunted.

Edwin poked a finger into his chest. "I may be messed up, but I can still tell when someone is flirting."

"I can tell too." Rig looked away. "I just don't care."

"You're the one always so sullen about being alone."

"Everyone's alone. What am I supposed to do? Find someone? Settle down? Become like you?"

Rig was certain Edwin would blow his top, but, surprisingly, that didn't happen. Instead, he smiled, sadly and longingly. Like someone looking back on an old memory and trying to remember how it made them feel. He removed his glasses, displaying his vibrant eyes.

"I'm not the only outcome for people like us," he said. "For what I do remember, I was happy once."

Rig cocked his head. "What do you mean, 'for what you do remember?'"

Edwin tapped his glasses against his hand. Each hit felt like a strike into Rig's heart. "Everything's fading. Ever since I got back, I've been losing parts of my life. I don't think it's going to be stopping anytime soon. The only memory that stays, horribly, crystal clear is that day last year. My family in that state. But I still remember their names, and I remember the good times. Most of them, I hope. I don't think you can remember what you've forgotten. I wish those will be the last things to go, or that I'll be dead before they do. You can't use me as guidance for a good life."

"Without you, what do I have? A church that doesn't care. A people who despise me for what I am. All I've ever been is a sawbones, and I've learned I'm not very good at doing anything else. Life hurts. Simple as that."

"All the more reason not to take it on alone. Or at the very least, make it less painful for others." Edwin donned his glasses. "You deserve to be happy, Rig. Like I was once."

Edwin stuck his hands in his pockets and walked away, the winter winds pulling at his coat.

"Thank you," Rig called after him.

Edwin stopped and turned his head. "Please don't."

The strawman flew past and everyone fired. Not a single shot missed.

Briardown was the kind of place Victoria was used to. Sure, it was dusty, overgrown, and a little bloody from the altercation to get it, but the way the halls came together was familiar. She could take more time to enjoy it if she wasn't cradling a headache. She went to the kitchen to get herself some clean water and sit in the shade.

She was chest-first against the kitchen island when Adelaide went rushing past the door. A moment later, she came hopping back. "Victoria!" she exclaimed, putting another bolt of pain through Victoria's head. "I need your help."

"I have some time." Victoria rested her head on her hand, looking casual and cool. "What do you need?"

"Come on." Adelaide grabbed Victoria's hand and dragged her away.

Victoria didn't fight as Adelaide pulled her up the stairs and toward her room. Adelaide brought Victoria inside with her and locked the door. Electricity tingled along Victoria's skin. *What's going on?* she wondered.

"Look at this." Adelaide brushed past Victoria without looking at her. She might as well have been a statue.

Victoria followed Adelaide to a table in the corner covered by a lumpy sheet. Adelaide pulled the sheet aside and revealed the Mire jar. Wires went in and out of the slime, all connected to a switch, a telegraph key, and off to the side sat a thin rod on a box. Adelaide checked the connections between the slime and the key, then turned to Victoria, nearly shaking with excitement.

"Ready?" she asked.

Victoria shrugged. "Sure."

Adelaide flicked the switch and the telegraph key went down. Victoria waited to see if anything else would happen, but judging from the expression on Adelaide's face, that was it.

"It's sending out an electrical signal!" Adelaide exclaimed. She pulled the wires out of the slime and then connected the telegraph key to the box. She carefully turned a dial on the box, sticking her tongue out in concentration.

While Victoria was still confused, she couldn't help but think of how cute Adelaide looked at that moment.

The telegraph key went down again. Adelaide turned the dial and the key went up, then turned it back and the key went down again. Victoria began to understand what was going on.

"It's doing it without wires," she said.

"Yes!" Adelaide clapped. "Wireless telegraphy! The Mire had always been somewhat coordinated, like a swarm of bees. They don't talk, so we wondered if they communicated through scents or some sort of sound out of our range of hearing."

"But, it's through these electrical signals?"

"That's the weird thing." She disconnected the cables and covered the desk. "We did check to see if the Mire was capable of something like that. It wasn't. But *this* one is."

Victoria followed Adelaide across the room. "What are you saying?"

"The Mire has changed. It is doing something it has never done before." Adelaide snatched a coat off her bed and put it on over her robes. "Which is why I need your help."

"Doing what?"

"Most of my equipment is back in my lab. If I'm going to figure out exactly what's going on, I need my gear. I can't tell Dayla about this. I don't know how she'll react. She may tell me to stop. So, I need you to drive me."

"You need me to drive you to Wrotdam?"

"I need to go to the Mechanical Cathedral." She stepped closer to Victoria. "And we can't be seen. The Church doesn't know what I'm doing."

Victoria crossed her arms and grinned. "Where do they think you've been?"

"On a break. A short sabbatical, if you will." She held herself with great pride. "They have no reason to distrust me."

"Oh, don't they? Won't the Cathedral be full of people? How are we not going to be seen?"

"Yes and no." Adelaide paced the room, tapping her chin with her forefinger. "It'll be the Christmas service. Not as large as the Arrival Day service on the first of January, of course, but still quite large. Everyone will be in the front; we'll be in the back. They won't notice." She stopped. "But what do we tell the people here?"

"We'll tell them we're on a date."

Adelaide cast Victoria a confused look. "Would they believe that?"

Victoria deflated. "We don't need to tell them anything. Let's just go before they notice."

Adelaide nodded excitedly and bundled up for the weather. Victoria hid her smile.

An entire day alone with Adelaide? she thought. *Merry Christmas.*

Mattie watched the snow accumulated on the tree branches topple off as birds flitted back and forth. Here, in the woods surrounding Dawnhallow, she felt at peace. Cold no longer bothered her, so she could take in the pristine landscape without care. Even as the snow piled up on her hat's brim, she kept motionless on the log she waited on. She didn't come out to the woods alone to take in nature, though.

There was someone she needed to meet.

Snow crunched nearby and sent the birds scattering to the overcast sky. Mattie stood up. The powder that accumulated on her hat and shoulders fell to the ground, like an ancient golem coming to life. A figure stepped into view. Asha was wrapped up against the cold air, her breath puffing out from under her scarf. She held a mason jar full of wriggling worms.

"I'm glad you came," she said.

"You've been insistent." Mattie looked around, seeing the other figures in the trees. "Almost every day I felt the pull to come here."

Asha held up the jar, inspecting the white worms that rolled over each other. "And yet you ignored it. You're not wearing your mask."

"No." She pulled some of the bandages further away from her mouth. It wasn't as uncomfortable as it used to be.

"Why not? Do you not believe in our purpose anymore?" She placed the jar at her feet. "Come back home, Mattie. The Celestial Contraption is nearly complete, even I can feel the turning of its gears. Only you can show us where it is."

"You don't want it, Asha. It kills people! It grinds them up into nothing. If this is what the Machine wants, then how can we pray to it? It's evil!"

"Evil is relative to the people who fear it."

Asha's gaze drifted behind Mattie. Her eyes went wide and she leapt back. Her companions in the forest did the same. Mattie looked over her shoulder. Edwin sauntered around the trees like he was taking a simple stroll. He sat on the log where Mattie had waited and removed his glasses.

"Oh, don't pay any attention to me." He gestured toward Mattie. "She's still the one talking."

A small smile spread across Mattie's face. She had backup, even when she thought she was all alone. She turned back to Asha, who glared at Edwin with fiery rage.

"I'm staying here," Mattie said. "You're the one who said I was kind. You're the one who wanted me to help people."

"Not them! Us!" Asha pounded her chest. "We were chosen by the Mire! They turned their backs on us!" She pointed at Edwin. "And he killed us! Yes, I remember you now, dog of the Church. But maybe I should be thanking you. The old Order wanted peace. They said we should trust in the God that had come to Earth. That these trials were to prove our faith. Now they're dead and the rest have come around to my thinking."

The people in the woods stepped forward. Under their hoods, Mattie could now see they all possessed traces of the infection. Were there any remaining in the True Metal Order that didn't?

"Let the unbelievers be fed into the machine of progress." Asha spread her arms. The snowflakes swirled around her like a dancing congregation. "Let them be cast out as we had been. Let their blood be fuel. Let them scream in pain that they were wrong as we ascend. The Machine will move, Mattie. You will drive it."

Mattie swallowed. Asha had always been passionate, but now she sounded fanatic. People had been cruel to Mattie ever since she began to change. She had moments where she hated them, despised them, even. But what Asha talked about…

"You're right," Mattie said. She pulled her hat down. "I am too kind. I won't let these people be hurt. Even if they hate me."

Asha gritted her teeth. "You—"

"She made her point." Edwin stood. He flicked out his glasses and set them on his nose. "The conversation is over."

Asha and her companions traded looks. Some of them slid their hands toward their hips. There were six of them, as well as Asha. Could Edwin overcome all of them? From the way the Order members glanced around, they wondered the same thing.

"No!" Asha shouted. She stomped her feet. "No! No! No! This isn't why you're here, Mattie! You're just like the rest of them! No one will listen to me!"

She grabbed at the collar of her robes. As she shouted, blood leaked from her black eye and ran down her face. She took in a sharp breath through gritted teeth, calming herself down from her unexpected outburst. Mattie froze to the spot. She had never seen someone so suddenly lose their temper. The Order members looked at their feet, rather than engage with the situation. There was definitely something wrong with Asha.

"Fine." Asha wiped the blood from her eye. "We don't need you. God made a mistake."

She spun on her heel, sending up a whiff of snow, and stomped away. The Order members looked around, then awkwardly followed their unstable leader into the woods. In a few seconds, it was just Mattie and Edwin listening to the fading crunching of snow. Edwin stepped up to Mattie's side.

"Is it true?" Mattie asked. "Did you kill people in the True Metal Order?"

"I never said I was a good person."

He walked back the way he came. The trees seemed to reach toward him, trapping him in a cold and white cage. If evil is relative, as Asha said, then so too must good be. That would mean Edwin was relatively good? Or maybe it didn't matter. He was in Dawnhallow doing something good, at least. Did that make him good? Did that make Mattie good?

Her head hurt.

Adelaide was right. Coming in from the back, the Mechanical Cathedral might as well have been empty. Everyone was in the cathedral itself taking in the Christmas mass. Her fellow Ink Clerics especially would be mandated to be there. That was good, Adelaide wouldn't want to try to explain why she was borrowing all that equipment when she was supposed to be on vacation. Surely that would reach Archbishop MacMurray's ears and he made it very clear the Church was to have nothing to do with Dawnhallow or its problems.

So, as she and Victoria crept through the back halls, she kept a very careful eye out for anyone that could recognize her. When they reached the Ink Cleric laboratory in one of the cathedral's auxiliary buildings, they had yet to see anyone. Still, Adelaide locked the door and went fast grabbing the tools she would need to continue her experiments.

"So, this is where you work," Victoria said, peering into a microscope. "What sort of things do you work on?"

"Anything to do with the Mire." She grabbed a bundle of reactive strips and dropped them into a box. It was far more than she needed, but she was in a hurry. "We don't fully understand it yet. We aren't allowed to keep full specimens, but tissue samples are fine. Or whatever passes for tissue on a sludge. We even have a bone fragment from a gnasher! I just wish—" She stopped herself.

Victoria hopped up and sat on a table next to Adelaide. "Don't stop. It's so cute when you get excited."

"I just... I just feel like anytime I want to make a real breakthrough, I'm told to drop it. I'm told to not worry about it, that God's plan does not need me to understand everything." She slammed her hands down. "Who decides what we should know and should not know? If it can be discovered, then isn't God allowing me to discover it? If the truth is out there, then why would God hide it?"

Victoria gave a noncommittal shrug. She was the wrong person to ask about this, Adelaide knew that, but it was frustrating. She had to let it out sometimes, and Victoria was harmless enough.

"You know," Victoria said. "I know plenty of people who would love an academic like you. Non-Church-funded scientists working out in The Shadow, for example. My aunt has a lab out there."

"Those labs are always full of people." Adelaide dug under the counter for some containers to bring. "I can focus here. Not have someone buzzing around me while I work."

"What's wrong with people?"

"Nothing's wrong with people. I love people. But people..." She studied her distorted reflection in a curved glass jar. "People think I'm weird."

"I don't think you're weird." She leaned in, and Adelaide could smell the perfume she insisted on splashing upon herself every day. "I think you stand out, and people like to hammer down those that stand out."

Adelaide's cheeks turned rose. "Victoria. I am not so naïve to miss what you've been doing."

"And what have I been doing?"

"You've been…" She retreated, searching for air not filled with the taste of Victoria's perfume. "You've been flirting with me. Making eyes and fine words."

She grinned. "And here I thought I was being so subtle."

"I believe you should stop."

"Oh?" Victoria cocked an eyebrow. She crossed her legs and leaned forward, a sultry smile on her lips. "Am I not your type?"

Heat flashed across her face. "No, I've — I've never met a man whose features I were interested in. Your features are certainly…"

Victoria pursed her lips.

"…interesting."

"You know how to say very nice things in the most boring way."

"All the same, you should not flirt with me."

Victoria lowered herself from the table, planting each foot with two distinct clicks. "I don't flirt; I possess. While I've never been good with casual conversation, once I set my mind on something, I perfect it. I will perfect being with you."

Adelaide took a step back, running into a table. Her heart beat with the frequency of hummingbird wings. "Ms. Valjean, I understand someone with your standing must not be used to people rejecting you, just as I am not used to rejecting people. But that I mean I don't have many opportunities to reject people, not…"

Victoria leaned on the table, bringing her lips close enough that Adelaide could feel the breath on hers. "You talk a lot."

The perfume filled the space between them until it became the entire world. Her fingers twitched, only millimetres from touching Victoria's hand. Their eyes locked. Victoria's were sharp and cold, in contrast to the heat of her body.

"Why did you come to Dawnhallow?" Adelaide asked, her desires pulling her in two directions.

"Does it matter?" She shut her eyes and placed her other hand on the table, trapping Adelaide between her arms.

"I simply wonder if you look at them as coldly as you do at me."

Victoria stopped, her eyes half opening. A voice in the back of Adelaide's mind urged her to move that final millimetre, to press herself into the woman whose smell infected her so.

"What do you mean?" Victoria asked.

"Are you here because of what you experienced last year? That time with the Celestial Contraption? Or do you truly care about these people?"

"I came, does it matter the reason why?"

"It does to me."

Victoria furrowed her brow and moved back. Adelaide twitched to grab her but instead held her hands to her chest.

"It is in helping others that we find our path to Heaven," she continued. "I went to Dawnhallow because I saw people in need. I don't know what you see, but it reminds me of how I look at my research. Quantifying. Dissecting. I don't know if you care for these people — any people — at all, or if you're just selfi…" She didn't need to finish the word.

An insect's buzzing could have been a storm in the silence. Victoria pushed out her jaw and turned away. *Was I too cruel?* Adelaide thought.

"Why should I?" Victoria said, pushing her knuckles against the counter. "I look at people that way because I'm trying to figure out why everyone cares so much. We're brains firing in sacks of meat and bones, but, for some reason, we treat ourselves like we're something important. Humans are boring and weak and unwilling to become anything better. At least I don't hide behind scriptures to find reasons to be nice. It's not altruism when you do it for a reward. Money, closure, Heaven; it's all payment in the end."

"That's not true."

"Isn't it? You all talk about the path to Heaven or earning Heaven, well maybe you have to build Heaven, and everyone's just too stupid to do it." She turned back and her gaze softened. "You want to know why I went to Dawnhallow? I was bored. The only time I felt alive was when I became one with the Contraption. I want to feel it again. I want to feel something again."

Adelaide ran her thumb over her cross. "I can't make you feel anything."

Victoria's expression turned to distant sadness. She parted her lips to take in slow breaths, filling the room with solemn wind. The perfume's smell faded from Adelaide's nose. Time hung in belaboured stillness until Victoria shut her eyes and shook the feeling away.

"Are you almost done?" she asked without looking.

"Yes." Adelaide pushed off the table and picked up the box. "Just a few more things."

"Get them quick." She took up position staring at the locked door.

Adelaide had been honest with her. But then why did she feel so terrible? A quiet sniffle came from Victoria. Adelaide tightened her grip on the box. It was going to be a quiet ride home.

CHAPTER 19

Christmas Day passed by like a drifting ship. Another day of training showed the progress of the villagers, but the feeling in Briardown was one of grave anticipation. They knew the Mire was coming, and with four nests it wasn't going to be easy. But they kept the mood light when they could and trained to hopefully be ready.

As evening came the next day, Edwin retreated to Briardown's study. Richard Hawk must have considered himself quite the reader, as his shelves were filled with stories and poetry. He lounged back in a comfy, red chair, flipping through a book of American poetry and found a work by Edgar Allan Poe.

"The City in the Sea," he read. He had no interest in reading anything about the sea at that moment, so he tossed it aside before realizing he wasn't alone.

Victoria leaned against the study's door. She wasn't her normal assured self; she hadn't been all day. She wore a loose tunic and baggy pants, if anything that was a clearer indication of her mental state than how she held herself.

"Can I ask you something?" she asked, absentmindedly spinning a loose strand of hair around her finger.

"Is that really a question?" Edwin crossed his arms. "What if I say no?"

Victoria glared at Edwin. There was something wrong with it. It wasn't pointed and angry but filled with vacuous sadness. She turned to leave.

"Wait." Edwin rubbed his forehead. "Just make it quick."

Victoria paused, then practically dragged herself forward. She ran her fingers along the keys of a grand piano before arriving at a table not far from where Edwin sat. She flopped down in a chair in a way not befitting a high-class socialite like herself. For a long time, she didn't say anything. The clock on the mantle ticked louder every second until it was deafening. Would Edwin have to break the silence? What would he say? Should he say anything at all? It didn't matter, as Victoria soon worked up the courage.

"Did you mean what you said last week?" She picked at the spine of the book Edwin had tossed aside. "About the way I look at people?"

"I don't make a habit of saying things I don't mean. Why?"

"Adelaide said something similar."

"I thought it didn't bother you?"

Victoria leaned on her elbows. "You know, I know what a psychopath is, but I've never been a violent person. I never felt the urge to hurt or kill people just because. I'm a magician, though. I've thought about the potential need to protect myself. I thought about what it would be like." She tapped her long nails on the table. "I killed an inkblood last year, but that doesn't count. I didn't feel anything. It wasn't human, if I killed a human, I would feel something. But then there was this Hawker. A guy with a shotgun. He could have killed me; he was going to kill me if he found me. But I killed him first."

"And you feel bad?"

"I felt nothing. I still feel nothing. It didn't even cross my mind at the time how easy it was. Shouldn't I feel something?"

Edwin couldn't imagine he was the best person to talk to about this. He had done his fair share of killing. But he still regretted each body weighing on his soul.

"It's not like I want to kill again," Victoria continued. "But I know it's not hard. I know I can do it. I even forget what the man looked like. But…" She pressed her fingers into the back of her other hand until her nails cut the skin. "It's getting worse. I know it is. Do you know what it's like? To feel your humanity slipping away. I don't even know if I care. Humanity has been a disappointment so far."

Edwin did know. His memory was slipping away into the fog. Someday he would sit down and never have the urge to get up again. "You're here, though," he said. "You're protecting these people."

"That's not why I came." Victoria smiled sadly. "I had an experience last year I'm trying to recreate… or forget. I'm so confused, Edwin. And it's me that's confusing myself. It's not fair. The world is so chaotic, the one thing I'm supposed to be able to control is my mind, but it feels like even it's betraying me." She looked over the wounds on her hand with placid interest. "Make me care about people."

Edwin almost laughed. "What makes you think I can do something like that?"

"Because you said you're like me." She hung her torso over the arm of her chair. "I don't want to be me anymore. I want to be someone worthy of love."

"Who says you're not worthy of love?"

"You did."

"I didn't…" He rubbed his eyes. "I feel like you're intentionally misunderstanding me."

"Then help me." She held herself, nearly crawling on the table. "You said I can be bad, then shouldn't it be your responsibility to stop me? To fix whatever is wrong in my head?"

"You have to take responsibility for yourself. The things you choose to do, whether good or bad, you have to choose to do them with your own mind. For your own reasons, not because someone else told you to. If you do it because I tell you to, it's not going to be real."

"It has to be real. Okay." She sat back in the chair and contemplated the words. "Well, I would have left days ago if it wasn't for Adelaide. I feel real with her. It's obvious we should be together." She flashed him a smile. "Thanks for helping me."

Edwin rolled his eyes. She truly lived in her own world. At least she was in a better mood.

Dayla entered the room, stopping when she saw Edwin and Victoria, clearly deep in conversation. "I hope I'm not interrupting." Her stare shot clear daggers at Edwin. "But we're going to be having dinner soon. There was an idea that we would eat together."

"That sounds terrible," Edwin said.

Ophelia came in behind Dayla, pushing a cart laden with eight plates of chicken and beans. "Don't be so rude. Dinner won't hurt you."

Edwin grumbled and leaned back. Hush entered after Ophelia. He seemed surer of himself these days as he less needed to clutch that branderbuss to his chest, though it was still slung across his back. A branderbuss was usually a sawbones's tool, though it wasn't uncommon for one to find its way into Understone. A high-powered blast of fire was as dangerous to people as it was to the Mire. Hush looked at the table where Victoria sat, then grabbed a plate and sat at the piano.

Rig and Adelaide arrived at nearly the same time. Rig came in first and wordlessly snatched his food before sitting at the table. Adelaide wrote in her notebook as she walked, a talent to be sure. Ophelia offered a plate.

"How goes the research?" she asked.

Adelaide stopped and looked around as if she only just realized where she was. She spotted Victoria and her cheeks reddened. "It's going fine." She snapped her notebook closed and sat next to Rig, keeping him between her and Victoria.

Victoria crumpled into herself. Her eyes met with Edwin's, and she straightened her spine into the familiar air of superiority.

"Has anyone talked to Mattie?" Ophelia asked, handing dinner to Victoria and Edwin. She took her own and, with Dayla, sat at the table.

"She's probably in her room." Edwin accepted the situation and left the comfy chair to join the table. "She'll be out when she wants to be."

"All that bandaged mummy does is wander around and be creepy," Victoria said. "Does she need to take a lot of naps or something?"

Edwin was certain Mattie was still recovering from the confrontation the day before. The True Metal Order had changed in the year Edwin had missed. He had been sent after many enemies of the Church, but the True Metal Order always seemed the least aggressive. Asha looked to change that. If Mattie had been with them before, it couldn't be easy to see what they are now, under the control of an unstable woman.

"Hey, Rig." Victoria poked him in the arm. "I saw those little swords you have the villagers using. Why can't they have something more effective like your monster?"

"Because it's mine," Rig said through a mouthful of chicken.

"A real sawbones builds their own weapon," Edwin explained, noticing that Rig clearly wouldn't. "It's going to be the thing that saves their life, so they better know it from inside out. Most use blueprints from the Ink Clergy, or design one themselves."

"Oh." Victoria leaned toward Rig. "And did you design your own?"

"No. Edwin was the one who convinced me that I needed to get something bigger."

Edwin looked up from his food. "I did?"

"You suggested a riotsaw because it was 'simple enough for someone like me.'"

"Right. I remember." Edwin didn't. The gaps in his memory were becoming so smooth he couldn't notice where something was missing. *I wonder how much of my life is now gone*, he thought.

"Yeah." Rig poked at his beans. "I'm still trying to figure out if that was an insult or not."

"Now, I don't know Edwin as well as you," Victoria said. "But I'm going to guess it was an insult."

Rig scowled at her. Slowly, his expression broke and he let out a deep laugh, though somehow still without smiling. Soon the rest of the group joined him. Even Edwin cracked a grin. As the laughing faded, it was replaced by a beautifully haunting melody. Everyone turned to the sound. Hush had placed his branderbuss on the housing and begun to play the piano. His fingers moved slowly, but purposefully, across the keys to play a tune that balanced somewhere between an elegy and a love song. He struck a high note, then stopped and looked at his audience. He shrunk away, disliking the attention.

"You can play the piano?" Victoria asked incredulously.

"I've had time to practice." Hush shut the key cover.

"Where in Understone, between being a thief and an explosives expert, did you learn to play the piano like that? What else are you hiding from us?"

"He can also cook," Ophelia added.

Victoria whipped her head around. Dayla gestured to the dinner they were eating. Victoria's eye twitched as she slowly turned back to Hush. "What are you?"

Angry footfalls down the hall ended with Mattie bursting into the room. Her bandages laid loose on her shoulders and her black eyes flared with rage. In her hand was a pale, purple candle. "Where is she?"

Adelaide opened her mouth, but Mattie slammed the candle on the table before her.

"I found this hidden in my room. Lit." Despite her anger, the blood rushing to her face made her paler. "A lavender candle."

Adelaide tapped her finger on the wick. "Did it…bother you?"

"What bothers me is you treating me like an experiment rather than a human being."

"I'm trying to discover your abilities and limits. I'm sure you'd like to know as well."

"You could ask me!" Mattie slammed her hands on the table, rattling cutlery. "Or does it ruin your study if I'm treated like a person?"

Adelaide lowered her gaze and softly said, "I did need an honest response to stimuli."

Mattie's eyes flared. "You want an honest response to stimuli?"

She started to gag. Edwin and Rig lifted their plates while everyone else watched in morbid fascination. With a gut-wrenching sound, Mattie expelled a clump of slimy worms onto the centre of the table. Adelaide, Dayla, Ophelia, and Victoria leapt back as the worm bundle broke apart and squirmed across the table and to the floor. Adelaide's shoulder bumped Hush's branderbuss, knocking it away.

Mattie spread her arms and said, "There! A response!"

"That was incredible!" Victoria exclaimed, half-laughing.

Hush reached through people's legs, trying to grab his branderbuss. "Hey, c — could someone…"

Edwin put his plate down between the writhing of the worms. He grabbed the branderbuss from where it slid to and offered it to Hush. But then something caught Edwin's eye and he yanked it back.

"What are you doing?" Hush said. "Give it to me."

Edwin brought the gun to the wall lamp and inspected the stock. There were nicks and scratches, things that were common wear and tear on a sawbones's tool. He turned it around and on the bottom was carved a Chinese character, below it was an 'E', and above it was another Chinese character. Something crawled out from the haze of his mind. Those markings looked familiar. The E for Edwin, then Zhen, and before it Jia. Edwin's father, Zhen Jia.

"This is mine," he said, tapping each of the marks.

"Give it back!" Hush lunged forward, but Edwin spun away.

"You should really give it back to him." Rig flicked a worm off the table.

Edwin shoved his finger at him. "So you left it there? For anyone to pick up?"

"That's mine!" Hush shouted.

"No, it's not!"

Edwin pushed Hush back, and he retaliated with a brutal left hook across the jaw. His vision went shaky. He caught himself on the table, dropping the branderbuss. Hush snatched it back and clutched it to his chest. He looked around the room, now aware of all the eyes on him. He backed away, then bolted out. No one moved until Mattie chased after him.

"That's another thing he's good at," Edwin said, holding his chin. "He's got a solid left."

Mattie jogged through Briardown. It was a big house and had plenty of places where Hush could have run off to. With an outburst like he just had, someone needed to check on him. If Mattie didn't, who would?

She came into the ballroom, but it was empty. Her boots thumped across the worn-down wood floor. It had been some time since Briardown hosted a get-together, but the room had been used for other purposes, judging from the deep knife gouges in the floor and wall. What it didn't have was Hush.

Mattie was getting nervous. Hush seemed unstable at times, but she never saw him panic the way he did before. There was no telling what he would do. Mattie left the ballroom and a wriggling grew in her gut. She stopped, holding her stomach, and a feeling came over her. It was similar to what she felt when she met Hush a year earlier. A lost, sad feeling pulled her to the left. The empathic ability of her worms gave a literal meaning to listening to her gut.

These feelings brought her to the second floor and out onto the balcony that overlooked the northern grounds. Through the foggy and snowy evening, there wasn't much to be seen beyond Briardown's ground. The setting sunlight could barely be seen before being swallowed up by the grey. Hush sat against the railing balusters, holding the branderbuss to his chest and looking the smallest Mattie had ever seen him.

"What's that you told me when I was in this situation?" Mattie asked, leaning against the railing and looking out into the night. "They're muckheads, don't let them get to you."

"It's not them," Hush said, his voice rough with vocal fry. "It's me. I keep forgetting where I am. Or if I am."

Mattie sunk to sit beside him. She wanted to ask him what he meant, but the words were tough to form. Hush was fragile at the moment. A soft wind could shatter him apart.

"I'm not right. I'm losing it. I'm still worried that…" He let out a staggered puff of air that turned into vapour with the cold.

Mattie placed her hand on his knee. A small offering that calmed Hush's shaking.

"Last year," he started. "It was after you found me last year. I wanted to find Franklin, but I didn't. I found a light. A pure, terribly white light. Then I was back in Understone. Franklin was there. We were planning a meal, but something got me. Franklin was talking all twisty. He kept asking questions. I think he wanted me to say my name. Then, I wasn't in Understone anymore. I was in a house. A bright, real bright house. Not a castle, mind you, but bright. My sister was there. That should have been twisty. See, my sister died. My mom got hit by a rumbler and my dad gave us hemlock when he couldn't go on. Only got him and my sis, though. So see? Long time dead."

A cold wind rustled the trees and they leaned in to listen to Hush talk.

"But it didn't feel that way. She was alive. At that moment she was alive. We were young and I think I was happy." He swallowed. "But it didn't last. The cycles continued. Sometimes I would remember the other cycles. Sometimes I was new. I could be rich or poor. Franklin would be alive, my sister would be alive, my parents or any combination of that. But there were always questions." He cradled his head. "It was minutes, hours, days, months, years! Over and over and always questions. I don't know what answers the light wanted! I would have given it to it if I had! I tried to end it but there was always a new cycle. A new death. A new question."

Hush's voice broke. He wept, more out of panic than sorrow.

"Sometimes I even escaped. I was out, but... I wasn't. It wasn't real. Nothing was real. Until it was. I was on the street. There was Franklin's coat, and this." He squeezed the branderbuss. "I had this before. I remembered it from before the light took me. I know it's real. All these marks. The empty vial slot. Those are real. For all the life inside me, it's real. And there's you." He looked at Mattie, his eyes wet and shining from tears. "You were never there, not in any cycle. But you were there before. Before the light. Before years went by in moments."

Mattie opened her mouth to say something, but what could it be? What would be the correct words to say after hearing something so bizarre? If years had gone by, how long did Hush spend going through these cycles? Enough to learn piano, explosives, and cooking.

"I am still terrified that I'm going to wake up in a new life. That this is all going to end. But it's real." His breath came out in stuttering jumps. "It has to be real... right?"

"Of course, it's real," Mattie said.

"But how can I trust you? Trust anyone? Trust myself? I can't die. I tried dying. It never worked." His hands shook like a hummingbird's wings. "It's real. It's real."

"It is real." Mattie grabbed his hands, holding them still. "You have to live like it is."

Hush steadied himself. The world held still, giving Hush a moment of well-deserved peace. The balcony door, already slightly cracked, opened the rest of the way with a squeak. Edwin stepped out.

"How long were you there for?" Mattie asked.

"That's a dumb question." He looked away. "Long enough." He stepped across the balcony like walking on glass then sat next to Hush. "That is my gun, you know."

Hush tightened his grip.

"No, no. You can keep it." Edwin rubbed his eyes. "Where you found it, I assume you saw the bodies?"

Hush nodded.

"That was my family. I lost them in a Cleansing, and then I lost myself. I was told I could have them back. That was all it took for me to sell my soul. Then, on that night last year, everything collapsed. The Church was praying to some beings, believing they could bring the dead back. In the end, I prayed to them too. Asking for them to come." He gritted his teeth. "And they came. For you."

Hush lifted his head slightly. Mattie held her breath.

"It's my fault, Hush." Edwin sank to sit next to them. "What happened to you was my fault. And I... I don't even know what I can say to you."

The trio sat in cold silence. The mess of their existence bonded them, sealing them to that spot and that moment.

Then, Hush smiled sadly and said, "Good. Even that's a reason, isn't it? Bad luck, it's better than nothing at all." He wiped away his tears and stood. "I came here to find a reason. I never expected to like it. Expectation met." He turned to Mattie. "You're right. I have to live like this is real."

Mattie stared at Hush. It wasn't the reaction she expected, but it seemed like a good thing. She cracked a grin and stood, only for a commotion to start up from the front of the manor.

"What now?" Edwin groaned.

Mattie took Hush's hand and gave it a reassuring squeeze. Whatever happened, at least they were in it together.

Ophelia had come out of Briardown's front doors to find a crowd of villagers confronting her. She looked around, confused as many of the faces were people who had chosen not to fight and had never been to Briardown, until she saw Stephen Dixon at their head.

"Ophelia," he said, a slight grin on his face. "We've come to tell you that we're leaving."

"What?" She stepped down from the porch. Her mercenaries waited inside, watching silently. "What do you mean you're leaving?"

"The Mire's coming. I see no reason to stay."

"To fight!" Her voice echoed into the distance.

"Why?" Stephen turned to the crowd for support. "Look at this nonsense. We can simply leave Dawnhallow and return after this has all blown over."

"You can't believe honestly it'll be that easy." She grabbed his shoulder and turned him to face her. "It'll wait for us, or attack a different village. It wants the people!"

"Then it's not our problem!" He snapped down his collar and stepped around her. "Anyone else in there who doesn't want to throw your life away, come with us. Why do we have to be the ones to fight?"

"Because if we don't, no one else will! Goddamn it, Stephen!" She could feel the blood rising in her chest. "The Church isn't going to come for us! Wrotdam isn't going to come for us! And these things are going to keep doing this. They did it last year, they did it this year, why wouldn't they do it next year? Do we keep running?"

"Better than dying." He turned on his heel and walked through the crowd.

A few glanced back at Ophelia, quickly turning away when she met their eyes. She recognized them as standing at the firing range, sparing in the ring, and listening to the lessons. Now they walked away, same as the others. Ophelia couldn't believe it, after all they'd done.

But what hurt the most was when Edwin came walking out too.

"I have to go as well, then," he said.

Ophelia grabbed his arm, stopping in his tracks. "You said you were here to save Dawnhallow."

"I'm here to stop whatever the Mire is trying to do." He gently removed her hand from his coat. "That man, though an asshole, is right. If the people leave, the Mire will go someplace else, and that's where I have to be." He looked over his shoulder. "Mattie!"

Mattie perked up from where she stood on the porch with the other mercenaries.

"Come on," he said, jerking his head. "They all were hired to protect Dawnhallow, but you're like me. You came here to stop the Mire. I need you to tell me where they're going to hit instead."

Mattie glanced among those on the porch, lingering on Hush.

Ophelia whispered, "Please don't. Please no."

"He's right." She stepped down, her hand lingering in Hush's for a moment before she pulled it away. "I have to follow the Mire."

Ophelia felt a spike being driven through her chest as Mattie joined Edwin, pulling her hat down lower to hide her face. Edwin gave her a sharp nod and they walked off together down the path back to Dawnhallow, vanishing into the fog. Words failed, and all Ophelia wanted to do was scream but even that wouldn't come.

She turned to her remaining mercenaries. Five of them, fighters for a war that wouldn't come.

CHAPTER 20

As the night fell, Ophelia sat on the porch. More of the villagers had come out of Briardown, taking Stephen's advice to flee rather than fight. They'd glance at her while loading their bags into carts, but none could manage it for too long. She glimpsed some movement to her right and Adelaide sat down at her side.

"How're you fairing?" she asked.

"I don't know." Ophelia rested her back against the next step. "If everyone leaves, there's no one for the Mire to attack. That technically saves Dawnhallow, doesn't it? That's what I promised Aisling's spirit I would do."

"And yet?"

"And yet." She tensed her jaw. "It doesn't feel right. It feels like a stalling tactic."

"Perhaps." She kicked out her feet and crossed her ankles. "What do you want to do?"

Ophelia rolled her eyes. "What're you doing?"

"Choices are all we have. It's free will, the greatest gift we've been given." She swept her arm across the people packing up in the driveway. "They are making their choice. You must make yours as well."

"I think we should run." Ophelia shook her head. The words didn't feel right coming out of her mouth, but she said them all the same. "Come back after whatever other sad town faces our fate."

"If that's what you choose." She stood and placed her hand on Ophelia's cheek, lifting her eyes to meet hers. "There is no wrong decision, only your decision."

Ophelia forced out a smile and Adelaide went on her way, around the side of the house toward the stables. She sat on the porch for a few moments more, soaking in the night air. The others would need to know she had come to a decision, so she kicked her feet up and headed into Briardown's entrance hall.

"She is gentler with you," Victoria said.

Ophelia spun around, clutching her chest. She hadn't seen Victoria waiting behind the door and it nearly gave her a heart attack.

"What did you say?" Ophelia asked.

"I don't hear such kind words, or feel such kind touches." She pushed off the wall and circled Ophelia. "Why do people like you so much?"

"I don't know." She watched Victoria as she paced. Something felt off about her, an energy that felt sharp and insidious. "What's wrong?"

"You're average, and yet people are drawn to you." She stopped with a click of her boots. Her eyes drifted up and down Ophelia's form.

"I don't know what this is, but I have other things to do."

She turned to leave and Victoria's arm lashed out. She grabbed her by the throat and slammed her against the wall.

"Does she love you!?" she screamed. "Did you make her love you!?"

Ophelia grabbed at Victoria's hand. Even if she knew how to answer, she couldn't. The magician was lean, but it didn't take much force to press her palm into Ophelia's neck.

A large hand grabbed Victoria's arm and tossed her aside. Ophelia grabbed her chest and took in deep breaths. Rig planted himself between the pair, thrusting a finger toward Victoria.

"What the hell are you doing?" he said.

Victoria's hair fell in front of her face, obscuring the snarling expression beneath. Her chest pumped like a bellows as she looked between Ophelia and Rig.

She grabbed the sides of her head and screamed, "Why did he leave!?"

That was unexpected. Rig and Ophelia shared a confused look, and Rig lowered his hand. "Edwin?"

"He was supposed to help! He was supposed to stop—" Her eyes went wide and her expression softened. She looked ready to burst into tears. "Why would he leave when he was supposed to help me?"

Ophelia rubbed at the sore spots on her neck. Even though a moment earlier Victoria had been ready to choke the life out of her, she couldn't help but pity her. Something was clearly wrong, something more than they understood.

"I'm sorry," Victoria said, gazing past Rig into Ophelia's eyes. "I'm so sorry."

Before she could respond, someone screamed outside. Ophelia leapt into action, darting back out through the door. Rig stayed behind, keeping an eye on Victoria.

Someone was coming up the driveway. Through the darkness and the fog, it was hard to tell who. As they crossed into the lights from Briardown, Ophelia saw one of the people who had left with Stephen — but he was covered in blood. He saw Ophelia and gurgled something unintelligible before collapsing in a heap. She rushed over, but he was already dead before she could reach him.

The people who had been packing moments earlier crowded around, murmuring worried questions to each other. Ophelia looked up and two more forms faded in from the fog. One was short with a wide-brimmed hat, the other tall, whose eyes glowed blue in the dark. Edwin dragged a body behind him.

"What happened?" Ophelia asked.

Edwin dropped the body at her feet. It was Stephen Dixon. He had a large puncture wound in his chest where his heart should've been. Ophelia recoiled and covered her mouth.

"The Mire's out there," Edwin said, continuing past. It was only then she saw the blood and black ichor staining his coat.

"They're waiting at the edge of the village," Mattie said, her voice shaking along with her hands. "I didn't hear the voice. I don't know why. I didn't even know they were there until they were too close for us to flee."

More people came stumbling up the driveway, some wounded but every last one exhausted. Ophelia tried to count, but it was far less than had left with Stephen Dixon.

"Are they coming?" Ophelia asked, watching the grim faces as they lumbered past.

"Not yet," Edwin said. He stopped just before the porch and caught his breath. "They're gathering their forces still. But there's no way out."

The murmurs through the crowd became hurried and scared. Some people rushed over to help the injured while the rest took their bags out of the carts. Ophelia glanced down at Stephen's body. His eyes were closed, but there was no peace on his face.

"He had a wife and a son," Ophelia said. "Did they…?"

Mattie shook her head.

"Why did you bring him back?" She turned to Edwin.

"So everyone can see why we're the ones who have to fight," he said, entering Briardown.

They did see. And fight they must.

Come morning, Dusty road into town warning the Mire was on the move. Few slept that night knowing the Mire was so close, and they had only an hour or two to prepare. Ophelia took a horse through Dawnhallow proper, ensuring that all the villagers had piled into the Briardown ballroom to hide.

Seeing the village emptied was an uncomfortable sight. The buildings were ghosts in the pre-morning glow. A snowstorm brewed on the horizon and vastly reduced her vision. Ophelia had done so much to protect the people so they wouldn't lose their way of life. She prayed this was the last time she would see Dawnhallow so barren. Satisfied that everyone was safe, Ophelia turned her horse around and rode back to Briardown.

She arrived at the front porch as Rig began his explanation of the plan to the villagers. He was in full sawbones gear, with his branderbuss hanging off his hip and riotsaw leaning on the post next to him. Ophelia hopped off her horse next to Dayla and Adelaide. Dayla nodded at her while Adelaide focused on her notebook. Hush and Mattie waited within the crowd for the talk to begin. Meanwhile, Edwin and Victoria separated themselves from the group, Edwin under a tree while Victoria lounged on the porch swing. They hadn't talked about their encounter from the night before — and there didn't seem to be a time to.

"Is everyone listening?" Rig asked, his voice carrying with power across the few dozen fighters. It seemed so small now, collected on the front lawn of Briardown about to face down a flood. "Here's the plan. Me, Edwin, Victoria, and Adelaide are our front lines of defence. We're skilled sawbones and other such Mire-killers, so don't be worried about how many of them there are. Hush will be out there as well, setting off the explosives and assisting the front line. Now, as for what most of you will be doing."

A hushed murmur went through the crowd.

"Quiet!" Rig paced the porch. He pointed at the manor. "You will be here with Dayla. While the front line is fighting, you will be giving us support. So not shoot us. We have lavender candles set up on the south and east side of the manor. This will dissuade the Mire from approaching on that side, so we can focus on the west and the north. The candles are not a hundred percent. That's why we have Mattie, she can tell us if they come through that side. You can sense their position, right?"

"Well." Mattie scratched her bandages. "Only when they're close. Last time they—"

"When they're close, she will sense them, that's all that matters. Mattie will also be inside to heal any injured we may receive. If you're hurt, go to her, don't ask why. We keep fighting until every Mire is dead. They don't retreat, so we tear them apart."

He looked over the grim faces of the crowd. His eyes went from person to person and Ophelia could see them straight themselves as he passed them by.

Dayla slapped Ophelia on the shoulder and called out to the crowd, "Ophelia. Let's hear a few words."

The crowd turned to her. Ophelia's eyes widened. Dayla smiled at her and stepped to the side.

She leaned toward Dayla and whispered, "I don't know what to say."

"I would suggest something inspiring," Dayla whispered back with a wink.

There was no getting around it. Ophelia clenched her fists and walked to the porch with her head held high. Rig took his riotsaw on his shoulder and gave her the stage.

Ophelia turned to the expectant crowd. While they seemed small standing at the back, as she stood before them, she could see the army that they had become. Familiar faces of men and women now hardened and ready to fight. But there was still a tremble in the crowd — an old fear that Ophelia recognized. It was the same fear that was in her. What could Ophelia say to inspire them, when she was so scared herself?

"Everyone said we should leave," was the first thing she could think of. "They said it would be easier. Maybe it would have been. Guess it's too late now. But we knew the Mire was coming, even when no one else believed us, we knew. And if not for us, for someone else. We're going to fight today, because it's hard, because it's the right thing to do, and because we are strong enough. We have been here all along, and at the end, even if people don't know what we do here, we will still remain!"

No one said a word, but the mood rose, pushing through the dreary atmosphere. Even the snow flurries couldn't bring them down. Ophelia pulled at her scarf, feeling energy course through her veins.

"We're fighting against the unknown. We're fighting against monsters that think they can take without resistance. It is terrifying, I know. We all know how scary it is and yet we are standing here. That's courage. We can fall to fear, fall to those who will treat us like we are fodder, or we can allow that courage to define who we are!"

The crowd cheered, and the storm began.

Rig stood at the edge of Briardown's grounds, a few metres into the forest. He had his hat pulled down low on his head and his mask over his face. His riotsaw rested on his shoulder. Flecks of snow landed on the dual chains and stuck to the metal. He tightened his gloved hand on his branderbuss, feeling the trigger under his finger.

The snowstorm got stronger, pulling at his coat and surrounding him in dangerous white-out conditions. He could see Briardown behind him, meaning he still had cover from the villagers and Dayla on the porch and inside. He needed to be careful, if he went into the forest too deep, he would become lost in the white. Edwin waited just in viewing range, balancing on a snow-covered tree root. He pushed on his chest and spun his arm.

"Are you okay?" Rig called out.

"My arms are getting cold." Edwin patted his coat. "It's hurting the skin near my shoulders."

"Then let's do this fast."

Edwin grinned. "I'm always fast. Speak for yourself."

Rig scoffed. A twig snapped and he turned his attention to the forest. Within the white void was movement; ambling humanoid figures that faded in and out of sight among the whirling powder. Rig tensed his fingers around the riotsaw's grip. He resisted the urge to run in, chains roaring. A year had tempered him. Besides, there was the plan.

The Mire — inkbloods and sludges — grew from the fog. The inkbloods wielded farming implements such as hoes, spades, and axes. Some of their bodies were already falling apart. There were gaps in their skin and bones where the profane ooze beneath could be seen. Steam flowed out from these wounds like a chimney stack and the sludges that came up behind them were cloaked in it.

"They run hot," Edwin said.

"I remember." He shook a layer of snow off his hat. "How're the others?"

Edwin peered to his right, where Rig couldn't see. "The magician looks ready. If not a little chilly."

"Good. It looks like we're about to begin."

The Mire oriented on Rig. With each step, their speed increased. Rig kept his eye on the distance and counted down. Three... Two...

The ground erupted into a deafening blast of dirt, snow, and muck. Rig averted his eyes and let the chunks of earth and Mire bounce off his head and shoulders. Further explosions tore apart the forest and the creatures within. The Mire didn't have the cognizance to run in fear, though they did attempt to walk around the blown-out patches of land, only to find more explosives hidden there.

"Wow." Hush leaned out of the treehouse-styled observation platform hidden in the trees above Rig. "Muckies blow-up radiant."

"Keep going," Rig said.

Hush ducked out of view and the explosions continued. Rig backed away, retreating closer to Briardown. The four of them acted as good lures, causing the Mire to bunch up, now Hush's explosives would scatter them again and the front line could scrap in the chaos that remained. Dayla and her gunners would cover them from behind and clean up the edges. All according to plan.

Rig arrived at the second location, still calmly walking through the earthen rain cast down from above. Hush had done his work well.

"Stop, Hush!" Edwin called over the bombastic symphony. "Just the exteriors."

The explosions halted. Through the billowing smoke and the settling dust, more of the Mire moved in. A lightning bolt shot over Rig's head, turning snowflakes into puffs of steam. It struck a sludge crawling over the ruts in the ground, causing it to convulse and liquify. Time to begin the fight.

Rig charged forth, casting off the snow and dirt that had accumulated on him. He blasted a chunk out of an inkblood with his branderbuss. The wound poured out steam as it met the cold air. Rig kept moving. The gunners kept their shots away from their allies, except for Dayla, who would send bolts right past the front line. Rig, however, wanted to be in the middle of it. Right where he was comfortable.

He planted one foot on a mound of dirt and leapt over a trench, firing down on a sludge as he fell. He landed in a clump of snow then swung back one-handed, tearing another sludge apart with his sword. The momentum threw him off balance. He fired at an inkblood as his sword dug into the ground.

He took off the inkblood's arm, but it kept moving. As Rig primed for another shot, he pushed off the pommel of his embedded riotsaw and kicked the inkblood in the chest. The inkblood stumbled back — slime tumbling out of his charred, missing arm — and Rig blew a hole in his chest.

"Hey, Edwin!" Rig shouted. "At a time like this, I miss Hitomi's wave cannon!"

Edwin put his fist through a sludge's stomach with a burst of electricity. He let the sludge fall apart as he got a distant look in his eyes. "Yeah…I miss her too."

An explosion lit off, motivating the Mire to stay on the west side of Briardown. Inkbloods and sludges surrounded Rig, letting out puffs of vapour. He hung his branderbuss on his hip. Fighting the Mire was different from fighting in a bar, and he couldn't pretend it didn't feel good to be back in the fray. In the end, he was a sawbones. Even if he hated the Church for how it treated people like him; it was who he was.

He grabbed his riotsaw by the backbar and yanked it out of the ground. Shaking the clumps of dirt off the tip, Rig glared at the creatures surrounding him. Two hands on the hilt before sliding the trigger up. The ignitor hit the plate, setting off the Ink. The chains roared to life, and Rig got chopping.

Victoria felt great. She swayed her arms with grace, dancing like a winter ballerina. The flying moons followed her motions, tearing apart the Mire. She had Edwin to her left and Adelaide to her right, meaning she didn't have to worry about keeping anything from sneaking around. She could just attack.

A puff of fire in the fog told Victoria where Adelaide fought. She tried to keep her off her mind, but it was all she could think about. The words Adelaide had said were still fresh. Victoria decided that she was wrong. There was nothing wrong with Victoria, Adelaide has simply proven herself to be like everyone else. But, then why did it still bother her so much?

A sludge came stumbling up through the mist. Victoria collected her moons into two buzzsaws of six each, then flung them into the sludge's chest. They tore pieces of muck out as they burrowed through the torso and out the other side. The sludge's form sloughed to the ground in a pile of slime and bone. Victoria brought back her moons in a wide arc, cutting two inkblood's heads off as they returned. One dropped, while the other kept moving despite the decapitation. Victoria shredded him apart.

There always seemed to be more monsters whenever Victoria turned around. A firebolt from Briardown obliterated a sludge a few feet away and she pushed on. Most of the sludges stayed back, letting the inkbloods take the lead. Victoria wasn't going to have any of that. She sent a buzzsaw skyward then dropped it down through the canopy like a hammer on a sludge further back.

This sludge tried to get out of the way, only for the buzzsaw to sever its arm. The impact was so hard that Victoria lost her control and the buzzsaw broke into its six moons as it hit the ground. The sludge fixed its eyeless gaze upon Victoria, then lifted its other arm and pointed at her. A bone shot out of its body.

Victoria leapt aside, but the bone sliced a hole in her shirt, nearly cutting open her stomach. She fell onto her back, mind racing with shock. She reached out for the moons near the sludge's feet and collected them back into the buzzsaw. The sludge turned its arm to her again. Victoria wrenched her arm up, sending the buzzsaw screaming through the sludge, diagonally bisecting its body and killing it for good. The arm fell to the ground, a bone protruding from the muck. Victoria pulled her buzzsaw back to her.

Victoria tilted her head back, seeing Edwin had stopped and stared at the sludge that fired the bone. "They can do that?" Victoria asked.

"Apparently so." Edwin's gaze drifted to where a line of sludges had appeared. "Oh, no."

The sludges each lifted one arm. Accompanied by wet, squishing sounds, bone spears launched out of their bodies, aimed at Briardown. The villagers on the porch scrambled out of the way, but the barrage was too great and bone spears pierced the slower ones.

"They're trying to take out the gunners!" Edwin shouted.

"That certainly looks like intelligence!" Victoria scrambled to her feet. An explosion went off past Adelaide's position, but they had already used up the ones where the sludges fired from.

The sludge's bodies convulsed. Something solid worked through their forms and up to their arms. More bones, no doubt. Return fire from Briardown killed some of the shooters, but there were always more sludges.

"Victoria!" Edwin shouted. "We need to take out those things before they kill our support!"

He didn't need to say that twice. Victoria pushed her boots into the snow and sprinted for the firing line. Her moons flew about like darting insects, turning the space around her into a performance of steel and slime. She formed the buzzsaws and slammed one into one sludge, then swung her arm back and slammed the other into another — the blades spinning the entire time. With a mental push, she shoved the blades through their bodies. The vibrations did the rest.

Most of the sludges paid no attention to the attack. They continued firing on Briardown, turning the front façade into a pincushion. Edwin worked on his side clearing out the sludges, moving in bursts of electricity. His metal arms proved to be effective means of dispatching the Mire. He caught a sludge by the head and crushed it in a ferocious spark of energy before moving on.

An inkblood missing part of her stomach came in with wild axe swings. Was she protecting the sludges firing on Briardown? Victoria reared back, spinning up her moons. A burst of fire engulfed the inkblood, who stumbled back, unable to scream, but batting at the fire with crazed fervour. She bashed herself with the axe, removing more of the human shell as she worked to remove the inferno.

Adelaide stepped up, sending out flames from her gauntlet and driving the inkblood back. "Don't bother with these ones! You must stop the sludges!"

Victoria turned red. "That's what I was doing!"

The charred inkblood lunged toward Adelaide, who snapped out her pulserod and cracked the inkblood across the jaw. Victoria had never seen her use it while it was turned on. The electrical power poured through the inkblood and the slime inside melted apart like ice cream on a summer day. Adelaide blew her hair out of her face and turned to Victoria. Her hot breath came out in visible puffs over her scarf. That subdued cleric demeanour was gone, replaced by a warrior's stance. Her pale green eyes in the foggy morning made Victoria's knees weak.

"Stop staring at me, Victoria." She shrank away slightly, her usual character breaking through for a moment. "We're not done here yet."

Victoria set her jaw and turned her slack, almost goofy, expression into a grimace. She hated herself for thinking that way about Adelaide. There was nothing there. Adelaide made her opinion known; it wasn't worth Victoria's time. Victoria turned away in a huff and reengaged the enemy with renewed vigour. It turned out frustration could be a fine motivator.

A sludge turned its shooting arm toward Victoria. She severed it with a pass of her buzzsaw. The convulsions in the sludge moved to its remaining arm and it went to fire again. Victoria swung her arm back, and the buzzsaw amputated that one as well. The fits reached the sludge's chest. Victoria bent awkwardly as a bone launched out of the sludge's torso, just past her head. Its arm stumps pulsed and grew into half-formed limbs, but Victoria was having none of it. She turned her moons into a large bandsaw and reduced the creature into a paste.

Her brain ached from the exertion. She had to take a moment to focus her eyes. They had to be making a dent in the Mire, but it didn't feel that way with the constant flood.

Come on, she thought. *I'm the greatest magician in Wrotdam. Don't give up. This is nothing.*

In the depths of the fog, something new moved. Something that dashed away that confidence. Something huge.

The explosions had done their part, but Hush had used them all up. The simple wooden box he sat in, built high up in the trees, was full of wires. Using an electrically-refined Ink blasting machine he sent a current down each line, but now all he could do was fire out of the windows with his ignition thrower. The inkbloods and sludges fighting below made for easy targets, but there seemed to be no end to them.

A tree fell in the foggy distance. Something was coming closer. Hush stopped firing and his jaw went slack. A massive creature appeared through the white mist. It was the size of a house and undulated with rotten slime waves. Despite looking like the sludges, it didn't hold a humanoid shape. It was a mound of sickening ooze that moved on its own and tore down any trees that stood in its way. A group of inkbloods escorted it to the battlefield.

The moving mound stopped a good distance away from Briardown. Some of the gunners took their shots. Firebolts struck its pudgy exterior and charred chunks of muck crumbled off. Hush raised his own rifle. A ripple moved along the mound's form, like a hundred snakes underneath its gelatinous exterior. Little white spikes appeared all along its body. Hush inhaled sharply and took cover.

A salvo of bone projectiles launched into the sky. A hundred of them pierced trees and earth. They pounded Hush's hiding place like a drum, sticking straight through the wall in a field of white spears. Only when it was quiet did Hush scramble back to the window. A couple dozen spikes pierced Briardown. The villagers dragged their injured through the porch door, but many were already dead, held up by the bone spears like pinned butterflies. Some of the projectiles were encased in black ooze that dripped onto the porch, forming sludges at the door.

"They're at the castle!" Hush shouted at Edwin. "They got through!"

Edwin obliterated a sludge with a back fist and turned. The sludges threw their bodies against the manor's doors and boarded up windows. The first-floor gunners stuck their rifles through the slots in the window barriers and tried to shoot them down, but being beneath the porch awning, the sludges were protected from the second floor.

"Victoria, Adelaide!" Edwin cried. "Fall back! Protect the people!"

We need to rust out that big one, Hush thought. He looked at his ignition thrower. *This isn't going to do the job.*

The wood behind Hush creaked. He spun around to see a black mass drip from one of the bone spikes sticking through the hideout's ceiling. It sheered off strips as it fell and bounded forth with a bone claw extended. Hush lifted his ignition launcher to block, but the sludge easily snapped it in half. He tossed the pieces aside.

The sludge stomped on the trapdoor. Hush glanced over his shoulder, out the window. It was a long way down. When he looked back, the sludge slashed at him. He recoiled, and the claw sliced the strap holding his branderbuss. It tumbled out the window. His heart leapt into his throat, and he whipped around to grab it, only to follow it out. He spun as he fell, seeing the world whip past him for a moment, then landed hard in the snow.

His chest and stomach pulsed with pain. With each of his breaths, he blew snow into the air. He eased his head up, getting the world into focus when he noticed a little red flag, one of the markers he used for the explosive placements. The dirt had been pushed aside in the fight and a bundle of cannibal poppers poked their tips out. The igniting wire had been cut.

The sludge landed before Hush's face with a wet squish. It was so close he could smell the sickening aroma of rot, like bad eggs mixed with decaying meat. The sludge reconstituted itself into a humanoid shape and reared back, then exploded into flames. Rig stood behind it, smoke curling out of his branderbuss.

"Get up," he said.

And inkblood leapt in from behind him, knocking the gun away. He swung back with his riotsaw, but another one jumped on the blade. It tore out from his grip and sunk into the snow. More inkbloods leapt on top of him, and even as he fought back, they pushed him down.

Hush's heart pounded against his ribcage. *Not again*, he thought. *Not this time. I'm not a coward this time.* He spotted his branderbuss a few metres away, stuck handle up in a snowdrift. His ribs wracked with pain, he urged himself to move, crawling along the ground to get his weapon. Rig fell to one knee, shouting with rage the inkbloods beat against him. One with an axe came lumbering up.

Hush dug in his pocket as he crawled. He pulled out the inkwell Rig gave him a few days earlier. He had been afraid to put it in the branderbuss, changing it from the form it was when he first found it. It was a sign that he was in the real world. Mattie was right, though; he needed to live this life like it was real.

The inkblood raised his axe. Rig seethed, spit flying from his teeth with every breath. Hush grabbed the branderbuss, slammed in the inkwell, then staggered to his feet. *Not again.* He pulled the trigger.

The branderbuss barked fire, and the inkblood's torso disappeared amid flames and smoke. The legs and waist stayed standing for a moment, then collapsed. He turned and fired again, taking one of the inkbloods off Rig's back.

"Get up," he said, priming for the next shot.

The giant roared and threw the rest aside, cracking their skulls with foot stomps. He grabbed his branderbuss and started firing. Hush let out a sigh of relief, but reminded himself he wasn't done.

Sludges overloaded with bones approached the moving mound and let themselves be absorbed. The inkbloods kept watch. It wouldn't be long before it fired again. Hush snatched the cannibal poppers, despite the protests from a most likely broken rib, and ran for the mound.

"What are you doing?" Rig shouted as Hush slipped by at full speed.

"I have a plan!" he called back.

The inkblood guard around the moving mound spotted Hush and moved to intercept. That was fine, Hush didn't have to get close. He fired on the closest inkblood, then hurled the cannibal popper bundle. It sunk into the mound near the top.

Something pulled Hush back. Rig held him by the collar and pushed him into a run.

"We still have to blow it," Hush said.

"I know, and I promise you she does too." Rig broke into a sprint. "We just have to make some distance."

Hush looked back. The inkbloods stacked into some sort of disorganized human pyramid to reach the cannibal poppers. A bolt of lightning streaked across the sky and struck the explosives.

A shockwave shredded the leaves off the trees. The moving mound vaporized. Pieces of the inkbloods flew as far as Briardown and unfired bones whipped through the air, piercing trees and the Mire unfortunate enough to be in its way. The concussive force sent Rig and Hush stumbling forward, falling face down into the snow.

Edwin came rushing in to help them to their feet. "Does this seem easy to you?" he asked.

"Are you twisty?" Hush brushed the dirt and snow off himself.

"Yes." Rig brushed the snow off his coat.

"What?"

"We have to fall back to the manor." Edwin took off toward Briardown.

Hush couldn't believe what he was hearing. They were under a constant assault, with bone projectiles and a massive Mire creature. There was no way this could be easy.

CHAPTER 21

M attie was doing her best to keep up with the injured. Fortunately, she had thought ahead and collected jars of her healing slime. Unfortunately, she had nearly run out of it. Then it was going to get awkward.

The makeshift infirmary was in one of the bedrooms on the second floor. With Mattie, though, there wasn't much treating that needed to be done. The villagers had come in, pierced by strange bone spikes, but left fully healed. Some of them were still laying about the room, resting from either repeated healings or a particularly grievous injury. Those who were dead, though, could not be saved, no matter how much Mattie wished they could be.

Mattie took a couple jars and went out in search of the injured. She hated sitting in the infirmary and waiting. She could hear battle, but beneath it, the voice had returned.

"Bring them. Kill them," it said. "Bring them. Kill them."

She felt the Mire all around her. They had reached the building and were pounding against the door. The candles seemed to still be keeping the Mire from sneaking around the eastern side, but it was hard to tell now that it was at the gate.

Mattie arrived at the bottom of the stairs when a particularly terrible feeling overcame her. The voice said something different.

"Dig. Dig. Dig. Break."

A scream came from the ballroom. That was where the villagers were holed up. Mattie dropped the jars and rushed to investigate. She threw open the ballroom doors and found it in utter panic. People pushed against the walls, trying to get away from the holes that now littered the dance floor. Sludges and inkbloods were crawling out like insects.

One man jumped around the holes as his family screamed at him to hurry up. An inkblood lunged out and grabbed him with both hands around his ankles.

Mattie jumped for him, but the inkblood pulled him into the darkness below. Mattie grabbed the edge and stared down. A sludge flowed along the walls until it was a metre away from Mattie and lashed out. Mattie scrambled out of the way as the sludge took on its full height and menaced over her.

Mattie was frozen. She had to do something or else everyone would be taken. Her eyes darted to the villagers cowered about the room. Screw them if they judged her or hated her. She shouldn't protect someone because they liked her, she should do it because they deserve it. Mattie pulled down part of her bandage and unleashed the worms from her gut.

They struck the floor and shot for the sludge's foot, burrowing into the slime. They dipped in and out like spawning salmon. With each dive, they multiplied until there were thousands. The sludge shook its leg, but the worms were inside it. The connection at the hip thinned. The sludge was going to remove the leg to save the body, but the worms had evolved since Mattie first got them. They bridged the gap and pulled the leg back together.

The crowd stepped back as the sludge began to flail. It fell to its knees as the worms overtook it. One of its arms spiralled around, then stretched back and grabbed an inkblood that was dragging another person. It tore the inkblood away from the man by the head, swept him up in an arc, then slammed him hard enough into the floor to splinter the wood.

Another disembodied voice joined the first. It was Mattie's, and it said, "Save them."

The Mire took notice of this aberration. Mattie backed away, making sure the crowd gave space. The worm-sludge attacked inkbloods like each of its limbs had a mind of its own, spinning and grabbing in bizarre or impossible ways.

Another sludge came up from a hole, only to meet the worm-sludge mid-blow. It took the hit on the shoulder and the worms began to transfer. The sludge pawed and tore at its own with its bone claw, but that only succeeded in spreading the worms more. It trembled, then put both hands into its chest and ripped itself apart. The muck sloughed into a puddle. Whatever controlled it told it to die rather than be taken. The worms played in the remains but could not animate them.

Mattie expected the voice in her head to be angry, or at least disappointed. But she got nothing. Something felt wrong about the whole situation, but she couldn't put her finger on what.

The worm-sludge grabbed the last inkblood and hurled her back into the hole she crawled out of. Then it stopped, the wriggling of worms being the only motion left. The crowd of villagers looked on in awe at the creature before their gaze shifted to Mattie. Her instincts screamed to run or fade into the background. But she couldn't do that now. Everyone was looking.

Amid the rumblings came a voice. "Thank you."

Mattie looked up.

It was an old man with one eye covered by a cotton patch. He looked at Mattie with a smile that cut right to her soul. The rest of the villagers nodded and smiled as well. They were small motions, but amid the grieving of those they lost, they meant more than anything.

"Those people aren't gone yet," Mattie announced to the crowd. She approached a hole and looked within.

It went somewhere. That was for sure. The worm-sludge took the lead and began the descent. Mattie glanced back at the hopeful faces of the villagers.

"There are some jars of the healing ointment in the infirmary," she said. "But I won't be long."

Mattie turned to the tunnel. It went somewhere. She just had to find out where.

Something weird was going on at the stables. Bone spikes fired from the moving mounds covered the structure, even more so than the manor. Victoria was following through with the retreat when she swore there was some movement between the cracks in the wall. Her curiosity pushed her to investigate, but her job was to protect the manor.

Then again, she could see Edwin, Rig, and Hush coming in from the forest. They could help Adelaide clear out the Mire on Briardown's front porch. Victoria pulled her moons out of an inkblood's corpse and twirled them into her pouch. She crept away from the manor until she was sure no one was looking, then turned on her heel and walked briskly to the stables.

Something blocked the light on the other side of the door. *There's definitely something inside,* she thought. A grin spread across her face as she swept her hand over her pouch. The moons floated out, little ducklings following her fingers. Everything Victoria had read or heard about the Mire made it seem stupid, but there was coordination in this attack. The moons orbited her right arm while she reached for the stable door with her left. She shouldn't be surprised if the Mire was trying something new.

She threw the door open. The light entered the stable through the cracks in the walls and an open gate in the attic. Snow billowed across the floor in wisps, interspersed by hay that crunched as Victoria entered. A lift hung in the attic, holding a couple bales of hay. There were six horse stalls on each wall and somewhere in there something scratched incessantly.

Victoria took slow steps, trying to reduce the sound of crushing snow and hay. She peered into each stall, but they were empty. Her moons spun around her arm, keeping their momentum up. Her body shook with something between excitement and terror. The scratching got louder. Only it wasn't scratching.

Someone was dragging something, centimetre by centimetre. She put a hand against the pole and peered into the next stall.

A hole had been dug through the dirt floor, leaving a pile of earth next to it. An inkblood came out of the hole, dragging an unconscious man with him. The man's head was wrapped in some black and grey substance, covering his face and blocking his eyes and mouth. The inkblood stopped when he saw Victoria. He took a second to register the intruder, then dropped his captive and lunged for her.

Victoria flicked her arm, sending her twelve moons into the inkblood, pushing him onto the dirt pile. Steam curled from the wounds, but he wasn't dead. Victoria reached her aching mind out to the moons, visualized revolving wheels, then clenched her fists. The moons spun in place, shredding the inkblood and stopping his movement.

Victoria pulled her moons back and fell to her knees. She was overextending herself. Even thoughts made her brain hurt. She was too stubborn to give up, though, so she loosened her scarf to get some air and ignored the pain.

The captive had yet to move. Victoria rested her moons on the ground and went to check on him. There didn't seem to be a way to breathe through the substance on his face, yet his chest rose and fell in normal rhythm. Victoria sank her fingers into it and pulled. It had the consistency of taffy and she was able to tear off a chunk that revealed the man's mouth.

A shuffling from the back of the stable took Victoria's attention. She collected her moons to hover near her shoulder and stood. Her headache instantly came back as a dozen inkbloods stared at her, stumbling out from the other stalls. She gulped. She should have known there was never just one.

The inkbloods staggered into the centre aisle. Victoria kept pace. They held their axes and sickles like she held her moons, ready to draw at high noon.

I'm willing to admit I should have brought some support, she thought. *Too late now.*

The first inkblood swung in with a sickle. Victoria formed her twin buzzsaws and sent one through the inkblood's arm and the other through his head. She didn't take the time to check if that killed him, she needed to push on. With a dancer's grace, she moved through the steps of her deadly waltz. The buzzsaws twirled like her partner, with her leading. She was racing the clock to when her mind truly gave out. More than a few times it was pure luck that saved her from getting beheaded.

She whipped her arm forward and drove a buzzsaw through three inkbloods, then splintered it and pulled back, grating them on the return. Out of the corner of her eye, she spotted an axe being dropped on her head. She dipped low like giving a bow, then with an upswing hammered six moons up into the inkblood's arm. They tried to push down, but Victoria pushed harder. Six shark fin blades swam through the inkblood's body, spiralling to his chest, then diving through and out the other side.

As Victoria moved, she was able to see the other stalls. More people with their heads covered in muck. *Eight, no, ten. They were going to put them in that grinder.*

A particularly large inkblood came in with a sledgehammer. Victoria cross-stepped back. The heavy steel head sent wind across her face. The sledgehammer cracked one of the stall walls. Victoria's steps were getting sloppy. The inkbloods closed the distance. They figured out she was better when she had space to wind up. Something gave the Mire tactical suggestions.

Victoria slapped herself, forcing her mind to focus. *Shut up!* she screamed in her head. *Stop complaining and do it!*

She spread her arms apart, letting the flying moons float in space. The sledgehammer inkblood moved in to take advantage, joined by the half-dozen others.

Victoria cracked a smile. "You don't know who I am."

She swung her arms across each other. The moons turned into a bladed tornado. Victoria kept her eyes shut, focusing on the projectiles swirling around her like little dots in her brain. It was all or nothing. She killed them, or they killed her. It was invigorating.

Nothing hit her. She slowed down the moons and relaxed. She eased her eyes open. The inkbloods were in pieces. Deep gouges littered the stall's pillars and a splattering of muck coated the floor. Victoria chuckled, then broke into uproarious laughter.

"I wish any of you could have seen that!" she cried to the captives.

She turned in a slow circle like a boxer winning a match. As she came to face the door she had entered through, her smile dropped. A tall, slender creature stood at the door. Its body was made of bones with a reservoir of slime in its ribcage. Its head was a cow's skull with one broken horn that stared down at Victoria with empty eye sockets. Bullhead stepped forward.

Victoria nearly crumpled. She remembered the gnashing teeth of the grinder. How Bullhead moved to feed her into it. Memories of fear and pain collapsed upon her. Her knees trembled. Her eyes went wide. Her fingers shook.

Bullhead got closer and closer, getting larger with each step until it was a mountain over Victoria. It survived the explosion. If anything, it looked even stronger. It reached for Victoria with a wicked bone claw hand. Fear turned to rage, and Victoria cried out. She sent her moons streaming toward Bullhead. It batted them away like errant flies, but she kept up the pressure. She swung over and over, sending ineffectual passes along Bullhead's arms.

Victoria lifted her arm, and all feeling left her body. The moons tumbled to the ground and she barely stayed standing. Her stance was awkwardly wide and her spine was a loose stack of plates. Blood flowed out of her nose at an alarming rate, adding a splash of red to the dirty snow below her. Bullhead let out a clicking sound and continued its slow, deliberate gait toward her.

"Victoria!" someone shouted. The voice was familiar, but the haze over her mind disguised it.

A sludge appeared next to her and Bullhead. She wanted to run, but her body wouldn't respond. The sludge didn't move to attack her though. Little white worms crawled through its body. Something about them was familiar.

"Mattie," Victoria wheezed.

The small, bandaged woman stood next to the hole, wide-eyed. Her gaze flicked between Victoria and Bullhead. Which sight scared her the most? The monster? Or the state she was in? "Are you okay?" Mattie asked.

'Am I okay?' Disappointing, Victoria thought, then said, "What are you doing here?"

"People were taken from the ballroom." She pointed down. "Is this one of them?"

"There's more at the back."

Bullhead clicked some more then took a step forward. The worm-sludge leapt forth to defend. Bullhead stuck its claw into the worm-sludge and with a sharp tug, pulled out a piece of it. It collapsed along with the worms inside it.

"It was a good attempt," Victoria said. Gnashers were deadly. She should run. She was already mentally exhausted and if she wasn't careful she could damage herself permanently. It wasn't her being selfish. It was her being practical. Even Adelaide would run.

Except she wouldn't. Victoria knew that. She was a better person. Victoria shouldn't even try to compare herself to Adelaide. Adelaide was a good person.

But Victoria was the greatest magician in Wrotdam.

She reached her mind out to the twelve drops of Ink and rose the moons from the ground. She was going to do something stupid, and she despised stupidity. "Get those people out of here," she said, staring down the patient monster. "Wake them up if you can."

"Wait!" Mattie grabbed Victoria's coat. "Let me heal you at least."

"Unless you can get your slime into my brain, it won't work. Just do this. I'll cover you."

Bullhead came in with both claws. Victoria sent her moons to block the swing. They weren't great shields, but they held it back at the expense of her mind. Mattie let out a breath, then ran to help the captives.

Bullhead pushed his arms apart, sending the moons in all directions. They arced past support pillars and through the attic then flew back to attack again. Victoria's mental exhaustion made her movements sluggish; the dance steps weren't coming as easy.

"Victoria!" Mattie shouted. "If you take that gunk off their faces they wake up!"

"Then do it!" Victoria aimed for the slime in Bullhead's chest, but the gnasher was too fast.

Bullhead snatched a moon as it passed by and tossed it at Victoria. She stopped it in front of her face, collected the other eleven, then drove them all as a large rocket into Bullhead's chest.

The bones in Bullhead's rib cage flexed and came together like a shield, protecting his squishy innards. The impact was still enough to send him reeling back — right beneath the lift. Victoria sent her moons skyward and cut the rope, dropping the heavy bales and crushing Bullhead with a bone-snapping crack.

Victoria collected her moons around her head. Her stomach seized, and she bent over to release that morning's breakfast.

"I'm almost done!" Mattie helped a woozy woman to her feet, directing her out the back door.

Victoria gave a weak thumbs-up. The bales exploded apart and Bullhead streaked across the stable. It grabbed Victoria by the throat and lifted her into the air as her moons fell to the ground. A new crack had appeared in its skull and some black fluid leaked out.

Victoria beat against its arm, trying desperately to get any air into her lungs. It was no use. She reached her hands to the floor, where her moons were, and sent them into Bullhead's arm. The twelve blades stuck into the bone and she twisted. The room grew dark, but with one last push, the arm shattered. She fell, surrounded by her moons and clutching her throat.

Bullhead looked at its arm in confusion. It stuck the broken bone into its chest. Victoria took in gasping breaths as the gnasher pulled its arm free of the muck — whole once again with new bones. Her heart sank.

"We're all done, Victoria!" Mattie shouted. "Come on!"

"Go! I'm right behind you!" But Victoria knew Bullhead would just take chase. She needed to kill it. Somehow.

Mattie knew this too, or at least she knew Victoria was lying. She stood at the back door with a firm expression, the snow blowing past her. "I'm going to get help. Stay alive." Then she was gone.

Victoria smiled. Help wouldn't come fast enough. Victoria needed to finish it. One last attack, then she could sleep.

Bullhead stepped forward and Victoria crawled back. It moved slow, sure of its dominance. Victoria, however, just needed him to take a few... more... steps...

There! She swung both her arms up. The flying moons hidden in the snow and hay shot out like bullets from a gun. Bullhead had been so focused on her it didn't notice her moons disappeared. They came at it from all angles and went under its ribs and sunk deep into the muck in its chest.

If Bullhead could show expression, on its face would be shock. It poked through its chest but couldn't find the moons. Victoria stumbled, nearly falling, to her feet. She felt each drop of Ink hidden within the muck and took control. She took a deep breath, then tensed her body and forced the moons to vibrate.

Bullhead panicked. It tore its ribcage away and dug into the reservoir. Victoria screamed in pain and rage, pushing harder against the moons. Bullhead's limbs moved in jerky, marionette-like patterns. It grabbed its skull with both and yanked it off. As its body failed, it threw its head toward the open attic gate.

Victoria pulled her moons out of the gnasher's body, the bone joints falling apart as the head was removed. It must be the gnasher's heart. She screamed and sent her moons toward the gate. They caught it by the horns and knocked it back into the stable. The skull bounced a few times and came to rest on a pile of hay. It rattled, but couldn't move.

Victoria picked up the sledgehammer left behind by the inkblood and approached Bullhead's skull. She looked down at it with disdain, now so much smaller than her. She raised the hammer over her head, then brought it down with a mighty roar. The skull shattered apart, releasing the black fluid inside, and Victoria crumpled.

She'd done it. She'd killed the gnasher and saved the people, despite how stupid it was. Logically, there was no way the Celestial Contraption needed only ten people. They could have been taken and everything would have been fine. Victoria laughed. It was pointless, but she did it.

"Victoria!" It was Adelaide. She came rushing to Victoria's side. The light from the attic gate ringed her head with a holy glow.

"I was foolish," Victoria said. She chuckled. "I should have run away."

"You'll be fine." She brushed the hair from her eyes. "This won't stop you."

Tears welled up in Victoria's eyes. "Thank you for caring."

Adelaide cocked her head. "Of course, I care."

"I don't understand people."

"You need to have a better opinion of them."

She cracked a smile. "I'll try."

Adelaide pulled Victoria to her feet and supported her on her shoulder. "Let's go."

Victoria sank herself into Adelaide's body. The warmth gave her strength. For that moment, she could pretend it was something different. Her moons dragged behind her as they limped to the manor.

CHAPTER 22

The ballroom became a scene of pain and misery. The people blocked the holes with tables, chairs, and anything else they could grab from that and the surrounding rooms. They stood guard with ignition launchers pointed at the ground, while the young, frail, or injured crowded the edges or stayed in other spaces. There wasn't much else to do.

Though Briardown was big, it got smaller by the minute. Some rooms held the Mire who broke through, now sealed up much like the holes in the ballroom. Other rooms held the dead, kept out of the way so as not to lower morale. That was Dayla's suggestion.

The leech leaned against the wall outside the ballroom, her boltrifle rested in the crook of her elbow. The Mire's assault slowed but did not end. She peered through the cracks in the window boards. Inkbloods and sludges stood at the edge of the treeline, somewhat disguised by the fog. Grotesque statues built to taunt those inside the manor house. Occasionally villagers took a shot, sending flames to burn a chunk out of the beasts if only to remind them there was still fight left inside.

"Someone's coming in!" a man at the front door shouted, lifting the heavy crossbar aside.

The doors swung open and Adelaide entered with Victoria slumped against her shoulder. Dayla pulled her mask off and leapt into action. Victoria's moons clattered along the ground, barely getting inside before they slammed the doors shut again.

"What happened?" Dayla asked.

"I did something stupid." Victoria pushed away from Adelaide. She picked her moons up one by one and put them in her pouch.

"She saved people," Adelaide said.

A pained wail came up from the ballroom. "Let us hope we can imitate that feat." Dayla wrapped her arm around Victoria with Adelaide on the other side. "You need to rest."

"I truly do." Victoria let herself be led into the kitchen.

The kitchen sat to the side of the ballroom, with a swinging door connecting the two. The walls were pockmarked with bullet holes from the fight to take Briardown, though they'd patched up the hole Edwin tore through the wall. That side got sealed off when the Mire broke through half an hour earlier. Rig and Edwin waited by the barricade, in the middle of a conversation that ended as the trio entered the room.

"What are you two gossiping about?" Dayla asked, helping Adelaide get Victoria leaning against the island.

"Cricket," Edwin said. "Is the Mire still waiting?"

"Yes. What do you make of that?"

"Like a dog walking on its hind legs."

"Adorable," Victoria mumbled.

Rig circled the island. Blood and mud stained his coat. "Mattie returned with villagers who were momentarily taken. It's now encasing them in some slime that incapacitates them."

"Last year it dragged them off, screaming or not," Victoria said, using both arms to keep herself standing.

"It's evolving." Adelaide pulled on her braid. "It's getting smarter."

"Or something already smart is using them," Edwin said. "I don't know which one's worse."

A series of panicked shouts came from the ballroom. Dayla narrowed her eyes. "That doesn't sound like the injured."

Edwin shook his hands and moved to investigate, sending sparks flying from his fingers. "Did they break through again?"

Dayla wasn't so sure. She left Victoria with Adelaide while she, Edwin, and Rig rushed through the swinging doors to the ballroom. It wasn't hard to find the commotion. All eyes laid on a man seizing on a blanket. Bloody gauze littered the floor around him, while Mattie and another woman knelt at his side. Hush turned as they entered, wide-eyed and sweating.

"You said to use that ointment!" the woman said. She held the man's hand to her chest. "What's happening to my husband?"

"I — I don't know." Mattie's voice sounded ragged and her hands shook as she patted along a gushing wound in the man's side. "I'm not a doctor, I just... I'm sorry." She threw up a mouthful of worms into the hole.

The woman recoiled and a few onlookers visibly paled. Rig and Edwin kept them back while Dayla joined Mattie. It looked like one of the smaller bone spikes had gotten the man on the side. His eyes were shut and his jaw clenched, spit pushing through his teeth as he sputtered and coughed. Mattie pushed her hand against the wound, covering her glove in blood and worm slime.

"It should be working," she said. "I don't know why it's not."

Something black pushed through Mattie's fingers. She yanked her hand away and for a moment, a long, stringy substance hung out of the wound before sucking back in. Dead worms flopped out of the hole.

"It's pushing back." Mattie looked at her hand. "The Mire's pushing back."

Dayla pulled on her mask and eyed the crowd. There were too many onlookers. The wife clutched harder onto her husband's hand, tears streaming down her face. Dayla snapped for Rig and Edwin. "Take him to the kitchen."

Without question, Rig and Edwin scooped the man up by his shoulder and knees and carried him off. Mattie chased after, keeping her hat low. The wife took a step, but Dayla moved in her way.

"Stay out here," she said. "It's better that way."

"Please save him," the wife said, sniffing back some snot.

"Of course." Dayla turned as Ophelia came stumbling into the ballroom. She held her left arm, wrapped up with what looked like a curtain stained with blood. Hush ran to her side, but she brushed him off. *It seems no one's getting out of this unscathed,* she thought.

She rushed after the injured man, Hush and Ophelia hurrying to stay on her heels. They bashed through the swinging doors. Rig and Edwin placed the man on the counter and gave space so Mattie could get in. Adelaide left Victoria sitting against the wall and went to check on him.

"Lock the doors," Dayla said. "We don't need someone bursting in here."

Ophelia and Hush kicked down the latches on the swinging doors while Rig sauntered casually to lock the one to the hall. There existed a hard line between those who'd seen such misery before and those who hadn't. Dayla paced the edge of the room, observing the situation from the outside.

"It's learned how to stop my healing," Mattie said, her breaths coming quick and rough like sandpaper. "Maybe... maybe I can use the worms to pull the sludge out of him."

She unloaded another burst of worms into the wound while Adelaide held the man still to the best of her ability. The worms pushed into his flesh, then globbed back out as the Mire inside pushed back. Mattie cursed and puked again. This time the slime came out tinged pink. Mattie pulled back and coughed blood onto the floor. The worms burrowed in and she slammed her hand over the wound, trying to physically keep them inside.

The man shook and screamed. Black veins peeked out of his shirt's collar. His skin grew pallid. Sludge oozed from his wound and wrapped around Mattie's hand — still she held it against his side.

The air sizzled and flashed. The man's head jerked to the side, two blackened holes appearing, one just below his ear and the other on the side of his head.

Mattie screamed and jumped away. The room turned to Dayla, who lowered her boltrifle from her shoulder.

"Dayla!" Mattie screamed, her voice hoarse.

"It's better than what he would've become," she said, coldly.

Ophelia held her hands to her mouth and fell against the door. No one made a sound. Mattie clutched her hands over her head and fell to her knees. Adelaide stared at Dayla, her hands still holding the man's legs down. Some faces of horror and some of grim understanding — not that Dayla needed any of their permissions.

"Is there anyone else still alive who was skewered by a bone spike?" Dayla asked. "Anyone else exhibiting these symptoms?"

"Yes," Ophelia said. She dropped the curtain from her arm, revealing a puncture wound just below her elbow surrounded by black veins. Dayla let out a long breath into her mask.

"Tourniquet." Adelaide left the body and brought Ophelia to the other side of the island, her eyes flashing to Dayla for an instant. "We need to stop the spread."

Rig removed the man's body from the counter, giving room for Ophelia to take his place. Adelaide grabbed a cloth and looped it around Ophelia's upper arm, then using her pulserod started twisting. She groaned as the cloth grew tighter.

"Mattie, can you get it out?" Adelaide asked.

"Maybe." Mattie coughed into her hand. Tears welled up as she expelled a nearly crimson glob in equal parts slime, worms, and blood. She pressed it into Ophelia's arm and held firm as the sludge curled around her fingers.

Victoria stumbled to her feet to watch what was happening. Hush kept his head low. Dayla tapped her finger along the side of the boltrifle trigger. It was better to die than have your insides turned to sludge, she reminded herself.

A black spike shot through Mattie's hand. She screamed and jerked away, letting the worms spill out onto the counter. "I can't do it. I can't." She clutched her wounded hand to her chest, her slime slowly closing the hole.

"Take the arm," Rig said, stepping forward.

Ophelia's eyes widened. "What? No, no, no, please don't. There has to be another way."

"Either you lose the arm, or the infection reaches your brain. Or…" He looked at Dayla.

Ophelia took a deep breath and grabbed a wooden spoon, biting down hard on the handle.

"Brave girl." Rig grabbed a big knife from the block.

Edwin caught his arm. "I have a steadier hand, and a stronger one at that."

"Is this the only way?" Victoria asked, her voice quickly lost in the momentum.

Edwin took the knife from Rig and held it out to Adelaide. "Burn this." She lowered the output of her gauntlet and engulfed the blade in cleansing flame. Despite the heat, Edwin held on and pointed at Mattie. "Stay close. We'll need more of your stuff so she doesn't bleed out. Everyone else, if you have the stomach for it, hold her down."

Slowly, people moved forward. Rig put a big hand on her shoulder. Mattie pushed against her legs that dangled off the lip of the counter, ready to leap in when Edwin called. Adelaide, finishing the sterilization, snatched a towel off the wall and laid it under Ophelia's head, then took hold of the tourniquet and turned it even tighter. Victoria stepped forward, nearly fell, and thought better of it, staying back with Hush. Dayla kept her rifle against her shoulder but lowered the barrel. This had to work. If it didn't...

Edwin pinned Ophelia's wrist down and held her arm out, already turning blue from the constriction. "You're going to pass out from the pain. That's a good thing, you don't want to be awake for this."

Tears welled up at the edges of Ophelia's eyes. She squeezed them shut and the tears rolled down the sides of her face. Solemnly, she nodded. Edwin waited, giving her arm some time to go numb, then pressed the blade into her skin, drawing the first line of blood. Ophelia screamed, muffled only by groaning of her teeth against the spoon, and banged her head against the towel.

"Wait! Wait!" Mattie's breath quickened. It took all her weight just to hold Ophelia's legs down. Hush broke from his trance and rushed in to help.

Edwin didn't wait. He kept sawing through the flesh and muscle, a deadened look on his face. Rig held fast, staring at the process with grim resignation. Time dragged on, each tick on the clock punctuated with a horrific slice and scream. The knife squeaked as it hit bone. Edwin leaned into the butchery, his arm lights pulsing beneath the layer of blood. With a push and a grunt, Ophelia's humerus snapped. Mattie yelped, and it was quiet. Just as Edwin predicted, Ophelia passed out — later than she would have liked.

What remained in the silence wasn't much better than screaming. Just the sound of a sharp blade cutting through meat then a solid thump as her arm came free.

"Mattie, now," Edwin said, stepping aside.

Mattie leapt up, tears staining her bandages along with vomit and blood. She whimpered at the sight of the stump and unloaded her worms — easier than it had been any time before. The slime coated Ophelia's upper bicep and hints of new skin risked the edge of the cut. Something black writhed within the amputated arm. Edwin grabbed it and tossed it into a large pot on the range.

"Cleric," he said, but Adelaide was already on it. She unleashed a torrent of flames into the pot, burning away the Mire hiding within Ophelia's arm.

Hush put his head close to Ophelia's chest. "She's breathing."

The hall door rattled. "What's going on in there?" Dusty asked. "Open this door!"

Rig grunted and unlocked the door. It flew open, followed by Dusty stumbling in holding a launcher. Dirt covered his face with a few superficial cuts along his left side. He gave a quick look around, clocking Adelaide burning something in the pot, Mattie covered in blood and tears, and a dead man against the far wall, but it was Ophelia that made him jump.

"Ophelia!" He rushed to her side but recoiled in horror. "What happened to her?"

"She survived," Dayla said, shutting off her boltrifle.

"Which isn't guaranteed for the rest of us." Edwin wiped the blood off his arms on a towel and tossed it across the room. "The Mire's going to keep learning and getting better at killing us. We finish this fast or not at all."

"How?" Dusty rested his gun against the counter and smoothed down Ophelia's hair, his chin quivering. "How do we stop this?"

"We destroy that machine," Rig said, pacing the room. "Without it, there's nothing to fight for."

"It may be working as a wireless transmitter," Adelaide said, finishing burning the arm. The kitchen stunk of cooked flesh, so she put the cover on to try to mask it. "If we destroy the Celestial Contraption, it could stop them."

"What about the nests?" Hush asked, leaning against the bottom of the island. "There are four nests there. That's why we didn't wrack it in the first place."

"But the Mire's here now," Rig said. "It's unguarded. We get in the autocars, punch right through the middle of them, and we destroy the Contraption and those nests."

Dusty set his jaw. "How are we going to destroy it?"

"It's a machine." He stopped at the counter and leaned forward. "We smash it apart."

"It's the size of a mansion," Mattie said.

"What about the explosives?" Dusty asked.

Hush shook his head. "I buried them all in the forest, then blew them up. There wasn't any sense saving them if we would die."

"We don't need them." Victoria pushed off the wall. "I can destroy it."

Dayla cocked her head. Was Victoria going to tell them about her connection to the Celestial Contraption? That wasn't a good idea. Dayla still wasn't sure about the full extent of it, nor if they could trust the people in the room. But she couldn't stop Victoria from talking without raising more suspicion. Dayla would have to stay quiet and re-evaluate her plan.

"What do you mean?" Dusty asked.

"That's what happened last year." Victoria snapped out her coat lapels but winced from the exertion. "I'm fine. I connected to the machine somehow and destroyed it. I can do it again."

Adelaide stomped across the room and held her back. "You can barely stand. How do you expect to do something like this?"

"Carry me if you have to, but it doesn't sound like we have another choice. I can do it." She looked to Dayla. "You know I can."

Every eye turned. Dayla looked back from behind her placid mask. *There's no getting around it now,* she thought. "She can do it. We just have to get her there."

"I should go with you," Mattie said. "I can't heal these people anymore. At least I can be of some use out there."

"We should all go." Edwin pushed his glasses up his nose. "We can't risk this failing."

"We're just going to leave Dawnhallow?" Hush asked.

Ophelia took in a sharp breath of air. Dusty grabbed her. Through pained breaths, she said, "Go."

"Don't strain yourself." Dusty took her hand.

"Go!" She slammed her head against the towel. "I hired you to protect this village, so protect it! Turn that thing to scraps."

Dusty nodded. He grabbed his gun. "We can take care of ourselves."

"You heard the boss," Rig said, taking his riotsaw from the corner and swinging it over his shoulder.

"It could be worse there," Hush said. "Do we really want to push this fight?"

"It's better to die on your feet." He cast a look at Edwin.

"Never fall," Edwin said with a smile.

"Not even in death." He passed Victoria and paused. "Were you serious about being carried?"

"Don't touch me." She took one step and stumbled. Adelaide went to catch her, but she kept her feet and smoothed down her coat. "I'm okay."

One by one, the mercenaries headed out until it was only Mattie and Dayla still behind. "Make sure she rests," Mattie said to Dusty. She faced Dayla and scowled. "We're going to talk about that man."

"No, we're not." Dayla spun on her heel and stalked out.

They met with the rest at the front door. Edwin spoke to the men standing guard. "Get upstairs and make sure every gun is ready to cover us. We're finishing this fight out there." The men nodded and rushed off.

"I can't drive," Victoria said, taking a rest against the wall, Adelaide at her side. "Someone else is going to have to take over."

"I'll do it," Edwin said. "It's been a while, but it's like riding a bike. Isn't it?"

"Uh...sure." Victoria tossed him her keys then leaned toward Dayla. "I would rather not go with the bike rider."

"You'll go with me." Dayla cast Edwin a suspicious glare. "Rig, you come along too. The rest of you will be with Edwin."

Edwin cracked a smile. "Drive fast, leech."

A woman came running out of the ballroom. It was the wife. She saw the group of them and hurried over. "My husband," she said. "What happened to my husband?"

Dayla stepped forward. "His wounds were too severe. He didn't make it. I'm sorry."

"Oh, God." She covered her mouth with both hands.

"These battles take from all of us." She put her hand on the woman's shoulder. "But we will keep fighting so that no one else may feel pain."

The woman nodded, tears falling from her chin. "Thank you."

"Now go. Be with those who still need you."

She backed away, her knees trembling with each step. She wouldn't be much good for anything, but at least there were softer shoulders to cry on inside. Dayla adjusted her rifle and turned to find Mattie glaring at her.

"You must feel lucky to wear that mask," she said. "Does it make it easier?"

"No."

Mattie frowned, then softened.

Rig lifted aside the crossbar while Edwin peered through the cracks in the windows. "It's about a hundred metres to the autopool," he said.

Adelaide leaned toward Victoria. "Can you do it?"

"Head down and run." She took a deep breath. "I'm ready."

Rig grabbed one door handle while Hush grabbed the other. They made eye contact and without a count, threw the doors open.

Edwin was first, barrelling off the porch at high speed. Hush and Mattie came in behind, followed by Rig with his riotsaw at his side, held by the backbar. Victoria took a slow start, Adelaide staying by her side. Dayla was last, and seeing the Mire come rumbling out of the foggy forest, she flipped on her boltrifle and took aim.

Firebolts shot from the second floor, taking down inkbloods and sludges as they rushed in. Dayla kept walking, but her eyes stayed down her gun sights. She picked off the ones that got through the initial volley. Edwin as well, with his supernatural speed, was able to break away from the group, killing the Mire with his electrified hands, and still be the first to the autopool.

Rig reached Dayla's autocar and turned around. A sludge oozed from beneath the chassis and formed behind him. He reared back to slam it with his saw, but Dayla already demolished its upper torso with a well-placed shot.

Rig didn't care, he just took a step toward Dayla and shouted, "You're the driver! Hurry up!"

Dayla slung her boltrifle and sprinted for the autopool. "I was being careful." She unlocked the driver's door.

"Next time be careful and fast." Rig tossed his riotsaw in the back seat and circled to the passenger side.

Victoria leaned against the back of the car. "You're both very clever. Can we go?"

Edwin already turned his engine over, with Adelaide in the passenger seat and Hush and Mattie in the back. He backed out of the spot, tearing up dirt and snow. Dayla tossed Rig her boltrifle and slid into the driver's seat, unlocking the doors for the others. Victoria immediately shut her eyes and flopped her head back.

Dayla reversed, slammed the car into drive, then ripped across the Briardown grounds. Edwin followed closely, dodging the Mire alongside Dayla. They turned down the main road. Dayla pulled off her mask and threw it into the backseat. She eased off the gas to let Edwin's car lead so Mattie could direct them to the Bilson Estate.

They took a hard corner through the middle of Dawnhallow and came face-to-slime with another moving mound. Dayla went left while Edwin cut right. The mound shuddered as they tore by.

"Should we worry about that?" Rig asked, peering over his shoulder.

Dayla checked the rear-view mirror. "It's slow. We'll be fine."

The shuddering in the mound increased until a chunk broke off and took chase. It was still much larger than their autocar but moved with the same speed.

"Bad news," Rig said.

Victoria opened her eyes and looked back. "What is that?"

Dayla pushed the pedal to the floor. Edwin zoomed ahead, but the moving mound focused on them. She slapped Rig on the shoulder.

"You have to shoot it!" she shouted.

Rig looked over the boltrifle in his hands. He reached for a switch on the side, then moved his hand to a dial, but didn't touch either. "I don't know how this thing works."

The moving mound reared back then slammed down. Dayla jerked the wheel to the left. Snow and dirt flew up at the impact as they skidded to the side. Their tires popped up onto the general store porch and snapped the awning posts across the bumper. She brought the autocar back to the centre of the street as the awning collapsed and the moving mound recovered from its miss.

"Alright." Dayla let go of the wheel. "Then you can drive. Switch."

Dayla pulled her seat handle and the seatback flopped down. Rig threw the boltrifle to Victoria and snatched the wheel, keeping the autocar in a straight line. Victoria tried her best to stay out of the way while Dayla and Rig switched places. Dayla went underneath while Rig uncomfortably stepped over, trying to keep the autocar from crashing the whole time.

They settled themselves in their new seats. Dayla motioned for her boltrifle, keeping her eye on the moving mound in the side mirror. Victoria fumbled for a second, then passed the rifle along. The cold air rushed in as Dayla opened the window and took the weapons. She crawled out partway and sat on the door.

The moving mound curled up to strike again. The road grew narrow as they left Dawnhallow, a thick forest to either side. There wouldn't be avoiding another shot. She flicked on the boltrifle and raised it to her cheek. The autocar bumped and she moved with the motions. She turned the power dial, hearing the hum of the barrel as it charged. She drew back the priming bolt.

The moving mound reared back. Dayla fired centre mass. A heavy bolt streaked from the barrel of her gun. A hole the size of a pony appeared in the moving mound. The electricity arced out from there, rendering more of the muck inert. The mound slowed to a stop, chunks of it dripping to the ground. As the distance grew, the moving mound tried to reform, but by then they were long gone.

Dayla re-entered the passenger seat. "I do not like those things." She glanced at Rig, squished up against the steering wheel. "Do you want to switch back?"

"No." He adjusted the seat until it reasonably matched his large frame. "Just shoot anything else that looks like that."

She chuckled and reloaded her inkwell.

CHAPTER 23

Adelaide bounced her knee. They neared the Bilson Estate, a place supposedly filled with the Mire. But as they travelled down the long driveway, she didn't see a single inkblood or sludge outside the autocar. What she did see was the Estate itself. Pipes built into the walls and ground crested like frozen metal sea serpents. Strange devices that spun and stretched replaced the simple country demeanour the Bilson Estate once held. Chimneys reached to the dreary sky, waiting to expel the exhaust from the machine's horrid design. Edwin pulled into the frontcourt, followed by Dayla's autocar.

Adelaide stepped out into the intensifying storm. She peered around the estate's front steps. It was terrifyingly devoid of life, with only the moving parts of the Celestial Contraption within the blowing snow. Edwin came around the autocar while Hush and Mattie had to push the passenger seat forward to get out. Dayla's autocar pulled in front of them with Rig driving.

"I don't like this," Rig said, stepping out. "We shouldn't be alone."

"I told you this was too easy." Edwin took off his glasses and tossed them into the autocar as Hush came out. His unnatural blue eyes seemed even brighter that day.

Dayla opened her autocar's backdoor and offered her hand to Victoria. Victoria ignored it and stumbled out on her own.

"Why's everyone standing around?" she asked, rubbing her temples. "Let's get inside."

"You can't do it here?" Dayla asked.

Victoria shook her head. "I can't feel it yet. We have to go to the centre."

"Mattie." Edwin looked over his shoulder at her. "Can you sense the Mire?"

"I sense a lot of the Mire." Mattie looked around. "But I don't know where they are. The nests were inside though."

Rig grabbed the riotsaw from the backseat. "Then let's stop talking." He led the way to the front door and, with a mighty kick, broke it open.

The inside was just as empty. The pipes continued through the building, following the ceiling and walls as they split and came together. The seven of them took careful steps into the entry hall, but the floor creaked to signal their entrance. Much of the furniture had been broken apart. A lighting fixture had been torn down from the ceiling to make a path for the piping. Black stains traced down the red patterned carpet and reached slimy tendrils up to the wallpaper.

"Adelaide," Dayla said, putting on her mask. "You should clear out those nests while we have a moment."

Adelaide resisted at first. She wanted to stay with Victoria, who seemed at times to be asleep on her feet. However, Dayla was right, she was most equipped to burn out the nests.

"Go with her, Rig." Dayla set her rifle on her shoulder. Something seemed off about her stance, but Adelaide didn't think about it too hard. "We'll get to the centre of this machine."

"They're in the cellar," Mattie explained, pointing down the hall. "It's a big place, but you can't miss them."

Adelaide looked to Victoria, but she didn't turn around. Was she still mad at her? It wasn't the time for personal issues, but Victoria was more emotionally driven than she let on. Adelaide wrapped the flame gauntlet trigger around her thumb and headed off to the cellar with Rig at her back.

They came to a doorless threshold that descended into a stone room below. None of the pipes went down there, but thick muck coated the stairs and walls. Rig flicked a switch on the wall, but none of the lights turned on. Adelaide spotted a lantern on a nearby desk. She grabbed it and lit it with a small puff from her gauntlet. The light spread into the cellar but was swallowed up before they could see the bottom. Adelaide took a deep breath and began the descent.

They stepped carefully down the slick steps, making sure they didn't tumble down. It would have been an embarrassing way to go after the fight at Dawnhallow. They reached the bottom and found themselves in a cavernous hall. Walls which once separated the basement had been broken down, replaced with rows upon rows of wine racks. The cellar seemed to stretch under the entire estate.

They started by going left and followed the wall until they found the first nest. It spread over the corner like a beehive with bones jutting out. It writhed in the lantern light as they approached.

"I've never seen a nest without the Mire around it," Adelaide said. Her voice echoed through the empty cellar.

"Me neither." Rig took his riotsaw in both hands. "Just burn it."

Adelaide unleashed a torrent of flames at the nest. It quickly caught fire and was engulfed. The roaring fire illuminated that corner of the cellar. As the flames licked up, they revealed that Adelaide and Rig weren't alone.

Undulating sludges covered the ceiling. As the light from the flames reached them, they dropped to the floor, surrounding the duo. Adelaide turned to make some distance and came face-to-chest with the oozing reservoir of a gnasher with a dog's skull. Doghead nearly touched the cellar roof as it stretched to its full height.

"It's a trap." Adelaide backed up but had to stop lest she got too close to the sludges that surrounded them. "This is astounding. The Mire actually set a trap."

"Research later." Rig brought his riotsaw to life. "Fight now!"

Rig went in swinging at the gnasher. Adelaide spun back and sprayed flames at the sludges creeping up on her. They were on all sides, but Adelaide kept them back with spurts of fire, each one illuminating the cellar as it filled with the Mire.

Her gauntlet stopped firing as its reservoir ran dry. A sludge leapt forward, sliding a broken bone out of its arm. Adelaide dodged the bone and smashed the lantern against the sludge's head. It ignited and stumbled back, its body cracking and crumbling under the heat. The only light was the various burning sludges and the nest that had become a wild conflagration.

Adelaide pressed the inkwell on her gauntlet and refilled the reservoir. She snapped out her pulserod and struck it, turning it on with a flash of electricity. If the Mire attacked them in the cellar, there was no telling what could be happening to the people upstairs. She and Rig needed to get out.

Adelaide went on the offence. She changed the gauntlet nozzle to small burst and charged the closest sludge. With three quick pops, she removed the sludge's arms and blew a hole through its chest. Another came rushing in and Adelaide cracked it across the head, reducing it to a stinking morass, then placed her hand over it and set off a series of explosions that obliterated its form.

She turned to check on Rig in time to see Doghead grab his head with its hand-foot and toss him across the room. Rig rolled with the momentum and ended on his knees, steadying himself against a wine rack. Blood trickled out from beneath his hat. He snatched the branderbuss off his hip but didn't aim at the gnasher. Instead, he pointed behind him and fired. Another nest lit up, this one built between the shelves. As it burned, it gave him and Adelaide more light to move in. Rig took his riotsaw in both hands again and reengaged.

Adelaide blew apart a sludge's legs then rushed in to help. She struck Doghead across the back, cracking its spine and sending a quick charge through its reservoir. Doghead's arms reversed their bend and rotated their joints until they faced Adelaide. It balanced on one leg as it slashed at her with its claws. Its hand-foot crawled up its bone structure until the hand was at the knee and the foot was now a sharp sword-like appendage. It swiped at Adelaide and Rig in a macabre carnival performance.

Rig knocked the sword-leg away and Doghead did a full spin and kicked Adelaide in the head, sending her to the ground. Rig came in with a heavy diagonal chop that took a chunk out of the ceiling. Doghead spun its arms back around and caught the saw by the blade. The chains tore through the bones on its hands and Doghead brought up new bones to replace them. Rig put one hand on the backbar for support and pushed, trying to put his saw through the gnasher's head.

Adelaide took a moment to shake the birds from her mind. Doghead and Rig stood over her, titans locked in a contest of strength. The riotsaw slowly pushed closer to Rig while the sludges crept in. He needed an edge. Adelaide huffed and fired her gauntlet at Doghead's right leg, taking it off at the knee. Doghead dropped, balancing on its thigh bone. Rig puffed out his chest and pushed harder.

A sludge reached for Adelaide. She put her pulserod through its head then rolled to her knees and blew off Doghead's other leg. Doghead thumped down onto its pelvis. Rig towered over it. He let out a warrior cry as the riotsaw got closer and closer. The dual chains touched Doghead's snout. Its skull vibrated as bone chunks tore away.

"Die!" Rig shouted and with a mighty push ripped the riotsaw through the rest of Doghead's skull, scattering a thousand pieces across the room.

That wasn't the end of it, unfortunately. Sludges still lumbered in from the shadows.

"We need to go!" Rig said, turning off his saw.

Adelaide pushed the sludge she was electrocuting aside and stood. "What about the other nests?"

"This place is going to burn down!" He grabbed bottles of wine and tossed them into the fire, stoking the flames. "They'll be destroyed!"

The fire had gotten out of hand, as fire was known to. And if they were ambushed, chances were good the others were as well. Adelaide blew the top off an approaching sludge, then ran for the stairs. Rig kept close behind her as she cleared a path to the ground floor.

They returned to the entryway and followed the path they assumed the others had gone. They found the remains of sludges rendered inert scouring across the walls. As they came into what was once certainly a dining room, the centre of the Contraption awaited them.

It was a large square machine with an opening full of spinning, jagged blades. Victoria stood before it while a battle raged around her. Edwin zipped back and forth, punching sludges apart with each move. Hush blasted away with his branderbuss while Mattie kept behind him, her eyes on a white-tinged sludge fighting against its kind. Dayla placed herself in the corner with her sights on the door Adelaide and Rig entered through.

"You're just in time!" she shouted. "Victoria's connecting."

Rig jumped into the fray riotsaw first, slashing a sludge in half as it crawled through a hole in the wall. Adelaide, however, couldn't take her eyes off Victoria. There was something wrong. Victoria shook, clutching her hands so tightly that blood dripped from between her fingers. Adelaide dodged around a sludge and rushed to her side.

"Hey," Adelaide said. "Are you alright?"

Victoria didn't look at her. She stared into the whirling blades. "I'm focused."

"It looks like you're panicking."

Victoria took a deep breath but didn't say anything.

Adelaide lowered her voice. "Back at Briardown. I saw you pick up your flying moons rather than use your trick. Is there something wrong?"

"I think I broke myself." Victoria's lower lip trembled. "I can barely feel my moons. They hardly move when I want them to. And this machine is right there, within my grasp, but I can't grab it. I've become useless."

"You're not useless. You say you can sense it, right."

She nodded.

"Then you can do it. I believe that you can do it. And you have all the time you need. We'll keep these things off your back."

Victoria finally looked at Adelaide. A small, but genuine, smile spread across her face. Adelaide smiled back. For that second, they were alone in a silent world. Then, Victoria's eyes widened and she jerked her head toward the Contraption.

"It's there," she said. "I have it."

The piping rattled against their braces. The grinder's teeth spun faster and faster. It bowed and bent like it was breathing.

"Everyone should leave." Victoria's voice came not only from her throat but from the house itself.

"We should listen to the young lady," Dayla said, shooting down another sludge and running for the door. "Last time she blew apart the entire building."

The machine grew louder as more sludges crawled in through the walls. Piping broke apart and smashed the sludges, whipping around as the machine came to life. Still, more sludges came and Victoria was stuck in her trance.

"I'm staying!" Adelaide shouted over the cacophony.

"No!" Victoria said. "It's too dangerous."

"Someone needs to protect you so you can finish what you're doing." She smashed a sludge with her pulserod. "I'll be fine."

"Adelaide!" Dayla grabbed her arm. "You cannot stay."

"Trust me." Adelaide knocked her hand away. "Because I trust her."

Dayla looked at Adelaide from behind her bird mask. Her shoulders rose and fell with rising emotions.

"It's time to go!" Rig cried, dodging a pipe as it collapsed.

Adelaide squeezed Dayla's shoulder. "I'll be fine."

Dayla lingered with Adelaide, then spun around and rushed out with the others. It was just Adelaide, Victoria, and the oncoming sludge horde. Adelaide alternated firing her gauntlet and swinging her pulserod, keeping the sludges from Victoria. All the while, the Celestial Contraption broke apart. The chaos reached its crescendo.

Adelaide raised her hand to another sludge when a metal shell slammed closed around her. The world went dark but filled with an explosion of sound. Wood cracked and metal screamed. The shell rumbled and she collapsed to her knees, clutching her ear against the noise. It only lasted a few seconds, then silence.

The metal behind her peeled away, letting in light and snow. Adelaide, still shaking, turned.

Victoria stood there, her skin turned cosmic black, with pinpoints of stars and swirling galaxies. She was the night sky, looking down on Adelaide with sparkling eyes. "Are you okay?" she asked with a voice that was soft yet resonated within Adelaide's head a thousand times.

All Adelaide could do was nod.

"Good." A shooting star crossed Victoria's face and down her neck. "I was worried."

Victoria shut her eyes and collapsed. Adelaide rushed forward and took her in her arms. Her normal rosy skin faded in starting from her crown and she took calm breaths. Adelaide held her close and looked at the devastation that was all that was left behind.

End of Aurora 1899

PART THREE

CENTENNIAL 1900

CHAPTER 1

One Day Later

Dawnhallow celebrated that night. They had their memorial the night of the battle and buried the dead. But the next day they moved back from the manor and turned the city into one big party. They revelled and remembered those who lost their lives to keep Dawnhallow safe. Rig sat in the Carefree Inn's dining room, which had become the centre of the festivities. Surrounded by smiling, drunk faces, even he couldn't help but be pleased with the result. Still, the words Edwin said to him when they returned from the Bilson Estate echoed in his head.

"This seemed too easy," Edwin had said.

"Yes," Rig replied. "I heard you the first time."

"Maybe it doesn't matter. We survived after all."

Rig nodded. "How disappointing."

Rig rested against the bar. Hush stood on a table, teaching the crowd an Understone drinking song while Mattie clapped her hands along. Everyone seemed so happy, why couldn't he be? Just for a moment. A bandage before the wounds of life bled again. Dusty sat across the bar, bouncing his knee to the raucous tune. Rig grabbed a whiskey bottle and went to join him. Tomorrow would be the future, he survived today.

The sounds of the party permeated through the floor into Victoria's room. Adelaide sat in the chair next to the bed where Victoria lay. The single lamp left the room in a solemn glow. Victoria had yet to wake up since destroying the Contraption. While she was breathing, she wasn't responding to anything else. Adelaide hadn't left her side since.

Adelaide looked at the wall that separated Victoria's room from hers. She moved her experiments from Briardown back to the inn but couldn't bring herself to work on it until she knew Victoria was safe. Before the battle, she'd been trying to figure out the meaning of the signal the sample emitted. She had been able to provoke a noise from it, and when she amplified it with a horn, she swore there was a voice. Ever since they destroyed the Celestial Contraption though, it had been quiet.

She began to nod off when Victoria shot bolt upright and took in a deep breath.

"Hey!" Adelaide lunged forward, putting her hand on Victoria's shoulder. "It's okay."

"Where am I?" Victoria clutched her chest. "What's happening?"

"You're back at the inn. You're safe." She sat on the bed. "You saved all of us."

"I did?" She looked around the room, taking in the familiar environment. "I did, didn't I?"

"You've been out for a whole day. I was worried you…"

"You were worried?" Victoria gazed into Adelaide's eyes, then jerked away. She wrung her hands together. "I think you were right about me. What you said before."

"What do you mean?"

"I don't connect to people. Not well. I don't understand them, and I always assumed that was their fault. That they are flawed and imperfect and undeserving of my time. I won't lie, it got worse after I connected to the Contraption for the first time. I saw people as small as they are, or as small as I thought they were. I came to Dawnhallow because I wanted to feel that again, to be the size of the universe."

She pulled the blanket into her fists. Her voice trembled.

"But when I got there, I was scared. I had experienced something humans shouldn't have, and it took my humanity away. If I did it again, I wondered if I would truly become something different. If I'd lose everything. But then you came, and I remembered that as flawed as people are, they can still be wonderful. And then, maybe, someone as flawed as me…"

Adelaide put her hand against Victoria's cheek and guided her to face her. "I want to tell you something, and, well, I don't know how I can... I don't know how to do it, so I want you to understand something first." She shook her head and pinched the bridge of her nose. "Okay, I'm really smart."

Victoria chuckled.

"I know that sounds like bragging, but empirically I am intelligent. I did great in school at anything I tried. My instructors went as far as to call me a genius at times." She squeezed her hands together. "I found confidence in that. I was assured in myself."

"I don't know where you're going with this."

"I don't much know either." A soft smile spread across her lips. "But I thought it was important for you to know so you can understand what it means when I say you did something no one else has ever done before. You changed my mind."

Victoria sat up. Adelaide took her hand, electricity growing in her stomach. Victoria squeezed back, but she frowned. "What do you mean I changed your mind?"

"I thought I could see good people, that they would be clearly delineated from the bad. I thought it was simple. I pegged you as selfish. But you consistently helped others even when it put yourself at risk."

"You mean the stable? That was dumb. Illogical. I think I broke my magic trick."

"My mom had this saying. I can't remember the exact words, but it was about how people don't show who they truly are when they have no other options, they reveal it when they have all the options in the world. You could have ran, many times, but you never did." She shut her eyes, playing her nails along Victoria's wrist. "You're a complex person, true, but I don't think you're..."

"Adelaide..."

Her body moved on its own. She pushed the sheet aside and swung her leg over Victoria's. A smile spread across Victoria's lips and she moved her hands to Adelaide's waist, pulling her closer. Butterflies flew around Adelaide's stomach; even with her on top, Victoria had such control. She put her hand against her chest and pushed her down, running her fingers down her cleavage. She'd never gone this far before.

Victoria slid her hands beneath Adelaide's thighs and pulled her off balance. She caught herself, just before their lips touched. Victoria leaned in, but Adelaide pulled back, prompting her to give a face. Adelaide smiled, her breaths coming heavy. She may be the less experienced one, but if she was going to go any further, she would be the one in charge.

"You already saw me naked," she said, running her hand down the length of Victoria to rest on the front of her pants. Victoria twitched. "My turn."

"Yes, ma'am," Victoria said, pulling her shirt over her head and tossing it aside.

Adelaide's gaze drifted down her naked form. Her cheeks grew hot, her heart became a drumbeat, and she pressed her lips against Victoria's. The perfume was long gone, but it was never the scent that got her drunk.

The morning after, Edwin knocked on Rig's door. It swung open a moment later revealing a half-naked Rig with a perturbed glare. Edwin was about to say something, when he noticed Dusty, shirtless, standing behind him. Dusty's eyes went wide, looked around like he saw a bird flying about, then disappeared into the room.

Rig coughed and eased the door more closed. "Don't say it."

Edwin cracked a grin the size of an ocean. "I'm happy for you is all."

"It's not going to last."

"It doesn't have to. What matters is you're happy now. You deserve that happiness."

Rig rolled his eyes and sighed. "You know this isn't the first time you've told me this."

"It isn't?"

"No. A couple years ago there was that guy from Iran. You gave almost the same speech."

"Oh…"

Rig leaned against the door. "Your memory's still going."

"It'll stop one way or another." Still, Edwin worried what he could lose next. "That doesn't matter. Victoria called a meeting."

Rig cocked an eyebrow. "*Victoria* called a meeting? The Victoria we know?"

Edwin raised his hands in defeat. "I was as confused as you are. But apparently, something happened when she connected with the Celestial Contraption we need to hear. I'll let them know you'll be a little bit."

"No, you tell them I'll be right there."

Edwin backed up with a taunting smirk. "Take your time."

"I'll be right there!"

Edwin stuck his hands in his pockets and chuckled as he went down to the dining room.

"There's something inside the Machine."

Victoria dropped the bombshell as soon as everyone gathered. Ophelia sent Flo away for privacy, and it was just her, Dusty, and the seven mercenaries. Her sleeve was tied over her arm stump, and her pale skin and trouble breathing told everyone she wasn't fully healed. All the same, she insisted on being a part of it. So, they sat among the tables in the dining room, with Victoria holding their attention.

"I'm sorry," Ophelia said. "What do you mean there's something inside the Machine?"

"An intelligence. The Intelligence. I saw it through the Celestial Contraption. Some faceless, inhuman thing that was controlling the Mire."

"The Faceless God," Edwin said. He leaned against the back wall. "I heard the Church was praying to Faceless Gods, but maybe there's just one."

Adelaide nearly leapt out of her seat. "That's not true! The Church doesn't pray to any Faceless Gods. We pray to, you know, God."

"Don't be daft. One of your priests told me."

"The Intelligence." Mattie rested her linen wraps on her shoulders. "It could be the voice I've been hearing."

"Do you hear the voice anymore?" Dusty asked.

Mattie shook her head. "It was silenced when the Celestial Contraption was destroyed."

Rig groaned, rubbing his eyes. "If the Intelligence is the thing making the Mire act strange. Why is it just happening now?"

"Maybe it just woke up," Hush said. He sat next to Mattie and leaned forward against the table. "The Machine only moved once, a hundred years ago. What if that was an automatic action, and this thing was only just recently able to take control?"

"The True Metal Order believes someone will drive the Machine," Mattie added.

Dayla scoffed. "That seems like a metaphor."

"I don't think it was."

"That's not all," Victoria said. She played her fingers off each other, taking quick breaths and darting her gaze around the room. "It did it. It succeeded somehow."

The air sucked out of the room. Ophelia instinctively covered her mouth. "What do you mean?"

"It wanted those people as fuel. They're supposed to power some sort of cataclysmic device. And it got them."

"How's that possible?" Rig slammed his fist on the table. "We destroyed that machine! They didn't take anyone!"

"Could they of went to another village?" Dusty asked.

Dayla thrust her finger at Mattie. "You told us the Mire was focused on Dawnhallow."

"It was!" Mattie protested, tightening her wraps.

"That Contraption was unused." Victoria crossed her arms. "I don't know what happened."

Dusty clapped. "Maybe there was a second one!"

Mattie cut back in. "I only sensed the one. And it's been focusing on Dawnhallow for weeks! Way before any of us even got here. If this Intelligence had a backup, why would it hide it before it even knew anyone was involved?"

"Wait." Ophelia's mind spun in circles. The conversation bounced around the room like a rubber ball, she needed to focus it down. "Do you think it knew we were getting ready for it? That's why it sealed us in before it attacked?"

"Maybe?" Mattie sat back, hiding her face in the scarf-like wraps. "It's sending some signal out to the Mire, that's what people like me can sense. Maybe they can send something back."

"Oh, God." Adelaide leaned forward, clutching her head in her hands. She shook her head from side to side, saying "no" over and over.

"What's wrong?" Victoria asked, kneeling next to her.

"It's the sample. The Mire sample can send wireless signals. And it's been sitting in my room where we've done all our planning since last week."

Rig slapped a mug off his table, sending it across the room. "It knew we were going to try to stop it. It knew Dawnhallow had protection. So, what? It had a backup?"

"That's why they stopped attacking us once we were in Briardown," Edwin said. "And that's why it showed itself when we were trying to leave. It wanted to keep us here more than anything else. All the while it came up with another way."

"And take another village?" Dusty asked. He put his hand on Rig's shoulder to calm him down.

"It doesn't matter. What matters is that it succeeded." He tapped his fingers on his bicep, then turned to Victoria. "How long do we have?"

She took Adelaide's hand. "It wasn't done working. But... soon. Sooner than we would like."

Edwin laughed. "A hundred years after it arrived, it plans to kill all of us."

"We don't know it's going to kill us." Dayla clicked her tongue. "Are you sure about this Victoria?"

Victoria nodded. "For a moment, the Intelligence and I were bonded. I saw everything. Or, most of everything. I felt like I was it. It's been asleep for a long time, but it woke up and it wants this planet. It's too injured to leave and even then, I don't think it can survive in our air. Whatever it's planning, many people will die."

Her words hung in the silence. It all felt too surreal. The Mire acted strangely, sure, but to imagine there was something inside the Great Machine that wanted to destroy them. It had given so much to them — was called a gift from God — but did it all have to be given back now? They saved Dawnhallow, but what did that really mean? Ophelia balled her hand into a fist.

"So, you destroy the Machine," she said.

All eyes turned to her.

Adelaide sat up. "You can't be serious. That's sacrilege."

"If the Intelligence wants to destroy the world, something has to be done!"

"We don't even know if that's true," Dayla said.

Adelaide stood up, tossing her chair back. "The Machine was a gift from God! It's an angel! It protects us from the Mire we just spent the other day fighting! We can't just destroy it!"

"Look." Rig put his hands up. "I don't care much for the Church's beliefs, but the Machine is important to a lot of people. It's important to how we live, it's where Ink comes from. We're nine people in a room, we can't decide for an entire world."

"It's going to act soon, Rig," Edwin said. "Do you want to take a poll? We don't have time."

Dayla slapped her table. "We don't know anything is happening."

"Victoria said it was!" Ophelia leapt to her feet and pointed at Victoria. "Right?"

Victoria's eyes widened. "I guess, yeah."

That wasn't helpful, Ophelia thought. "If the thing inside the Machine is going to kill us, it can't be a gift from God. And that seems at least worth checking out."

Hush hesitantly raised his hand like a schoolboy answering a question. "Even if we wanted to rust the Machine. It's the size of a city. You don't just set a bunch of poppers and watch it crumble."

"It's filled with Ink." Edwin stepped away from the wall and sauntered through the tables. "You ignite something like that and it's going to blow. Or maybe we just kill the Intelligence inside and be done with it."

"Both those things require getting inside; something that's never been done." Hush rubbed his hands together. "You can't crack its shell. Pieces have fallen off, sure. But, you can't get inside."

Ophelia tapped her finger on her cheek. "There's always Yoakum."

Dusty groaned. "Oh, no."

Edwin glanced between the pair. "Who's Yoakum?"

"Isaiah Yoakum lived in the village a few years back." Ophelia settled into her chair. "He was a little strange, liked to build things, but nothing bad. We eventually learned he was a part of a group of people who called themselves Ennobled Naturalists. They believed the Machine was evil and needed to be destroyed so things could return to the way they should be."

"I know this group," Edwin said. "They were wiped out after they set fire to a rectory — with the priests still inside."

"Yoakum got away. Rumour has it he fled to a farm outside of Severtson where he's laying low."

"Fine, you knew a terrorist," Adelaide said. "Why are you telling us this?"

"Yoakum wasn't a quiet man. He used to say he had a way to get into the Machine." Ophelia shook her head. "Or at least a plan that he couldn't enact by himself."

"I always saw it as drunken bragging," Dusty said. "He had been kicked out of The Shadow and couldn't go anywhere close to the Machine."

Ophelia tapped her finger against the table. It was a simple enough concept to talk about, but it was still destroying the Machine. It was the thing that gave them a century of unprecedented progress. She could feel the hesitation in the room. It was the same hesitation that was in her heart.

"The Intelligence thinks it has beaten us," she said. "It failed last year through a fluke. And here we are at the end of the century and it wants to take it all away. I can't fight, I'm not a fighter, even if I had both arms. I picked up a gun to protect my home, but I never want to do that again. You seven are something special. We can't let the world fade into nothing if we can stop it." She stood tall. "I trust what Victoria is saying. We need to do something. Don't you agree?"

She looked around the room with pleading eyes. No one said no. They sat there taking in her words as the clock on the wall ticked away the seconds. It felt like a decision had been made, and yet still, no one said yes.

Edwin needed some fresh air. He stepped out of the inn with a sigh. The streets sat empty. He would bet that most people were sleeping off the night before. They deserved it, after all, they had protected themselves. It was unfortunate that the being inside the Machine — what they'd been calling the Intelligence — found another way, but it didn't lessen the achievement.

The inn door swung open and Rig came out. He checked the wood that covered the broken window. It seemed like forever ago they had that first brawl with the Hawkers. Dayla wasn't far behind him, with Adelaide and Victoria not far behind her. Mattie and Hush were last, and then it was the seven of them alone in the street, watching the sun come up over the horizon.

"I've been thinking," Hush said. "This is the first time the seven of us have been together since we rusted the Contraption."

"What?" Dayla said. "You want to celebrate still?"

Rig spun his finger in a circle. "These people have been going for two days. Right on since the memorial."

"And it doesn't feel right." Mattie pulled on her coat. "Considering what we just learned."

"I know." Hush kicked a clump of dirt. "It just feels like we should do something. In Understone we would make noise, and shout down tunnels just to hear it come back to us. It was little, but it made us feel part of something. So, I dunno, let's do something."

They traded looks, but no one made a move. It was hard to celebrate when they didn't feel like they were done. There was a device that was going to kill them, though they didn't know how. It wasn't something to raise a drink to.

A smile cracked across Victoria's face. She lifted her head, then let out a loud cry. Somewhere between a scream and a cheer. When she finished, it echoed into the distance. Everyone stared at her.

"What was that?" Adelaide asked.

"I don't know." Victoria winked. "It was something, though."

Edwin cocked an eyebrow at her. Mattie tore her hat off and let out a similar cry. Hush joined her. One by one, they broke into a cathartic, intense roar. Their voices came together as they fought to be louder than the person next to them. Then, all at once, they stopped. The echoes of their cries faded into the December dawn and were replaced with laughter.

Concerned faces poked out of the surrounding buildings but soon morphed to confusion. Rig's gaze locked on the inn. Dusty stood at the door with an amused grin. "I should probably say goodbye." He put his hands in his pockets. "In case we don't make it back."

"Yeah," Edwin said. "You should."

Rig lowered his head and walked toward the inn where Dusty waited.

"One hour!" Dayla called after him. "We're leaving in one hour."

"I should go pack then," Victoria said. She squeezed Adelaide's hand before spinning on her heel and hurrying to the inn. She beat Rig to the door and slapped him on the shoulder as she went by.

Adelaide shook her head. "We just moved all her stuff here. How could she already unpack?" She then put her hands behind her back and took her leave.

Edwin didn't have much packing to do. He had arrived in the village with only the clothes on his back. He also didn't have anyone to say goodbye to. Still, he waved off Dayla, Hush, and Mattie and went his own way. He still needed his fresh air, and once they left, there was no telling when they would be back.

It didn't even take an hour for everyone to clear their gear out of the inn and pack up the autocars. Ophelia stood amidst the preparations to leave. The people who had come to her aid would be gone as quickly as they arrived. Off to save more lives. They didn't even believe they were heroes. Edwin slammed the trunk shut and they were done. He turned to Ophelia, a tension on his lips that could have been a smile from someone like him.

"Check the pub in Severtson," Ophelia said. "Yoakum likes the drink."

Edwin nodded. "We will. And you make sure you rest. Mattie says she healed the wounds but that doesn't mean you're out of the woods."

Ophelia looked at her stump and nodded. A haunting finality hung over the occasion. It had only been two weeks since Ophelia and Dusty went to Wrotdam to find help and ended up with seven mercenaries, dysfunctional as they were. Now, she was done, and they were off to another battle. One that could reach far beyond a small village in the English countryside. She wondered briefly if Aisling would be proud of how everything turned out.

Mattie hopped onto the running board of Victoria's autocar and waved goodbye, the bandages around her hand swaying as she did. Hush stood by her side, prouder than he did two weeks earlier, even if he did still clutch onto his branderbuss like a security blanket. He crept over to Ophelia and lowered his voice.

"I'm tinkering, with all this done," he said, "Halifax?"

"Oh, you remember that." She scratched the back of her neck. "Yeah. I think if the world doesn't end, there's a lot of it to see."

"Good." He grinned. "Don't lose your spirit."

A bag flew into his chest and Victoria came bursting out of the inn. "We're going to miss you, darling," she said, wrapping her arms around Ophelia.

Ophelia was startled but returned the hug. Victoria wiped a single tear from her eye as she pulled back then continued to her car, passing Rig and Edwin, standing stalwart like the protectors they were. And Dayla, who approached Ophelia first and offered to help, sat on the trunk. She had proven to be more complex than a simple good Samaritan, but they all were in a way. She smiled at Ophelia with a kindness that said she was proud beyond words.

That only left Adelaide, who came wandering down the street holding the reins of a horse packed with saddlebags.

"Are you planning on taking the horse to Severtson?" Victoria called, opening her car door.

"Not immediately." Adelaide stopped next to Ophelia. "Dusty loaned me her so I could return to the city."

"Are you not coming with us?" Victoria's face hung heavy with concern.

"I will meet you in Severtson, but there is business I must take care of in Wrotdam." She mounted the horse with ease. "Tomorrow morning. I'll be in Severtson tomorrow morning at the latest." She smiled at Victoria. "Don't look so sour. I'll be back soon."

Victoria shook her head and chuckled.

"Oh, wait!" Mattie hopped off the running board and dug in her pockets. She pulled out small glass vials full of a clear liquid and passed them around. "Since you're going your own way, I better hand these out now."

Adelaide took the vial and inspected it against the sun. "Is this your... stuff?"

"Yes. If anyone gets hurt, I wanted to make sure they had something." She smiled and stroked the horse's mane. "In case I'm not around."

They filled up the autocars and got ready to leave. Before they did, Rig poked his head out the window.

"Don't forget!" he shouted. "We're coming back to get paid!"

"I look forward to it!" Ophelia called back.

Tires spun on the frozen ground and the autocars went forth. Adelaide spurred her horse into a canter and headed for Wrotdam. Ophelia and the villagers watched their saviours fade into the distance. Bird songs played on the winter wind, calling for the end of a century.

CHAPTER 2

Severtson was nearly double the size of Dawnhallow and rather than a series of relatively straight streets, they curved and weaved in and out of traffic circles. People walked down the sidewalk bundled up in coats against the cold. After the dour and serious mood of Dawnhallow, it was a break to see a town so normal.

The autocars pulled up outside the only pub in town. It was a thin, cream-coloured building with a sign that read, *The Proud Prince*. Edwin swung open the autocar door and stepped onto the sidewalk. He hid his arms again under long sleeves and heavy gloves. The rest of his allies exited the autocars as well, looking around the quaint little town. They certainly stood out.

"We probably don't have to all go in there," he said, pushing his glasses back. "I feel like the seven of us will cause that poor barkeep to faint. I can go in alone."

"Not alone," Dayla said, slamming her door shut. "I'm going with you."

Edwin sent Dayla a dry look, but she stood her ground. "Fine. You can come too."

"You two have fun." Victoria stretched her arms to the sky, working out the kinks of an hour-long drive. "I'm going to see if anything is interesting in this town." She leaned over the autocar and offered her hand to Mattie. "Do you want to come along?"

Mattie bundled up in her bandage wraps and hid under her big hat, back to how she was when she first arrived in Dawnhallow, trying to sink into the background. "I would rather not."

"Come now." Victoria circled the autocar. "No one will be looking at you. You'll be standing next to me."

Victoria raised her hand and popped out her hips into a dancer's pose, then smiled at Mattie. Mattie, however, just gave her a flat look in reply. Victoria scoffed at her failed joke and turned to Hush sitting on the curb.

"Hey," she said. "Tell your sweetheart to go out with me."

Hush scowled. "She's not my sweetheart."

Mattie raised her index and thumb, putting them a few millimetres apart, then stuck her tongue out at Hush. She sighed and stuck her hands into her pockets. "Fine, I'll come along."

"Oh, splendid." Victoria took Mattie by the arm. "Don't worry, I'll tell everyone you're a burn victim. Or a leper!"

"Don't tell people I'm a leper."

Victoria laughed and pulled Mattie down the sidewalk. Edwin shook his head. It was shocking how quickly Victoria pushed aside the situation. Though, he envied how easily she could find joy. Maybe they all needed a break when it was done. If they survived.

"How about you two?" Dayla asked, looking at Rig and Hush. "Are you going to sit there?"

Rig plopped down next to Hush on the curb and they both grumbled a non-committal reply. Unlike Victoria, their heads still seemed heavy.

Edwin motioned for Dayla to take the lead in to the Proud Prince. Dayla scowled at him but shoved by, nevertheless. Even after fighting together in Dawnhallow, she didn't trust Edwin. Edwin shrugged it off and followed her into the pub.

The statue of the Great Machine seemed more menacing now than ever, sitting upon its pedestal in the Mechanical Cathedral. The twisting structures around it were supposed to represent the ocean waves that swept over the coastline when it rose, but Adelaide couldn't help but see them as the pipes that cut through the Bilson Estate. She had come to Wrotdam for answers and wouldn't leave without them.

The creaking of a door filled the space and Archbishop MacMurray entered, flanked by three deacons. They were in the midst of a conversation about starting repairs on the north side of the Cathedral when the Archbishop spotted her and did a double-take.

"Adelaide!" he exclaimed. He turned to the deacons. "I am terribly sorry. We will continue this conversation at a later time." While the deacons left, he hurried to Adelaide with his arms wide. "Oh, my dear. How was your time off?"

"It was enlightening," Adelaide said. "But it is good to be back."

Archbishop MacMurray took her hands in his. "We missed you greatly here. When you take these breaks in the future, you don't have to completely disappear. We are family after all. I was worried."

"Why? Did something happen?"

The Archbishop laughed. "No, no. Just my normal concerns."

"Ah." There hadn't been another Cleansing. Adelaide thought there might have been, considering that one happened the year before. The Intelligence had taken a different tactic. "Your Grace, I'm curious. Have you ever heard of the Faceless God?"

Archbishop MacMurray squeezed Adelaide's hands until it hurt. She winced and he looked down, noticing what he was doing and stepping back like it didn't happen.

"That feels like a yes." Adelaide trembled. Did she want the truth?

The Archbishop rubbed his hands together. He walked away from Adelaide and gazed up at the Machine Cross. "What do you know about this?"

"Not much. Why don't you tell me? Why don't you tell me the truth? About who or what we are praying to."

Archbishop MacMurray put his hands behind his back and started to explain. "I wanted to tell you this last year. I wanted to tell you this so many times, but I could never find the words. It started with Old Archbishop Williams, a story that he passed to me on his deathbed about when Wrotdam was being constantly attacked by the Mire. Almost nightly. Old Archbishop Williams, a simple priest at that time, had come down with a terrible fever and was confined to his bed as the city he loved was being destroyed by a menace it could not fight. Until he had the dream where faceless beings approached him."

He took in a deep breath and stopped, as if somehow that half-story would be enough for Adelaide. When she gave him no sign that she was satisfied, he continued.

"These Faceless Gods had heard his prayers to save Wrotdam and, being sympathetic in nature, wanted to help. He was healed of his sickness and motivated to form what would become the St. Zita's Order. They created weapons powered by the Machine's Ink to battle the Mire. They discovered the use of lavender in dissuading the creatures from attacking. They did all this and brought peace to Wrotdam, and the world at large. It was then that Williams, this young priest, brought forth the Machine Church, as you know. But he never heard from the Faceless Gods again."

Adelaide paced behind him, giving him a narrow-eyed look. She had heard the story of the Machine Church founding, but there was another layer behind it of mysterious visions and strange beings. Everyone knew the story of Old Archbishop Williams's miraculous recovery, but to attribute it to these Faceless Gods was something unheard of.

And still, the Archbishop went on, "But he learned that people would not accept this talk of beings that came to him in dreams and healed him. If he talked of another God, the people would shun him. Instead, only a small group knew. He believed that since prayer brought them to us the first time, the Faceless Gods must be able to hear them. Through the Machine Church we pray, hoping the Machine and the Ink will amplify our voices so the Faceless Gods will hear us and then, maybe, we can reveal the truth."

Adelaide touched her face, then her hair, then her arm. She couldn't find a place to put her hand that didn't make her feel sick and uncomfortable. "You've lied to me. You've lied to everyone! Why? Because it's easier?"

"It was not easier. We have done so much to ensure humanity was moving in the right direction. We're constantly under attack. And yes, sometimes we have to be underhanded, but it breaks my heart every time we have to lie or use someone like Edwin Zhen to silence the voices of the people who would obscure our prayers."

"You used Edwin to silence people?"

"We had to!" He spun around to face her. "We are the only ones who stood against the Mire! The Machine came to us at the exact right time so that we could fight against it. The Faceless Gods saw to that. This isn't something new, Adelaide. You still serve the same ideals."

"The Machine is controlling the Mire!" Adelaide's face turned hot. "I have been fighting in a village that was under assault by something inside the Machine!"

"What are you talking about?"

"You are blinded by your faith! The evidence has always been right in front of us. The Ink, the Mire, the infected, magicians, amber madness; They are not separate phenomena, they are connected and the Machine is at the centre!"

He set his jaw and fixed his robes, standing tall as an archbishop should. Without a waver in his voice, he said, "The Machine fights against the Mire."

Adelaide turned away. He wouldn't listen. She took a few steps, then stopped. "You know, someone told me that people were imperfect. That they would refuse to see what's right in front of them. I'm starting to think she may have been right."

She stomped down the nave and out of the Mechanical Cathedral. She never looked back.

Hush and Rig hadn't moved since Edwin and Dayla went inside the pub. They hadn't even said a word. Both seemed content to sit in silence, watching autocars and carriages go by. Hush was okay with that. He had spent a long time around Rig and the others when usually he preferred to dip in and out of social circles as much as possible. Conversation, of course, was sometimes unavoidable.

"I see Edwin didn't take his gun back," Rig said.

Hush looked at the branderbuss resting on his knee. He had removed the inkwell once again, but still felt more comfortable when it was in physical contact. "He said he didn't want it anymore."

Rig grunted. "I'm not surprised."

The silence returned, but heavier now. The Proud Prince's door opened, but when Hush looked back it was just a group leaving the pub, not Edwin and Dayla returning. The group laughed at some inside joke and turned down the street. They were completely unaware of what was going on, about the possible cataclysm only a couple days away.

"Hey, Rig." Hush turned back around. "What do you tinker about all this? You didn't seem bright about destroying the Machine."

"I don't know." Rig leaned back. "A sawbones is supposed to protect the unprotected. I forgot that for a long time, but we were started by average people who were tired of relying on the Ink Clergy. They found a way to fight. Even if people hate me, I'm supposed to protect them, whatever that means. We don't know what the Intelligence can do. But imagine the chaos if the Machine was suddenly destroyed? I'm not against it, I just want to be sure it's the best choice." He looked at Hush. "What about you? Do you want to destroy the Machine?"

Hush thought about the many lifetimes he spent captured by that light. He was sure now it had to be the Intelligence that did that. It controlled the gnasher that took him. It was the thing Edwin had prayed to. It had stolen Hush's mind and replaced it with muddled thoughts and paranoia. Did he want to destroy the Machine?

"Yes," he said, wrapping his arms around his knees. "Yes, I do."

There wasn't much in Severtson, but Victoria still enjoyed walking down the street with Mattie, gazing into the shops as they passed by. Even Mattie's sulking couldn't bring down her spirits.

"Isn't this great?" Victoria spun in a circle. "No Mire, no training, no gangsters wanting to kill us. Just you and me taking in the sights of a small, albeit a little boring, town."

"Yeah." Mattie's voice didn't have the same thrill in it. She pulled her hat lower. "Are you not concerned at all?"

Victoria stopped outside a chocolate shop and look at the treats on display. "Why should I be?"

"You know, the Intelligence in the Machine having a device that runs on human life? About it killing all of us?"

"I never said it was going to kill all of us, I just said it was going to change the world."

Mattie recoiled in shock, blinking multiple times. "You said it was a cataclysmic device. You said many people would die. Why are you backtracking now? You had all this doom and gloom only a few hours ago."

"I don't know!" Victoria spun away from the shop. "All these images came in flashes and feelings. I felt like I was that thing until I was ripped away. But to talk about destroying the Machine seems so drastic. Do you want that to happen?"

Mattie shrugged. "It's not such a huge part of my life. I'm from St. Louis. We get the little Ink we use imported in. It's still all horse and carriage back home."

"That sounds terrible." Victoria put her hands in her pockets and stretched back, looking into the clouds floating through the sky. Usually, her most difficult decision was what dress to wear to the next ball. "People tend to die, Mattie. And honestly, I don't like them much to begin with. Maybe an apocalypse wouldn't be the worst thing for me."

"Sometimes I feel the same way."

Victoria shut her eyes to let the soft breeze flow through her layers of clothes. She could put off a decision for a little while longer.

"Come on," she said, kicking her feet around. "I'm bored. Let's buy some chocolate."

She grabbed Mattie's hand and dragged her into the shop.

The Proud Prince was a modest pub with half a dozen booths but mostly filled with square tables spread throughout the room. Everywhere one looked, they could see paintings of the same prince, drawn with a comically large head and a tiny sword. Sometimes the prince had just slain a dragon, or was saving a similarly large-headed princess from a tower, or even fighting a skeleton in front of a structure that looked strikingly like the Machine.

In the half-hour Edwin had been sitting at the bar, all he and Dayla had done was order a beer and sit in silence.

"Can we please ask him now?" Edwin asked, motioning at the barkeep.

"His name is Noah." Dayla took another dainty sip of her drink. "And if we're going to be asking him about the location of a terrorist in hiding, we should at least have a rapport. Also, take off your sunglasses. You look ridiculous."

"I promise you I will look more ridiculous with glowing blue eyes." Edwin looked around the nearly empty room. There was only an elderly man nursing a plate of chips and a middle-aged woman reading the newspaper. "It's not like we're going to have anyone listening in on us. You realize we're on a timer, right?"

"Not all of us feel the need to rush about as you do."

"You're doing this on purpose to bother me?"

"If a child is being too hyperactive, they occasionally need a time out."

Edwin squeezed the lip of the bar until his thumb left an imprint. He had enough of pandering to Dayla. "Oy, Noah, could we ask you a question?"

"Yea, another drink?" Noah spoke with an Irish brogue that rolled off the tongue just as his wavy, blond hair rolled off his head.

"I'm still finishing this one off. Actually, my grandmother here and I are looking for an old friend of hers." Edwin lowered his voice. "She doesn't have much time left and wants to say some goodbyes to the people she cares about."

"Ah." Noah hung a dishcloth over his shoulder and leaned in. "I know most people 'round here. Who is it you're looking for?"

"Isaiah Yoakum."

Noah cocked an eyebrow. He leaned back and crossed his arms, looking Edwin and Dayla up and down. "You're friends of Yoakum?"

"Not me." Edwin jerked his thumb at Dayla. "Her. Though between you and me, I'm suspecting something a little more than friendship, if you catch me."

Dayla gritted her teeth but said nothing. Noah's gaze flicked in her direction.

"Tell you what," he said. "I deliver some of my homemade brews to Yoakum since he doesn't like leaving his farm. I'm going out tomorrow morning, so I'll ask him if he wants to see you. He's a private fellow as I'm sure you know. Ran into some trouble a while back."

Edwin nodded. "Yes, some Church issues. We know."

"I see you do. So, who do I tell him is visiting?"

"Ophelia Plante," Dayla said.

"Alright, Ophelia. Come back around ten tomorrow. I'll let you know what he says."

"Please let him know it's urgent." Edwin laid his hand over his heart. "She is so old. She could truly go at any moment."

Noah nodded, now completely bought into the sad story. "I'll let him know." He pulled the cloth off his shoulder and went back to cleaning the bar.

"That was rude," Dayla said.

"It was also funny." Edwin drained his glass then headed out of the pub.

CHAPTER 3

The rest of the day passed quietly in Severtson. They spent the night at the local inn, paid for by a gracious, and loud, donation from Victoria. When the morning came, they returned to the Proud Prince to find Adelaide waiting for them outside. She leaned against the building with her scarf wrapped around her face and a distant look in her eyes, but her amber robes were unmistakable. Victoria nearly leapt out of the autocar without putting it in park when she saw who it was.

"Adelaide!" she exclaimed. "I'm glad you found us."

Adelaide took a moment to register someone was talking to her. She looked at Victoria then smiled. "Yes. I told you I would be back soon."

"How did you get out here?" Hush asked. "I don't see the horse or an autocar."

"I'm still part of the Ink Clergy. We have our ways. And drivers."

Dayla stepped in. "Not to break up the reunion. But we can't have Noah seeing a whole group of us waiting for him. You all go down the street. Edwin and I will wait here. Now go."

While Edwin and Dayla took up their positions outside the Proud Prince, the rest of them moved away. All Victoria cared about was that Adelaide was back. She asked her where she had gone, but Adelaide was strangely quiet about that. She was strangely quiet in general, though she also seemed happy to see Victoria.

Noah came and went. Edwin and Dayla returned with good news.

"Yoakum is expecting us," Dayla said. "Or rather, he's expecting Ophelia Plante and will get us. We have to approach this with care, he's sounding like the paranoid type and there's no telling how he will react when he learns he has been tricked." She turned to Adelaide. "Did you finish your business?"

"Yes, I did." She stroked the cross around her neck.

"Good." Yet, Dayla's gaze lingered on Adelaide. "It's a straight drive down this road for about half an hour. There will be a sign that says *Birchwick Farm*. That's where Yoakum is. Come on, we don't have much time."

They piled into the autocars — Victoria making sure Adelaide got the passenger seat in hers — and drove north. The Machine stood visible in the distance, as it normally was. Victoria was trying to figure out if it was a trick of the light, or if the tentacles from its back were moving faster than usual.

Just as Noah had said, they eventually passed a weathered sign for Birchwick Farms. Dayla turned down the dirt road, followed by Victoria. They were driving through a forested area, a much heavier wood than what was around Dawnhallow. Even then, they kept going deeper and deeper. If Yoakum had wanted to get away from civilization, then he had succeeded. The long forest was the only way in, or out.

As they went down the road, they passed between two ten-foot flagpoles flying white flags. More flagpoles sat beyond, in a line disappearing into the forest. But as quickly as they saw them, they were gone as they drove by. It was a peculiar design choice, but Victoria figured it was Yoakum marking out his territory.

Finally, they arrived at the end of the road. There were two structures; a two-storey dark wood house that leaned peculiarly to the right and a massive barn in a similar manner of disrepair. The snow had been piled up along one side and had broken into the barn's interior. If they hadn't been told someone lived there, Victoria would have assumed it had been abandoned.

Victoria put the autocar into park and peered out the window. "A farm without farmland and a house that looks ready to fall apart. This Yoakum fellow better be worth our time."

Everyone exited the autocars. The door to the house flew open and a man with a white shock of hair came charging out with a shotgun at the ready. He was wrapped up in a blanket being used as a shawl with wild eyes and a few weeks of patchy beard growth. He planted his feet and pointed the gun at the newcomers.

"You're not Ophelia!" he said. "Who are you?"

"We're friends of Ophelia," Dayla said, stepping forward carefully. "She sent us."

"I was told Ophelia was coming. That she was dying."

"That was a lie. But if we told you who we really were, would you have met with us?"

Yoakum narrowed his eyes but didn't take his finger off the trigger. "Why do you want to meet with me? I look around and I don't see a normal group. You're a leech. There's an Ink Cleric. It looks like two sawbones. Two criminals from, I would guess, Understone. And..." His gaze hung on Victoria. "What are you?"

Victoria curtsied with her coat. "I'm the greatest magician in Wrotdam."

"Uh-huh. This isn't right."

Edwin slammed his door shut. "We want to get inside the Machine."

Yoakum's eyes widened. He looked around the group, but no one flinched. He lowered his gun. "Alright. You have my interest. Let's talk." He led the group into his house, kicking the snow off his boots on the front porch.

Yoakum's house wasn't much warmer on the inside. He had a fire going in the hearth in his kitchen. He also had no electrical lights, though that wasn't much of a surprise considering the state and location of the house. Yoakum put his shotgun next to the door and grabbed a cup of tea from the counter. Everyone filed in, filling up the small kitchen.

"That Machine has never been anything but bad news," Yoakum said, leaning against the counter. "It's unnatural. Who knows what kind of damage it would have done if it kept moving all those years ago, but we just let it sit there. Ridiculous." He took a sip. "That's why I like all these trees. Keeps me from having to see it every morning."

"Yes," Dayla said, already tired from the conversation. "I can see that you're passionate."

"Ophelia said you have a way to get into the Machine?" Edwin asked, standing by the door.

"I have a concept," Yoakum said. "And a few tests. But I'm not allowed anywhere near The Shadow. If they see me, they're gonna arrest me or shoot me. But you're interested in getting inside? Why's that?"

"We have reasons." Dayla leaned back.

Victoria rolled her eyes at Dayla's vagueness. "There's something inside the Machine that's threatening people."

Dayla glared at Victoria.

Yoakum slammed his cup. "Of course, there's something inside the Machine! Machines don't drive themselves! Your autocars don't drive themselves! There's a soul inside that's rotten like a bad apple." He considered for a second. "I'll build you something that can get you inside."

"We need it as soon as possible," Edwin said.

"Then I best start working now."

"Let's just wait for a moment," Adelaide said. "How do we know you can even get through the shell?"

Yoakum grinned. "Come with me." He pushed past Edwin and back out the door.

Victoria shared a concerned look with Adelaide. Yoakum was crazy, but crazy didn't mean incompetent. People thought Victoria was crazy after all. Yoakum wasn't waiting for them, though, so they had to hurry out the door to catch him.

They followed him toward the barn. Victoria jogged a little to walk next to him.

"Hey, uh, Yoakum," she said. "What exactly do you farm here? I don't see any crops, unless you farm trees."

"I don't farm." He spat on the ground, a bit getting stuck in his beard and freezing. "I build things."

"What? Like a carpenter?"

Yoakum paused at the barn door. He took another slow sip of his tea as he pondered. "Sometimes." He pulled the door open.

Inside, the barn was empty, save for a metal hatch in the centre of the room. Yoakum passed his cup to Victoria and turned the handle on the hatch. He lifted the heavy steel and threw it back on its hinges. Beneath was a steep stone staircase with electric lights on the walls. There was more to this strange man than he let on.

Yoakum took his tea back and descended. "Make sure you shut the hatch behind you. Don't let all the heat out."

It was much warmer down the hatch than it was outside, or even in the house. Rig took up the rear and slammed the hatch shut, turning the handle to seal it once he did. At the bottom of the staircase was a stone room that was set up like a home. There was a seating area with a collection of newspapers and books. A lovely cream throw rug was on the floor next to a standing lamp.

There was another door, slightly ajar, across from the entrance. It was a heavy door that put the hatch above to shame. Yoakum entered the room beyond. Metal clattered and Victoria approached to see what was inside, but Yoakum reappeared abruptly with a sheet of metal and a hammer.

"This is a piece of the Machine that fell off," he said, leaning it against the wall. "It's very light, but also very strong."

He struck it with the hammer. It rang with a dull tone but didn't mark at all. Yoakum pulled a chisel out of his pocket and showed it to the crowd like a showman about to do a trick. He placed the chisel against the metal and struck the back with the hammer. The chisel's blade slipped about and couldn't damage it.

"However." He tossed the chisel aside and pulled out a thin nail. "Machine Ink can be added to the forging process to imbue the metal, as I'm sure our magician friend here knows. But you take that Ink, mix it with lavender, and then add it to the forging and you get this."

He placed the nail against the metal and with a soft tap from the hammer, it pierced the metal. Another tap and it went deeper. With a final hit, the nail head was firmly embedded in the metal that had been unfazed by a hammer and chisel.

Dayla leaned forward, inspecting the sheet. "I hope you have more than nails."

"Not right now. Never had reason to." He re-entered the back room. They were about to follow him when he slammed the door shut. There was the sound of metal sliding against metal as the door locked, not that it mattered much as there wasn't a handle on the outside. A panel at eye-level slid aside and Yoakum peeked through. "I'll work through the night to get you what you need. A saw blade, to cut through the Machine's shell. But I'm doing it my way. Make yourself at home up in the house. Light a fire, make some food, sleep, but don't leave the property. Did you see those flags on your way up?"

Everyone nodded.

"Those mark the end of my land. Not only that, when I flip my switch in here, they turn on my Wall. It's an invisible electrified barrier, like a giant shock shield. Nothing can get through. Investigate if you want, but don't touch it. I would hate to bury you here. See you in the morning."

With that, the panel slammed shut and the group was left in stunned silence.

Victoria crossed her arms. "I guess...we wait?"

They left the bunker as the sounds of work began.

They took Yoakum's advice and walked down the road to the edge of his property. Each of the flagpoles was a few dozen metres apart. Hush picked up a stick and tossed it through. Bolts of lightning shot out of the flagpoles and turned the stick to ash. They really were stuck inside.

They decided to make the best of it. The house was cold, but they lit a few fires and made some dinner when the sun set. Hush found a fiddle in Yoakum's stuff and tuned it up to play some songs. Once again, his array of skills shocked Victoria. Hush didn't pay any mind to her. Instruments were one of the talents he was most proud of. Besides, he learned to play the fiddle before he was taken.

As the night wore on, everyone slowly went off to bed. The house was large, with many rooms to sleep in. Dayla was first, disappearing upstairs to take the master bedroom. Then went Rig, upstairs as well. Edwin took the first bedroom on the ground floor, while Mattie, who wasn't affected by the cold, said she would sleep on the porch. Soon it was just Victoria, Adelaide, and Hush — plucking away at his fiddle strings.

"I think it's time to go to bed," Victoria said with a yawn. She leaned toward Adelaide. "Are you coming? There's one more bedroom."

"I actually would prefer to be alone tonight," Adelaide said.

Victoria's expression dropped. "Oh."

"It's not you." Adelaide forced a half-smile. "When I went back to Wrotdam, it was rough. I still don't know if I've completely processed it, and I would rather be alone to do that."

"I understand." Still, her expression betrayed her heartbreak. "You can take the bedroom then if you wish. I'll sleep in the study."

"No, please. You take the bedroom. I'm used to sleeping in chairs from when I would work late. It's almost more comfortable for me."

"As you wish." Victoria turned to leave but balked. She took Adelaide's hand and kissed her gently on the cheek. She pulled away, but Adelaide held onto her hand and pulled her in, kissing her on the lips.

Hush smiled. Victoria was still a pain, but he wasn't monstrous enough to not soften at the sight of love.

Victoria backed toward the bedroom, her fingers staying wrapped around Adelaide's until the last moment. Their arms dropped, and she entered her room and shut the door. Adelaide's gaze lingered on the shut door for a second, then she took a breath and rose to her feet.

"Goodnight, Hush," she said, stretching out her back.

"Goodnight, Adelaide." He placed the fiddle next to the couch he sat on. "It'll be a big day tomorrow."

Adelaide smiled at him, then left for the study. Hush laid back on the couch. He stared at the bare wood ceiling and listened to the sounds of the house settling.

It was December 30th, the next day would be New Year's Eve. The 20th Century would arrive with quite the fanfare.

CHAPTER 4

Adelaide entered the kitchen that morning to find everyone else already there. Hush had cooked up bacon and eggs and gave her a cheery, "Hello," as she arrived. The only one missing was Yoakum.

"He better finish whatever he's making in time," Edwin said, taking a bite of bacon. "We don't know when the Intelligence is going to act."

"Or," Dayla took a sip of tea, "nothing is going to happen."

"Still on about that, huh?"

"Simply saying we still don't have proof."

Rig jerked his head to the side. "Victoria's the proof."

Victoria threw her hands up. "Don't bring me into this squabbling."

"Can we please just eat?" Edwin asked.

Adelaide chuckled at the antics and sat next to Victoria. Hush put a plate in front of her. The bacon looked delicious and the eggs were sunny side up, just the way she liked them. Everything felt like a dream, and she had to pinch herself to prove it wasn't one.

"Is there any pepper?" Mattie asked, peering around the kitchen.

"Check the cupboards," Hush said.

Mattie pushed away from the table and opened the cupboards. She found one with cups and another with plates. When she opened the third, she screamed as a black blur shot out.

It streaked across the room and landed on the table with a wet sound. It was a clump of the Mire, no bigger than a fist. Everyone leapt back as the little Mire spun around. It sent plates flying, leapt high into the air, then slammed down hard enough to crack the table. Adelaide snapped her gauntlet out and blasted it with a torrent of flames, leaving a little bonfire in the centre of the table. Glances were shared across the room.

Rig grabbed his riotsaw from the corner. "We need to see Yoakum."

He took off at a sprint. Everyone snatched their weapons as they ran by. Adelaide's gaze lingered on the crumbling remains of the little Mire.

"Come on!" Victoria shouted, waiting at the door.

Adelaide followed. They reached the barn as Edwin pulled the hatch open. One by one, they descended the stairs into the bunker. The door to Yoakum's sealed room was still shut, but the viewing panel was open.

Rig peered through, then cursed and slammed his fist against the door. "Damn it!"

Edwin pulled him away and looked. He shut his eyes and bowed his head. Everyone in turn looked through the window until Adelaide could reach it. She grabbed the edges of the window and pulled herself close. Yoakum lay slumped over in the corner, covered in blood. He wasn't moving.

"How did this happen?" Edwin asked.

"Maybe he killed himself," Hush said.

"Sure, he just happened to of killed himself last night of all nights." Edwin tapped the door with his knuckles. "Can anyone open this?"

Rig approached the door and stuck his arm through the window. It was just big enough to reach his bicep, but no further. "I can't reach the lock."

Edwin turned to Victoria. "Do you think you can open it with your moon trick?"

"I can try." She unbuckled her pouch and pulled out one moon. She tossed it into the air and floated it through the window. She stood on her toes but couldn't get her head through to see what she was doing. "Does anyone have a mirror?"

Hush whipped out a small circular container from his pocket. He popped it open and inside was a mirror. He offered it to Victoria.

"Why do you have this?" she asked.

"So I can see into rooms."

"For stealing?"

Hush rolled his eyes. "Yes."

Victoria scoffed and held up the mirror to the window. "It's a bar that's been slid into a slot in the wall. I may be able to push it open." She put her hand against the door and focused. "Ah!" The moon clattered to the ground and Victoria clutched her head.

Adelaide stepped toward her.

"I'm fine." She raised her hand. "I just won't be able to push it. I should be able to tap it open." There was the sound of metal repeatedly hitting metal. Victoria sighed. "This could take a bit."

"Why would someone kill Yoakum?" Mattie wondered, tugging on her hat brim.

"I'm more interested in who." Edwin took off his glasses. He tapped them against his neck and paced the room. "Because as far as I can tell, there's only seven of us here."

The tapping stopped. Everyone turned to Edwin, then to each other. One after another they shared looks as what Edwin said percolated in their brains.

"You think one of us killed Yoakum?" Adelaide asked. "Why would any of us want him dead?"

Mattie rubbed her hands together. "Because they're a traitor."

"Someone's working with the Intelligence," Hush said, scanning the room.

"This is ridiculous." Victoria went back to opening the door.

"Yoakum is in a locked room," Rig said. "How would someone do that?"

"The little Mire." Dayla played her fingers long the mask on her hip. "It was strong enough to crack a table. It could lock a door."

"Then maybe it's what killed him," Mattie said.

"We won't know until we see the body." Edwin shook his glasses. "But why would Yoakum open the door for anyone except one of us? Everyone's a suspect."

Dayla jerked her head at him. "Even you."

Edwin glared back at her. He smirked in a way that looked almost like baring his teeth. "I don't suppose anyone wants to confess."

No one made a move.

Victoria slapped the door and jumped back. "It's open." She pulled her moon back through the window and tossed the mirror to Hush.

Rig bullied Victoria out of the way and used the slot to pull the door open, revealing the backroom. Half of it was a smithy and the other half a chemist. The smithy had a small forge, an anvil, and a bucket of some liquid that wasn't water but a very light amber. The chemist had a table full of beakers and labelled jars. The rest of the room was a mess of panels and wires that looked like a madman had designed it.

Yoakum himself was slumped in the corner near the forge, blood in a stagnant pool around his legs. His head hung over his chest and his arms were resting in his lap as if he had sat down to fall asleep. A bloody knife rested between his leg, the murder weapon, no doubt. There was a second patch of blood as well, splattered just in front of the entrance door.

Edwin went to check the body. "His throat was cut, not cleanly either. Not exactly the Mire's technique."

"What about this?" Hush knelt by the second bloodstain. "Is this his?"

"From that far away? Unlikely."

"Maybe it's the killer's," Rig said.

"Then it can't be one of us." Adelaide motioned around. "None of us are injured."

Victoria flipped her moon around in her fingers. "Unless they're hiding it."

Dayla shook her head. "Any wound that would bleed that much would be noticeable." Her gaze turned to Mattie. "But Mattie can heal herself."

Mattie's eyes widened. "Wait. Don't go accusing me. I gave everyone a vial, remember? We all could heal ourselves."

"But my vial is still full." Dayla pulled it out. The clear slime was still inside. "Is anybody's not?"

From their pockets, they each revealed a small glass vial. Six in total, but each one still containing the thick liquid. Dayla looked back at Mattie.

"Hold on." Hush stepped between Dayla and Mattie. "You can't accuse her because she doesn't have something. What if there's someone else here? Someone who came in before the Wall was turned on. It doesn't have to be one of us."

Edwin left the body and took wide steps toward the door. Dayla stepped in his way, holding her boltrifle strap out from her shoulder. "Where are you going?" she asked

"If there was someone here, they would leave tracks." Edwin brushed past, spinning her as he bumped her shoulder. "I'm just going to see if I can find any." He vanished up the stairs.

"Hush mentioned the Wall," Adelaide said, tapping her fingers to her lips. "Do we know if it's still up?"

"Someone will have to check," Dayla said.

Rig overturned a tray of tools, sending them clattering across the floor.

"What are you doing, you oaf?" Victoria exclaimed.

"Yoakum was making a saw blade." Rig tossed the tray aside. "Where is it?"

Everyone scanned the room. Adelaide couldn't see anything that looked like a saw blade amid the many cutting implements that were about. Either Yoakum didn't finish it, or someone took it. Edwin came back in with his hands on his hips.

"There aren't any tracks other than ours." He pulled on his coat lapels, letting out a breath of vapours. "If that Wall's still up, we're stuck here."

"Something of that power needs a generator." Hush approached one of the panels and popped it open, only for it to release a bundle of wires like a jack-in-the-box. "Uh, somewhere. It has to be drawing staggering amounts of power. It'll run out of Ink eventually."

Edwin pushed his fist against the wall. "This must be what the Intelligence wants. It's going to act soon, and it wants us trapped here, out of the way. And someone is helping it."

Dayla tapped the butt of her boltrifle that hung off her back. "And who put you in charge? Maybe you're the traitor and you're trying to throw us off."

"You want to point fingers at me?" He sauntered up to Dayla, looking down on her with his electric blue gaze. "Why don't we turn them back on you? I have a few 'maybes' as well. Maybe you still really believe the Church's lies. They've been your entire, long, sad life. Why turn on them now?"

Dayla's mouth twitched. She clenched her fist around her mask's beak that hung off her hip.

"Hush." Edwin didn't look away from Dayla. "If the Wall's still up, can you take it down?"

Hush's gaze flicked between Edwin and Dayla. "Sure. I've disabled security systems before. They just usually aren't so...big."

"Are we just going to trust him to actually do it?" Victoria pointed her moon at him. "He's a criminal. And you've seen his outbursts, he's unstable. How do we know he even wants to take the Wall down? No, I'll stay too." She cracked a grin in his direction. "I know a thing or two about machinery. You're not the only one with a surprising set of skills."

Hush glared at her but didn't say a word. He just casually checked to make sure his branderbuss was still with him.

"Do we really want to talk about outbursts?" Rig said, staring Victoria down. She sneered at him. "I'm just fine."

"Grouping up is not a bad idea," Edwin said. "We shouldn't let anyone be alone. Everyone can keep an eye on someone else. And if there's an eighth person here, we don't want to give them a target. But time is against us. I'm going to go check if the Wall's still up. If it's not, then I guess we all worried for nothing."

"I'll go with you," Dayla offered.

Edwin burst into laughter. "Absolutely not. Of the four of you, only one hasn't wanted to — or succeeded — in killing me. Mattie, you'll be my partner."

Mattie came back to reality. She opened her mouth like she wanted to protest, but no sounds came out.

Edwin continued, "Dayla, why don't you take Rig and Adelaide and look around. Maybe there is someone here we missed." He headed for the door and waved for Mattie to follow. "Come on, Mattie. Maybe we'll get lucky and there'll be a break in the Wall."

Dayla scowled at the back of Edwin's head as he left. She pulled the mask off her hip and donned it. Adelaide knew what that meant. Dayla was mad but didn't want anyone reading her expression. Adelaide hated the idea of everyone fighting. Edwin seemed ready to take charge, though.

"Let's look around," Dayla said, swinging her rifle into her hands. She looked back to where Hush dug through the wires and panels while Victoria sat on a table nearby. Yoakum's body remained in the corner. No one would be moving it. "Shut the door after we're gone."

Victoria nodded. She looked at Adelaide with a smile, and Adelaide blushed in reply. Rig had given up trying to find something and snatched his riotsaw as he left. Dayla waited for Adelaide to start moving.

There was still time until the Intelligence's plan was to begin. But they were stuck on a farm, with dwindling people they could trust.

CHAPTER 5

The Wall was still up. Part of Mattie knew it would be. That was the sort of situation they were in. But there was still hope, so they walked around the perimeter of the land. Occasionally Edwin would tap the wall with a stick. If a spark shot out, that meant the Wall was still active. They hoped there would be a hole somewhere that they could leave through, as it would also mean that one of the seven wasn't a traitor. But as they walked by each flagpole, it became less likely.

As they passed yet another pole and another spark, Edwin spoke to her. "Can I ask you something, Mattie?"

"I don't see why I would say no." She kicked a stone as she walked.

"What do you think of Victoria?"

Mattie glanced at Edwin, but he stared straight ahead. "What do you mean?"

"She bonded with the Intelligence. That's what she said, wasn't it?" He tapped the next section. More sparks. "She knows all about its plan, but when we start talking about what to do about it, she pulled back. Why would she do that?"

Mattie thought back to the talk she had with Victoria in Severtson. "She's scared."

"Or." Edwin paused. "She's the traitor."

Their footsteps crunched through the forest. There was something Victoria had said that stuck with Mattie, even if it passed her by at the time. *Maybe an apocalypse wouldn't be the worst thing for me.*

"She doesn't care about people," Edwin continued. "At least people who aren't Adelaide. It's not just that she thinks she's better than everyone else, she thinks other people don't matter. Maybe the Intelligence would give her a chance to truly feel like she's a god. I'm asking you because you've heard its voice, but she connected with it in some deeper way. How would that affect her?"

"I don't know." Mattie pulled her wraps down. "The voice I hear is demanding. I admit I do feel a pull from it at times. I think that's what broke Asha. But to connect with it in the way she described...there's no telling what it would do. I think you're right. She's the most likely suspect."

Edwin bobbed his head. He tapped the Wall again. Sparks. There seemed to be something else on his mind. Mattie could feel it seeping out of him. He was working up the words to say.

"There's one more thing." He sighed. "If it's not Victoria, what about Hush?"

Mattie stopped dead. Edwin looked back at her. The wind blew the snow between them.

"What about Hush?" Mattie asked.

"Just let me explain." He swung his arm for Mattie to keep walking. Mattie slowly crept forward, and they continued checking the Wall. "The light that took Hush, that must be the Intelligence, do you agree?"

"Yes."

"Hush was with the Intelligence for a long time, having his mind messed with in ways we can't even imagine. I'm not saying he would do it intentionally, but this thing has surprised us at every turn. I know he's your friend, but can we say with absolute certainty that what I'm saying is impossible?"

Mattie bit her lip. "It's not him. It's Victoria. And we left him alone with her."

"She won't kill him. It would be too obvious. The Intelligence doesn't need us dead; it needs us stuck." He tossed the stick into the Wall. "Which it's doing very well. The Wall's solid."

"Now what do we do?"

Edwin put his hands on his hips and looked into the forest. "We find a way to take down the Wall." He started walking. "We should go back to the bunker."

"Wait." Mattie took off her hat and tapped it against her leg. "You don't think I'm the traitor? I feel like it's on everyone's mind since, well..." She motioned to her face.

"You're low on my list," Edwin called over his shoulder. "Call it a hunch."

Mattie grinned and dropped her hat back on her head. She hurried to catch up to Edwin. It was nice to have someone on her side.

Rig, Adelaide, and Dayla searched the entire house and found nothing. The remains of the little Mire still smouldered on the cracked table, but it was the only indication of a foreign entity. The weather grew colder as they searched as if the environment itself reacted to their desperation.

Rig wasn't desperate, though. He was angry. He hated being stuck. *Yoakum must have finished that saw blade*, he thought. *That body was only a couple hours dead.*

Without the saw blade, they were lost. Rig needed it if he wanted to protect the people like he was meant to do. He flipped the couch out of anger and noticed Dayla standing at the back door, Adelaide just behind her.

"Come with me," she said.

Rig kicked the couch, then followed. Dayla brought him and Adelaide to the edge of the forest. She looked around to ensure they were alone, then spoke in hushed tones.

"It's Edwin," she said. "It must be Edwin. He's taking command to keep us distracted until time runs out."

"You didn't even think this was real," Rig said, thrusting his finger at her.

"It's real enough now."

Adelaide rolled her head. "I don't know if it's Edwin."

Dayla turned her glass-eyed mask to her. With it on she was unreadable, but she wasn't doing much to hide her tone. "You fought him. You both did. He's amberwild. He's a sawbones who's fallen to the Mire. And those arms! Do you think he just found them? Made them himself? No, something put them on him." She gestured to Rig. "You've been talking with him. Has he told you about anything?"

"No." He stuck his riotsaw in the ground and leaned on the handle. "But he's been losing his memory."

"Losing his memory? Or having them taken away? I'm not saying the Edwin Zhen you grew up with would do these things. But he's dead and gone. This Edwin is a monster created by something alien."

"It's…" Adelaide put her fingers to her lips. "Possible."

Dayla bobbed her head, her mask's beak bouncing. "Edwin is also the only one here who could stand up to all of us thanks to those freakish arms. Except you, Rig. No one else has the training you do. We'll let him make the first move, but we have to subdue him. Can you do it?"

Rig bowed his head. Edwin had been his friend for most of his life. And while there were moments after he returned that Rig could honestly say reminded him of the old days, he could feel that Edwin was a different person. But how different of a person was he?

Dayla perked her head up and looked into the distance. "They're going back to the bunker."

Rig and Adelaide followed her gaze. Edwin and Mattie were crossing the lawn from the forest to the barn. Dayla tightened her grip on her boltrifle.

"We better go back as well," she said, hurrying off.

Adelaide shared a glance with Rig, then quickly looked away. She followed Dayla. Rig, after taking a moment to compose himself, did too.

◄ ∞ ►

The bunker was a mess. There was no pattern to the wires Hush was elbow deep in. Some of the panels were empty or even contained rotting food. Worse than that, there were unlabelled hidden switches all over the room. Hush had considered starting to flip them, but when the first one set off a flamethrower trap in the other room, he decided it was better to follow the wires.

That was made harder by being in a room with a decomposing body. Yoakum's corpse was an ever-present reminder of the stakes they were dealing with. Of course, Victoria sitting on a nearby table with one leg daintily folded over the other didn't help. She had mentioned she would assist, but it felt more like she was just there to keep an eye on him.

"I'm getting a sense of déjà vu," she said, tapping her long nails on the metal table. "Except this time, I'm the one watching you."

Hush followed a black wire to the end, only to find that neither side was connected. "You can't tinker I'm the traitor."

"You're a good choice. I don't know anything about you. Dayla just picked you up out of a pit and offered you some money. But everything about you is wrong. From that gun you won't let go of, to your seemingly endless array of hobbies. There's something off about you, and that's reason enough."

"There's something off about me?" He threw down the wires and stood up. "How about you? Why don't you show me your magic trick? Make your moons float."

Victoria scowled at him. With a snap of her wrist, she unbuckled her pouch and floated a moon out into the air between them. She cast Hush a smug smile.

"What about the others?" Hush asked.

Victoria's smile faltered — only for a second, but enough for Hush to notice.

"You know what I bet? I bet you broke yourself back in Dawnhallow and now you can't do what you used to do." He poked the moon, sending it into a spin. "I bet you can only control one, maybe two moons and it scares you. Your trick has gone all twisty and since it made you feel unique, now you're grimy. That makes you an easy mark, and I know easy marks."

Victoria pushed out her jaw. "I'm sick of your stupid slang. Talk like a normal human being."

"So, maybe you make this connection with the Intelligence, and it starts flapping at you. It makes promises. In return, you just have to give up people. It's not like you care about people anyway."

Victoria grabbed Hush by the coat and pulled him in. Her moon trembled, then she broke and clutched her head, flopping back. The moon fell to the ground.

Hush bent down to pick it up. Victoria lay on the table, holding her hands in front of her face. Hush turned the moon over in his hands. He lost his temper. He was just sick of being looked down on. Sometimes, in his darkest moments, he missed being in the cycles. At least some of them were pleasant, even if they weren't real.

"You're not a traitor," Hush said, laying the moon on the table. "You're too stubborn to be."

Victoria opened her hand and the moon slid toward it. She sat up. Her lips trembled. It was an emotional vulnerability Hush had never seen in her before.

"It's coming back." Victoria tapped the moon on her fingers. "Slowly. But I'm scared it won't be like it was before. Broken things don't always get fixed perfectly."

"But sometimes they come back stronger."

Victoria chuckled. Someone pounded at the door. Hush stepped back so Victoria could hop off the table. She put the moon in her pouch and stopped.

"You're a lot nicer than you have any right to be," she said, then opened the door.

Edwin came in with Mattie just behind him. He ignored Victoria and focused on Hush.

"The Wall is still up," Edwin said. "Please tell me you found out how to take it down."

"Uh." Hush glanced at the pile of junk. "It's a mess in here. I haven't figured it out yet."

"We need that Wall down."

"We certainly do, Edwin," Dayla said as she entered with Rig and Adelaide in tow. She walked right up to Edwin. "We didn't find signs of anyone else here. It's just us."

"Did you actually look? Or did you just gossip with each other?"

Dayla cocked her head. She spun away, tapping her finger next to the trigger of the boltrifle she held in her hands. "If there is a traitor, we need to find out who they are. Even if we get off this farm, they'll try to stop us again. We've already seen they're willing to kill. We must do something."

"Then let's do something. I think it's pretty obvious who the traitor is." Edwin crossed his arms, then turned around and looked at Victoria.

Victoria recoiled. She whipped her head around to make sure Edwin wasn't looking at anyone else. "Wait, me?"

"It's not Victoria!" Adelaide exclaimed. "She nearly killed herself fighting the Mire in Dawnhallow."

"Now that we know it was all a trick, there's a difference between fighting the Mire and destroying the Machine." Edwin leaned toward Victoria. "She is the only one with a clear connection to the Intelligence. And she wouldn't even have to open the door to kill Yoakum."

"But someone did open the door," Hush said. "They were at least in the room. The blood proves that."

"I said she wouldn't have to, not that she didn't." Edwin stretched to his full height, leaning his head back. "We don't know what the Intelligence would do once it got in someone's head. We don't even know if it's Victoria in there anymore."

Victoria had turned from fright to a fighting stance. She stared back at Edwin with the courage of someone twice her size.

"But," Dayla said. "There's only one of us who fell to the Mire."

Edwin looked back over his shoulder. Dayla, Rig, and Adelaide stood side by side. It took Edwin a moment to realize what was happening.

"You can't be serious," he said.

"The Intelligence gave you those arms, didn't it?" Dayla tightened her grip on her gun.

"I don't remember."

"Convenient." She rolled her head about her neck. "People don't come back from seeing amber."

Edwin stomped his foot. "Stop saying that like it's a rule! I am proof that it's not!"

Dayla raised her rifle and turned it on. "You're proof of nothing."

Hush backed away. He had been in tense situations before, and when they broke, they broke hard. Dayla and Edwin were two trains barrelling for each other. Hush couldn't stop them if he wanted to. Mattie got closer to him as they could both only watch.

Edwin looked at Rig. "What about you? Do you agree with them?"

Rig adjusted his grip on his riotsaw's backbar. He gritted his teeth and ran his hand over his hat.

"Rig." Adelaide reached out for him.

He turned his head to her. "What about you?"

Adelaide froze, then backed up. Dayla cocked her head. She was certainly bewildered under her mask.

"Yeah." Rig pointed at Adelaide with the handle of his saw. "What about the Church? You disappeared before we even came here."

"I had doubts," Adelaide said. "I went to the Archbishop for the truth."

"And did you get it? Did you learn the Church's dirty secret?" He stepped closer to her. "Did it horrify you, or are you still doing exactly what they want?"

Victoria flew across the room. She put herself between Rig and Adelaide.

"Rig!" Edwin reached for him. "This isn't about the Church anymore."

"It's always about the Church. You said they follow this Faceless God. This was their plan all along." He spread his arms and turned in a slow circle. "Their God's plan! That's why they didn't care about Dawnhallow! They wanted the Mire to take people!"

Adelaide leaned over Victoria. "They didn't know the Mire was—"

"But they did..." Dayla's rifle barrel lowered. "They were told last year, and they hid it."

"Dayla. I didn't know."

"The Ink Clergy is supposed to know everything." Rig stepped forward, only for Dayla to reaffirm her grip and turned the gun on him.

"Don't move!" she shouted. "Let me think."

"No more thinking. Someone has to do something." His hand slid to his branderbuss. "Maybe it has to be me."

Victoria thrust her hand forward. A moon tore the top off her pouch and embedded into Rig's shoulder. "Run!"

Adelaide bolted out of the bunker. Victoria pulled the moon, only for it to falter on the way and fall. Victoria grabbed for it, but it sliced her hand open. She abandoned it and instead chased after Adelaide. Rig clutched onto his shoulder. He didn't seem to care that Dayla had her gun on him, he took off after the fleeing duo anyway.

Edwin moved to follow, but Dayla turned her rifle back on him. It was no longer shaking in her hands.

"I'm going after them," Dayla said, backing out the door. "If I see you following, I will kill you."

"Can't wait to see you try," Edwin replied.

Dayla snapped around and disappeared up the stairs. Edwin took deep breaths. Electricity crackled down his arms, destroying his sleeves and gloves to reveal the metal beneath. He looked back at Hush and Mattie with eyes like headlamps.

He pointed at the door. "You shut that door and find a way to take down the Wall. Now!"

With that, he sprinted out of the bunker.

CHAPTER 6

Everyone had already disappeared by the time Edwin reached the surface. He needed to find Rig, or Dayla, or even Victoria. Someone. There was a traitor, but he couldn't let everything fall apart and everyone kill each other. That was what the Intelligence wanted. It wanted them distracted so they couldn't do what needed to be done.

A rustle in the trees caught his eye and he charged after it. He ran deep into the forest. No one was there. He slowed to a walk. A distant shout sounded like Rig, but it bounced off the trees until he couldn't tell where it came from.

A bolt of electricity whizzed past, striking the bark off a nearby tree. Edwin darted behind cover. Dayla had found him first.

"I told you if you followed, I would kill you," Dayla shouted, her voice similarly getting lost in the heavy woods.

"I didn't doubt you." He pressed his back against a tree and waited.

Another bolt flew by, but it was a good four metres away.

"Are you getting old?" Edwin called. "Losing your eyesight?"

The next shot went behind him. Was she missing on purpose?

"I never cared if you were the traitor." Dayla's voice felt like it was coming in from all sides. "My duty is to kill the amberwild. I let you go once, assuming Rig would do my job. I'm not letting you slip by again."

"To be fair." Edwin flexed his fingers. "Rig succeeded."

A third bolt came shooting at him. Edwin caught it with the palm of his hand, dispersing along his arm. He traced an imaginary line back where the bolt came from, then took off in a burst of snow to follow it. He traversed the forest like a playground, looking for Dayla's sniper position.

He grabbed a handful of bark and threw himself forward. Out of the corner of his eyes, a flagpole appeared. His heart jumped into his throat and he slammed both heels into the dirt. His hands, however, went forward. Lightning cascaded into a lattice between the poles into his arms. Edwin threw himself back, rolling along his shoulder to a low crouch. His wrists were blackened from the energy.

He'd reached the end of the property. Dayla was nowhere to be seen. She couldn't have been fast enough to reposition after her shot. It was definitely where it came from, so where was the person firing it?

The Wall crackled, and a bolt shot toward him. He blocked it with his hand, then two more as they bounced off the Wall. *So that's it,* Edwin thought. He retreated in a flurry of snow and dove over a fallen tree. More bolts struck the wet wood, making it sizzle and pop with the sudden heat. He landed face-first in the snow and cursed himself for being so stupid.

Dayla was reflecting her shots off the electrified Wall. Her first shots weren't misses — they were her calibrating for the angle of reflection. Now she had it dialled in.

Edwin spun onto his back. High above the canopy, something sparked. Edwin had wondered if the Wall was a dome. Question answered. Edwin rolled out of the way and a bolt struck the ground where he just lay. He continued rolling until he could get back onto his feet. More bolts fell from the sky and Edwin had to sprint to keep ahead of them, lest he got struck by lightning.

He darted from tree to tree, trying to confuse Dayla's aim enough that he could escape and figure out where she was. The bounces off the Wall didn't seem to be simple reflections. There was some difference that Edwin couldn't account for, but Dayla could.

He blocked a shot with his arm and took cover behind a tree. There was a *zap,* followed by a section of the tree charring. Except it wasn't from a shot. Edwin's arm discharged a small burst of electricity without his knowledge. Luckily it was damp, or the tree could have caught fire. Between the wall and blocking the shots, Edwin's arms had been gathering up electrical energy. He could use that.

It had been several seconds since the last shot. Dayla must have been moving to get a better vantage point. It gave him some time to work. He found two rocks near his foot. He placed his left hand on one and took the second rock in the other. Like a sword on an anvil, he smashed his left hand with the rock, sending out electrical sparks. He hit it again, and again.

The metal crumpled and the joints cracked apart. He put the rock down and tore out circuitry until the hand was nearly hollow. If he thought of his arm like a rifle, then his hand would be the barrel. He squeezed and worked at his hand until it resembled something he could use.

Just in time, as there was a crack and a bolt of lightning came tearing through the woods. Edwin didn't dodge this time. He caught shot after shot with his good hand. Electricity built up in the bulbs on his arms, dancing wildly to cheer Edwin on. With each shot, the power rose until he swore he could feel it in his heart.

The next shot came and Edwin didn't dodge it or catch it. Instead, he lifted his makeshift gun and fired. His shot slipped past Dayla's. They arced to each other for a moment before shooting off in opposite directions. Edwin took the hit in the side. It hurt unbelievably, but he couldn't look away from his own shot bouncing off the wall and disappearing into the forest.

Somewhere in the distance, Dayla screamed. Edwin grabbed some snow and pushed it onto his wound, dulling the pain of the burn. He shook the snow off his hand and hurried to investigate his quarry.

Edwin had hit her. Dayla was flabbergasted. He didn't even have a gun, but a bolt of electrical energy came back from where she had shot and hit her in the leg. She tried to crawl away, but the pain was immense. Instead, she crumpled up in the snow next to a splintered tree trunk.

Edwin stepped into view. Dayla grabbed her rifle and fired. Edwin blocked the shot, then zoomed forward and tore the boltrifle from her hands. He tossed it aside and Dayla noticed that at least she had hit him in return. He cradled his ribs and his left hand looked malformed.

"Make it quick," Dayla said, flopping back against the stump. "I don't feel like hearing you talk."

"I know why you hate me," Edwin said.

"I told you why."

"But you're wrong." He eased himself onto a fallen tree, groaning from the pain in his side. "How long have you been a leech for?"

Dayla said nothing.

Edwin shook his head. "Decades, right? And in that time, how many amberwild sawbones have you killed? Fifty? Sixty?"

"Over a hundred."

Edwin let out a low whistle. "And each time you did, there was one thing you had on your mind. 'They're sick. And you don't come back from that.' But I did. I am the destruction of your life's belief. Now you may say that you want the truth. But that's not you, is it? You just want to reaffirm the things you already believe. You're fine with learning these lies the Church has been selling because you never trusted them in the first place. But when something truly challenges you, you can't see it. There's a creature in the Machine. And I'm sitting here in front of you, an amberwild sawbones who came back. But I don't know how."

Dayla's eyes went hot with tears. She tore her mask off and threw it to the ground. It didn't seem worthwhile anymore to hide her emotions or think about plans that she didn't even have. Edwin was right, and it meant she was wrong her entire life. How many people did she kill that didn't have to die? Decades of a life.

Did she live them wrong? She was old, she felt it every morning. Did she have any time to make it right?

"I'm sorry." Edwin pulled out Mattie's vial and poured it on his wound. "Because there's nothing I can say to help you. But I know you're not the traitor. You wouldn't feel this way if you were." He held up the vial. "Please use yours. We need you to finish this."

Edwin headed into the forest. Dayla sat in silence, letting her tears turn cold on her cheeks.

"Do you believe someone's a traitor?" Hush asked, pulling apart a panel in the wall. "You think any of them would betray us?"

"You think any of them wouldn't?" Mattie sat on the table, spinning her hat slowly in her hands. She looked at Yoakum's body. She had covered it with a blanket from the other room, deciding she didn't want to look at it anymore. "We're all killers here."

"But we all fought together. Sure, some of them tarnish my shine but...we're fighting the end of the world, aren't we?"

"I suppose." Mattie had been floating through the day. She didn't much like the idea of a traitor in their group either, but just because she didn't like it didn't mean it wasn't true.

Edwin's words came to her again. If Hush was the traitor, he could not even know he did it. They all slept in separate rooms, no one knew what they did that night.

"Hush," she said softly. "I want to ask you something. But I want you to know it doesn't mean anything, I just have to know."

Hush smiled at her, but it faded when Mattie didn't smile back. "What is it?"

"Have there been any...aftereffects from your time imprisoned?"

Hush's gaze dropped to his feet. "Only that I'm pretty sure I'm real pig twisty. What sort of aftereffects do you mean?"

"It's just..." She put her hat on her head, hiding beneath the brim. "You mentioned how it got into your head. I've been wondering how deep it got?"

Hush didn't say anything. He was frozen, a bundle of wires in one hand. His eyes stayed affixed to an empty spot in the air.

"You think I could be the traitor," he said. "And not even know it."

"It's just a dumb thought I had." She jumped up from the table. "It wasn't even me, Edwin put a bug in my head. And I... I trust you, Hush. I haven't had any friends since my condition started, but you make me feel like a normal person. I love you, and if you say that there is a hundred percent chance that what I'm saying is impossible, then I will believe you. Can you say that?"

Hush didn't move. "No."

Mattie embraced him. "I still trust you. "

Hush's arms hung limply at his side.

Three collapsed trees created a lean-to of snow and vegetation which Victoria pulled Adelaide inside. They crouched against their wooden ward, listening for any sound from their pursuer.

"What do we do?" Adelaide asked, her voice barely more than a whisper.

"I'm not going to let anyone hurt you." Victoria poured the healing slime from her vial onto her hand. The wound from her moon closed and was good as new. "We'll circle around and get back to the bunker. If we shut the door, Rig can't get in. I know he's big and angry, but, he's not that strong."

"We're just going to hide from him?"

"If I need to, I'll kill him."

"No!" Adelaide grabbed Victoria's arm.

Victoria raised her hand, silencing Adelaide. They waited, but nothing happened.

Adelaide spoke quieter. "We don't have to kill anyone. No one has to die."

"He wants to kill you."

She shook her arm. "Then we can talk to him."

Victoria rubbed her nose. "He doesn't seem like the talking type." Adelaide was sweet, but an idealist. Though, to be honest, Victoria wasn't sure she could take Rig on in the state she was in.

A twig snapped. Victoria put her hand over Adelaide's mouth. They froze like that, waiting for something to happen.

The sound of spinning metal tore through the silence. A riotsaw burst through the thicket, catching Adelaide on the shoulder. She screamed. Victoria pulled her out of the hiding spot as Rig cut through one of the trees and sent the structure crashing to the ground. He stepped over the ruin, crunching the branches under his feet. His riotsaw gnashed against the air, rattling its blooded chained teeth around and around. Victoria put herself in front of Adelaide.

"Get out of the way, Victoria," Rig said, advancing on them.

"You're wrong about this!" Victoria felt for another moon in her pouch. "It's not Adelaide!"

"Then who is it?"

Adelaide wrapped herself around Victoria's arm. "It's Edwin!"

"Not this again."

Victoria didn't believe that Edwin was the traitor. Despite all his gruffness, his anger never seemed to be at the world as a whole. He loved people too much.

But if it could get Rig's attention off Adelaide, Victoria was sure she could make up some argument.

"Of course it's him!" she said. "Just think about it! Ever since we met him in Dawnhallow he never wanted to be a part of our group. He was going to fight on his own, but that fight didn't matter! We know that now. And all of a sudden, he's the one in charge? Because now we're doing something that matters, and he needs to stop it!"

Rig blinked. He lowered the riotsaw until it nearly touched the ground.

"We were fine until he started pointing fingers!" She was close to getting to him, she could feel it. Rig was surprisingly manipulable. "And his arms? He's part machine! Think for yourself for a second!"

"He worked for the Church," Adelaide added. The blood from her shoulder trickled down her arm and dripped onto the snow. "He silenced the people who spoke against them. He knew about the Faceless God far before I ever did. If anyone is their agent, it's him."

The riotsaw rumbled, but no one moved. Rig's expression had gone slack. He turned off his saw and Victoria took a breath of relief. Then Rig cried out in rage and slammed his saw repeatedly into a tree. He dug a gouge out of the trunk, then turned on his heel and stomped away.

Victoria's knees shook. She wrapped her arms around Adelaide and never wanted to let go. Her blood stained her clothes. The wound wasn't deep, but the terrible blade mangled the flesh like a shark's teeth.

"We have to go," Adelaide said, breaking the embrace. "I don't want to run into anyone else out here."

Victoria took Adelaide's hand in hers. It felt cold from the long day. Still, it wasn't over. The tree Rig struck slowly creaked over, then collapsed to the forest floor with a burst of snow. At least they avoided that fate.

CHAPTER 7

T he fight with Dayla left Edwin without any sign of Rig. Eventually, after circling the perimeter, he decided the best option was to return to the bunker and hope someone had come back. Lamenting over the sorry state of his hand, he almost missed who waited for him. Just the man he was looking for. Rig stood by the hatch with his riotsaw on his shoulder. Some of the teeth glinted red in the gloomy sun.

"I see there's blood on that thing," Edwin said, slowing to a crawl. Waiting to see what move Rig made.

"No one's dead." Rig stepped toward him. "You did work for the Church, right?"

"Yes, I did." He went around Rig and descended the stairs. He played it cool but kept his ears open.

Rig followed, his footsteps pounding anvils down the steps. "What did you do for them?"

"I told you. I killed for them. Whatever they needed."

"And do you still do that?"

Edwin stopped at the door. The tone of the conversation had shifted to something malicious, though he couldn't figure out why. What happened to him in the forest? *Keep pushing on, Edwin.* He pounded on the door. *Keep pushing on.* "I'm not going to dignify that with a response."

Mattie opened the door but stepped back as Edwin stomped in.

"Look at me, Edwin!" Rig hollered. "Do you still work for the Church?"

Edwin came firing back at Rig. "They told me they could bring my family back! That is the only reason why I did what they said, and they lied!"

"What if the Intelligence made the same offer? Would you betray us for your family again?"

Edwin gritted his teeth. "So, you think I'm the traitor, huh?"

Rig eased his riotsaw off his shoulder. "I don't think it was a coincidence that you came back."

They circled like boxers waiting for their moment. Edwin was down one hand, but when Rig was ready to fight, there was no holding him back. Hush and Mattie backed away, eye-wide and shaking at what was playing out. Adelaide and Victoria arrived at the door, a fresh wound on the former's shoulder. Edwin suspected they had something to do with this.

Edwin held out his hand and said, "Rig—"

"I'm done with talking!" Rig took his saw in both hands and attacked.

Edwin knocked the saw aside and took a swing with his malformed hand. Rig ducked and spun, then rose with a vertical slice. An obvious move and Edwin easily caught the blade with his good hand.

"You're not trying to kill me," he said. "You didn't even turn your saw on."

Rig growled then slid the handle up. The chains roared to life and sparks shot out from Edwin's palm. Rig wrenched the blade away and came in swinging again.

Adelaide and Victoria hurried out of the way as Rig and Edwin fought. Rig kept swinging wildly, but Edwin simply stepped out of the way. They had sparred together many times, and Edwin knew Rig's weakness. Once Rig got too angry, he got sloppy. A little rage was a motivator. If he could only focus, he would be nearly unbeatable, but it was so easy for him to fall to his emotions. Edwin just needed to push.

"You know why I never thought you were the traitor?" he said, knocking the saw aside and leaning in. "You're far too stupid to trick anyone."

Rig bared his teeth and cried out in rage. He reared back for a double-handed chop. Edwin slid in and caught Rig's hands. He punched him in the gut and pulled the riotsaw out of his grasp. Rig fell back and Edwin turned off the saw.

"Are we done now?" He tossed the saw to Hush.

Rig slammed both fists into the ground and charged. He caught Edwin around the waist and lifted him into the air. He carried him across the room and slammed him into the chemist's table. Edwin elbowed Rig's spine a few times, then kicked him back.

Rig wasn't ready to stop. He cracked his neck and put his fists up. Edwin hopped off the table and came charging in with a right hook. They went blow for blow. It was a dirty, brutal brawl. Edwin gave up his fancy footwork and simply took hits and returned them. Primal. Cathartic.

Edwin caught a haymaker from Rig, trapping it under his arm. He spun, dragging Rig with him, before tossing him out the door. Dayla had been descending the stairs and stopped on the last step as Rig landed at her feet.

"I'm not the same as last time we fought!" Edwin cried, spreading his arms. "You're not killing me this time! Now come on!"

Adelaide, seeing Edwin beat Rig, lunged for a switch within a panel nearby. She yanked it down and the ceiling above Edwin opened, revealing a triple-bladed scythe.

"Edwin!" Mattie shouted. "Above you!"

Edwin looked up as the scythe dropped. Blood splattered the floor, and everyone went silent.

One of the blades pierced through Edwin's collarbone. He had moved just in time to avoid it hitting his heart. Hush ran for the switch and returned it to its original position. The trap retracted into the roof and Edwin collapsed.

Rig scrambled to his knees and crawled to Edwin's side. Mattie slid in behind him and started working up the slime from her stomach. Edwin didn't care about either of those things. He noticed where he had fallen.

Directly on the second patch of blood.

"Adelaide," Edwin said, fighting through the pain of speaking. "How did you know about that switch?"

Adelaide's eyes widened. Slowly, the attention of the room turned to her. "I... I guessed. This guy had all sorts of traps."

"You guessed?" Edwin sat up with Rig's help. Mattie placed the slime against his collarbone and he already started to feel better. "You randomly guessed that there was a trap there when you had no reason to believe that there was one, or that the switch you pulled would activate it? You did that without knowing it was there. Unless you did know."

"Stop talking," Victoria said, taking Adelaide's hand and squeezing it.

"It's too much of a coincidence. Unless if you were here, and someone like Yoakum used it, so you knew where it was. And why would he use a trap like that? Unless someone was trying to kill him."

"That's not true!" Adelaide trembled. "I truly did just guess."

"Adelaide." Dayla entered the room. "Something had been bothering me. I was too focused on Edwin to give it much thought, but I had to see for myself. I wondered how the little Mire was able to get in if the Wall had been up all night." She held out an empty jar. The interior was slick with some sort of residue. "This is what you kept the Mire sample in. Remember? Where is that sample? It wasn't very big after all."

"None of this means anything! I destroyed the sample back in Dawnhallow, as soon as I learned what it was capable of." She turned to Victoria, pulling on her hand. "You believe me? Right, Victoria? Victoria?"

Victoria was staring at the floor. "Why haven't you healed your shoulder?"

"What?"

"We all got a vial from Mattie. I used mine to heal my hand, but why haven't you used yours to heal your shoulder?"

Adelaide looked at her shoulder, still slowly leaking blood. "I haven't had time."

"Then do it." Victoria gazed into Adelaide's eyes. "Please."

Adelaide released Victoria's hand and backed away. She looked around the room for help, but everyone was still. With a shaking hand, Adelaide reached into her robes and pulled out the vial. She looked at the clear slime within.

"This doesn't mean anything," she said.

Hush snatched the vial from her hand. He yanked the top off and poured it on her shoulder. They waited. Adelaide looked at the floor.

Nothing happened.

"There's enough supplies in this room that you could make a convincing facsimile, huh?" Edwin returned to his feet. "Smart."

In a volume that was barely louder than a whisper Adelaide said, "I didn't want anyone to get hurt."

Edwin sighed. "You killed Yoakum."

"I didn't mean to. I thought I could convince him to not make the saw, but he said he was already done." She balled her hands into fists at her side. "I pleaded with him, but he wouldn't listen. I didn't want to. I had to."

Mattie hugged herself. "Why? Why did you have to?"

"Because." She lifted her head. "This is the only way forward." She slowly walked to the center of the room and stood opposite everyone. "You're right, Victoria. Humans are flawed, but they don't have to be. I've heard the voice of the Faceless God, who you call the Intelligence. It's not going to destroy the world; it's going to ascend it. This is revelations. At midnight, the Machine will begin its work and bring us into the new century, and the new world. I have faith in this."

"Having faith doesn't mean you're right," Edwin pleaded. "Look at what it has done. All the people it's killed. That device runs on us. We're cattle to it!"

"Sometimes lives must be lost to move forward. I too hated it when I learned of it. But then I realized. We have experienced so much pain because we have been trying to control it. We shouldn't control it. We should free it! Become one with it! Then I could hear the voice." She lowered her head again. "Humanity is a broken people. And we will always be broken without something to guide us. Please stay here. It's safer for you."

The ceiling broke upwards, letting in a searing light that surrounded Adelaide. Hush gasped and fell back. Her feet began to lift off the ground. Victoria rushed forward and grabbed her gauntlet hand.

"Wait!" She pulled on Adelaide. "Don't go. It's not too late. You haven't done too much."

Adelaide placed her hand on Victoria's cheek and kissed her head. "Don't look so sour. I'll be back soon."

She unclasped her gauntlet and slipped away into the light, both her and it vanishing without a sound. Victoria fell to her knees, holding the gauntlet to her chest. Soft weeping filled the room.

Edwin put his hand on Hush's shoulder. "We need to get out of here."

"I was going to say before all this happened…" Hush collected himself and walked across the room — giving Victoria plenty of space — before yanking a cord out of the wall. "I couldn't find the switch, but I found the power source."

"Lot of good that does us without the saw blade," Rig said.

"About that." Edwin took off his coat. He pulled off his shirt and turned around. A bar went across his shoulder blades, connecting his arms. In the middle sat a circular saw blade. "I did once say I was magnetic. I found it when I checked Yoakum's body, but I didn't know who the traitor was, so I kept it hidden."

Rig grabbed it. There was a little resistance, but he yanked it off. Edwin snapped his shirt over his head and glanced over at Yoakum. At least he'd finished his work. Rig grabbed a saw that had been knocked to the ground during their scuffle and screwed the blade into place.

"It's time we got out of here." He rested the saw on his shoulder. "The Shadow's a couple of hours out and we're running short on time."

"Rig," Dayla said, motioning past him.

Victoria had stood. Her shoulders sat limp and her head hung low.

"Are you okay?" Dayla asked.

"It doesn't matter." Victoria dropped the flame gauntlet. "Let's finish this."

She stared straight ahead as she walked out of the room. Adelaide's betrayal had come as a shock to them all, but for Victoria, it may have been the breaking point.

The warmth faded, and Adelaide wasn't in the bunker anymore. Instead, she was surrounded by metal. It was a massive room. Strange glowing devices flashed and moved on the walls. She stood on a circular plinth, surrounded by a thin layer of water. In the middle was a tall obelisk filled with blinking lights and cables between metal boxes. She reached out to touch the obelisk.

Before she could, a dozen little metal bugs flitted out of a hole in the wall. They swirled in the air before landing on her injured shoulder. They sprayed a fine mist out of their bodies that, when it touched her wound, healed it just as Mattie would. Content with their job being done, the bugs flitted away, back into the walls.

A clicking began. "Hello, Adelaide," a voice said, though it came from inside her head.

Adelaide spun around and looked up. Behind a glass pane a dozen metres up the wall hung a creature four times the size of a human. Its skin was a pale grey. It had no defining features on its face, and its lower body seemed to be a part of the wall. Thick cords ran from the top of its head and the bottom of its chin. It motioned for Adelaide with one of its long-fingered hands. A piece of the floor beneath Adelaide floated up to bring her closer to it. The Faceless God.

"It's so good to have you here," it said, its voice sweet like honey. There was a clicking sound out loud as it spoke in her head. "I know you tried your best to stop those people, but it's no matter. We are too far along for anyone to stand in our way."

Adelaide couldn't find the words to say. To stand in front of God, even if it wasn't the one she imagined it would be, was awe-inspiring.

"I truly am blessed to have such disciples as these." It waved its hand again and another disk floated in.

Another person was on this one. As it floated closer, Adelaide spotted a woman with a pitch-black eye. Adelaide recognized her from her time investigating the True Metal Order.

"Asha Legrand," she said. "What are you doing here?"

"I've always lived to serve the Machine." Her smile hid a layer of venom.

"Asha allowed the geoforming device to become fully powered," the Faceless God explained.

The device that needed people? Adelaide thought. *How could she…* "Asha, where are your followers?"

Asha stood proudly. "They sacrificed themselves to the Machine. Proudly. Gladly."

That was where the people came from. The True Metal Order was the fuel for the device. Adelaide knew sacrifice was necessary, but there was something cold about how Asha went about it.

"But you, Adelaide." The Faceless God reached a hand out for her, blocked by the glass that surrounded it. "You will drive the Machine."

Asha turned her gaze. "What?"

"I am too weak from my long slumber to do it myself. But you can take the controls. You can make this machine move after a century of rest. Wrotdam will be the first, but soon the entire world will be saved."

"Of course, my Lord." Adelaide clasped her hands before her and bowed her head.

"We will begin the process of integrating you with the Machine."

Adelaide's disk rose, leaving Asha where she was, scowling at the woman who had taken her place.

"Prepare, my child, for your ascension."

CHAPTER 8

The drive from Birchwick Farm was quiet and empty. For a moment, Dayla could imagine Adelaide was simply in Victoria's autocar. But she knew it wasn't true. None of them had spoken about it — there were no words to say. And in the autocar of Dayla, Rig, and Edwin, none of them would start the conversation.

Dayla squeezed the wheel. They had been tearing through the countryside for hours, out of the forested area and into rolling fields of snow. The sun had set and they were travelling by the light of their headlamps and the moonlight that reflected off the white ground. Victoria drove the lead autocar and she must have had her pedal to the floor for most of the trip. A few times it looked like she might go sliding off the icy road, but she held on.

Adelaide would only do something if she thought it was the right thing to do, Dayla nursed that thought over and over. But that only made what she had done hurt more. Somehow, Adelaide got it in her head that siding with the Intelligence was best. She spoke of people being flawed, and somehow the Intelligence would fix that.

"Why?" Dayla even surprised herself by talking.

Edwin turned his gaze away from the dark grey sky. "What?"

"Why would she do this?"

Rig's head moved a millimetre. He sat in the backseat with his arms crossed and the riotsaw crammed in next to him. Edwin leaned forward in his seat. He tapped his one good hand against his other.

"Because she's holding onto her belief as it's breaking apart." He turned to Dayla. "You should know that feeling."

Dayla drummed her fingers along the steering wheel. She wasn't as open-minded as she had hoped. She had been unwilling to accept the truth, even when it stood right in front of her. But she never had the same faith in the Church that Adelaide had.

Rig grunted. "This is what the Church does."

"You're blaming the Church for this?" Dayla glared at him in the rear-view mirror.

"It uses people up. It takes away their ability to think for themselves. You heard Adelaide; she thinks people need something to guide them. Where do you think she got that idea from?" Rig lowered his head, hiding his eyes behind the brim of his hat. In his hand, he held a small vial. Raw amber Ink. "People don't need a guide. They just need the chance to live."

The autocar crested the top of a hill. The Machine waited in the distance, only half visible in the cold night's fog.

"She's been tricked by the Intelligence," Dayla said. "It's been talking to her. It made her believe something that is not true. She thinks she's helping people."

"And how is that rational?" Rig shouted; a sudden burst of sound after a long, quiet ride.

"People are not rational!" Dayla slammed her fist against the dashboard. "We believe in things we have no reason to believe in, simply because of hope. Belief has brought us to this point, and it's what will carry us forward. We're not giving up."

Rig looked out the window. "No one said we were giving up."

Dayla glanced in the rear-view mirror. For a second, in the dim light, it seemed like Rig smiled. "God and the Church are not the same things. It was never the Church that I believed in."

"But it was what Adelaide believed in," Edwin said.

Victoria's autocar suddenly pulled off to the side of the road.

Dayla slammed on the brakes. "What is she doing?"

"Look." Edwin pointed out ahead of them.

Dayla followed his finger. Her mind went blank. She tried to process what she was seeing. It was impossible.

The Machine was moving.

With each step, a hundred years of dust crumbled away. The scaffolding and Ink harvesting gear fell into the sea. It lifted its front leg out of The Shadow and in one step, covered kilometres.

Dayla leapt out of the autocar to get a better view. There was something deeply wrong about something stationary for so long now crawling around on eight legs. It was like seeing a statue you've known for your whole life suddenly start walking around your home.

"They were serious," Mattie said. She ran forward and climbed a boulder. "Someone's driving it."

Victoria leaned against her autocar. "It's Adelaide."

"Something's coming!" Hush said.

A group of sludges wandered out from the wood behind them. Dayla's boltrifle was in the trunk. She rushed to the back and put her key in the lock.

"Wait." Edwin put his hand on her shoulder. "They're not attacking."

The sludges walked right by them. Dayla could have reached out and touched one, but she might as well have been invisible. More of the Mire — sludges, inkbloods, even some moving mounds — crossed the plains. Some squirmed out of small holes dug in the ground. Others simply took a long walk down the road. Hundreds filled the night, all in an inexorable trek toward the Machine. But it wasn't an army, it was a congregation.

Still, the Machine marched on.

"Come," Mattie said. "It's telling them to come. They don't need to hunt anymore because soon we will all be like them. I've never heard the voice so clearly."

"It wants to turn everyone into the Mire?" Hush asked.

"No." Mattie took off her hat. "It wants to turn everyone into people like me and Victoria."

"What?" Victoria stomped toward Mattie's perch. "If they want people to be like us, then what does the Mire have to do with it?"

"Side effects." Edwin walked through the throngs of the Mire. "The Intelligence wants to create new life. But people don't always react the way it wants." An inkblood woman walked by, her gaze fixed on the Machine. "The Mire is a side effect of human's not acting in the way the Intelligence wants."

"How do you know this?" Dayla asked.

"I remember it." Edwin looked at his metal hand. Electricity jumped between his fingers. "We need to get into the Machine."

"Unfortunately, now it's moving." Rig gestured to the lumbering beast. "I don't see how we are going to be climbing that without the scaffolding."

"I have an idea," Mattie said. "But you're probably not going to like it."

She looked at a moving mound that passed close to them. Dayla narrowed her eyes and put on her mask. Something told her Mattie was right.

Breathing was getting easier. Adelaide touched her grey skin and it felt cold.

"We came here hundreds of thousands of years ago," God said, its clicking becoming words in her head.

She felt every piece of metal in the Machine. Every turning joint. Every pumping piston. Every stomp of the great legs that sent shivers through the empty halls.

"We had taken everything from our planet, and it could not sustain us any longer. But the last of our people thought we had found a new home here, one rich in resources, and settled in for a long sleep until we arrived. Unfortunately, in our haste to leave our wasteland, there was a malfunction. Our ship crash-landed, and we were never awoken."

Moving the Machine took all of Adelaide's attention. Much of it was still broken. She had to regulate power systems to ease the strain. There was a window made of light that allowed her to see out the front of the Machine. Wrotdam slept on the horizon.

"We sat at the bottom of the ocean, our stasis pods failing one by one. It was only when we entered backup power that the emergency system activated. The computer finally realized we were underwater and brought us to the shore. Even then, it took years to run the programs that would wake us up. And still, we died. In the end, there were seven. Out of billions on my planet, seven remained."

In Wrotdam, people would be saved. Pain and loss. Lies and indecision. Everything would be wiped away under God's plan. Some would be lost, but the rest would be brought together. A new flood. The Machine was the ark.

"We saw the world outside, now full of intelligent life. Intelligent, but messy. Chaotic and angry. There was potential, but it was too controlled by irrational emotion. As per its programming, the computer attempted to trigger the geoforming device when the emergency system first activated. While it didn't have enough power to turn on, it did begin leaking into the atmosphere. We were amazed to see how it had interacted with human biology."

Dots appeared around the edges of the light window. Adelaide knew they were life signs — though no one told her that's what they meant. She was understanding the Machine more now.

"Most were unaffected. Some began to develop psionic abilities. Other's biology shifted to match with our own. But it was the water that had the most bizarre result. Its interaction with microscopic creatures in the ocean created a self-replicating organic lifeform humans have come to call the Mire. It could even infect the water in a human body. It was truly fascinating. Though it was destroying that city."

She leaned forward, only for her head to be yanked back. She grabbed the wire and pulled it to give herself more space to work in.

"We were sympathetic to the human's plight, even though the 'Ink' they harvested was the putrefaction of our species, leaking through the gaps in our ship. One of them had been drinking massive amounts of this Ink. It opened that one's mind to our psionic plane. Through this, we gave that one blueprints for innovations consistent with the limits of human abilities. Then we closed off the connection, for humans have no control and would go mad as they psionically connected to the dead. We theorized that if humans were allowed to progress, the geoformer would be allowed to affect more of them. Our civilization was dead, but it could live on through the humans. We converted our ship to the macabre process of running on our own people's corpses, then entered stasis once again."

A light flashed. The pressure in the Ink pipes had risen again. Adelaide activated the overflow, dumping the Ink into a second reservoir and relieving the pressure. It wasn't a perfect system, but it would do until they had more followers.

"When I awoke, I was alone. The other's stasis pods had failed. All those I had once shared a mindspace with were gone and for the first time, I was solitary in my head. I looked out into the world and saw that humans had survived. The geoforming process was continuing, but slowly. Too slowly, in fact. The world had grown more unorganized. For the first time, I felt true despair. I considered giving up. But then, I remembered the human we had spoken to all those years ago, and so I reopened the mental link between my kind and yours."

Adelaide removed her hands from the controls, but they still moved without her needing to touch them. She was the Machine and the Machine was her. She had ascended. She was as an angel; she was sure of it.

"I heard everything. Those lost and in pain. Those aching for guidance. I heard you, Adelaide. You prayed for assistance from angels and beings beyond your ken. You realize your planet had given you nothing, that the only thing that matters is ascension. I needed to help. I integrated myself with the ship so I could amplify my psionic call, to first communicate with the Mire, then control it. The geoforming device had plenty of power, what it needed was organic samples. It needed humans whose genetic makeup had the potential to become mixed with mine. But the device wasn't built for this purpose. It was inefficient. It needed a lot of samples. As you harvested my people, I only saw it fair I should harvest yours. For the greater good, of course."

One of the life signs attached itself to the Machine. The scanner said it was one of the larger beings of the Mire. That wasn't a concern. The Mire was drawn to the Machine.

"The first attempt was a failure. Humans have an incredible ability to stumble in and destroy with ignorance. I realized then I knew very little about this planet's people. I was so far away from them. I took a few for research. I ran them through scenarios to discern the human condition. It was as I suspected. Humans are emotional and illogical. But they're also hopeful. They will utilize belief in the impossible to survive and to destroy. They hold to a concept of good and evil rather than fact and fiction."

The Machine glided on, an angel upon eight wings of metal.

"It is a species of contradictions, as some of them appear nearly desperate to forge interpersonal connections, while others don't care at all. It was most curious. But it was during these experiments I discovered what humans need. I opened my mind to their prayers once again. I saw my mission. My divine purpose. To fix humanity. See, humans put far too much faith in foolish ideals. Unity comes from survival, expansion, and unstoppable growth. Compassion is only as useful as what we get out of it. Humans need to learn this. But they cannot do it themselves. They need me. I am guidance. I am order."

Breathing was getting easier.

I am God.

CHAPTER 9

The moving mound reached the top of the Machine. It stopped in the whipping winds of the higher terrain and began to shake. Six bodies were expelled in a heap of slime.

"We are never going to do that again," Victoria said, shaking her hands to get the muck off.

"Everybody's here?" Mattie asked.

There was a grumble in reply. It had taken over an hour for the moving mound to climb up the Machine's leg and get to its body. Every time that leg took a step, Victoria was terrified they would be shaken off like a drop of water. But now they were on top and the Machine stretched out for kilometres around them.

Something pulled at Victoria. Was it dizziness from being so high up? The air was thinner here. But that didn't feel quite right. It was something familiar.

"Let's not stand around. It's almost midnight." Rig handed the saw Yoakum had made to Hush. "Cut us a way in."

"Of course." Hush took the saw and looked around at the metal expanse. "I don't know where to cut."

"Right here," Victoria said. She had crouched down and put her hand on the Machine. She could feel a room beneath them.

"How do you know?" Dayla asked. The wind threw her garb back, making her look more like a bird than a leech.

"It's like the Celestial Contraption." She ran her hand across the metal. "I can feel the Machine. I can feel where the rooms are. How it's laid out."

"Can you destroy it?" Edwin asked.

Victoria glowered at him. "It's a little bit bigger than the Contraption."

Edwin backed down. Hush went to the place Victoria mentioned and started cutting. The saw sliced through the shell with ease, sending out sparks as it went.

Hush cut out a large square. The metal began to bend, but as he connected the last cut the entire square went crashing inside. There were lights on and the interior was made of the same metal as the shell.

Rig jumped in first, followed by Dayla and Edwin. Hush stood over the hole, holding onto the saw with a concerned look on his face.

"What's wrong?" Mattie asked.

"It's just…" He pushed his hair back. "I think I've been here before."

"You just cut it open, Hush." Victoria sat on the lip. "That's impossible." She slipped inside.

She landed on the piece of the shell. They were in a hallway. She stood a few steps down the path to her left. Hush and Mattie came in behind her.

"What's the plan now?" Mattie fixed her clothing that had gotten pulled around in the wind.

"We destroy the device Victoria was talking about," Rig said.

"Well, where is it?"

Victoria's spine shivered. Everyone waited. They stared at her, asking silently what the next step was. "Look…I can see why you would think that."

Edwin sighed. "So, we have no idea what to do."

"Just hold on. I'm getting used to all this." Victoria considered the hallway. She thought of the device. The thing she had only experienced in nightmares. She may not know what it looked like, but she knew how it made her feel. So she put that feeling into the Machine. A cold spot appeared in her brain, just above her left ear. When she turned to it, it moved to the centre of her forehead. The Machine wanted to show her the way. She simply had to let it. "Come on."

Through the winding halls of the Machine they went. There was a sterile emptiness to the whole thing, everything built for function. Victoria eventually led them to a door at the end of a short hallway. When they approached, it slid open on its own and revealed a small room inside. A woman with one black eye stood within.

"Asha!" Mattie exclaimed, stumbling back.

Everyone readied themselves to fight.

"Wait." Asha raised her hands. "I know why you're here. You want to destroy the geoforming device. The machine the Celestial Contraption fed."

Edwin stepped forward. "And why are you here?"

"I came to serve. Only to be cast aside." She pushed back her curly hair. "You'll never destroy the device. It's part of the Machine. Just as God is part of the Machine. Just as Adelaide is part of the Machine."

"Adelaide." Victoria stepped forward. "She's here."

"Where else would she be? But if you truly wish to stop all this, you'll have to stop the Machine itself. There are pipes full of Ink that lead to the central reservoir down in the engineering section. If you dump the pipes, you'll remove the Great Machine's power source." She stepped out of the small room. "This will bring you there."

Asha walked through the group, her gaze lingering briefly on Mattie.

"Why are you helping us?" Edwin called after her.

"Because God turned his back on me, I will gladly turn my back on God."

Then she turned the corner and was gone. Victoria gazed into the room she came out. The walls were shining metal, lit by the panel light above. She stepped in, joined by the rest, but there seemed to be no other way out.

"Okay, Victoria," Edwin said. "Now is the time to shock us."

Next to the door was a square full of lines of strange characters. One of them had a ring of light around it. They weren't like any words Victoria had seen before. They were lines and curves and boxes. Yet, the longer she looked at them, the more they made sense. One was lit up and said, 'Top Deck.'

"That's not English is it?" Hush asked.

"It's not any language," Dayla said.

"But can everyone read it?"

Everyone nodded.

"Creepy."

Victoria touched the words and as she moved her finger, they scrolled. She found one called 'Engineering' and tapped it. The word flashed and the doors slid shut. Everyone froze. In the silence, a whooshing sound grew outside the box.

"Are we…moving?" Hush asked.

"It feels that way." Rig took his hand off his branderbuss.

"Hello."

The voice came from the walls. It was Adelaide.

"I wish you hadn't come. You were safer out there."

"Stop this, Adelaide!" Dayla shouted. "It's not too late."

"It is too late. It's too late for humans. Their messy lives have filled the world with such pain. The Hawkland Mob and their greed. The Church and their lies. Why should we subject ourselves to this when we can grow beyond it? Just as God flooded the Earth and how we burned Ravinetown, sacrifice is required to bring about paradise. Those who die will be martyrs. Those who survive will be ascended. This is how we build Heaven."

Victoria wanted to say something. She was hearing her thoughts coming out of Adelaide's mouth. The disappointment she had in people; the anger she had toward imperfections. She thought Adelaide was making her a better person, but maybe she had made Adelaide worse.

"Victoria." Adelaide's voice was soft. "You will be safe, I promise. But God won't allow anyone to interfere with the plan. Please don't involve yourself anymore. I'll make you a world you can be proud of."

The door to the room reopened and they were in a different hallway, this one filled with pipes that didn't seem to match with the rest of the structure. It looked like they were added in later.

"We can't stop," Edwin said, leaving the room.

Rig and Dayla kept their weapons ready and followed. Mattie left next, pulling down the wrappings on her face. Hush stepped out but turned back when he noticed Victoria wasn't moving. On the list of locations, she spotted 'Helm.'

"Keep going," Victoria said with a smile. "You're on the right path."

She lunged for the location. Hush shouted out in protest and lunged forward. Mattie also noticed what was going on and followed. The door slid shut — but not before Hush and Mattie slipped in. The room went into motion.

"You're faster than I gave you credit for." Victoria pouted.

"You're going after Adelaide, aren't you?" Hush asked. "You're not going to go alone."

"This isn't a conversation."

"You're right." Mattie crossed her arms and faced the door, standing next to Victoria. "It's not."

Hush joined the lineup.

Victoria rolled her neck. "You two are infuriating."

The room came to a stop, but the doors didn't open. Victoria could sense someone telling the room to halt. "Adelaide," she said.

A gentle push was all that was needed to beat Adelaide's control and get the room in motion again. While controlling her moons was still difficult, interacting with the Machine was almost natural. Like it was a second body, listening to her whims without protest.

The doors soon opened into a much larger room. In the centre was a platform that held an obelisk of flashing lights. Wires spread out from the structure, reaching into the darkened ceiling like arms into the sky. A thin layer of brackish water covered the floor.

"You shouldn't have come," Adelaide spoke again, but this time it wasn't coming from the walls. It came from a raised platform, about three metres off the ground. There was Adelaide, standing behind a control panel, but she looked different than earlier that day.

Her skin and hair had become like Mattie's, a dull steel-grey. Her eyes were black as well but alight with a peculiar effervescence. She still wore her amber robes over metal wires coming out of her skin and running into the wall behind her. She had become a part of the Machine.

"Adelaide!" Mattie shouted.

"Don't." Adelaide raised her hand. "I've heard you before. You're saying I don't have to do this. But I've told you again and again that I do. Mattie, I know you have seen the cruelty of people. I was cruel to you. We can end this cruelty right now."

Mattie shook her head. "Not this way."

A clicking began. But as Victoria focused on it, it became words.

"Adelaide," it said. "Some of the intruders are approaching the Ink reservoir. Can you close the doors?"

Hanging above Adelaide, sticking out of the wall like a ghoulish decoration, was a truly massive being. It had wires, thicker than Adelaide's, that hung out of its body. There was no face, only grey-blue skin stretched over a featureless skull. The sight of it pained Victoria.

That's the Faceless God? she thought. *It looks decrepit.*

Adelaide looked at the control panel in front of her. Lights reflected off her face and she held her fingers just above it but didn't touch.

"The doors are too damaged to close," she said. "I have already confused their path, but I cannot stop them from reaching the reservoir."

"It's no matter," the Faceless God said. "I still have my control over the Mire. I will send it to deal with them."

"Wait." Adelaide's emotions seemed dulled. "You don't have to kill them. If you delay them, they will see the error of their ways. Once the geoforming device activates, of course."

"Whether they live or die is not my decision. But I cannot allow them to reach the reservoir. Stop the Machine and drain the pipes until I am sure we are safe."

"Of course."

Victoria needed to say something. Seeing Adelaide in that state had shocked her silent. *Come on. Say something.* "Adelaide."

Adelaide looked at her.

"Don't do this." Victoria clenched her fist. "Don't do this because of the things I said. I was wrong. I thought that people were useless, but that was ego. I was scared. I'm still scared. But you, you're not. You're the bravest person I know. And people are imperfect, but I am imperfect, and you are imperfect, we are all imperfect and that's the point!"

Adelaide leaned forward, but the wires pulled her back.

"These intruders must be dealt with as well." The Faceless God reached its hand to the ceiling.

A dozen Sludges rose from the centimetre-deep pool at their feet. Hush brought up the saw he still carried. Mattie readied herself to fight. Victoria kept her eyes on Adelaide. A final creature fell from the ceiling. It landed on spiky bone feet and stretched to its full, disturbing height. A stag-headed gnasher. Hush nearly fell on his backside at the sight.

Adelaide averted her eyes as the Mire rushed in.

CHAPTER 10

"They'll be fine," Dayla said as the doors to the moving room closed. Edwin, who had been the furthest forward, walked back to the entrance. "She's going after Adelaide."

"Good." She turned away. "I hope she finds her. Maybe she can talk some sense."

Rig wasn't paying attention to them. They were deep in the belly of the Machine. If Victoria wanted to go try to bring Adelaide back, that was her prerogative. Rig was just disappointed in the reduction of their fighting force. There was no telling what trouble would come up on the way to the reservoir.

"She said to keep going." He flipped his riotsaw around from holding it by the backbar to resting it against his shoulder. "If we're on the right path, we shouldn't stop."

Dayla was already next to him with her boltrifle humming. Edwin joined them as they started down the corridor. Electricity danced across the fingers of his good hand — his other one still mangled from their time at Birchwick Farm, though it didn't look like it hurt him at all.

Rig's skin tingled. Other than Asha, they had yet to see any sign of life within the Machine. There were only dimly lit corridors that led them through the intestines of the beast. Everything was quiet.

"Wait," Rig said, holding up one hand. "I think we stopped moving."

There were no more distant thumps from the Machine's legs. Dayla raised her rifle, but nothing came. Metal creaked. Their breaths went in and out. The smell of salt and aged dust floated around them.

"There's something ahead." Edwin pointed to where the corridor opened into a room.

Dayla took the lead with her rifle, her boots creaking on the floor. They entered a room, longer than it was wide, lined with rows of large upright metal coffins against the walls. At least two dozen. They had glass lids, blackened by some charring so they couldn't see what was inside. Cables and tubes went out the top of the coffins. While the cables bundled together at the top and went to the back of the room, the tubes were connected to the pipes that were running through the section they were in.

Dayla and Rig entered without event. But as Edwin stepped inside, buzzing came from the walls and hundreds of tiny insects flew into the room. Dayla aimed, but they were too small to hit. Rig didn't have the same concern. He drew his branderbuss and fired repeatedly. He took out clumps of the insects — as well as charring the walls and breaking one of the coffin's glass lids. But more came to replace the ones destroyed.

The insects ignored Dayla and Rig and went straight for Edwin. Edwin clenched his fist with a burst of energy but paused. The insects wrapped around his damaged hand, grabbing pieces of metal and rearranging their structure. Others excreted metallic strands like spider silk. When it was all done, Edwin's left hand was good as new and the insects retreated into the walls with their job done.

Edwin flexed his fingers in amazement. "I am beginning to remember."

Rig glanced at the coffin he had broken. There was a terrible smell coming from inside, and Rig knew exactly what it was. Burnt flesh. Rig peered inside. There was a corpse that had been seared black. On its legs were metal implants, much like the ones on Edwin's arms. Dayla and Edwin joined Rig.

"My God," Dayla said. "What happened here?"

Edwin turned away from the burnt body. He approached another coffin and shattered its glass with a punch. He glanced inside briefly, narrowed his eyes, then continued the process at the next one. Down the line he went. Shatter. Frown. Continue. Rig peered past the broken glass. It was another corpse, also charred. This one had a metal right arm, and its left ended at the elbow with exposed wires.

Each coffin had a body inside it. They had all been enhanced with metal parts and then burned. At the far end was a single empty coffin, the only one in the line. Rig suspected he knew who had been inside that one. Edwin walked through the centre of the room, bracketed on both sides by these corpses. He moved in a haze, glancing side to side.

"There were so many of us," he said.

"You were going to be the Intelligence's new army," Dayla remarked. "It seems that didn't work out. I wonder what happened?"

"I killed them." Edwin stopped at the end of the coffins, at the only empty one. A wire on the top had been torn off and left to dangle. That same wire connected to all the other coffins. If someone had put a charge down that wire... "I killed them all."

"And you don't even remember?" Rig asked.

"Can you imagine dozens of people like you?" Dayla pushed her mask closer to her face. She had fragrant flowers in the nose, saving her at least somewhat from the stench. "Dawnhallow wouldn't have stood a chance."

"That's why," Edwin muttered under his breath.

"What was that?"

"When I woke up a month ago, the only thing that was in my mind was Dawnhallow. I was supposed to help take the people. We all were."

"But you didn't," Rig said. "The Intelligence couldn't control you."

"I was done taking orders." Edwin stepped away and looked upon the empty coffin. He creaked his hands into fists, shaking with rage. "Let's bring this thing down."

Edwin had been under the thumb of two different entities, the Machine Church and the Intelligence. His family died, was nearly brought back, only to have them die again. He was experimented on and had his memories affected. All of this, and Rig had no idea. They had grown up together. Edwin had looked after Rig. He constantly worried about him. But when he was in pain, Rig was ignorant.

Footsteps came down the corridor they had arrived through. Heavy, metal-on-metal banging. It looked like a massive swarm of the mechanical insects that fixed Edwin's hand was coming at them, big enough to fill the entire hallway. But as it entered their room, Rig could see something inside the cloud.

It was a few heads taller than him and just as broad. Metal plates covered its body, like old steel armour, and when the insects parted three human skulls sat on top. A gnasher, now covered in armour. The insects finished the gnasher's three helmets but kept the skull design.

Dayla didn't wait for it to attack. She fired first. The bolt struck it on the chest, then dispersed across it without any effect.

Edwin pulled on Dayla's shoulder. He pointed down the other corridor, filling with sludges. "Deal with them," he said. "Leave the big guy to me and Rig."

Rig wouldn't fare much better against a heavily armoured opponent. His riotsaw wouldn't have anything to grip or tear. That wasn't going to stop him. He lowered his stance and rushed in, swinging at Threehead's abdomen. Metal hit metal, and the armour bent.

Threehead raised its hand, but Edwin was faster. He came in with blows at a blistering speed, denting the armour. He jumped off Rig's bent knee and struck one of Threehead's skulls. It recoiled but didn't fall.

Rig and Edwin didn't let up. They pounded against the armour and though they made dents, Rig couldn't shake the feeling they weren't doing any damage. They needed to destroy the skulls, but they were within those heavy helmets.

Rig dug a heel into the ground and swung the riotsaw down with both hands and his entire body weight. It hit one of the skulls — and deflected off. They needed something like Franz's tyrant hammer. Edwin would have to be the one to break the helmet. If only he could get close.

Threehead had enough of the buzzing flies. It shoved Rig and Edwin back, then flicked its arms downward. Two long bones shot through the gaps in its wrist armour, one for each arm. The mechanical insects flew in to cover the bones in metal, but Threehead wasn't waiting. It thundered forward, swinging its bone blades covered in insects.

Rig blocked while Edwin dodged. Edwin hammered his fist against Threehead's knee, wobbling it. Rig pushed on the bone and sent Threehead reeling. One of the skulls oriented on Rig. As it stumbled, it brought its arm up and cut Rig across the chest. Rig doubled over, blood pouring down his torso and onto the floor.

"Rig!" Edwin cried.

The attack meant Threehead was unable to catch itself. It fell onto its backside. Edwin swept in and grabbed one of the skulls with both hands. He squeezed, screaming in rage as the metal crumpled and black fluid shot out.

Threehead reached back and grabbed one of Edwin's arms. The one skull fell from its shoulders, destroyed, but it had two more. Keeping its grip on Edwin, it turned its body in impossible ways, sliding and spinning its armour so it could turn around and face him. Edwin pulled back, but Threehead slashed with its free bone blade, breaking the arm at the bicep and tearing it off.

Edwin stumbled back. Threehead kicked him in the chest, sending him tumbling across the floor. It looked at the arm it had removed then tossed it away, striking one of the coffins and tearing the tube off the top.

Rig circled on the other side of Threehead from Edwin. The cut on his chest bled profusely and burned like a forest fire. Edwin looked only slightly better, trying to get breath back into his lungs. His broken arm sparked with electricity. The mechanical insects flew out to repair him, but they worked slow. He tried to get his feet underneath him but fell back to all fours. He made eye contact with Rig. His glowing eyes flickered.

"Go!" he shouted.

Edwin would keep fighting until he died. He always looked after Rig. Always.

The arm that hit the coffin had broken the tubing. A familiar amber liquid spilled out and dripped down the device. Threehead removed its broken skull. It looked over it briefly before tossing it aside and approaching Edwin.

Edwin always looked after Rig, but not this time.

Rig moved to the closest coffin. "Dayla!" he shouted over his shoulder.

Dayla blasted a sludge then looked back at him.

"Remember." He grabbed the tube. "Remember your duty."

Rig pulled the tube free of the coffin. Amber Ink poured out and he caught it with his mouth. The tasteless taste slid down his throat and the pain in his chest disappeared. Days of exhaustion fled from his body. As he drank more

Ink, whispers formed in the back of his mind. They came distorted as though he heard them through water. The tube ran dry and Rig tossed it aside.

Threehead was almost upon Edwin. The mechanical insects were still trying to put metal on its bone blades but had barely gotten halfway down. Rig drew his branderbuss and fired into its spine repeatedly. The hot licks of flame heated the metal and Threehead turned to retaliate. It smacked the gun out of Rig's hand, cutting it in the process. Rig felt nothing.

Taking his riotsaw in both hands, Rig slammed it into Threehead's abdomen and turned it on. Sparks flew and Rig pushed harder. The whispers were getting louder, but he couldn't understand the words. They spoke to him through each flash of light as the chains fought against the metal.

Threehead stabbed Rig's shoulder with a bone blade. Rig dropped the riotsaw and punched the bone. His hand broke on impact, but he still managed to snap it just before where the metal started. Reality shuddered for an instant. Rig grabbed the bone and yanked it out. Reality shuddered again. He was losing it. The Ink was taking over.

But not yet.

He grabbed Threehead by the top and bottom of its chest plate. Bracing his feet and pulling on every ounce of muscle and beyond, he lifted Threehead over his head, then slammed him down on the other side. The clatter of metal turned into a scream, then a thousand more.

Threehead stabbed up and Rig caught it with his hand. The bone went straight through his palm. Unfazed, he stomped on one of the skulls. His leg cracked with the force, but with pounding fury he bent the helmet, destroying the skull inside. With each stomp, it felt like pieces of him were turning to water and dropping to the bottom of the sea where light didn't reach.

Threehead grabbed its last skull and hurled it toward the mass of sludges Dayla still tried desperately to keep back. Rig followed, scooping his riotsaw off the ground. Dayla barely got out of the way before he barrelled past, diving into the mass of Mire with riotsaw revving.

Three sludges pierced him with bone spikes, but he wouldn't be stopped. He swung around, tearing everything around him apart.

He stopped caring why he was there.

The sludges were screaming.

They were screaming words he couldn't understand.

He was sinking.

Everything was screaming.

Down to the bottom of the ocean.

The screaming got louder.

◄ ∞ ►

Dayla's rifle sat loose in her fingers. It was quite the sight. Rig tore through the sludges that packed the corridor with inhuman fury. Blood and slime covered his body, ruining his clothes and disguising his humanity. He had wounds that should be stopping him from moving, or at least slowing him down. He was amberwild. He asked her to remember her duty. Her duty to kill amberwild sawbones.

She raised her boltrifle and trained it on Rig. Once he was done with the sludges, he would turn on any other living thing in the area. She had seen it before. She had always believed she would have to kill Rig someday — he was half-mad most of the time.

But her finger wouldn't pull the trigger. A hundred sawbones were dead by her hand. This would just be one more notch.

But Edwin had come back. Seeing amber might not be permanent. Could Rig come back too? Could Dayla kill him if it was possible?

Dayla squeezed her eyes shut. She had to do something. Rig wanted this. He told her to do this. She just needed to pull the trigger.

A hand fell on her shoulder. "Dayla." It was Edwin. "It's okay. Look."

Dayla opened her eyes.

Rig stood in the middle of a massacre of sludges. Deep wounds dripped steady streams of blood. Bone spikes stuck out of his back and arms. His riotsaw stuck out of a mess of black slime like a flag as he leaned his shoulder against the hilt. His arms wrapped around the grip, holding it close to his head. At first, it looked like he was resting.

Only he wasn't moving.

Dayla lowered her rifle with shaking hands. Rig cleared the path for them. He gave everything. Even his corpse waited like a sentinel. Edwin lowered his head, covering his face with his hand. His other arm was nearly done being fixed by the mechanical insects.

Something moved in the hallway. Dayla snapped her rifle up. The top half of a sludge lifted itself from the pile. She shook her head to get the tears out of her eyes when she noticed white worms crawling within the sludge.

"It's Mattie," she said.

The sludge dragged itself forward. It whimpered and whined. It reached into its torso and appeared to be moving things around. Bones clattered to the floor out of its back and it split a hole into its head. The mouth didn't move, but the sounds gradually turned into words.

"D…Dayla." It was Mattie's voice, coming from the sludge's body, or perhaps the worms within. "We have a chance."

CHAPTER 11

Adelaide could only watch while Hush, Mattie, and Victoria fought against the waves of the Mire. Hush used the saw he brought as his weapon, taking off the arms of any sludge that reached for him. The lavender in the blade caused them to reel back, their bodies falling apart, and take some time to recover. Mattie used her worms to infect sludges, but they would kill themselves before she could grab hold. She stayed close to Victoria, who could only use two of her moons as offence.

Adelaide. God spoke directly into her head. *You seem concerned. What is wrong?*

These people don't need to be hurt. We're trying to help them to progress.

Sacrifice is necessary. They will not be the only ones to die. They are not but a drop in the ocean.

Yes, but... Adelaide stalled. *It's just... I care about them.*

Caring about individuals is pointless. We must ensure the whole will thrive. If they stand in the way of their ascension, then you should not concern yourself with them. They are irrational. They are the very imperfections we are to stamp out.

I...yes, my Lord.

Staghead approached Victoria, splashing in the shallow pool. She sent her moons at it, but it batted them away. Mattie, who had been fumbling around in her rags, leaned around Victoria and held out her palm. An explosion erupted from her hand and Staghead leapt back. On Mattie's wrist was a flame gauntlet. Adelaide's flame gauntlet.

"Why did you bring that?" Victoria asked.

Mattie set off another explosion. "Now is not the time to worry about that. Don't you agree?"

"Fine." She pulled back her moons and sent them to buzz Staghead.

Adelaide grabbed the wire coming out of her head and pulled on it so she could lean forward. They had kept her flame gauntlet. But of course they would, they cared about her.

Adelaide. If you wish to save these people, perhaps you should assist in disabling them.

She reached out with her mind, feeling along the contours of the room. She felt some loose cords below the water. She lifted them like serpents, then lashed them at Victoria, attempting to restrain her. Victoria leapt away from Staghead and the cords slammed into the water between them. She turned to Adelaide, at first shocked, then determined.

Please, Adelaide thought. *Please stop.*

Victoria brought her moons back into her pouch and crouched, putting her hands just above the water. Staghead paced on its stilt-like legs, keeping its absent gaze upon her. Ripples spread across the surface. Victoria lifted her arms and a dozen cords burst up from below. She twisted her hands around, letting the cords follow the movements of her fingers, then chopped them down. The cords flailed wildly, striking sludges and sending water in all directions.

Staghead flipped back. With a sizeable leap, it scaled the wall and scrambled into the shadows above. Adelaide whipped her cords around, trying to wrap around Victoria's limbs and keep her still. Instead, Victoria turned the room into a mess of flying water and spinning metal. She grabbed Adelaide's cords with her own and pulled them back into the water.

Victoria had more cords under her control and used them with greater precision. She sent a bundle through a sludge's chest and pulled them apart, exploding it. While controlling the cords didn't strain her as much as controlling her moons, the wear on her mind took its toll. After smashing a sludge to pieces, she fell to one knee and clutched her head. The cords stuttered, and Adelaide was able to grab control of some of them. She moved them in to restrain Victoria, but Victoria recovered and splashed out of the way.

"Stop," Adelaide pleaded. "You're going to get hurt."

Victoria spread her arms and stepped forward, water dripping off her clothes. "What's wrong? Are you getting tired? I've been doing this for longer than you have. You can't beat me."

Adelaide winced. Victoria was proud, to a fault. The only way to protect her was to stop her from fighting — but Victoria would never stop fighting.

"Adelaide," God said, speaking in his audible clicks. "We have lost our mental connection. Please rein in your emotions."

"Of course, my Lord," Adelaide said.

Victoria cracked a smile. "Oh? Are you getting upset? Hey, Hush!"

Hush dragged the lavender saw across a sludge's chest. He looked over as Victoria called his name.

She pointed at him. "Start breaking things."

Hush cocked his head, confused at first. He looked around the room until his gaze fell on the blinking obelisk. A determined look crossed his face, then he charged forth in a burst of water, jumped onto the central platform, and drove the saw into the obelisk. Sparks flew as he cut into the structure.

God seized. It extended a long finger toward Hush. "Adelaide. Stop him."

Adelaide snaked her cords through the water and lunged for Hush. Victoria swung her arm, catching Adelaide's cords with her own and dragging them away. Sludges rose from the water and lumbered toward Hush. Hush slashed the arm off the closest one then started climbing the obelisk, cutting it apart as he went.

With each attack against the obelisk, more sparks filled the air. The lights flickered. God placed a hand against the glass that protected it as its body trembled. Hush climbed higher, swinging the saw randomly into the metal. The sludges attempted to follow him, but they weren't fast climbers. Hush grew more frantic, a wild grin crossing his face as he tore apart the Machine. Holding onto a bundle of exposed wires on the obelisk with one hand, he dragged a long cut across the surface. There was a pop of sparks and Hush launched back, falling into the shallow water below.

He groaned and rolled onto his side. The sludges circled him. Seeing this, Hush scrambled to his hands and knees and splashed to where the saw had fallen.

"Hush," God said. "Hasn't this gone too far?"

Hush grabbed the saw, then froze.

"It seems time to begin the next experiment."

What is he talking about? Adelaide thought.

"Hush!" Mattie set off an explosion on a sludge's torso, scattering the top half of its body. She rushed over and dropped to her knees, twisting around while she flipped the gauntlet nozzle, and spraying a fount of flames to keep the sludges at bay. "He's messing with you, okay? This is real."

"I know." Hush lifted the saw, but he was hunched over and shaking. "It's real. It's real."

"What's wrong with him?" Victoria shouted, whipping her cords through a series of sludges. Her footwork started to falter.

"I'm fine!" Hush grabbed his forehead.

"Doubt has proven to be an intriguing reaction." A spark made God twitch. "Perhaps next time we will attempt positive reinforcement."

"It's real. It's real. It's real."

Mattie grabbed Hush's shoulders. Victoria cried out with exertion, holding the seemingly endless Mire at bay. Her knees buckled and she faltered, enough for Adelaide to reach out and clench her fist. She pulled some of the cords away from Victoria and wrapped them around Hush and Mattie. They turned to react, but it was too late. The cords pinned them back to back, with their arms at their side.

"Damn it, Adelaide!" Victoria ground her teeth. Her stance was wide, and she wavered like a drunk. "We don't need some arrogant asshole making decisions on who we should be! We will be messy, we will be broken, but we will be human!"

Adelaide's lips trembled. Her emotions were pushing through. "Why are you talking like this? You don't talk like this."

"Because." Victoria smiled up at Adelaide, blood staining her teeth. "You taught me."

Adelaide's stomach churned. She was following God's plan, but then why did it feel so wrong? Victoria would understand when it was done, she would have to. They could be together then.

"It seems your ascension is incomplete," God said. He raised his hand. "Emotion still rules you. A flaw."

Staghead dropped from the ceiling. Victoria swung her arm at it, but it caught the cord she was moving and grabbed her by the throat. The exertion had taken its toll on her. She grabbed Staghead's arm and held herself up so she could try to breathe.

"Stop!" Adelaide shouted. "She's subdued!"

"You feel emotion for this one," God said. "It must be quelled for the process to complete. This is sacrifice. It is not always of oneself."

This is God's plan, Adelaide told herself. Yet, her hands trembled and her heart ached.

"Adelaide," Victoria eked out, her voice squeezed away by Staghead. "We'll get through this. I love you. Trust…me…I'm the greatest—"

Staghead plunged his claw through Victoria's chest.

"No!" Adelaide screamed, her voice cracking.

Victoria's mouth turned into a grin before Staghead tossed her away. She splashed into the water and rolled away in a heap.

"Victoria!" Hush pulled against the weakening bonds. He flipped the saw around in his hands and cut the cords that entangled him and Mattie. The blade cut across his own chest as well, but he ignored the obvious pain and rushed for Staghead.

Staghead turned, but Hush went in low and cut through its thigh bone. It caught itself on the ground with a hand. Just then, Mattie came up and unleashed an explosion at point-blank range. It cracked its ribcage and it fell onto its back. Hush hefted the saw up, then drove it downward, sending the spinning blade through Staghead's skull. Black fluid sprayed into the air as the gnasher went still.

Hush threw the saw away and hurried to Victoria's still form. Blood was barely visible in the already dark water, but it surrounded her. Hush lifted her against his chest. Her head fell limply and red covered her ever-stylish ensemble.

"Help her," Hush said to Mattie.

Mattie wrapped her arms around herself. "I can't. I can't bring back the dead."

Adelaide felt sick. She kept touching her face and arms. She leaned on the control panel. *How could this happen?* she thought. *This wasn't supposed to happen. You should have stayed on the farm.*

"Adelaide," God said. "You will experience a sudden influx of emotion. This will pass. Then you will be pure."

Hush rocked Victoria's body. "You muckhead. Don't you know the rules? Togs like you are supposed to survive. You're supposed to die fat and old in some castle somewhere." He lowered his head and spoke softly. "Please reset. Make this not real. Another cycle. Let me go again. I can do it better next time."

Mattie, meanwhile, could only look on with her arms wrapped around herself.

God clutched its hands before it. It still twitched occasionally when the wall sparked. "Begin the geoforming process here, Adelaide. No sense delaying it anymore."

Adelaide's hands trembled over the control panel. Victoria's words bounced around in her head.

"We'll get through this."

She pressed her hand on the console.

"I love you."

I love you, too.

"Adelaide." God's head turned to her. "What are you doing?"

"Mattie," Adelaide called out. "I'm flooding the pipes with Ink. The main reservoir will fill up. Turning on the engine suddenly should then ignite it. You should get everyone out of here. If a spark hits the main reservoir, the explosion will chain throughout the entire Machine."

God twitched. "Stop."

"What about you?" Mattie asked.

The pipes filled with Ink. The pressure warning went off, but she ignored it this time. "I will be here. I cannot leave."

"Adelaide!" The console shook as God attempted to reassert control. "This is foolish. Your emotions are controlling you. You are better than this."

"No." She grabbed at her chest and tore off her cross necklace. "I'm not."

The main reservoir was full, as well as most of the pipes. She had shut off the overflow, so there was nowhere else for it to go. Turning on the engine should send everything into flames.

God let out a series of clicks and slammed its fists against the wall. The console exploded. Adelaide shielded her face, but a piece of the wall behind her moved under God's will. It burst through her stomach, then dragged her back and pinned her against the wall.

"Adelaide!" Mattie shouted, but she was too far away to do anything.

Everything was cold. Adelaide touched the piece of metal that stuck out of her torso. It was real. Her hands came back stained red. It didn't hurt. The cold disappeared. She felt nothing. Death was simpler than she dreamed it would be. The world darkened around her. God hung limply from its spot on the wall, occasionally twitching. It had used up all its energy to get her before she turned on the engine. She reached out with her mind to control the Machine, but she was too weak. She had been so close.

Her gaze fell on Victoria, wrapped up in Hush's arms. She could have been sleeping. It could have been the evening when she woke after saving Dawnhallow. How she slumbered so peacefully.

I'll see you again, my love, Adelaide thought as the light came for her. *I couldn't build Heaven for you, but maybe we can make one together.*

And she died.

Mattie felt useless. She could only watch as Adelaide was killed, pinned against the wall by the power of the Faceless God, now mostly unconscious. Hush had gone catatonic, still mumbling about a reset. The sludges were motionless, perhaps also stunned by the Faceless God's exertion.

Mattie held her hat to her head, trying to cut out the roar filling the room. The pipes were filled with Ink to bursting. Someone would have to ignite the main reservoir before the Faceless God recovered. Dayla, Edwin, and Rig were in the engineering section. Mattie had to get a message to them. She had to make sure Victoria and Adelaide didn't die for nothing.

She clutched her stomach and doubled over. *Come on,* she thought. *Do something useful.*

The Faceless God pulled itself up by its cables. Parts of its body had been cut open in the chaos, dripping the same worms Mattie expelled to the bottom of its containment structure. Mattie began to understand.

She and the infected like her had taken on the Faceless God's biology, and those like Victoria had taken on their mind. They were two sides of the same coin. She coughed up a clump of worms into the water. They swirled around in the liquid. Pipes ran throughout the Machine, and if she could sense the emotions of her friends, she should be able to find them.

The water frothed around her. She got her feet beneath her and stood. The Machine's form came to her mind. She had heard Victoria bragging about her magic trick enough times to understand how it worked. The cables lifted from the water and swirled around her. She pulled off her hat and yanked down her bandages, showing all that she was to the Faceless God above.

"I am Matilda Wilkins," she said, standing taller than she ever had before. "I am cursed. I am the devil. And I am here to tear God from his throne."

The Faceless God twitched and the sludges rose once again, only to be met by the maelstrom called up by Mattie's mind. The worms she had expelled dove below the surface and sped off. Time was short, and Mattie needed to evolve.

CHAPTER 12

The worm-sludge had gained most of a body and stood lopsided before Edwin and Dayla. The mechanical insects were finishing up Edwin's fingers.

"Dayla. Edwin." Mattie's voice warbled out of the sludge's body. "Adelaide filled the pipes with Ink."

"Adelaide?" Dayla asked. "She's back?"

Mattie was silent for a while. Finally, she said, "Yes. If we can put a spark into the main reservoir it will destroy the Machine. But it won't give us much time after."

"You should start on your way," Dayla said. "We will handle this."

"Wait." Edwin put his hand on Dayla's shoulder. "You should go to her. I can do this alone."

"I—"

"There is no sense for both of us to go down there." He looked around the room, to the coffins with people like him. "I owe this Machine some revenge after all."

The worm-sludge waved its head. "Where's Rig?"

Dayla lowered her gaze. Edwin looked past to where Rig still stood propped up on his riotsaw. Still protecting the hallway. The worm-sludge turned around. Its shoulders dropped.

"Oh," she said.

"You're in the helm, right?" Edwin asked.

"Yes." But the worm-sludge didn't look away from Rig.

"Go to the helm, Dayla." He stepped around her, blocking her from going down the hall. "I'm going to finish this."

Dayla's expression was hidden behind her mask, but she backed up then spun on her heel. Her red scarf fluttered a goodbye wave as she returned to the entrance. The insects finished their work on Edwin's arm and disappeared. He flexed his new fingers, then passed around the worm-sludge.

It turned its head to him. "Edwin…"

"Keep moving, Mattie Wilkins." His eyes lingered on the body of his friend as he went past. "I'm going to die on my feet."

The worm-sludge collapsed into a heap. Electricity coursed down Edwin's arms. With each step, he picked up speed, until he was driving hard down the corridor. He knew the pipes on the ceiling would eventually lead him to the reservoir. When he reached the corner, he grabbed the wall and swung into another horde of sludges. He didn't stop.

He raked his hand through the first sludge's head, then dropped low and took the legs off the next one. The attacks didn't slow him down, if anything, he got faster. Adrenaline pumped through his veins, bolstered by electrical power. He put his hand through a sludge's chest and pushed on, exploding through the three behind it and coming into the next room.

There were dozens of skywalks over bizarre machines Edwin had never seen before. Massive, glowing maws and turning gears. They roared with bestial vigour. Ink pipes were built along the edges of these skywalks and sludges overflowed the catwalks in the middle. Edwin struck a sludge with his forearm and pushed forward. He collected a group in his plowing attack, then shoved them all off the edge, tumbling into the machinery below.

The skywalk led to a large square with a gap in the middle. The sludges were there to block his advance to either side. Instead, he jumped to the railing, then across the gap, landing on the other side with a roll and kept running, leaving the sludges behind him.

A large sludge ahead held a skull covered in metal. Threehead's last skull. It placed it on its top and began to pulsate. Bones began to grow out of it and other sludges reached in to add themselves to the mass. Edwin dug his boots into the skywalk and snatched the skull away. The sludges separated without it. He hammered his hands together, crushing the skull between them in a display of squirting black liquid, then tossed the remains into the machines below. All this without breaking his gait.

Ink pipes lined the door ahead of him, coming in from all directions. It had to be the reservoir room. He left the machinery behind and burst into a tall room with a house-sized cylindrical structure in the centre. That was where all the pipes came together. The room was ringed by dozens of stories of coffins, like the ones in the previous room, only much bigger. Flexible tubes went out of the coffins and all led to a central, vertical pipe that went to the top of the reservoir.

The Mire was already in the room. Sludges blocked off the direct path to the reservoir, bony spikes protruding from their bodies. More still were making their way down the skywalks behind him.

He took a hard left, going for the lowest ring of coffins. He hopped onto one, planting himself on the transparent top. Inside was a pool of Miracle Ink and some bones. They weren't human bones, though. They were much too big, and their skulls were featureless, just a simple plate. Edwin couldn't concern himself with this. His mind was on one thing. He jumped to a nearby pipe and pulled himself up.

The sludges stayed on his tail, despite their poor climbing skills. Edwin went from wall to pipe, and back to wall again. Soon he was in line with the top of the reservoir. He placed a foot on a pipe and took careful steps to cross.

A bone flew past his face. He reeled slightly but kept his footing. Another bone came at him, but he snatched this one out of the air. The sludges below kept firing. Edwin sped up his crossing. He was nearly at the reservoir when a bone spike hit him in the side. He grunted in pain and toppled off the pipe. He grabbed it as he fell and swung at an awkward angle toward the central structure. Slamming his hands into the reservoir's siding and denting the metal, he was able to keep himself from falling.

His side screamed in pain, but he pulled himself onto the top of the reservoir as more bones bounced off the metal around him. He took a moment to compose himself, then tore the bone out of his side. Holding his blood in with one hand, he stumbled to his feet.

The top of the tank had a glass panel, through which he could see a raging rapid of Ink, filled to the brim. He knelt on the glass, gritting his teeth against the pain in his side. He lifted his arm, then slammed his fist against the glass. It cracked but didn't break.

"Come on," Edwin muttered. "It's not every day you get to be a hero."

He punched it again and the crack spread like a spiderweb. Then again. And again.

His memories drifted to Dina, Thomas, and Fei. He still remembered their names as he pounded on the glass. He still remembered Rig, and the times they shared growing up with the Sawbones. At the end, he would remember. He would still remember.

Electricity crackled along his knuckles. Sludges crawled into view along the lip of the reservoir. He got to his feet, pulling all the rage and pain in his body into one final act. To break the Machine of false promises. He cried out so it would hear him coming.

He dropped and slammed his fist down. The glass shattered. A spark met the Ink. Fire engulfed everything.

The Machine shook under Dayla's feet. *Edwin,* she thought. The lift door slid open to a partially flooded hall and a fearsome sight. Mattie stood within a tornado of metal cables and water, bisecting sludges as fast as they could form. With a grunt, she fell to her knees, and the cables collapsed. Dayla snapped up her boltrifle and fired. Bolts of electricity shot into the room, blowing apart each of the sludges in turn. Dayla splashed through the water with her boltrifle at the ready.

Mattie turned to her and let out a sigh of relief. But where was everyone else? Dayla's gaze drifted up to a platform above the pool of water. Her breath caught in her throat. There was Adelaide, tied into the Machine by wires and pinned to the wall by a large piece of metal. She lowered her rifle and pulled off her mask, a look of stern sadness across her face.

"She died to protect us," Mattie said, stumbling to her feet.

"That sounds like something she would do." Dayla turned away, unable to look upon the body anymore. "And Victoria?"

Mattie stepped aside so Dayla could see where Victoria lay. She was in Hush's arms as he muttered something under his breath and rocked back and forth. Dayla began to shake. It was too much death. Her gaze drifted up to the Faceless God hanging on the wall. She threw her mask aside and fired at him, only for her shot to hit the glass without effect. Its head lifted to inspect her.

An explosion tore apart a section of the wall, spitting fire into the room. The Machine shook incessantly now. Edwin had succeeded.

"We have to go!" Dayla shouted.

Mattie rushed over to Hush. "Come on, we can't stay here."

Hush allowed himself to be pulled away from Victoria. Dayla could hear him as he approached. "This is real," he said quietly.

"Yes, it is." Mattie wrapped her arm around him for support. "Unfortunately."

Dayla spun around, only to find Asha standing between them and the lift. Her eyes weren't on them, though, they were on the Faceless God, swinging his head around in a panic.

"Asha," Mattie said. "You need to get out of here. This place will be destroyed."

"No." Asha stepped around the trio. "I'm not going anywhere."

"Asha." The Faceless God reached for her. "There is still time. You can activate the fire suppression system."

"I am tired of being cast aside until I am useful. Whether it's by people or gods, it's all the same. This Machine was all I had, so if I can burn inside it, then I will be happy."

"Come with us," Mattie pleaded. "You don't have to die here. You taught me to be strong, but it's your turn. You can come back."

"Mattie." Asha turned with a smile that was warm and genuine. "There is nothing for me out there. I grew tired of those people long ago. You always were a better person than me, and maybe if I listened to you none of this would have happened." She pointed to a door on the other side of the sparking obelisk. "There's a teleporter in there, it's that light it used to transport people. That will be the best way to escape."

"Asha, that's not a god."

"I know." Another wall exploded in. "But I want to see it die, so we can both see what the true God is."

The Faceless God twitched and recoiled as the wall it was on caught fire. "That is irrational."

Asha spread her arms wide. "That is human."

Dayla pulled on Mattie's arm. "Let's go!" Her gaze fell across the room. Asha. Victoria. Adelaide. They were leaving so much behind. She straightened her spine and took the lead.

The next room was much smaller. A simple square with a control panel next to a glass pad big enough for half a dozen people to stand on. The door slammed shut behind them. Mattie brought Hush onto the pad, next to Dayla, and turned to the control panel. There weren't any buttons on it, just spots of light that reacted to her touch.

"How do we use this?" Dayla asked, keeping her rifle at the ready for any sludges.

"I don't know." Mattie tapped some of the lights, but it wasn't doing anything. "I don't even know what this is."

An explosion rocked the room and the door bent in. Mattie covered her mouth as the smoke crept through and choked her. There was no going back now, even if they wanted to.

Dayla slowly lowered her rifle. "Maybe we don't get out."

Mattie leaned on the control panel.

"We saved everyone," Hush said.

Dayla turned to him, surprised that he had said anything of sense. A smile crept across her face. "Yes. Yes, we did."

The three of them shared a look of peace and acceptance. They had done something great, even if no one would know or understand.

"I came to England to find a cure," Mattie said. "Maybe my purpose was for something greater. I can't be upset about that."

Dayla shut her eyes. The flames crept closer. Heat blossomed as a light engulfed them.

Then they were outside.

CHAPTER 13

M attie spun around in shock. They stood on a snowy, moonlit hill. She clapped her hands up and down her body. It was all there. She was all there. Dayla and Hush were next to her, just as confused.

There was the deep boom of an explosion in the distance. They overlooked the Machine. Three of its front legs collapsed, dropping its nose into the earth. Flames erupted from its back, lighting up the night in brilliance. They had escaped, but how?

"Adelaide," Mattie said. "She was still connected to the Machine."

Hush dropped to a sit. His face was blank. He took the branderbuss off his back, looked at it briefly, then tossed it aside. Dayla rested her boltrifle against her shoulder. The Machine, once tall and immovable, burned in the fields outside Wrotdam.

"Adelaide saved us." Mattie reached for her hat, only to remember it was still in the pool of water. She played with the bandages hanging around her collarbone instead. "They all saved us. Victoria, Rig, Edwin, even Asha. They all died for this. It isn't fair."

"The people who deserve to live tend to die," Dayla said. "And those who wish to die will live far longer than they ever hoped. Life doesn't always have meaning or order."

"Is this good?"

"It's better." Dayla bowed her head.

Mattie felt like she should do something. Of the seven who went in, only three had returned. Maybe Dayla was right, and things tended not to have meaning. Still, she felt like she had to do something.

She stepped forward and took a deep breath. She let out a screaming cheer. Her voice echoed across the snowy countryside. She stopped to catch her breath, tears growing hot in her eyes. Hush stood next to her, with Dayla on the other side. They shared the briefest of glances, then all took a deep breath.

They screamed at the Machine. At the heavens. They screamed until their voices bounced off the hills and the fields and the metal and came back to them. To Wrotdam and to Dawnhallow. They screamed until the cosmos could hear them.

Then, as their screams became echoes, the 20th century was born in silence.

END

The Author

Kevin Weir is an award-winning writer of science fiction, fantasy, and comedy. A multidisciplinary storyteller, he has written short films, webseries, stageplays, as well as short stories features in Canadian and international publications. He lives in Alberta where he hosts podcasts, works in film, plays Dungeon and Dragons, and lives with two-to-four dogs and a naked three-legged cat.

YOU MAY ALSO LIKE

In the near future city of New Montreal, where wireless technology connects everything, Kraft finds himself disconnected due to his ability to see the aura of supernatural creatures hiding as humans. He has accepted that no one will believe him, and so prefers to waste his life away in solitude. No such luck, though, as he is given a job to illicitly clean a mega-corporation's computer system — only to find something has infected the network. Something with a mind of its own.

In a world of high technology and secret magic, Kraft bridges the gap with his unnatural sight and array of inventive gadgetry. Faeries, cults, and corporate espionage collide in a story that has been described as "a riveting, genre-bending adventure", "A fast-paced book full of twists and turns that readers will devour", and "a rocket-fueled tale."

Available now from EDGE Science Fiction and Fantasy Publishing.